DAINDRETH'S SORCERESS

By

Elisabeth Wheatley

CHAPTER ONE

Amira

"Are you nervous?" Sairydwen asked, hands working deftly as she braided strands of ivy into Amira's hair.

"No," Amira answered, voice flat. "Not about the wedding, anyway."

"It's alright to be nervous," Cyne said. "I was a bundle of nerves the day I married your father."

"I'm not," Amira answered, her tone harder than she had intended. She inhaled a long breath, exhaled, and bit her tongue.

The Istovari women had been surprisingly agreeable ever since she and Daindreth had returned from Kelamora.

They had gone to free more than twenty children stolen by the Kadra'han and Vesha. In the process, Vesha captured Amira and Daindreth and tried to unleash Caa Iss upon the world. She had almost succeeded.

Caa Iss had plagued Daindreth and his father before him. A cythraul from the Dread Marches, Caa Iss was the embodiment of evil, or as close as Amira could imagine.

But something had gone wrong. Captain Darrigan—Vesha's most loyal Kadra'han—had made a deal with Vesha's familiar, a cythraul called Saan Thii.

Saan Thii had possessed Darrigan, allowing him to break his Kadra'han vows. She had expelled Caa Iss from Daindreth in exchange for giving her a corporeal body.

Amira still didn't understand the full of what had happened. She'd known Darrigan disagreed with Vesha's dealings with cythraul. She hadn't thought he would go so far as to commit treason.

But Amira and Daindreth had killed him. Amira kept remembering that fight, guilt plucking at her every time she recalled the way Darrigan had looked up at her when the blade pierced his chest.

He'd been relieved. She was sure she had seen that.

1

Captain Darrigan had made a deal with Saan Thii, and then counted on Amira being able to kill him once he was possessed.

There was so much Amira wished she could have asked him. What secrets had died with Darrigan? What had made him take such a risk?

He couldn't have known for sure Amira would be able to stop Saan Thii. But he had gone out of his way to give her and the rangers a fighting chance.

Kelamora had been left all but unguarded that night. The guards he should have had posted were clustered around Vesha, as if she had been the only important thing in that whole monastery. Amira had learned later that two serving girls had been found by Thadred and the rangers and they revealed a side passage through the monastery's water door. Darrigan had threatened those girls to the point they'd fled.

He had planned it. All of it. Yet he couldn't have planned all of it. Could he?

Amira would never know now. Darrigan was dead and Saan Thii had been sent back to the Dread Marches.

Caa Iss was no longer inside Daindreth, but no one was quite sure where he was. He seemed to be a spirit caught somewhere between the world of flesh and the world of the dead.

Amira didn't think he could harm anyone in this state, but she didn't want to leave him at large in the world. At the same time, just how were they supposed to go about finding him?

Amira closed her eyes. Tomorrow. Tomorrow, she would worry about this. Today was her wedding today.

Amira had thought getting Istovari approval would be difficult, but it being easy was almost worse. She kept thinking that there was something she had missed, some caveat she had overlooked.

By her reflection in a slab of broken glass, she could see her mother, Sairydwen, and several women her mother said were distant cousins. The women were hard at work to finish her hair, paint her eyes, and finish last touches to her dress.

A shadow crossed her mind. She barely knew these women. Strangely, Sairydwen was the one she felt the most connected to, even more so than her own mother. Sairydwen at least seemed grateful to Amira, Daindreth, and Thadred for saving her life and protecting her son.

Amira had never thought about who would be surrounding her on her wedding day. She had only recently begun to think that she would ever have a wedding. But now…

Her sister should have been here. Fonra would have been happy for her, she thought. Fonra would have been smiling and giggling with a pink blush to her cheeks.

When they returned to the lowlands, Amira planned to see her sister. She would go to Fonra and tell her everything. And for the first time, there would be no Kadra'han curse forcing her to hold anything back.

"Do you have any questions?" Cyne asked, her voice too quiet, like she was trying hard to sound casual.

Amira shot her a glance in the glass's reflection. "About what?"

Cyne blinked twice. "About tonight?"

Amira frowned. "What about it? I thought we were feasting around a bonfire."

Cyne cast Amira a pointed look in the mirror. "After, Amira."

It took Amira another moment to realize what her mother was saying. "Oh," she said. "No, I'm not worried about that."

"Are you sure?" Cyne frowned. "It is your first time, isn't it?"

Amira bristled at that, anger simmering down her spine. "I don't see what business it is of yours."

Cyne's nostrils flared, though her hands didn't slow as she worked the braids. "I am your mother. Of course, it's my business."

Amira was getting everything she wanted—Daindreth. The right to call him her husband, and the guarantee that no one could ever keep her from him again. Now wasn't the time to pick a fight with this woman.

It was her wedding day. It was going to be lovely and hopefully brief.

When she thought about *after* the wedding, her stomach tangled in knots, but not from fear. She had craved Daindreth

3

for what felt like forever.

In some ways it was strange to long so intensely for something she hadn't experienced. She'd been told it might hurt, that the first time might not be what she hoped, but at this point she didn't care. Even if tonight was a total disappointment, she would have Daindreth, and they would have a lifetime to figure out that side of their life.

Tonight couldn't come soon enough.

CHAPTER TWO

Daindreth

"I don't know why you're nervous," Thadred scoffed. "You're not the one about to perform a ceremony in front of a whole damned tribe."

Daindreth glared at him. "You said you were willing."

"I am." Thadred peered out the curtained window, barely pulling back the curtain like he feared being seen. "By gods they have garlands of flowers. *Garlands*. Is this a wedding or a Maying Day parade?"

"It is customary for Istovari weddings," Tapios said from his post by the fireplace, stiff as an oak tree as if he feared wrinkling his best linen tunic. "Let the women do their work."

Thadred was unimpressed. "Well, it's not customary for imperial weddings."

"Your archduke didn't want to wait for an imperial wedding," Tapios clipped. "As you'll recall."

Daindreth thrummed his fingers on the edge of his wicker armrest. It wasn't so much that he and Amira didn't want to wait—even though they didn't.

It was more the matter of their position being stronger as a married couple. If Amira was Daindreth's wife, King Hyle would have a good reason to back him as the rightful emperor. Once they swayed King Hyle, it would be much easier to sway the other kings and barons of the central empire.

No one wanted to be first to back a new ruler, but everyone wanted to be early, especially when it appeared that new ruler would soon take power.

Not to mention that the Istovari had agreed to a treaty ending hostilities between them and the empire.

None of that happened unless Amira was his wife—his empress, really.

"Emperor," Daindreth said.

"What was that?" Thadred snapped the curtain closed, though Daindreth was sure no one was trying to look.

Bridegrooms were much less interesting than brides.

"Emperor," Daindreth repeated, making his voice project the way he did when he was at court. "I am the rightful emperor and Amira is my rightful empress. Or will be in a few hours. We need to get used to saying it now. Before we go back to the empire."

Thadred muttered something under his breath.

"You're right," Tapios nodded. "We must be the first to recognize your claim. I shall call you my emperor from here on."

Daindreth inclined his head in thanks. Relief swelled in the back of his mind, grateful he didn't have to argue the point.

They were inside Tapios's home, the barrow he shared with his sister and her son. Sairydwen was with Amira and Rhis was with the children gathering flowers. Tapios had been helping the two men ready themselves.

They had shaved, bathed, and dressed. There was not much more to do now but stand around in their wedding clothes and wait for someone to come fetch them. Amira was taking much longer to get ready, but Daindreth expected it wasn't her fault. She would have married him in the ruins of Kelamora if he had let her.

"At least you finally decided to give me land," Thadred muttered. "I just hope it has soldiers we can rally."

Daindreth had ceremonially signed several imperial tracts to Thadred. Hylendale required wedding officiants to be landowners. They'd need the records keepers of Mynadra to finalize it, but it was sufficient for now. Amira hadn't wanted her grandmother or mother to officiate and Sair had refused out of respect for them, so Thadred was the compromise. He was an imperial knight with Istovari blood. Everyone agreed he was acceptable.

Daindreth frowned at him. "Soldiers?"

Thadred exhaled a long breath. He stepped away from the window and marched to take the wicker chair beside Daindreth. "What happens when we get back to Hylendale? Back to the empire? We don't know where Vesha is. It's been weeks. She could have been rallying her forces this whole time."

Daindreth had studied the same histories Thadred had. He

6

knew as well as his cousin that an heir seizing control from a regent, especially one who had reigned this long, rarely happened peacefully. These things often ended in war, but there didn't have to be a war. This could be settled without bloodshed, though he must be forceful. Vesha would need to be put down swiftly.

Daindreth clung to hope his mother would not force them into armed conflict, but at least a part of him agreed it was inevitable. What else would Vesha do when Daindreth emerged, calling himself emperor?

"My mother might be rallying the army, or she might not," Daindreth said. "As of now, I doubt she had reason to. But either way, she will not have made what happened in Kelamora common knowledge."

"She could publicize her own version of it," Thadred said. "Say we tried to kill her. She could rightly say her guard captain died protecting her. Many in Mynadra considered him respectable or even a friend."

It was true. Captain Darrigan had earned himself a reputation as a man who put the best interests of the empire first. Many would be saddened to learn of his passing—not that Daindreth wasn't. But his death would lend credence to Vesha's claims.

"She can tell any story she wants so long as she tells it first."

Daindreth let a breath out his nose. "That's why I need to marry Amira and get us all back to the empire."

Thadred nodded and inhaled sharply. He sat back, running a hand through his hair. "Marry Amira. Right. We can see to that. Pardon me for trying to keep us alive and such."

"You're right, Thadred," Daindreth said. "You know you're right. But this is exactly why we need to get home."

Thadred nodded shortly. "Right."

The door creaked and Daindreth nearly jumped out of his skin. He spun around to see Rhis's round face poking through the crack.

"Mama says they're ready," the boy said.

"Thank you, lad." Tapios shuffled like a great bear toward his nephew.

7

Thadred rose to his feet. "Let's be getting you married, then." He clapped his cousin on the back. "You only have to do it once."

Daindreth swallowed and willed his legs to stand. Letting go of the wicker chair was harder than he had expected.

Outside, it seemed that spring was in full bloom, even though that shouldn't be for another few months. Where the Istovari had found all the flowers and garlands, he had no idea.

Rhis led the way skipping with Tapios behind him and Daindreth with Thadred bringing up the rear. The Istovari village was livelier and more vibrant than Daindreth had ever seen it.

Children carrying garlands ran in all directions. Women of all ages had braided their hair with flowers and the men had draped their shoulders in garlands of leaves and wild blossoms.

When they saw Daindreth approach, they smiled and hurled handfuls of petals at him. "Good fortune to the bridegroom!" they cried. "Make way for the bridegroom!"

Daindreth had assumed that he and Amira would be married at the center of the village, but Rhis didn't lead them toward the center. Their small procession came to a space between several barrow houses that sat like four massive tortoises. Streamers of cloth had been strung overhead to create a canopy. Children ran around the tops of the barrows while the adults gathered below.

The Elder Mother and other women Daindreth recognized as the clan's ruling council waited near the edge of the canopy. Each one of them wore flowers and metal bangles that made soft chiming sounds. When she saw him approach, the Elder Mother smiled at Daindreth.

Though his decision to let Thadred legitimize the wedding had been a controversial one, it seemed that argument was behind them.

Thadred greeted the Elder Mother with one of his charming smiles.

"Do you think you can remember all the necessary parts?" the Elder Mother snapped.

Maybe Daindreth had assumed the best too soon.

Thadred smirked. "Worried your granddaughter will get with

a bastard tonight?"

Daindreth immediately flushed with heat. "Thadred!"

"Sorry." Thadred looked to the Elder Mother. "What I meant is that I can remember everything that will make the marriage legal."

The Elder Mother opened her mouth to reply, but then the voices of children rang out over the tops of the barrows.

"Here he comes! He's coming!"

Daindreth's heart leapt into his throat as petals hurled from the rooftops and excitement shivered through the crowd. People pressed around him and, in that moment, Daindreth thought that every Istovari in the world must be crowded under the makeshift canopy.

Purple-white petals rained around him as the people started singing an upbeat, jovial tune that sounded more like a child's song than a wedding ballad. Everyone threw themselves into it and even Thadred clapped along to the tune.

Where had all these flowers come from? Everything was white and dreamlike and beautiful.

"Nervous?" Thadred punched his arm.

"Go on, son," the Elder Mother gestured, her smile returned. "Your bride awaits."

Daindreth's throat was suddenly tight and his tongue dry as kindling. Amira waited for him.

"Let's not keep her waiting, then!" Thadred whooped. He grabbed Daindreth's hand and hoisted it into the air. Cheers erupted on cue as Thadred half-led Daindreth under the shade of the canopy.

Under the canopy of streamers, it was as chaotic as any Maying Day parade Daindreth had ever seen—much more so. People pressed in all around him, singing, shouting, stomping, and twirling. Tambourines clanked to the song's rhythm.

It was song and dance and celebration worked into a euphoric frenzy. Daindreth had never experienced anything like it before and doubted he would want to again.

Dancers—men and women of all ages—stomped bare feet on the grass as they formed what seemed to be ranks, lining up behind him and sweeping him along their edge.

He felt as if he were in a current, being sucked along by its force. No one had prepared him for this, but Thadred still held his hand high in the air, making sure everyone could see where the bridegroom was.

"Daindreth!"

He turned at the sound of her voice. There she was. And just like that, the noise and chaos of the wedding party meant nothing.

Amira wore an undyed linen dress belted with cords of green. She had no jewelry, except the ivy braided into a crown around her head and the garland of flowers draping her like a shawl. She stood with her mother, Sairydwen, and several other women as her attendants.

She held her hands out to him. The early morning sun shone down through the canopy, radiant as the dawn.

Daindreth caught her hands, and she pulled him in close. Her lips found his and she kissed him soundly on the mouth while the cheering around them somehow grew louder.

"Hello, husband," Amira purred in his ear.

Daindreth pulled her closer. "I'm not your husband yet," was all he could think to say.

"Let's fix that," Amira whispered. She nipped his ear and Daindreth nearly choked in surprise.

This would never have been acceptable in an imperial wedding, but none of the Istovari around them—not even the Elder Mother—seemed surprised or displeased. Quite the opposite.

The cheers continued until Thadred succeeded in quieting them down enough that his voice could be heard above the clamor.

"Ladies and gentlemen," Thadred began. "Venerable Mothers," he swept a gallant bow to the council of nine women. "Most valiant keepers of the purple blossoms," he said, sparing a nod for the children still at work raining flowers around them. "Are you ready for a wedding?" As he said it, Thadred flung out both arms to the crowd.

A roar of cheers went up. Daindreth couldn't have asked for a more enthusiastic crowd of witnesses.

Amira giggled as Daindreth kissed her quickly, stealthily, as if no one had seen them kiss the first time.

"Then good people, by Eponine and the great god Demred, I will give you a wedding!"

Cheers went up again as Amira laughed against Daindreth's chest, her body warm and comforting against his even amid the chaos.

Daindreth had assumed that they would be married in Mynadra, where hundreds would pack the cathedral and thousands would crowd the streets for a glimpse of the first imperial wedding in almost thirty years. It would have been declared a holy day, thanking the empire's patron gods for the continuation of the imperial line.

It would have been a spectacle for a generation.

This was far more intimate. Where he could see the face of every onlooker and feel their heat pressing in around them.

Thadred was speaking to the Elder Mother and Cyne, asking if they gave their blessing or if they knew of any reason their daughter shouldn't marry. Both women gave their assent, though the Elder Mother's blessing was spoken much more easily than Cyne's.

"Daindreth?" Amira looked up at him from under her ivy crown. "Are you alright?"

"Fine," Daindreth coughed. "Just not used to having this many people this close."

"You've been to balls before," Amira reminded him.

"That's different." Balls were more ordered. More decorous.

"Excellent!" Thadred shouted at that moment, whirling around to face Amira and Daindreth holding hands at the center of the canopy. "Amira, your mothers have given the blessing of this union. Who will give blessing for this man?"

"I give my blessing," Sairydwen said from behind him. Daindreth hadn't even realized she was there. "I swear that he is a man of honor, good character, and there is no reason he cannot pledge his troth."

"Perfect, perfect." Thadred nodded. "Amira Brindonu, daughter of Cyne, princess of Hylendale, do you freely enter covenant with this man for so long as you both draw breath?

11

Will you devote yourself to him and no others? Do you so swear?"

Amira looked straight at Daindreth, her smile radiant. She seemed happier than he had ever seen her. "I do so swear."

Then it was Daindreth's turn. Thadred said words and Daindreth said words back, but he forgot what they were a moment later. The rest of the world, even the pressing crowd, seemed to shrink in comparison to the woman standing in front of him.

Amira's red hair turned copper in the morning sun. She was beautiful. So beautiful.

"Do you witness?" Thadred called to the gathered onlookers.

"We witness!" The shout was so loud, Daindreth stumbled into Amira from the force.

She held onto him, still giggling. She kissed his neck as garlands of flowers were wrapped around them by the onlookers, tying them together in a fragrant bundle.

"This is very snug," Daindreth murmured to Amira, her temple pressed against his jaw as they were wrapped tighter together.

Amira laughed. "That's the point, my love."

"As you are bound in body, may you be bound in spirit," cried the Elder Mother's voice.

"Be bound in spirit!" the crowd joined in.

Then there were cheers all around them.

It seemed these Istovari had wanted a reason to cheer for a long time and now that they had one, they were making the most of it.

Amira found Daindreth's mouth with hers and she kissed him as the others began unwrapping them. The garlands came off one at a time and then her hands were on his face as she pulled him closer.

The garland pinning Daindreth's arms came off and he wrapped them around her. He splayed his hands over her back, savoring the solid warmth of her.

Amira purred in his mouth, still kissing him as the last of the garlands were pulled away.

12

Thadred said something and the Elder Mother said something. He wasn't sure what, but it was said solemnly and with a resounding clap of hands from the crowd.

"Wife, behold your husband," Thadred said. "Husband, behold your wife."

Daindreth's face split with a grin between kisses. He smiled down at Amira, trying to hold this moment tight enough to keep it forever. "Wife," he said.

"Husband," Amira said back.

He opened his mouth, but then she was kissing him again and he was too lost in the delirium of her caresses to remember what he wanted to say.

CHAPTER THREE

Amira

Amira leaned against Daindreth's shoulder by the light of the bonfire, toes stretched toward the edge of the circle of stones.

The party had lasted all day and involved more wine than she had seen outside a religious festival. Daindreth had his arm around her, finishing his third cup.

Around them, the celebrators sat off together in huddles, speaking in low voices by the light of the fire. A lute still played and the last few of the dancers had formed a circle on the grass, skirts flaring as the women spun together in time to the music.

The Istovari knew how to celebrate.

As best Amira could tell, not one person had returned to their own home. Children had fallen asleep on their parents' shoulders or at their feet.

Thadred appeared to have made friends with Tapios and several other rangers. They were sharing yet another round of drinks. The Elder Mother and the older women sat quietly talking beside the bonfire and several younger men appeared to be trying to pull sticks from the flames.

Amira and Daindreth had been toasted more times tonight than she could count. She couldn't imagine being more celebrated if they had been in the center of the imperial city surrounded by well-wishers.

Amira looked to her husband by the light of the fire. The laces at the collar of his shirt were undone, exposing just the barest hint of collarbone. She leaned over, slipping one arm around him. Nuzzling the side of his neck, she kissed him gently, lips just brushing along his skin.

"Mmm." Daindreth tilted his head back, giving her better access.

Amira's lips nipped along his throat, up to his ear. She nibbled at his lobe, tugging him ever so slightly toward her.

Daindreth flinched. "Not quite that hard."

Amira let go with her teeth and instead traced the shell of his ear with her tongue, licking the sweat off his skin.

A shudder went through him at that, and he grabbed her arm. "Playing with me, are you?"

"Yes," Amira grinned against his ear. "I am playing with you."

Daindreth's hands found her face in the dark and he pulled her in for a kiss. A long, slow kiss that took its time.

He stroked along the neckline of her dress, fingers running along her collarbone and throat, teasing, toying, eager. Asking permission.

"Come to bed with me." Amira hadn't realized she was out of breath until she dared speak. "Husband."

"Seductress." It was Daindreth's turn to nuzzle her neck as he breathed in the smell of her hair. "Always you tempt me," he whispered. "You tantalize me."

"I'm glad I tempt you." A little thrill of excitement ran down Amira's spine. "Is it working?"

"Show me to our room," he said.

Amira and Daindreth had been given a room for tonight and for as long as they stayed in the Haven. But Daindreth didn't know where it was, yet.

Amira took his hand in the dark. "I'll show you to our room."

"And then show me what you want me to do in it," Daindreth said. It was impossible to make out his expression in the dim firelight, the flickering patterns casting him in shadow. But she was sure she caught a devilish tilt to his mouth.

Amira's heart raced. "I have lots of things I want you to do in it."

Daindreth made a low sound of approval. "Lead the way, wife."

Amira squeezed his hand tighter and stood. "Come with me."

She lifted her skirt with one hand and tugged him through the maze of sleepers and drowsy celebrants. No one even seemed to see them.

In imperial weddings, Amira had heard that the bride and

groom were escorted to the bridal chamber amid pomp and pageantry, cheered on by the court matrons and married men. Amira much preferred this quieter, more private tradition of the bride and groom leaving when they wished.

Amira led Daindreth back to the large main barrow of the village. A few torches had been left lit, at least enough to see by. Amira pushed open the main door of the hall. No one was present save for a few older men who sat around one of the tables, deep into their cups. None of them acknowledged the couple as Amira and Daindreth slipped inside.

It took Amira a few moments to remember which of the many doors led to her bridal chamber. Everything looked different in the dark. But she was able to find her way to the right room and push the door open.

The chamber was sparse compared even to Hylendale, that much was certain. The rough wooden furniture looked more suited to a farmhouse than the bridal suite of an emperor. Nonetheless, the bed was lined in furs and the low fire cast the room in an amber glow.

Flowers and garlands lay strewn on the floor, filling the air with a sweet aroma. Two narrow chairs waited beside the fire atop the skin of some large animal. Amira took in the room with a deep breath before facing her bridegroom. He had not been looking at the room at all.

He shut the door behind them, eyes on her. "Amira."

Amira stepped back out of his reach, but closer to the bed. "Daindreth." She wasn't sure why her breath hitched.

She had waited for this, longed for this, been so impatient she had felt it would tear her in half. Why did her nerves flutter now?

"Is everything alright?" Daindreth closed the distance between them, resting his hands on her arms. "You're shaking."

"Nervous is all," Amira whispered. Damn it, her mother had been right. Maybe she should have asked questions when she had the chance.

Daindreth pressed a kiss to her forehead. "We can go slow," he said quietly, hands stroking up and down her arms. "It's late. We can just go to sleep."

Amira balked. "What do you mean?"

"We don't have to do this tonight."

Amira blinked up at him. "What?"

"We can—"

"I will *not* leave my wedding night a virgin, Your Majesty." Amira took a step away from him, reaching for the belt of her dress.

Daindreth chuckled. "You have strong feelings about this."

"Yes." Amira located the knots around her waist and ripped them free. "I want you, Daindreth."

Daindreth watched her, eyes following her every movement. "And I want you."

The ties of her dress came free too slowly and at the same time too fast.

Amira's heart hammered in her chest, sick with both excitement and fear at the same time. Her dress fell easily, sliding off her body like water off a fish's scales. It pooled around her ankles on the floor, leaving her naked in the firelight.

Daindreth's heated gaze drank her in from head to foot, taking in every slope and curve of her. His eyes lingered on the scars slashed across her sides and the pale marks left by blades on her arms.

When his eyes met hers again, he smiled. "Beautiful."

Amira swallowed, unable to speak and unsure why.

"Come to me," he beckoned softly, holding out a hand to her.

Amira obeyed, trembling with a strange tangle of sensations and emotions.

Instead of taking her hand, Daindreth fit his hand against her side. He pulled her against him, mouth finding the side of her neck. His tongue stroked a path to her ear, then back down her throat.

"Mmm." Amira pressed closer against him, forgetting her nervousness as his hands stroked her bare back.

"You want me?" he whispered, leaning down.

"Mmm-hmm." Amira found the hem of his shirt and tugged it up, just a few inches.

"Say it."

17

"I want you." Amira's voice came out hoarse and ragged, like she had been running.

Daindreth pulled away from her.

"What's wrong?" She felt the lack of his closeness like a loss.

"Nothing." Daindreth finished untying the laces at his collar. "I want to match you." He pulled his shirt over his head and tossed it to the side.

Amira took in the lines of his body by the hearth's glow—toned chest and arms that rippled when he moved. These past weeks on the road had given him a leanness and toughness that he hadn't had back in Mynadra. He was fitter with just a hint of toughened strength he hadn't had before.

Daindreth was already kicking off his boots and reaching for the belt around his waist. Amira watched, not moving as he undid the clasp and shucked off his breeches, leaving them to join her dress on the floor.

Amira looked him up and down the same way he had ogled her, studying the parts of his body she knew and the parts that were unfamiliar. Her eyebrows rose and she grinned at him in approval.

"This is nice," she said, not meeting his eyes just yet. "I can work with this."

Daindreth smiled. "I'm glad you're pleased, wife."

Amira beckoned to him this time. "Come to me, please."

Daindreth dove for her, grabbing her waist and scooping her up. She could have twisted out of his grip, but she let him sling her over his shoulder.

"Daindreth!" Amira couldn't stop the giggle that escaped her then.

He carried her across the room and knelt on top of the bed, lying her on the furs. He straddled her, trapping her under him.

Amira stroked the coverlet, feeling the softness of the pelts. "I like this," she murmured, squirming under him.

"Me too." Daindreth leaned over her, pressing her deeper into the mattress. The pea shells inside the mattress crackled under their weight. He traced a line of kisses along her jawline, then down her throat to her collarbone, but this time he didn't stop. His kisses continued down her sternum, over her heart,

18

slowing as they went lower.

Amira rested her hands on his sides, his back, feeling how his muscles tightened and strained as his breathing quickened. "Daindreth," she gasped. "I love you, Daindreth."

"My love," Daindreth murmured between kisses as his mouth ventured farther and farther down her body. He caressed the skin just below her navel, tongue sliding along the curve of her belly.

Amira's breath hitched, desire welling in her until she could feel it wrenching in her gut.

"My wife," he whispered, one hand finding its way to grip just behind her knee. He guided her knee up, parting her legs as he pressed a gentle line of kisses up the inside of her thigh.

Amira gasped, back arching as his touch sent shivers through her whole body.

"My empress," he whispered.

And then her moans drowned out whatever else he might have said.

CHAPTER FOUR

Vesha

Caa Iss perched across from Vesha in the carriage, bulky arms folded across his chest. He was visible only to her, the maids and servants of her retinue moved past and around him, completely oblivious.

"Are you ready to do what needs to be done?" the cythraul rumbled. "I need to know."

Vesha looked away from him, watching the rocky landscape slide past. She ignored the demon as she usually did when she didn't want to argue with him.

She traveled with her Kadra'han guards, twenty or so soldiers, and her handmaidens. The Kelamora Kadra'han had parted ways with her group at the first port city they'd reached. The grandmaster had been rather tight-lipped about his plans, but Vesha couldn't exactly force him and his acolytes to join her. She'd gathered her people, found a ship, and sailed to here—the Kelethian Colonies.

The estate of Viceroy Serapio of Volaine was a grand thing edged with palm trees. Though summers here could be brutal, the palm trees often died during the region's harsh winters and had to be replaced. Serapio refused to learn his lesson, though, and insisted on having new trees shipped in from his homeland every year to replace those that died.

It was extravagance, even by the standards of the empire, but Serapio could afford it. Not only had he risen to become imperial viceroy for the Kelethian Colonies, but he had been given stewardship of the continent's largest alum mine. The precious powder was used across the empire, mostly for clothmaking, and there never seemed to be enough of it. The empire had too many people needing to be clothed.

Growing children needed to be clothed most of all and the empire had an excess of those in recent years. Fewer famines meant larger families.

The carriage rounded a bend in the avenue, bringing the

manor house into view. The building was blocky with large windows and doors. Today, the windows of the upper stories were open, leaving thin curtains to dance in the breeze.

The carriage pulled under the carriage porch. Footmen and servants rushed out to greet them. The servants were dressed in loose white clothing meant for the warmer weather and many of them even went barefoot.

A step was lowered and one of Vesha's Kadra'han opened the door. The empress alighted on the gravel outside as her small army of maids flocked around her to adjust her hair, straighten her skirts, and fix her mantle.

"Your Imperial Majesty," cried a woman's voice—a melodic soprano so much like their mother's.

It had been years since Vesha had last seen her sister in person. She thought she should feel something—her and Zeyna had once been as close as two girls could be—but Vesha had not felt much of anything these past weeks.

The woman in front of her was tanned with freckled arms, her hair bleached a dull brown. Vesha had always told her sister not to ride without a veil and long sleeves. It appeared Zeyna had not listened, though that was hardly a surprise.

"Welcome to my home, Your Majesty," Zeyna said, dropping into a curtsy. They were sisters, but Zeyna was a countess and a viceroy's wife. Vesha was the empress of the largest empire in the known world.

Vesha extended a hand to Zeyna. "Rise, sister. No need for formalities."

Zeyna took Vesha's hand in both of hers. "We are honored to have you with us. Long have I hoped you would come to see my home."

"It is quite lovely," Vesha said. "I hope you are happy here."

"Very happy." Zeyna hooked their arms together as if they were children again.

It was a small breech of protocol, but Vesha allowed it. It would have been different if they were back in the central empire, but these were the colonies. Things were more lax.

"You must meet my children," Zeyna chattered, sounding exited. "They have heard so much about you."

21

Vesha thought to herself that she knew Zeyna's firstborn better than the woman herself did. Thadred had been left behind when Zeyna went away to marry Serapio.

Serapio had kept the engagement even after he learned that his bride to be—whom he had only met twice—had just given birth to another man's child.

Many people had speculated at the time. Perhaps he had learned that Emperor Drystan was secretly courting Vesha? Perhaps he had rightly seen the advantages in marrying the sister of the empress.

Zeyna led Vesha toward the manor house as servants scurried around them, hurrying to unload Vesha's luggage, such as it was. A trio of young women in ironed frocks greeted them at the threshold. They ranged in age from early twenties to what Vesha guessed was barely twelve.

"Your Majesty, allow me to present my daughters and your nieces, Vespasia, Aelia, and Calpurnia."

Each of the girls dropped into an easy curtsy as her name was spoken. None of them were as tanned as Zeyna, though Vesha noticed dirt under the youngest one's nails.

Zeyna continued. "Their brother, Flavius, is with Serapio."

Vesha considered that a moment. "Isn't your son a toddler?"

"Flavius turns seven next month, Your Majesty,"

"Oh."

"I know!" Zeyna said. "I lose track of time, too. It seems only yesterday he was playing hide and seek in my skirts."

Vesha tried to show no reaction. Only her sister would have allowed a male child to hide in her skirts. What had their mother thought of that?

Zeyna led Vesha deeper into the manor house. Red tiles lined the floors and mosaic reliefs splashed the walls. White curtains waved in the open windows and every square inch had been decorated with designs of lacquered red and white. No expense had been spared in decorating this manor. Servants lined up and bowed, their white-starched uniforms far more orderly than anything Vesha would have expected from her sister's household.

Kadra'han guards fell into step at Vesha's back. Caa Iss

lumbered behind them, though if anyone else could see him, they gave no sign.

"Oh, Vesha look," Zeyna said, probably forgetting that she was still supposed to address Vesha as empress. "This was done just last summer. Don't Mama and Papa look grand? Serapio had it commissioned from one of the best portraitists in the colonies. I only say 'one of the best' because there is some dispute over who is actually best. But I think he did a fine job, don't you?"

Vesha looked up at the life-sized painting that stretched along the side of the wall. It was of her parents, even if their skin was less wrinkled and their faces rounder than she remembered. Her father had been posed standing with a hand on his sword belt—though he'd never been a soldier—and their mother was seated with a bouquet of flowers—though she'd never been a gardener.

"It's lovely," Vesha said, thinking that was what Zeyna wanted to hear.

"Isn't it? Mama and Papa haven't had their portrait done since you were married. Did you know that? When I heard, I insisted that they had to have one done. It's such a shame and I want the children to be able to remember their grandparents." At this, Zeyna looked fondly over her brood of daughters.

Vesha focused on a vase in one corner of the portrait and kept her comments to herself. Her nieces and nephew at least had someone to remember. Her own son barely knew his grandparents.

Ambassador and Lady Myrani had visited Zeyna every summer since her self-imposed exile. They had never visited Vesha and Daindreth. Not since Emperor Drystan's death.

"Your sister is something, isn't she?" Caa Iss chuckled. "Nothing like you. I like you much better."

A spaniel with a silk ribbon around its neck trotted into the hall. Immediately it stopped. Its whole body stiffened with its hackles raised. Barking, the little dog stared in the direction of Vesha. The pugged snout twisted into the most ferocious snarl one could expect from a dog shorter than knee height.

"Hush, boy," said the oldest of Zeyna's three girls. "Quiet."

The little dog kept yapping, its whole body jerking with the force.

The middle daughter, Aelia, scooped up the spaniel, but then another appeared around the corner and another. Each dog wore a different colored ribbon, but otherwise they might have been shadows of the same dog.

Soon no less than four little spaniels blocked the hallway, barking and howling at Vesha. No, not Vesha...

The dogs were staring straight at Caa Iss.

The cythraul rolled his eyes, corded arms across his chest. He hissed at the dogs, and they yelped, shrinking back before barking louder.

"I am terribly sorry," Zeyna said as servants rounded up the spaniels and herded them out of the room. "They're not usually like this."

Vesha frowned. Animals had never responded to Saan Thii like this. How were the dogs able to see Caa Iss now?

It was probably nothing. But it still rankled Vesha.

Caa Iss had said that the veil was thinned around him, that he was caught between the world of the living and the Dread Marches. It made him different from an ordinary familiar, he said. But Vesha still didn't understand how.

"You must be exhausted," Zeyna said over the barking of her dogs. "Come, let me show you to your rooms. Only the finest for my sister."

Zeyna's two younger daughters helped the servants corral the animals into another room.

"I'm terribly sorry," Zeyna said as the dogs' barking faded behind them. "Serapio hates barking dogs, and these ones hardly ever do it, I promise. I don't know why they're being so naughty."

Caa Iss stuck out his forked tongue after the dogs. Could no one else see him?

Vesha wished Captain Darrigan was here. Well-versed in the sorcerous arts, he had always been her first and best counselor when it came to the cythraul. Not that she had heeded most his advice.

Zeyna showed Vesha to a room with soaring ceilings and broad, open windows. Incense burned in one corner, pungent

24

spices that weren't native to the colonies.

Vesha's servants had already rushed ahead and were airing out the sheets, arranging her trunks, and unpacking her clothes.

Vesha took in the room. It was less than her rooms back in Mynadra, but everything was. Nothing compared to the Mynadra palace. It was the ancestral home of Demred's sons for a reason.

"If we'd had more notice, we would have had a whole new villa built for you," Zeyna said. "I've always told Serapio we should. Then our parents could stay there."

Vesha bit her lip. She had never told them the secret of her husband then her son, but she wondered if a part of them didn't know. Had they somehow felt that their imperial grandson was cursed? Like those dogs, had they been able to sense the cythraul's taint?

Caa Iss swaggered into the room, peering down at maidservants and waggling his talons before oblivious hall boys. A footman scuttled past with an armful of linens and Caa Iss shot out a misshapen foot.

The man tripped, scrambling to regain his balance while clinging to the pile of sheets. He apologized to the maidservants as he nearly crashed into them and scuttled away with his head down, ashamed.

Caa Iss stared at the man with rapt interest. He thrummed his claws on the floor as if thinking. Perhaps not even he had realized he could do that.

"We are truly honored to have you," Zeyna said. "Even if it was a surprise. Will Archduke Daindreth be joining us?"

Vesha considered that question. The sister she had known was a creature of parties and pastimes. She had always shied away from talk of court, politics, trade, or anything that hinted at unpleasantness.

But Vesha had known the maiden—the girl who had one too many trysts with a guardsman before she considered the consequences. Vesha had never known this woman, this countess who had lived in this strange colony for longer than they had lived in their parents' house.

As much as Vesha might want someone to confide in, that

25

person wasn't Zeyna. Her sister couldn't be trusted.

"The archduke will not be joining us," Vesha said simply. She should have added something to that. She should have said "unfortunately" or hinted that Daindreth had wanted to come. But she hadn't the will for it. Not right now.

"I do hope he is doing well," Zeyna said. "He's a man grown now, is he not?"

"He is," Vesha answered. Why that came out sounding so sad, she wasn't sure.

"Serapio and I are planning to visit for the wedding." Zeyna folded her hands in front of her. "The girls are so looking forward to it. What is she like? The Hylendale princess?"

Vesha wasn't sure if her sister was prying for information or if it was genuine curiosity. But they were exactly the questions she herself would have asked, though probably for different reasons.

"Amira is a good match for him," Vesha answered honestly. "Beautiful as she is cunning."

Zeyna's brow furrowed at that last part, but she pressed on. "I heard that her beauty is so great that the archduke fell in love with her at first sight. That he begged her father for her hand in the place of her sister."

Vesha forced courtly graces to the surface and pasted on a smile best she could. "My son is smitten with her, for certain."

"I'm so glad to hear it." Zeyna smiled, one hand fluttering at her throat, as if she'd been about to cover her mouth with her fingers and then thought better of it. "When we heard the wedding might be delayed, we were a little concerned."

Vesha froze, mind reacting slowly to her sister's words. Delayed. Wedding. Yes. Officially, Amira and Daindreth had gone for a visit to the countryside with Thadred as chaperone. Amira was overwhelmed by court life and needed more time to prepare. That was what Vesha had told the court.

Vesha wasn't sure many had believed it, but what were the courtiers going to do? Call Vesha a liar to her face?

She had planned to put Caa Iss in charge of Daindreth and bring him back to Mynadra to smooth things over. Let him invent some story about whatever had happened to Amira.

But now…

Amira and Daindreth were alive. They were together. They would no doubt be plotting with those Istovari sorceresses. Under Amira's influence, Daindreth would no doubt try to take over the empire.

That would be a disaster for everyone. Without the cythraul's protection, decades of misfortune, disease, famine, and unrest would begin ravaging the land. Vesha owed it to the people of the empire not to let that happen.

Vesha needed to get in front of them. She needed to stop Daindreth and get another bargain with the cythraul in place. That was why she was here.

"Your Majesty?" Zeyna leaned over, daring to touch Vesha's arm. "Are you well?"

Vesha jumped, realizing she had fallen silent. "Yes. All is well."

"The wedding will still take place?"

"I see no reason why not," Vesha answered. "Hylendale is a strong ally of the empire and both my son and his betrothed are eager for it."

"I am sure you are as well!" Zeyna said.

"What?" Vesha let her genuine confusion show before she remembered herself.

"Well, if your son is about to be married, he seems a bit old to have a regent. Have you discussed a date for the coronation?"

Vesha's eyes narrowed. Was her sister asking because she looked forward to another party, or was she asking if Vesha would step down?

In her original bargain, Caa Iss was supposed to be unleashed as soon as Daindreth had secured an heir. The cythraul would have ruled the empire in exchange for its protection and prosperity. For that reason, Vesha had allowed rumors that she would be resigning from regency soon.

But now…

Her plan had been shattered and her preparations were coming to stab her in the back. She needed time.

"No date has been set for the coronation as yet," Vesha said. "My son and his bride will be going on a tour of the empire after the wedding. We had planned to discuss arrangements after."

It was a lie, but feasible enough.

"I do understand," Zeyna answered, head bobbing as if she accepted that response. "The first months of marriage were definitely the hardest for me."

Annoyance flared through Vesha. She wanted to make her sister leave her alone. So, she said the one thing that was sure to do that. "Thadred is doing well."

Zeyna blinked. "Who?"

"Your son." Vesha didn't bother to hide the venom in her words at that.

"My son is—"

"Your firstborn son," Vesha snapped. "I understand if you forgot his name. I named him, after all."

Zeyna shot a look to her daughter, the eldest who had followed them into the guest suite.

"Mother?" The girl looked to Zeyna.

"Wait outside, Vespasia," Zeyna said. "Go!"

The empress studied the young girl's confused expression. Realization struck a moment later. "You never told your other children?" Vesha said, looking straight to her niece. "I'm impressed, to be honest. Everyone in the central empire knows Thadred Myrani is your son." Vesha looked back to her sister. "But I suppose that is one advantage of living in a backwater colony. You can leave out any gossip you want to."

"Vesha!" Zeyna screamed.

The whole room stopped.

Vesha's guards stared at the two women, the servants froze with boxes and trunks in their hands, and even Caa Iss looked on with piqued interest. The girl Vespasia gaped at her mother, agog that Zeyna would scream at the ruler of the known world.

Zeyna recovered herself a moment later. "Forgive me. I think we have troubled you long enough." She dropped into a curtsy that was stiff, formal.

"Yes, make her fear you," Caa Iss growled. "As she should."

Tears pricked the corners of Zeyna's eyes as familiar guilt plucked at Vesha.

Zeyna kept her head down as she moved toward the door,

28

shoving her daughter out of the room with one hand.

"Sister." Vesha almost reached for Zeyna, then stopped herself. It was better for them both—safer—if Zeyna was away from her right now. "Will there be a family meal tonight?"

Zeyna stopped, eyes fixed on the floor. "Yes, Your Majesty," she said, reverting to formality. "It should be at the second bell."

Vesha nodded once. "I will see you then."

Zeyna scurried out of the room like a frightened animal, dodging the questions her daughter was already asking.

Vesha hadn't meant to reveal a secret of her sister's so casually. But what had the woman expected? Especially if she had come to Mynadra for Daindreth's wedding, Thadred would have been there at the center of the festivities.

Thadred would have ridden in the jousts, stood at Daindreth's side, and sat at the high table. Everyone in court knew who his mother was and there would have been no way for Zeyna to keep that secret.

But Zeyna never had been one to think things through, especially unpleasant things. She'd hidden her pregnancy from their parents for the first five months while begging Vesha not to tell. By the time their parents found out, Zeyna was too far along for the matter to be handled discreetly.

It seemed that at least, had not changed.

◆◆◆

Vesha waited until the servants finished unpacking before having her maids disrobe her of her traveling clothes and bring her a dressing gown. She dismissed them all, asking them to return an hour before dinner, saying she needed to rest.

In the quiet after they had left, she went to her cosmetics box and found a pair of tiny scissors meant for trimming her nails. Pulling her hair up, she snipped off a few strands near the base of her neck, where it wouldn't be noticed.

Caa Iss looked on, licking his chops.

"You find this appealing?" Vesha sneered.

"I find this world appealing, my dear. Anything to keep me in it, I can appreciate."

Vesha tossed the strands into the incense burner. The sharp stench of burning hair filled the room, mingling with the sweet incense. Vesha wasn't sure how long it would be before her servants noticed the smell of burning hair filled any room where she was left alone.

Perhaps they had already noticed. Not that it was the most eccentric thing she had done, but Darrigan was no longer here to help hide her arcane pursuits.

"Say the words, Vesha dear," Caa Iss purred.

"I give this offering willingly and for your strength."

Caa Iss leaned over the narrow stream of smoke, inhaling deeply. The tendrils swirled into his nostrils, and he closed his eyes with pleasure, like an opium addict breathing in the vapors.

"Tell me more about this bargain you propose." Vesha returned her scissors to the cosmetics box.

"Well, you see, Vesha dear." Caa Iss still breathed in the smoke, taking his time. "The best way to appease my mother after a broken deal is, in my experience, to offer her a better one."

"I offered her my firstborn and only child," Vesha snapped. "What better deal is there?"

"Hmm, what indeed." Caa Iss adjusted his tattered wings. "I will have to think on this."

"Liar," Vesha snapped. "You know, you're just refusing to tell me."

"Yes," Caa Iss conceded. "But are you ready to hear it?"

"Yes." Vesha clenched her hands at her sides. "Tell me."

"My mother wants power in this world, true. But I think—I know, in fact—that she desires what I desire."

"And that is?"

"Freedom from the Dread Marches."

Vesha didn't speak for fear that she might give herself away. "Freedom? For Moreyne?"

"Yes. My mother was imprisoned with us all those ages ago. My brothers and sisters and I have had respite from time to time, but our poor mother..." Caa Iss let off a dramatic sigh. "It's a wonder that the imprisonment hasn't driven her mad."

Vesha wasn't so sure about that. None of the cythraul she

30

had dealt with were exactly *sane*. "I suppose we'll find out." She ran a hand through her hair. She had enough of it that she might be able to keep up her offerings to Caa Iss indefinitely without anyone noticing. "You said there are places of power near here? In Kelethian?"

"Yes," Caa Iss agreed. "Places your kind have forgotten, but we remember well. Your people once called them holy."

"Holy?" Vesha scoffed. "I should think a holy place is the last place you want to be."

"Such a thin line between the holy and the profane," Caa Iss purred. "So easy to mix up, sometimes. Even for me."

"What is that supposed to mean?"

Caa Iss shrugged. "Holy places are just powerful places that have been given over to holy things."

"Who gives them?" Vesha asked.

"You, darling," Caa Iss answered. "Humankind. The rules don't just apply to cythraul. Gods and devils alike, you are the ones who grant us power."

Vesha considered that for a long moment, working to show nothing on her face. "Saan Thii never shared this with me."

"Saan Thii held back many secrets," Caa Iss replied. "She manipulated you."

"You aren't manipulating me?" Vesha shot back. She had been able to use cythraul this long only because she never trusted the creatures.

She trusted them to keep their bargains, but nothing more. If there was a way to weasel out of their end, they would find it.

"Good girl," Caa Iss smirked. "Never trust a demon, especially me."

Vesha disliked being called *girl*. She was a woman well past forty who had never felt like a child to begin with. Selfishness was the true luxury of childhood—a luxury Vesha had never had. For as long as she could remember, there had been someone to protect, someone to look out for. First her sister, her parents, and eventually the entire continent. But it wasn't worth arguing with the demon.

Vesha inhaled through her nostrils, the scent of her burnt hair still thick in the room.

Caa Iss made a rumbling sound in his throat. "But I have a greater interest in seeing you succeed than watching you fail, believe me."

"Hmm." Vesha wished she could believe him. But she had only trusted—truly trusted—one man these past years. Not only was that man now dead, but he too had betrayed her in the end.

CHAPTER FIVE

Amira

Amira woke up with Daindreth's arm around her and his bare chest pressed against her back. His face nestled into her hair.

Amira stroked her fingers along his forearm, enjoying how his body cocooned her in warmth. Slowly, she reached out with her awareness of *ka,* feeling the world around them.

Life moved sluggishly outside the walls of their bedroom, almost like the world was hesitant to wake. She could sense a few smaller shapes moving about, probably children at their morning chores.

The fire had died sometime during the night and the room was lit by a narrow shaft of sunshine from a window near the eaves.

Amira kissed the back of Daindreth's wrist and he stirred, his arm tightening around her. His breath tickled the back of her neck as he nuzzled behind her ear. "How long have you been awake?"

"Not long," Amira whispered back, hugging his arm against her.

"Hmm." Daindreth's grip on her loosened and he shifted back, giving her room to turn and face him.

She'd seen him when he'd just woken up before, but this was different. Daindreth looked down at her with an expression of gentle affection and a hint of satisfaction in his smirk.

"How are you, my love?" He played with her hair, coiling a single strand around his finger.

"Excellent." Amira cradled the side of his face with one hand. "A little sore, but…"

"You're sore?" Daindreth's brow flickered with concern and his smile wavered.

"I'm fine," Amira assured him. "I've heard this might happen. Especially the first time."

Daindreth had been beautifully patient and gentle—almost

enough to make her cry. He'd taken the time to explore her body, covering her in kisses. He'd made her feel things she'd never felt before and filled the room with her moans of pleasure.

They'd laid in the bed together for a long time after, not speaking, just holding each other, and breathing in each other's scent.

Daindreth kissed Amira's knuckles, smiling. "Congratulations, my love. You've had your way with me."

Amira giggled, rolling onto her back. "You were the one in control last night."

"No," Daindreth whispered, his lips finding her neck. "No, you were in control, my empress.'

Amira quirked one brow. "We remember the night very differently, then."

"You have mastered me," Daindreth said between kisses, leaving feather-light caresses on her collarbone. "You bring me to my knees. I exist only for your pleasure and to hear your cries of ecstasy."

Amira grinned at him, pushing him back so she could see his face. "You're being dramatic."

"A little," Daindreth admitted, leaning down so that their foreheads were touching, their noses brushing against each other. "But not by much."

Amira slipped a hand around the back of his neck and kissed him. "I love you," she whispered. "I love you so much."

◆ ◆ ◆

Amira had never thought she would have Thadred as a fellow pupil, but here they were.

The two of them sat in the Elder Mother's personal study, practicing while the Elder Mother herself worked at her spinning wheel. Amira had shown up late for this lesson. Thadred and the Elder Mother had seemed surprised she was here at all. It was the day after her wedding, after all.

The Elder Mother had them practice a simple spell for binding, this one specifically for metals. There were general spells for binding, but also more specialized ones for metals,

34

wood, cloth, stone, and even leather. The pattern of weaving *ka* was slightly different for each—cloth could be woven together with *ka* as a guide, wood could be fused using the residual *ka* from the tree, and so on. When it came to weaving spells to bind metal, the *ka* needed to be almost barbed. The Elder Mother said that made for a better bond.

Amira and Thadred each had a pile of nails they were binding together. The Elder Mother called them "nail houses." The structures did look like little houses as they began taking shape.

Amira held two nails on opposite sides of a third, binding them so that they balanced each other out. She took another pair and steepled them together, fusing their tips at the same time she bound their heads to the base of her nail house.

Ka leapt readily to obey her now. It came so easily into her hands, Amira barely had to work for it.

When she looked up, the Elder Mother's stare had settled on her, not looking away.

"What?"

The Elder Mother looked pointedly at the two nails on opposite sides of the nail house. "You are shaping multiple lines of *ka* at the same time."

"Yes." Amira picked up another nail. "I am."

The Elder Mother shook her head. "You have served the archduke well. It has made you strong."

"Emperor," Amira corrected.

The Elder Mother's nostrils flared slightly at the correction. "Yes. The emperor."

"Like I haven't," Thadred quipped, not looking up.

Amira didn't respond to that. They both knew Amira's greatest breakthrough in power had come when she'd almost killed herself. Breaking her curse had been the single greatest thing she had done for her power.

Though he disagreed, Amira could see Thadred growing stronger, too. He noticed *ka* now without needing to be told—when people were close, when the Istovari children were practicing magic. Here he was working spells, something that he had once said he couldn't do.

35

"You're strong," the Elder Mother said to Amira. "If things had been different, I would be able to train you more. As it is, you will have to learn under your mother's guidance."

If things had been different, Amira would not have been bound in a Kadra'han's curse. While that would have spared her much pain and suffering, it would probably have meant she would never have the amount of power she had now.

"I'll be taking my lessons from Sair," Amira said flatly. "I've already discussed it with her and my mother."

The Elder Mother blinked at Amira. "Is there a reason you don't want your mother to teach you?"

Amira bit her tongue. There were many reasons. Chief among them was that she didn't trust Cyne. It was hard enough learning from the Elder Mother these past weeks.

"Sair knows what she's doing," Thadred muttered, probably sensing the tension between the two women. "She'll be able to handle it."

Of all the sorceresses in the Haven, Sair was the one Amira trusted the most. The bar was low, but Sair had been their first ally among the Istovari, and despite a rocky first meeting, Amira was grateful to her.

She could accept Sair as her teacher. Even if Sair's magic was somewhat weaker than Cyne's, Sair was well-versed and competent.

The Elder Mother settled back into her seat. "Are you prepared to face what you must back in the empire?"

"Yes," Amira said, not hesitating. In truth, she didn't think she would ever be ready. But each day they delayed was another day Vesha had to get ahead of them. Waiting was a losing game.

"Are you? The schemes of the courts and the intrigues of the nobles? Are you truly ready to face that?"

"Nobles are nobles," Amira said flatly. "The more they're different, the more they're the same. I survived my father's court. I can survive Daindreth's."

"You need to do more than survive, Amira," the Elder Mother countered, going back to her spinning. "My husband was an insignificant baron who served the last King Hyle. Yet my daughter married the prince."

36

"And your granddaughter married the emperor," Amira said, balancing on the edge of her stool. "Congratulations."

The Elder Mother shot her a look. "You must learn the courts, Amira. As empress, you cannot be just a sorceress or just an assassin. You must learn politics."

Amira almost said that if she was a good enough assassin, she wouldn't need politics.

Thankfully, Thadred interrupted. "Remind me what I'm supposed to do with this now?" He gestured to his completed nail house. It had taken him a few moments longer, but from what Amira could see, his spellwork was just as sturdy and good as hers.

The Elder Mother squinted at Thadred's nail house, probably inspecting the lines of *ka*. "Very good," she said, sounding genuinely impressed. "Your spell work is excellent, Sir Thadred."

"Wonderful. If I need to impress Vesha's Kadra'han with parlor tricks, they will be helpless." Despite his words, Thadred's eyes sparked as he studied his handiwork.

Amira suspected he was thinking along the same lines she was. If they could bind metal at will, there were countless possible applications. Granted, they both needed much practice.

The assassin sensed a pillar of *ka* headed in their direction and turned. The door creaked a moment later and Daindreth's face showed in the doorway.

"Forgive me." He looked to Amira and smiled. "But I must speak with my wife and cousin."

The Elder Mother made a shooing motion.

Amira slipped off her stool, going straight for Daindreth.

He planted a firm kiss on her lips, seizing her waist as if she might try to run away.

Amira deepened their kiss, stifling a giggle. It was an open and brazen show of affection that would have been scandalous in the imperial court. Amira savored his kiss, pressing her body against the length of him.

"Disgusting," Thadred said with a deep sigh. "Newlyweds. Blech."

"You may find use for this." Something thudded from

behind them.

Amira pulled away from Daindreth long enough to see that her grandmother had set a heavy tome on top of the table. It was at least as wide as Amira's palm and the outside had been wrapped in a careful outer covering of oilskin. The front was unmarked, but a sizeable latch held the cover closed.

"More than I, anyway," the Elder Mother said with a note of sadness.

"What is it?" Thadred took the volume, his brows rising when he lifted it. "Heavy."

"My personal spells," the Elder Mother said. She looked to Amira with a forlorn expression. "I can no longer use most of them. And those that I can use, I have memorized." She waved to Amira and Thadred. "Use it to continue your studies."

Amira dropped her hand to grasp Daindreth's, though she did face her grandmother. "Are you sure?"

A sorceress's spell book, especially one so large, was the compilation of a lifetime's experiments and studies. To give one away was like a master artisan giving away his tools.

"I am sure," the Elder Mother said. She let off a long breath. "You will need all the help you can get."

Amira wasn't about to argue with that.

The Elder Mother broke eye contact. "In this book are the spells I used to summon Caa Iss."

The room went cold at mention of that name.

"More accurately, it has several spells I used together to summon Caa Iss. Perhaps with it you can find the means to banish him."

Amira nodded solemnly. Caa Iss was not gone. As much as they would have liked to believe that, Amira and Daindreth both had every confidence that Caa Iss was still at large.

They needed to find a way to banish him back to the Dread Marches along with any other cythraul Vesha might have let through. Unfortunately, no one seemed to know how to do that.

"I would go with you, but..."

This had already been discussed at length. The Elder Mother and the other women who led the Istovari would stay here, in the protection of the Haven with most of their people.

Some of the rangers would be coming as escorts and Sair would be coming as both envoy and as instructor to Amira and Thadred. Once they confirmed that the Istovari would be able to leave the Cursewood safely, Amira and Daindreth would invite them to their court. Whether the two of them would have to set up in Hylendale or another kingdom, or if they would immediately be able to claim Mynadra was unclear.

"We'll send word when it's safe," Amira promised.

The Elder Mother nodded. "We have made a good life here, I think. But I would like to see Hylendale again."

Amira nodded. This woman now had a vested interest in seeing Amira and Daindreth take the throne. She would be an ally out of necessity if nothing else.

"We will do our best to get you there," Daindreth said.

"Yes." Thadred tucked the heavy spell book under one arm and ambled toward the door. He was steadier on his feet these days, but the silver-capped cane sword was still at his side. "Now," Thadred cleared his throat, "did you actually have questions for the two of us or was this just an excuse to come fondle your wife?"

"Perhaps I had questions for you and fondling my wife at the same time is an added bonus." One of Daindreth's hands wandered daringly low on Amira's back. "I do need you to help prepare the horses. Tapios and the rangers are having a time of it. Amira, your mother has asked for your help in readying the women."

Cyne had spent the last several weeks preparing a handful Istovari women for their journey into the empire. Most of them were too young to remember life in the lowlands, much less life at court. Though most the women were rangers going as bodyguards, Sair and Cyne were going as sorceresses and envoys.

"Go," the Elder Mother said. "Nothing I can teach you in the next few hours will make a difference."

Amira looked to her grandmother at that. The old woman cast her a sad look. Amira wondered if she didn't see grief there, resignation.

If Amira and Daindreth succeeded, the Istovari would be pardoned and welcomed back into the empire. That was part of

Daindreth's agreement to ally with them.

But when compared to the magnitude of Vesha's power and the strength of her alliances...how could a thwarted heir and a young sorceress hope to oust her? Vesha had already ruled longer than most emperors.

Amira and Daindreth may very well be going to their deaths along with everyone who sided with them.

CHAPTER SIX

Thadred

Thadred paid one final visit to Iasu the morning before they left. No one was really sure what to do with the angry little man.

Iasu sulked in his room inside the large main barrow. One wrist was chained to the wall, and he sat on the floor despite the presence of a bed. He stared toward the narrow window, meager sunlight bleeding through.

Iasu's dark eyes flicked up the moment Thadred entered. The knight had to stoop and squeeze through the door.

"Good morning, Iasu." Thadred rested both hands atop his cane. He carried it more out of habit than need these days, but it was still good to always have a weapon.

Iasu sniffed, looking Thadred up and down. The small assassin had a way of conveying both disdain and disappointment with that one gesture. It was annoying.

"We're leaving, but don't worry. The Elder Mother and her people will look after you."

Iasu turned back to the window. "My sister did not see fit to come herself?"

Thadred shrugged. "She's busy. Newlywed bride and all that."

Iasu's lip curled. He seemed to revile Amira's marriage, but he also seemed to revile everything in general. "What is to become of me?"

"You'll be held here until we have somewhere better to keep you."

"Prisoner for life?" Iasu folded his exceptionally muscular arms across his chest. Despite being at least a head and shoulders shorter than Thadred, his biceps were the same size.

"Prisoner until Vesha's dead, more likely," Thadred said mildly. "Then Amira will most likely demand your vows."

Iasu smiled, which was somehow worse than scowling. "My liege lady dies, and my vows pass back to the grandmaster of

Kelamora."

Thadred arched one brow. "The Kadra'han vows are for life. They end when one of you dies." That had been in the terms of both Thadred and Amira's vows and also Darrigan's, as far as they knew.

Iasu shook his head, still smiling. Something about Iasu's smile made Thadred want to punch him. "It's a modification that Kelamora Kadra'han make to our vows. If our liege dies, we go back to the monastery."

"Well, the monastery was burned down, in case you didn't notice."

Iasu made a disgusted sound. "The grandmaster's corpse wasn't there, in case *you* didn't notice."

Thadred had noticed, as it so happened. Amira had noticed as well. They'd probably have to deal with the Kelamora Kadra'han at some point, but that was a problem they would face in the future.

One of many problems they would face in the future.

"Yes, well. Thank you for letting us know. I'll make sure you aren't released until everyone's dead, then."

Iasu's voice dropped into a growl, low and threatening. "I told you that you should just kill me."

"Don't worry, Amira agrees with you." Thadred halfway agreed, too, but Dain was adamant. Iasu was to be kept alive, at least for now. "Unfortunately for you, Dain is a kind and merciful man."

"He's a fool."

Thadred heaved a sigh, glancing to the ceiling. "Sair says that your leg is better. You should be able to walk again soon."

"I can walk just fine now," Iasu snapped. "Better than you, I reckon."

"Ah yes. Cripple jokes. How original." Thadred toyed with the head of his cane. He briefly thought about thwacking Iasu's bad leg with it, but just briefly. "Anyway, I wanted to let you know that you will be in the Elder Mother's care for the foreseeable future. She and a few of the rangers will be guarding you."

"You make me not only a prisoner, but the prisoner of an

old woman."

Thadred snorted. "You were expecting torture, I imagine. But no, we sentence you to the care of an aged grandmother."

Iasu rolled his eyes. "If I get the chance, I *will* kill you."

Thadred found that deeply funny for some reason. "Get in line, my friend. There's an empress, a goddess, and a few demons ahead of you."

Even Iasu's endless fount of mockery stopped at that.

Thadred shook his head. "Anyway. Enjoy sulking and complaining for the rest of your miserable existence."

Iasu jerked forward, snapping his chain taunt. "I will be free, knight. One day. And when that day comes—"

"Goodbye, little brother," Thadred interrupted. "Maybe you'll be able to convince the Elder Mother to kill you. If anyone could do it, I'm sure you can."

Iasu shouted threats and curses after him, but Thadred squeezed back out into the hallway.

He didn't know what to do with that one. None of them did. Iasu was useless as far as information went. He couldn't reveal Vesha's secrets even if he wanted to, but on the other hand, he had to know a good many of them.

Iasu had knowledge, training, and skills that were invaluable and yet he was effectively worthless. He was like a fine gold brooch in a remote desert oasis. They kept him in case they ever had need of him, but no one had any idea when that might be.

Thadred tried to push thoughts of the furious little Kadra'han aside as he made his way out of the barrow complex. Outside, the Istovari were readying horses and pack animals, preparing for the journey to the lowlands.

The dappled grey gelding Amira had bought for Thadred was lost back in Lashera, but he was counting on another horse joining them once they left the Haven. He saddled his gear— such as he had—onto a pack mule and prepared a hackamore bridle without a bit for Lleuad. He also had a saddle blanket ready but wasn't yet brave enough to try putting a full saddle on the kelpie.

"Are you ready?"

Thadred jumped at Amira's voice behind him. He whirled

around to face her. "Don't sneak up on me like that."

"If you were more aware of *ka*, I wouldn't be able to sneak up on you at all," Amira clipped back, though her tone was mild. She must be in a good mood. She been in a fairly good mood ever since her wedding.

Thadred wondered if those tips he'd given Dain before the wedding were helpful. His cousin hadn't asked for more advice, so probably.

"Almost ready," Thadred answered. He glanced over the top of his horse to where Cyne was handling a long-limbed palfrey. "Are you sure about this? Bringing your mother along?"

Amira looked past him to her mother and shrugged. "No. But everything we do is a gamble at this point."

"Eh." Thadred finished securing the last buckle to the mule. "Fair enough."

"If I have to deal with my parents, I think it's fair they have to deal with each other," Amira said.

"You mean to play them against each other?" Thadred cast her a knowing look.

"I'd rather not. But I will do what I must. Vesha is coming."

"Yes," Thadred agreed. "She won't go down without a fight."

"No matter what Daindreth thinks," the assassin added.

"Yes." Thadred didn't understand it himself, but Dain still seemed reluctant about the idea of fighting Vesha outright. Thadred saw no way around it and neither did Amira. The former empress would not be one to bow out gracefully.

"Hello, wife." Dain came up and slid an arm around Amira's waist. He pressed a kiss to her temple, then looked to Thadred. "Tapios and the others are ready to head out. Rhis is asking to ride with you."

"Absolutely not," Thadred clipped. "I have no idea how Lleuad would take that."

"Sair already told him as much." Dain grinned. "I think he's just embarrassed about having to ride with his mother."

"I'll find him a pony in Lashera," Thadred said. "Or maybe King Hyle can give us one. Something slow and stubborn and prone to biting."

Amira arched one eyebrow. "Do you hate that child?"

"What? No. But every child's first pony should be a *little* evil. It builds character." Thadred picked his cane from where it was leaning against a tree.

One of the rangers—a blonde girl with freckles whose name he could never remember—mounted her horse and just like that the Istovari were saddling up.

"I think we're ready to go." Amira pulled away, but touched Dain's arm affectionately as she did.

Dain pulled her back in for a kiss before releasing her. "Are you good to walk to the edge of the Haven?"

"Gah." Thadred swung his cane at Dain, but it didn't come close to hitting. "Worry about yourself and that pretty wife of yours."

"I will," Dain said it with a grin. "But since I'm already worrying, it's no trouble to throw you in with the rest."

"Go," Thadred said. "I'll catch up."

The group of mules and horses began to head toward the edge of the Haven. Tapios was in the lead and dozens of Istovari men, women, and children had come to see them off.

Dain clapped Thadred on the shoulder. "Good luck."

Amira rode up on her little bay mare, holding the reins of Dain's sorrel. The archduke—emperor—mounted up easily and the young couple headed after the rest of the group, riding side by side.

Thadred watched them go. They were a good thing. He hadn't trusted or even liked Amira in the beginning, but...they fit together.

"Are you going to be alright?" Sair asked. She rode a flea-bitten grey gelding with Rhis gripping her waist. The little boy didn't look happy about the arrangement, but he'd live.

"I *can* walk, Sair," Thadred retorted, using the shortened name he'd given her. Only he, Amira, and Dain used it. "Don't worry about me. Lleuad will catch up with the rest of you faster than you can miss me."

Sair looked uncertain. "You are sure he will come?"

Thadred swung his arms out. "Why does everyone doubt it?"

Sair exhaled a short breath.

"I'm sorry. But I've braved worse things than a hundred paces walk to the edge of the Haven."

"I know." Sair looked about to say something else, then closed her mouth.

"Can I ride the kelpie?" Rhis asked, squirming behind Sair.

"No," Thadred answered flatly, his face a deadpan. "They eat little boys like candy."

"What's candy?" Rhis asked.

"I'll get some for you in Lashera," Thadred promised without thinking.

"Thadred…" Sair made an exasperated sound.

"Fine, I won't give him candy."

"That's not…" Sair opened and then closed her mouth.

Thadred took a step closer to her horse. He almost put a hand on her knee, then thought better of it, touching her horse's neck instead. "I'll be fine, my lady," he said, the title slipping out habitually. He managed to smile up at her. "Go on. Or your brother will wonder where you are."

Sair nodded. "We'll see you shortly." She kicked her horse into a brisk walk after the others. She didn't look back.

"Mind if I join you?" The Elder Mother appeared at his elbow, a walking stick in one hand, though he suspected she didn't need it.

"Of course." Without waiting, Thadred began his trek after the horses and mules. They were all ahead of him by now, the first of the animals already disappearing into the border of the Cursewood.

"I hope you will continue your studies," the Elder Mother said.

Thadred glanced to her sideways. "I plan to." He had thought that was the point of Sair and Cyne coming with them. He and Amira needed instructors.

"You have a gift, one that will only grow stronger as you continue to serve the emperor."

Around them, Istovari villagers called out well-wishes and blessings. Some wept, others gave joyful shouts. Those who were leaving would either come back with word that it was safe for the Istovari to return to the lowlands, or they would never come back at all.

"Yes," Thadred agreed. Already, he had discussed with Sair and Amira ways that he might use spells to make him stronger in fights. On horseback, he could still hold his own. On the ground, he needed help.

Sair had some promising ideas already.

"You are the future of our people, Thadred," the Elder Mother said. "You and Amira."

Thadred glanced at her and then to the dozens of Istovari villagers racing around them. "Pardon?"

"You are untainted," the Elder Mother said. "Your magic is not bound to the Cursewood."

"What if we broke the Cursewood?" Thadred suggested. Amira had brought it up before but had been summarily dismissed.

"It's not that simple," the Elder Mother replied. "You and Amira are our only hope."

Thadred didn't like the sound of that. "Then I'd give up now," he shot back.

"Thadred—"

"It's been a pleasure, Elder Mother, but I really must be going." They had reached the edge of the Cursewood, where the green grass and vibrant foliage of the Haven gave way to inky decay. Thadred was the last one, the horses and pack animals already disappeared into the forest.

"May Eponine guide you," the Elder Mother said.

"Hmm." Thadred ambled into the forest alone, the Istovari gathered around, shouting farewells. They were mostly meant for the people who had gone ahead of him, but it still felt strange. How odd it must be to be missed.

A path had been carved into the Cursewood, courtesy of years of rangers heading into the forest to scout and hunt. Thadred stepped over a knotted obsidian root and around the trunk of a massive tree that had been an oak before it was strangled by the curse.

Silence descended around him. He looked back and could see no sign of the Istovari village. Already, the Cursewood had separated him from the Haven.

Thadred rounded the tree and let off a curse. A stocky black shape blocked his path.

"It's rude to sneak up on people," Thadred said, looking over the stallion. The horse looked feral—mud splattered up his legs and what might have been blood on his shoulder, but otherwise fine. "You want to come with me, boy?"

The kelpie snorted and stomped, shaking his mane.

"You sure? We're going to the lowlands." Thadred stepped up beside the small black horse and spread the saddle pad over his back.

The kelpie stomped and shifted uneasily but didn't shy away.

Thadred slipped the hackamore over his head. The kelpie flinched when Thadred touched his ears but allowed it.

"Good boy." Thadred finished buckling the hackamore in place and scratched the horse's neck. "Are you ready?"

Lleuad snorted and ground his teeth.

Thadred took that as agreement. Grabbing a handful of mane, he swung aboard the stallion's back.

"Let's be off, then." Thadred hoped to start training the kelpie with reins, but for now kept a loose hold on the hackamore. "Find me the others, alright? Dain and Amira. You remember them?"

Unsurprisingly, Lleuad broke into a steady trot through the trees. His gait was smooth and easy, hooves stepping high over roots and rocks. He carried his head a little high for a saddle horse, but Thadred would work on that later.

It took them no time at all to break through the trees and straight to the column of riders. Three arrows were nocked and pointed in their direction as soon as they emerged.

"Excellent work, everyone," Thadred said, offering a mild bow from Lleuad's back. "Very good. Just testing your reflexes."

"Thad." Dain sounded a little too relieved, like he had been worried Thadred wouldn't arrive at all.

"Yes, I am fine." Thadred tested the hackamore's reins, gently nudging Lleuad to join the column.

"Is that the kelpie?" exclaimed a young voice from inside the column.

"Yes, hush," Sair chided.

Thadred pulled Lleuad back a little and joined the riders just beside Sair and Rhis's horse.

Lleuad wasn't particularly impressive by equine standards. He was built for endurance and survival in the wetlands. Stocky, a bit shaggy, and with sticks tangled in his mane. Lleuad would easily be overlooked when compared to one of the massive imperial destriers.

"His eyes really are white!" Rhis gasped. "Uncle Tapios, look!"

"Yes, Rhis," Tapios called from the front. "Yes, I know."

Thadred grinned at Sair and she shook her head with a tired smile.

"Can I touch him?" Rhis asked, stretching out his hand toward Lleuad.

"Yes," Thadred answered. "Tonight, when we camp. You still can't ride him, though."

"But—"

"I can barely ride him," Thadred pointed out. "And I am a master horseman."

Sair quirked one eyebrow at that. "Master horseman?"

"Yes," Thadred repeated. "I've been undefeated in jousting tournaments for years."

Sair frowned at him. "Really?"

"You sound cynical," Thadred pointed out.

"It's just...undefeated?"

"It's true," Dain called from ahead of them in the column. "Thadred has trounced every eligible knight in the empire."

Sair still didn't look convinced.

"Anyway, as I was saying, Rhis, I am a master horseman and even I find Lleuad a challenge. Besides, your mother would never forgive me if Lleuad ate you."

"You're right," Sair said. "I wouldn't." Her expression was serious, but Thadred detected a slight sparkle of mischief in her eye. "And like Thadred said, kelpies eat little boys."

Thadred nodded in agreement. "Especially ones that don't listen to their mothers."

Rhis's nose wrinkled. "You're teasing me."

49

"Of course, I am, lad," Thadred sighed. "Or maybe not. Why don't we let Lleuad smell your arm and see if he takes a bite?"

Rhis yelped and gripped his mother's waist tighter. "He wouldn't!"

Thadred and Sair laughed at the same time. Sair had a nice laugh. Gentle and kind. It made him want to hear it again. Better yet, he'd like to be the one to make her laugh again.

"Thad," Dain called from the front.

"Pardon me, sir," Thadred said. "Madam." He nodded to Sair. "My emperor calls me." He nudged Lleuad into a faster walk. Though he had only limited time riding the stallion, they had worked out the commands to make him go faster and slower.

Lleuad marched past the other Istovari and their horses and though he pinned his ears at a few of them, he didn't bite. Thadred was proud of him for that.

The two of them reached the front, coming alongside Dain and Amira. Cyne rode behind them silently, watching Amira's back.

The newlyweds weren't holding hands, but their horses were close together. From the way Amira was shifted slightly toward Dain, Thadred had the feeling they would have been holding hands if it had been possible.

"You called?" Thadred asked.

His cousin nodded. "Can you take the lead? Lleuad has been outside the Cursewood in Hylendale. He should know the way out."

"He has?" Thad glanced down at his horse, though he wasn't sure why. It wasn't like Lleuad could give him an answer.

"We met a farmer who lost a ram to a kelpie," Amira explained. "We thought it must have been a wolf or something, but then…"

"Then you met Lleuad." Thadred scratched the horse's thick crest, where his mane joined his neck.

"Yes. Anyway. I am hoping not to spend days in this forest if we can help it."

"I see." Thadred straightened on his saddle pad and patted

50

Lleuad's neck. "I'll see what we can do."

Thadred pointed the little stallion at the front of their column and coaxed him into a trot.

Thadred passed Tapios and the ranger who had been put on point. He nodded to the others, feeling smug at their looks of wide-eyed awe. It seemed the Istovari would never get used to the kelpie.

"Lowlands, boy," Thadred said to the horse. "Do you know the lowlands?"

Lleuad stopped, chuffing at a low stream in front of them. The water was dark grey, putrid.

"Come on, boy," Thadred urged. "What's wrong?"

Lleuad refused to move, still chuffing at the water's surface.

The other horses caught up with them. One by one, the horses came to a stop at their backs.

"What's the hold up?" Tapios called.

"I'm not sure, I—"

A screech rent the air and an explosion of motion burst in front of them. Someone shouted and Thadred turned in time to see a long, serpentine shape rear up out of the stream.

Lleuad caught the thing in his jaws and a wet crack rent the air. Thadred grabbed the stallion's mane and held on with all the strength he had.

The other horses shied back, but Lleuad snapped his head from side to side like a dog. The stallion squealed, batting with his front hooves and bashing the snakelike creature against the ground.

As quickly as Lleuad had grabbed it, he dropped the thing. It hit with a hard thud, but the stallion kept stomping and smashing it until the thing was a bloody pulp on the ground.

The creature looked like an eel, but at least six feet long and big enough to have swallowed Rhis whole. It lay on the mud beside the stream, not moving.

Lleuad snorted and stomped again.

"I think you got him, boy," Thadred muttered.

"Thad!" Sair cried.

"Thad? Are you alright?" Dain was there, close, but keeping his horse back from Lleuad's kicking range.

Cyne and Sair had both drawn extra *ka,* ready to use spells. Amira had a bow drawn as did several of the rangers. When had she started carrying a bow?

"I'm fine," Thadred brushed off their concern. "Alive." He squinted down at the mutilated creature under Lleuad's hooves. "Whatever it was, my hell steed seems to have crushed it to death."

As if to accentuate the point, Lleuad snorted and blood sprayed from his mouth.

"It's a wood eel," Tapios said, peering down from his own horse. "A big one, too."

"Well, it *was.*" Thadred looked down at his horse. "Good job, boy."

"Are there any others?" Amira asked, getting straight to business.

Thadred patted Lleuad's neck. "Nothing else you want to kill before we move on?"

Lleuad snorted and pawed at the ground. After another moment, he hopped over the stream and the mangled corpse of the wood eel.

Tapios's horse came next, then the rest of their group. Thadred glanced back long enough to see Sair and Rhis make it across. The other horses shied from the carnage on the mud, but after the first passed over it, the rest followed, if a little reluctantly.

Thadred turned back to the front of their column and light smacked him in the face. He raised an arm to shield his eyes as they adjusted.

Without warning, they were in a meadow with clean, lush grass. The sun was shining bright and Thadred looked around. It seemed to be an ordinary, late spring day, even if there was a bit of a chill on the wind.

Tapios was the first to break out of the dark line of the Cursewood. Next came several of the rangers, Dain, Amira, Cyne, Sair with Rhis, and the rest.

Their horses visibly relaxed at being free of the Cursewood while Sair, Amira, and the other sorceresses took deep breaths. They had described to him what it was like to be oppressed by the Cursewood's tainted magic. Thadred still couldn't tell the difference.

"That was quick," Dain said with a sigh. "Barely half an hour, I would say."

Considering that they had previously spent days in the Cursewood on their way to the Haven, Thadred had to agree.

"Lleaud knows where he's going." Thadred grinned proudly. "Off to Lashera now? Which direction?"

"Southwest," Amira said, studying the treetops with the Cursewood at their backs. "That should take us toward Lashera."

"As you wish." Thadred nudged Lleuad in that direction. He wasn't sure how the kelpie would react to life in the empire. He wasn't sure about how the people of the empire would react to Dain coming for his throne, either. But in both cases, there was nothing left to do but roll the dice and hope for the best.

CHAPTER SEVEN

Vesha

Caa Iss had stopped needling her and that was how Vesha could tell he was nervous.

Vesha reclined in the palanquin, carried by three men on either side. She watched the world through the gauzy white curtains meant to give her privacy.

Kelethian was a lovely country, beautiful in every way, though this was a less civilized corner of it. The outskirts of Iandua still reflected its primitive origins as a mining town. The theatre, central forum, and even the new monastery were all projects undertaken by Serapio's family in the past thirty years.

Vesha had never visited this land before, but it was a far cry from what she had been brought to expect. Zeyna had bettered and beautified the world around her as she always did. Even as children, Zeyna had always been the one to bring flowers into their playroom or add lace to her dresses.

Beauty and leisure—those were Zeyna's areas of expertise.

But Vesha was not here for either.

Caa Iss lumbered along, ears twitching like an animal's, red eyes flitting in all directions. Just what did he expect to happen? He claimed to be certain that there were no other cythraul loose in the world. What else did he have to fear? Perhaps he was not as certain as he said.

Most dogs barked at Caa Iss and cats avoided him altogether. Horses seemed oblivious for the most part, but this morning one of her brother-in-law's prize colts had panicked and nearly dislocated a groom's shoulder. A donkey in the market had brayed and shied away when Caa Iss had come close. When Caa Iss had kept coming nearer, the little beast of burden had kicked out with its back hooves, hitting nothing but air.

The animals knew Caa Iss was unnatural, that he was *wrong*. The cythraul were monsters, evil and corrupted. But like fire, they could be useful when controlled.

Vesha had used them to ensure peace and prosperity for

almost two decades. If she quit now, years of held-up misfortunes would come raining down on her people.

She couldn't let that happen.

"This is the place," Caa Iss confirmed, sniffing the air.

Vesha turned to her servants. "Stop here."

The palanquin shuffled to a halt in a quiet corner outside the market quarter. The palanquin lowered and one of her Kadra'han stepped up to assist her from the litter.

"My empress," he said with a bow. His name was Cashun, a bit young for a captain of the guard, barely out of his teens, but he was the most senior of the Kadra'han with her now.

Darrigan had rarely kept lieutenants with him for more than a few years. He'd always worked with them until he was satisfied with their character and skill, then sent them off across the empire. Cashun had been with Darrigan just under two years, but Darrigan had trusted him to protect his empress while Darrigan himself went on a suicide mission.

Suicide. To protect her, of course. The same as Drystan.

Men kept thinking that she needed protecting from the cythraul. Vesha meant to master the beasts instead.

Hiding her frustration, Vesha let Cashun help her out of the palanquin. Behind them, the palanquin carrying Zeyna stopped and Vesha's sister joined them a moment later.

"What is this?" her sister asked, looking surprised. "I thought you wanted to see the city."

"I do," Vesha said, eyes fixed on the crumbling building before her.

"Your Majesty," Zeyna said, hands clasped tight. "This is a bordello."

"I can tell."

The building was old, but still looked as if it would outlive every person in Iandua. Large columns graced the front in the shape of women in chitons carrying baskets. Those stone baskets had been filled with fresh flowers, most of which had wilted in the midday sun.

Through the open doors, Vesha could see a courtyard with a fountain in the center. Around the fountain lounged women in varying states of undress, some combing their hair, washing in the fountain, and others sitting with fans in the shade of palm trees.

"Allow us to secure the place first, my empress," Cashun said, inclining his head.

"Go," Vesha agreed with a nod.

Cashun signaled to several of his men, singling out a few in armor. "We're clearing this place for the empress's use."

"Your Majesty," Zeyna's expression turned horrified. "What business do you have in…in a house of pleasure?"

Vesha didn't even look at her sister as the Kadra'han marched up the steps of the brothel. "You are free to return home, Zeyna," Vesha said. "I have business to attend to."

"It's not proper for us to go in there!" Zeyna protested, her voice taking on a high-pitched, wheedling sound that was too girlish for Vesha's liking. "Think of the scandal if—"

"If what, Zeyna?" Vesha demanded. "I am reigning empress of the Erymayan Empire. Nowhere is forbidden to me, not even by gossips and busybodies."

"I…I thought you were regent," Zeyna stammered.

Vesha whirled away. "Thank you for accompanying me, sister," she clipped. The term was at once an acknowledgement of their relationship and a slight by leaving off Zeyna's title. "My men will escort me back to your home."

"Your Majesty, I—"

At the entrance to the brothel, three Kadra'han approached, only to be stopped by a man as broad as an ox. He folded his arms across his chest. "The price is four apiece. Imperial silver only."

Vesha's brows rose. That was at least twice the price of a brothel visit back in the mainland and Vesha would know— brothels provided some of the best tax revenue in the empire.

"We're not buying," said the officer in front. "You and your lot will be clearing out by imperial order."

The bouncer looked toward Vesha, Cashun beside her, and the palanquin behind her. "What business has a fine doll like you got in a place like this?"

"You will not address Her Majesty, dog," Cashun said. "You will inform the other residents of this place that they are to vacate at once."

Vesha looked on as Cashun and the others took a few more minutes to convince the big man to move. Once he did, the three officers entered.

"We won't be long," Caa Iss said.

It took some time for the officers to clear the brothel to their satisfaction. Vesha sat back down in her palanquin to wait. The prostitutes were herded into the street along with their burly protector, and an indignant, sputtering middle aged woman that must have been the madam.

The madam stormed up to Vesha, face twisted into a scowl. Her hair had been drawn back into a tight bun and her dress came down to the ankles. She looked more like a governess than a flesh peddler. "We have an imperial charter and the deed on this building for the next ten years! You have no right to throw me out of my own establishment!"

Vesha almost laughed.

Cashun stepped forward, as did two of the other Kadra'han. The woman had no idea how seriously she had just endangered her own life.

"I will be taking this to the viceroy!" the madam screamed.

Vesha almost laughed at that, too—threatening her with her own brother-in-law? How ironic. She waved down Cashun and the other Kadra'han, looking past the madam to the huddle of prostitutes cowering in the shadow of their large protectors.

"What's your name?"

The madam ruffled. "Mistress Hawthorne." She mimicked Vesha's accent in a clear mockery.

Caa Iss snickered at Vesha's side. "This spell doesn't require a blood sacrifice," he said, "but I can always use one if you want an excuse."

"You are addressing Her Imperial Majesty, Empress Vesha Myrani Fanduillion of the Erymayan Empire," Captain Cashun snapped. "Get back in line, whore."

The madam looked between Vesha and the guard captain, as if she wasn't sure if she believed him or not.

"Mistress Hawthorne, how old are those girls of yours?" Vesha looked appraisingly at the prostitutes. Several looked young. Too young. Some hid their faces from Vesha and the guards, others looked on with blank expressions, not seeming to care. "Do you have age certificates for all of them? Filed with the city clerk?"

"Of course, I do," the madam snapped back. "This is an upstanding establishment. Fully legitimate."

Vesha doubted that. Three years ago, she had passed a law banning the use of prostitutes under the age of sixteen. It was the first time brothels had truly been regulated beyond taxes and while there had been many dissenters at court—mostly nobles who owned brothels—few had been willing to outright oppose the law to Vesha's face.

Vesha had been proud of that law, but it was still hard to enforce with so many corners and crevices in the empire. Proving a girl's age could also be difficult, especially in regions with few clerks. In some kingdoms, children's births weren't recorded until their one hundredth day or sometimes even their first birthday. It left a lot of time for the task to be forgotten. Many children of the slums and remote farms had no official record of birth.

"I would double check your documents," Vesha said simply, not blinking as she stared at the madam. "There's no need to file a complaint with the viceroy. I shall have his agents here as soon as I have the time. I would make sure your records are in order before then."

The madam looked between Vesha and the guards, finally speechless.

"You may think the law is on your side," Vesha said coolly. "But I am the law."

Her Kadra'han deposited several more figures outside the brothel—a skinny man still pulling his pants on, and two older women wrapped in blankets who were so similar in appearance, Vesha wondered if they were twins. Their faces bore the marks of hard living and one of them had an exposed sore on the back of her shoulder.

Vesha had always hated brothels as a rule. They were cesspools of disease and worse. Though Drystan had outlawed slavery not long after he had been crowned—even before he had met her—brothels were one place where the practice was often carried on through roundabout means.

The soldiers jogged up and reported to Cashun, who in turn went to Vesha.

"Your Majesty." Cashun bowed to her. "The building is secure."

"Thank you, Cashun." Vesha took his arm and he escorted her up the steps, past the misplaced prostitutes, their useless bodyguards, and the disempowered madam. Vesha's handmaidens followed close behind.

"Look what they've done with the place," Caa Iss chuckled. "Long ago, the temple was the only thing on this godforsaken hill," Caa Iss went on. "A village, and then a city was built around it over centuries. And then you people forgot about it, as you do."

The building inside was a central courtyard with a well in the middle. Blue and white tiles lined the floor, chipped and worn, but swept clean. Two levels of doors faced them on either side with stairs leading up to the top levels at the far end.

Everything was stone and most of it was designed after the older style from when the first Erymayan colonists had settled here. Some brighter, smoother stone marked where repairs had been done over the years, cobbled together with the original designs.

"This way," Caa Iss beckoned. The cythraul crouched at the center of the courtyard, leaning over the edge of the well.

"Here?" Vesha stepped up to the central well and looked down.

Caa Iss nodded, horns waving above his head. "It was once a holy well kept by the allegiants of Hezra, the goddess of doorways and crossroads."

Vesha looked down the well and frowned. "It's so small."

"Your people wanted to be small back then," Caa Iss replied. "You had to make room when gods walked the earth."

Vesha shot him a look, but he chose not to elaborate.

"Here is where we will work." Caa Iss shuffled his wings and searched their surroundings.

Vesha turned to Cashun. "Secure this place. Bring in all our

Kadra'han and keep the other men outside to wait. Then close the doors."

Cashun saluted and hurried to obey.

Vesha didn't wait for them to finish securing the brothel. She heard her sister outside, half in hysterics.

"Help me take these off," Vesha ordered her handmaidens. "All of my jewels."

"Your Majesty?" one of them peeped nervously.

"Come, girls. All the jewels. My overdress, too."

The handmaidens removed the massive earrings Vesha had worn, along with her bracelets, necklace, and the belt of gold they had so carefully selected that morning. Vesha's soldiers stood watch but didn't speak.

Vesha insisted the girls remove her silken overdress until there was nothing but the white chemise underneath. After that, the Kadra'han avoided looking straight at her.

Lastly, Vesha removed the pearl pins from her hair. That left her hair in a long black braid down her back. Vesha stepped up to the edge of the well, stripped of all her signs of office, except the Fanduillion signet ring on one finger. She looked to Caa Iss.

"The offering," he urged. His face was calm, but his tail twisted and writhed the way a man might twiddle his thumbs.

"The box I gave you, Shelaine," Vesha said to the nearest handmaiden.

The girl held it out tentatively. Each of them was used to Vesha's experiments and dark rituals. But while they had supported her in the past, everyone was hesitant since the death of Darrigan.

Vesha opened the small wooden box, wholly unobtrusive and unremarkable. Inside was the broken tip of a claw. It had taken a whole lock of burned hair to make Caa Iss substantial enough to give it. One of his claws was now shorter than the rest, but he had said it would grow back.

"Say the words I taught you and then toss the claw in," Caa Iss snapped. His tone was harsh, but his feet shuffled.

Vesha narrowed her gaze at him. She thought about responding but preferred her people didn't see her talking to the air.

Tossing the claw into the well, Vesha watched it sink. The stone around the well was grey and weathered and covered in moss. This whole brothel appeared worn, dilapidated, and a step away from neglect. It was hardly the kind of place she would have considered holy.

"Grant me entry to the homeland of this creature." Vesha waited until the claw vanished from sight.

Nothing happened.

Vesha looked at Caa Iss with one quirked brow.

"Wait!" he hissed. "Just—"

Hot wind gusted up from the well as the water rippled back. Vesha shielded her face against the heat as the well became a doorway down into a barren land of basalt and ash. Lava glowed in the distance and there was no sign of life as far as the eye could see.

The Kadra'han balked and the handmaidens trembled. Someone screamed.

Looking at the vast, hostile expanse of the Dread Marches, Vesha realized a part of her had hoped this wouldn't work. She inhaled the cool, fresh air of her own world, wondering if she would ever breathe it again.

But it didn't matter. This had to be done. For the sake of her people, for the sake of the empire.

"Your Majesty!" Cashun cried.

Vesha schooled her face into one of calm and turned to the guard captain. "You will keep watch here for one day and one night," she said. "Let no one come in and no one interfere. If I have not returned by the second sunset..." Vesha's throat tightened, but she forced the next words out. She had given it careful thought and was settled that this was the right decision. "You and the other Kadra'han are to seek out my son, Daindreth Fanduillion, and give your allegiance to him."

"Your Majesty, please," Cashun protested. "If someone must go, let it be one of us. Do not endanger yourself."

"These are my commands, Cashun." Vesha stopped beside her crying handmaidens. "It's alright, girls," she whispered softly, touching their shoulders. "Don't weep."

"Your Majesty, are you really going into that place?" Shelaine gasped, looking on the wasteland that was the Dread Marches.

"Yes," Vesha said, hardly believing it herself. "Yes, I am." She stepped up to the edge of the well.

Caa Iss nodded to her. He shuffled, keeping her between himself and the yawning portal. "You will do well, empress. Remember the things I told you."

If Vesha was gone too long, Caa Iss would lose his tether to the mortal world and would be drawn back to the Dread Marches. This was a risk for him, too.

"If you die in the Dread Marches, you will find no escape," Caa Iss warned her. "You will become a cythraul, trapped to wander the wastes, but weaker than all of us, the plaything of my siblings for eternity."

Vesha didn't ask what that would entail, but she knew enough about cythraul to guess. She said nothing to the demon as she stepped down through the portal, her feet meeting black basalt. Ash and soot stained her skirt almost immediately. She looked up to see the sky one last time, but the portal had already closed.

She was in the Dread Marches now. And she had no choice but to succeed or die trying.

CHAPTER EIGHT

Amira

Amira didn't know if it was dread or excitement that tied her in knots. They kept to the main roads, but avoided the farms and towns.

Thadred's kelpie became more irritable the closer they came to civilization, but he managed to control it. At night, he would rub down the stallion with the help of Rhis, usually while Sair looked on. Thadred spent more and more time with Sair and her son. Daindreth had noticed it, too, but neither mentioned it to Thadred.

Thadred's liaisons at court were legendary, but a relationship with an Istovari sorceress couldn't be so casual—especially one with a child. Anyone could see Rhis was growing fond of the knight. Sair and Thadred were adults. Rhis wasn't.

Amira had warned Sair about Thadred's reputation, only to find out Thadred had already told her.

Was there a chance Thadred might settle down? It seemed outlandish and yet more and more possible.

On the third day, they camped in the forest a few miles from the city walls. It was royal land, owned by the king, and no one was supposed to hunt game or graze livestock without an imperial charter. A cave complex crouched near a natural spring and the ragtag group set up in the shelter of the rocks.

Sair and Cyne, with Amira and Thadred's help, threaded spells in a mesh all the way around their camp to alert them if anyone approached.

The rain had returned and that made the woods hazy with golden *ka*. To a sorceress's eyes, it was beautiful. To a practical assassin, it made them all wet and grouchy.

Even though summer was almost here, Amira and the others spent the entire time drenched or struggling to get dry. Sheltering in the rocks helped, but it wasn't a solution.

Sair was the first to venture into the city. Amira had volunteered, but Sair had contacts in Lashera and had practice sneaking in and out.

Their plan was to see if Cromwell would be willing to get them an audience with the king. From there, Amira and Daindreth would work on swaying her father to their side.

The small group sheltered in a cave, listening to the rain and waiting for Sair's return. Tapios taught Rhis how to wax a bowstring with the rangers near the entrance. Amira, Daindreth, Thadred, and Cyne sat closer to the back with the horses.

Lleuad had been left loose outside with just his hackamore. The water horse seemed to be the only one enjoying the rain. He twitched his tail happily as he nibbled the ferns.

Amira perched on the edge of a rock beside Daindreth, her grandmother's spell book open in her lap. She had studied it dutifully every night since leaving the Haven.

"She's been gone almost six hours." Thadred tossed a rock at the wall.

"She knows what she's doing, Thad," Daindreth reminded him. "She captured you well enough."

Thadred scowled at that. "The imperial Kadra'han may expect us here. They could already be here. If they sense her magic..." Thadred threw another rock. This one thudded into the wall, breaking off a flurry of smaller rocks. "I don't know."

Amira sat on a rock with her elbows on her knees, chewing her lip. "We all knew this was a risk. But Sair avoided detection for years. I think she'll be fine for a day." Despite her words, Amira had to stuff down her own gnawing sense of anxiety.

Amira considered Sair a friend and she didn't have many of those. They didn't know what kind of traps Vesha might have left in place for them. Had the former empress anticipated their return?

Word could travel slow across the continent. It was possible that by the time Amira and Daindreth had been captured, Vesha's agents had just received the orders to secure Lashera.

"I'm worried about getting to the king." Daindreth leaned forward, resting his elbows on his knees. "I don't know if my mother has returned to Mynadra yet. She might be spreading any manner of stories through the empire."

Amira rested a hand on his back. "We'll deal with her when

64

we have to." It was a bold statement from a woman who spent most of this week thinking of ways to kill her mother-in-law.

Vesha was powerful, charismatic, and dangerous. Amira knew enough about the ebbs and flows of power over the centuries to know that regents rarely gave up their power willingly. Especially ones as successful as the empress.

After being betrayed by Saan Thii, Amira was hopeful that Vesha would think twice before making another deal with the cythraul. But while she hoped, she also planned and prepared.

She had read and re-read her grandmother's spellbook, trying to truly understand just what the Istovari had done. Cyne helped where she could.

Amira had spoken at length to them and the others who had survived the tower. Unfortunately, there were several conflicting accounts of which spells they had used and in which order.

None of it helped her understand how Vesha had summoned a cythraul as her familiar or how they could banish Caa Iss.

The rangers stirred at the mouth of the cave. Tapios stood.

Amira tilted her head to one side, concentrating. It was hard to sense when the forest was a smog of *ka,* but something large was coming. Something large enough to be a sorceress and her mount.

"Sairydwen," Tapios called.

"Mama!" Rhis stood so quickly that the bow in his lap clattered to the ground.

"Careful with that!" protested one of the rangers.

Thadred was the first of their group to stand, hobbling toward the cave's entrance.

Daindreth took Amira's hand without looking, like he could sense where she was without needing to see. Amira tucked the spell book under one arm and went with him to meet the sorceress.

At first glance, Sair and her horse appeared fine, if a bit wet. Sair smeared hair back from her face, telling Rhis to calm down as he hopped around her.

"How did it go?" Tapios asked, taking her horse's reins.

"It went as well as it could, I think." Sair's nose was red and her cheeks pale. "I wasn't spotted, at least." Sair's eyes went to Amira and Daindreth. "Cromwell has been imprisoned in the royal dungeons."

"Imprisoned?" Amira wasn't sure she had heard correctly.

"As best I could learn, the Kadra'han who chased us knew he helped you escape. He wasn't executed, which is probably a testament to his cleverness. But they did have the king imprison him to await their return."

"You're sure?" Amira pressed. "He's alive and a prisoner?"

Sair nodded. "My contacts said Vesha also has soldiers stationed in the royal palace."

Amira chewed her lip. She'd expected as much.

"Are they Kadra'han?" Cyne asked.

"I couldn't confirm." Sair shook her head. "It's possible that they have no access to spells, even if they are." She glanced sideways to Thadred. A few weeks ago, Thadred had been a Kadra'han who thought he had no access to magic.

"Is there another way we could get a message to the king?" Daindreth asked. He looked to Amira, then Cyne. "Anyone who might still be loyal to you?"

Cyne shook her head. "Everyone loyal to me was either banished or learned better."

"Can we approach through regular channels?" Tapios suggested. "If he knows his daughter is here, might he grant you an audience?"

"We can't risk it." Thadred braced his hands atop his cane. "Vesha's agents are in the palace. Maybe all over this city. They'd be on us before we finished talking."

Daindreth pinched the bridge of his nose. "Even if we get a message to the king, we have no way of making sure he's on our side before we get him to meet us."

"Renner will kneel to whoever he fears the most," Cyne clipped.

The others kept speaking, discussing their options. Thadred suggested riding onto another fiefdom with a more sympathetic ruler, but that was quickly shot down. They needed Hylendale, if only so that the Istovari would be able to aid them without being threatened from the south.

"What of Princess Fonra?" Amira hated herself even as she asked it. The last thing she wanted was to put her sister in danger, but if she and Daindreth failed, it wouldn't matter anymore.

"She is here," Sair answered. "I asked about her, as you requested. She is in good health, and she is expected to visit Mynadra soon, for your wedding."

Amira frowned. Was the empire still planning an imperial wedding?

"What news of Amira and I?" Daindreth asked.

"People seem to think that you are both in Mynadra, or at least the central empire," Sair answered. "But news might just be taking time to reach this far north."

"Vesha must be trying to maintain the image of control," Cyne guessed. "If that's the case, she will try to cover up your disappearance as long as possible."

"Bloody hell." Thadred looked to the ceiling. "What if we could break Cromwell out somehow?"

"From the bowels of the royal dungeon?" Tapios gestured in a circle. "There are less than twenty of us."

"And most of you have barely been outside the Cursewood," Cyne agreed. "If we—"

"I can get Cromwell," Amira interrupted.

All eyes turned to her.

Daindreth gave her a long, hard look. "You can?"

Amira shrugged, arching one eyebrow. "My father paid a lot to train the perfect assassin. Time he got to see me in action."

Daindreth's tone turned serious. "Amira—"

"I don't mean like that," Amira assured him. "I know we need the king alive. But I spent my whole life in that palace. I know my way around it blindfolded." As a child, she had spent many hours avoiding her stepmother, but she didn't mention that part. "And I know how to get in and out unseen. If Cromwell is able to walk, I can get him out."

"Your father knows how you used to get in and out," Daindreth reminded her. "He will be expecting that."

"I don't think so. I've thought about this." Amira had thought about it, almost as much as she'd thought about killing Vesha. "Even if he is expecting me, he will be expecting me as I

67

was, not as I am. I'm stronger now. I know more spells and I can sense *ka* much farther out. I will be more powerful than any of Vesha's Kadra'han," Amira was only confident saying that now because Captain Darrigan was dead.

"This could be a trap," Daindreth argued. "My mother could have planned for this."

"Yes," Amira agreed. "Yes, it might be a trap. But we need allies and right now Cromwell is our best start."

Sair nodded. "Cromwell's spy network alone would be a great blessing."

Amira had been thinking that, too. "Cromwell knows he is a traitor to Vesha. He will have to throw his lot in with us. And he will know how to sway King Hyle to our side."

Cyne's mouth pressed into a tight line. She studied Amira closely, not speaking.

Daindreth gripped Amira's shoulder, pulling her toward him. "This is too dangerous."

"It is dangerous," Amira agreed. "But either I do this, or we wait here for Vesha's agents to find us. I must try. We both know it."

Daindreth shook his head. "I don't want you needlessly risking yourself. You don't have to do things alone anymore."

"It won't be needless." Amira rested a hand on his arm. "Also, I have no intention of doing this alone." She braved a small smile and added in the one thing she knew would sway him, "We can avoid bloodshed this way."

CHAPTER NINE

Vesha

Vesha picked through the land of basalt and soot. Her hands were stained, and her chemise smeared in black. She'd blow a strand of hair from her face only to have it fall back down. Her chemise had left her feeling overexposed back in Iandua, but now it felt thick and oppressive. She wanted to strip it off, but then would have had no protection against the raining soot.

Caa Iss had given her directions, of a sort. Even he had admitted he had no idea where in the Dread Marches she would find herself when she went through that portal.

Light filtered through the sky from behind the gauzy haze of clouds and smoke. Vesha was grateful for the cloud cover. Something told her that she'd rather not see whatever sun hung in this sky.

After walking for what felt like hours, Vesha found what she was looking for—tracks. They were vaguely human, but the toes too long, the heels too pointed. How many there were, she couldn't have said. When she had visited the beach as a child, she had once chased a flock of seabirds into the air. The ground they left behind had looked like this slope did now—scarred in more prints than she could count.

Vesha steeled herself and followed them. Not for the first time, she wondered if Caa Iss was tricking her. It didn't matter, though. She was committed to this course and had no choice.

She followed the tracks into a rocky outcrop and then into a maze of deep gashes in the stone. It was as if the landscape had been clawed by some giant beast.

Vesha lifted the hem of her chemise with one hand, finding her way over the rocks at the bottom of the gorge.

"What's this?" croaked a garbled voice.

Vesha resisted the impulse to jump. She forced herself to turn around slowly to face the voice. As she did, she had to bite back a scream.

Just a few feet above her head, hundreds of red-slitted eyes watched her with a hungry glint. The creatures were no larger than cats with hooked claws and skin mottled in burn marks.

No two were exactly alike. Some had mangled wings that hung off their backs at impossible angles—much like Caa Iss. Others had spiked tails, and extra limbs. A few had ears like rabbits and she saw at least one with pincers like a scorpion.

They were cythraul, but different from Caa Iss and even Saan Thii. Bones showed beneath their skin and soot coated every one of them.

Vesha had been told by both Saan Thii and Caa Iss that cythraul had hierarchies like any creatures did. While Caa Iss was a prince and Saan Thii was what amounted to a member of the gentry, there were many other castes beneath them, including the imps, the lowliest of the demons.

If Vesha had to guess, these were imps. Their size seemed to fit with that.

"It's a human," purred one of the imps, Vesha couldn't see which one.

Vesha gagged back her horror. "I would seek an audience with the Goddess of the Second Moon."

The imps let off a chorus of laughter that was like the sound of claws on steel.

"We should eat her nose first," said one of the imps. "Humans look funny without their noses."

"Start with the arms and legs," squealed another. "I like to see them wriggle around on the ground. Like grubs!"

Vesha forced down the panic in her chest and raised her chin. Caa Iss had warned her not to show fear.

It had been a long time since Vesha had been in a situation where she had no real power, where she had to bluff. But she hadn't gotten this far by being a coward.

She spoke. "I am Vesha Myrani Fanduillion, Empress of Erymaya and the witch of Caa Iss, formerly the witch of Saan Thii."

At the name of Caa Iss, the imps hesitated. According to Caa Iss, his name would hold some weight with the lesser demons, but cythraul were conceited and prone to arrogance. Who knew if he was telling the truth or not?

"Caa Iss has no witch," one of the imps sneered, a creature with too-large eyes and a pugged snout that made their voice sound wheezy. "Caa Iss has a vessel."

"Saan Thii betrayed us both," Vesha said simply. "When Caa Iss was vulnerable, Saan Thii expelled him from his host." Vesha didn't give the imps time to discuss more. "I come to offer a bargain to your mother."

"You broke your bargain to our mother," hissed the big-eyed imp. "The goddess of pacts and bargains does not take kindly to those who break them."

Interesting. The imps knew exactly who she was and how she had failed to let Caa Iss take control of Daindreth. Was she famous in the Dread Marches? That could be a good thing or a very, very bad thing.

"I did," Vesha admitted, not making excuses. Caa Iss had warned her against making excuses. "But I come to offer her a better one."

"You failed our mother!" squeaked a toadlike imp, crouching at the very edge of the rocky outcrop. "Failure is sin!"

Several other imps joined in. "Failure is sin!" the creatures chanted. "Failure is sin!"

How odd that demons had a concept of sin. Vesha wondered how many priests would be dizzied by the idea.

"You will take me to Moreyne," Vesha commanded. "I will submit myself to her judgment and her judgment alone." Then she spoke a phrase Caa Iss had taught her, "May the Second Goddess be second to none."

The imps looked to each other, suddenly unsure.

"If we take her to Mother, Mother might give her to one of the princes instead of us," protested the toadlike imp.

Another spoke up. "If we eat her and Mother finds out—"

"Mother always finds out!" wailed a small imp with tentacles waving like a mane around its neck. "Mother will know, and she will punish us!"

"Mother hasn't had visitors in…how long has it been?"

"If you want a chance to be free from this world," Vesha interrupted, "you will take me to your mother." For a moment, the only sound was the distant rumble of the lava flows and the thud of Vesha's heart. A bead of sweat trickled down her forehead, but she was already soaked in sweat. What difference did it make?

Vesha faced down the creatures, not flinching. Unless she wanted to be eaten alive, she would stay the course and finish this.

The pug-nosed imp was the first to speak. "We will take you to Mother. If Mother does decide to kill you, I will ask that we get to eat you, since we found you."

"We will take you to Mother," the imps chorused in agreement, their voices overlapping and clamoring. "We will take you to Mother." The troop of imps scuttled overhead, moving along the gorge.

Relief flooded her though she did her best to hide it as she followed them. But with every step, her easiness faded as the destination became all too real. She was headed to the Second Goddess.

That was assuming that these imps didn't trick her. Her only consolation was that Caa Iss would probably spend the next century skinning, gutting, and boning every single one of them if they did.

Vesha was his last hope of being permanently freed from the Dread Marches. She was valuable. She could only hope that Moreyne would feel the same way.

Vesha followed the flock of imps through the basalt trenches. The trenches never rose much higher than her head as best she could tell, but it rankled her not to be able to see.

The imps eventually led her out of the trench and up onto a flat plain. The ground was black soot that stuck like charcoal to her shoes and rubbed the dark stains even deeper into her chemise.

She must look like a mad woman, and she supposed she was. Sane women didn't enter the Dread Marches to make bargains with fallen goddesses.

The imps scuttled around her, not coming close, but circling her from behind and both sides as well as the front.

"She does smell like him," one of the imps whispered. "The

72

Firstborn's stench is on her."

Vesha assumed they meant Caa Iss.

They led her on and on. Vesha saw distant shapes moving on the basalt flats, but they were too far away for her to make out the details. All the same, she could have sworn the shapes stared at her.

The heat continued to buffet Vesha. It was like inhaling the putrid breath of a brimstone dog. Her lungs burned and her nostrils stung, yet she couldn't seem to get quite enough air.

Massive white rocks jutted up from the ground, almost like pillars, but bent and unnatural looking. They were stained with soot like everything else in this place.

"Here we are," croaked the toadlike imp.

Their little group parted, making room for her to go forward. Vesha looked around them. "What do you mean?"

"This is Mother's house," rasped the imp with overlarge eyes.

Vesha blinked back at the massive red eyes, bigger than Caa Iss's, but in a body a fraction of his size. "Do you think me an idiot?" She let anger well in her breast. Anger was more useful than fear with these creatures.

"We're not lying," the imp coughed, seeming almost offended. "This is Mother's house? See? This way. This way."

The creatures beckoned and Vesha followed them onward, around the slope of the grimy basalt, down the other side. A massive boulder rose into view as they rounded the slope of black sand.

"Here," the imps said again.

Vesha followed the creature's pointing claw and had to stifle a gasp as she realized what this was.

A massive skull loomed before them on its side, as high as any parapet in Mynadra, sitting like its own hill. What she had mistaken for boulders were the cracked remains of broken teeth. The jutting rock pillars weren't pillars at all, but the cracked remnants of a titan's ribcage. The broken jaw lay open in the death throes of the giant's final scream.

"In there," the imps urged her. "Mother is in there."

Vesha glared down at the bug-eyed imp. "If you are trying

to trick me…"

"We're not!" swore the imp, ears lying flat against its head. "We're not lying!"

A voice shook the ground, like the whooshing of the wind, the pull of the waves and the rumbling of the earth combined. "Criin Moor."

Vesha stumbled back as the other imps scattered.

The imp that had addressed Vesha dropped into a crouch, ears pinned back and tail between its legs. It cowered, a pathetic whimper escaping its throat.

"What have you brought me, my child?" the voice rumbled.

The words were affectionate, but their tone was anything but. Something in them made Vesha cringe even as the imp—Criin Moor—did the same.

"A guest, Mother," the cythraul whimpered. The imp was nearly flat with the ground, though nothing moved from the mouth of the cave. The creature groveled and whimpered, pressing itself deeper and deeper into the sand like it was trying to burrow away.

"A guest?" the voice drawled back, confusion lacing its powerful boom.

Vesha inhaled the hot air, forcing her lungs to breathe in and out. Something in the voice chilled her bones and made everything in her want to scream. Dread welled up from somewhere deep inside her, a primal, instinctive terror.

"Yes, Mother," the imp whimpered, whining as if it was in pain. "She came seeking you."

"Who is she?" the voice demanded. The hint of anger was slight, but Vesha felt her spine chilling at the voice's displeasure.

The imp yelped and whined. "Forgive me, Mother. She says Caa Iss sent her."

Vesha's heart thudded in her chest, beating against her ribs so hard she could feel it through her entire body. Sweat trickled off her in drops, leaving streaks on her soot-covered skin, yet a cold fear crawled along her body, plucking at her spine.

Every second seemed to last an eternity.

"Caa Iss…" the voice repeated, dropping into a growl. "Where is he?"

"I don't know, Mother. I don't know!" the imp wept.

Vesha was surprised to see massive tears rolling down the imp's pugged snout.

"Please! Forgive me. I only—"

"I asked, who is she?" the voice—the voice of Moreyne—roared.

"Caa Iss's witch," Criin Moor wheedled. "Please, Mother."

"You lie," Moreyne snarled. "Caa Iss has no witch."

Vesha forced herself to take a step forward. She had come this far. She would not back down now. "I come to treat with you."

"You think you have the right to treat with me? In my own domain?"

"No," Vesha said. "But I would bargain for your right to mine."

"Your domain?" Moreyne scoffed. "What do you have to offer me?"

"I am Vesha, Empress of Erymaya."

"You are Saan Thii's witch," Moreyne growled back. "Do not lie to me."

Vesha licked her lips. Did Moreyne really not know? Or was this some manner of test?

Vesha had assumed that Moreyne knew Saan Thii betrayed Caa Iss. She'd also assumed that the Second Goddess knew all the bargains her children made. But perhaps Vesha had assumed too much. She'd never thought Moreyne could be fooled or be kept ignorant of failure.

Whether Moreyne was testing her or not, Vesha decided it was best to tell the truth.

"Saan Thii betrayed us," Vesha said. "Caa Iss and I."

Silence as loud as thunder stretched across the basalt plains. Criin Moor kept groveling on the ground, almost flattened with the black sand. There was no sign of the other cythraul anywhere in sight.

"Enter, witch," Moreyne commanded. "Let us treat."

Vesha didn't give herself time to think. Placing one foot in front of the other, she stepped under the shadow of the giant's cracked jawbone.

Inside was dark, but it was more than the lack of light. Inside, she felt the darkness wrapping her like a shroud. Though nothing moved in the shadows, her spine crawled with the sensation of being watched.

"Come closer, witch," Moreyne ordered.

Vesha couldn't turn back now. Behind her, Criin Moor scurried away, running back into the dunes with their fellows.

Inside the skull, Vesha picked her way through broken teeth twice her height. The teeth were everywhere, some cracked in half, others lying haphazardly on the ground. She wondered what had been able to shatter this titan's jaw. How much power would have been needed to turn this giant's face into fractured splinters?

"How did you enter the Dread Marches?" The voice came from over Vesha's shoulder.

The empress whirled around to find nothing but empty shadows. Fear spiked in her veins. Gulping, she forced herself to speak. "Forgive me, goddess," she began, her voice hoarse. "I came to speak to you on behalf of Caa Iss."

A laugh reverberated through the skull. Vesha couldn't tell which direction it came from. It seemed to surround her.

"Does my son send a mortal to parley?" Moreyne laughed.

Vesha changed tactics. "I sent myself. Caa Iss helped me."

"You wished to see me?" Moreyne chuckled, sounding both curious and amused. "Few have been so foolish."

"I wish to bargain with you." Vesha wished her voice was not so shaky.

"So you have said," Moreyne muttered. "But we *had* a bargain. You forged a pact with me as Saan Thii's familiar."

A white shape swooped overhead, wings and claws and teeth.

Vesha ducked out of instinct with a cry, dropping to her hands and knees.

The shape flew over her, but Vesha heard claws scraping on a boulder at her back. She didn't dare turn around this time.

"We had a bargain, witch. Caa Iss on the throne in exchange for your empire's prosperity. I assume Caa Iss is not on the throne."

Clenching her eyes shut, Vesha continued. "I beg forgiveness, Great One."

From behind Vesha's back, she heard the grating of talons. "You lie to a goddess and then have the gall to enter my domain? Am I some nanny goat to be milked for favors?"

The air stirred overhead. Vesha realized that Moreyne had moved across to perch on a different tooth.

"I mean no disrespect," Vesha said, sounding pitiful even to herself.

"I will teach you respect," Moreyne growled. "You think you know fear, Vesha Myrani Fanduillion. You think you know pain." A hissing, seething growl emitted from the goddess. "I shall teach you pain, darling. I shall peel you apart inch by inch. Sinew by sinew and vein by vein. I will savor your screams until your throat frays like a shredded reed. Then I will heal you." If menace had a scent, the stench of it filled the air. "And we shall do it again. And again. For as long as you amuse me."

Vesha squeezed her eyes shut tighter. Seventy-eight thousand, four hundred, and eighteen. That was how many children under the age of five were in the empire according to the first census under her rule.

Seven years later at the next census, two thirds had still been alive. That was more than twice what should have survived according to past censuses.

Vesha had ensured good crops, prevented famines, and put an end to storms, earthquakes, and floods. Tens of thousands of children had been saved.

If she failed now, the empire's protections would be at an end. The power Saan Thii and her minions had granted Vesha would be lost and decades of held-up calamities would sweep the land. Devastation and death would tear the empire apart.

Vesha refused to fail. She was the empress—she was all that stood between her people and annihilation.

"You are my only hope!" Vesha cried, her voice echoing against the inside of the giant's skull.

"Now that," the goddess purred, "is something no one has ever said to me."

"Please." Vesha lowered herself closer to the ground. "I

have entered your domain myself because I would not insult you by sending an ambassador. I come to offer you a bargain, Moreyne, goddess of pacts and bargains. I would seek you as patron goddess of the Erymayan Empire. Your children shall be free to wander the lands as they will. The land shall be under your dominion."

Moreyne didn't speak. There was a faint swooshing, sweeping sound and Vesha guessed it was the goddess waving her wings.

Vesha dared open her eyes and had to choke back a scream. Before her, close enough that she could reach out and touch them, were a pair of paws with too-long toes and pointed claws digging into the black sand. The paws were white, as white as bone, with hair as fine as a mole rat's. The claws were pale, almost translucent. Vesha imagined what her own blood would look like spattered across them.

"You are a bold one," Moreyne hissed. She sounded angry, but she still didn't pounce.

Then again, why should she? Moreyne had all the time in the world. She was in no hurry. She could carry out all her threats ten times over and still have an eternity left.

Moreyne's white paws dug deeper into the sand before Vesha's eyes. "You have your gods," Moreyne growled. "Demred is patron of the empire."

"Demred is useless!" Vesha's words came out sharper than she had expected. "He is either deaf to our prayers, impotent, or indifferent. I prayed to every god in the pantheon. I sought favors from their clergy and bowed down at their altars, but none ever lifted a finger to help me." Vesha sank lower, prostrating herself deeper before the mother of demons. Hot droplets spilled down her cheeks and she wasn't sure if it was sweat or tears. "They did nothing to stop the rebellion and the killing that came after my husband's death. The burning of crops. The famines that followed. Only your children answered my pleas."

Moreyne let off a low sound that was part growl, but there was something else to it, almost a question.

Vesha took that as permission to continue. "I offered you

78

the empire before and my offer still stands, but this time, I would offer more."

Caa Iss had warned her that this was where Moreyne would be most likely to grow angry—when she was reminded of Vesha's past failures.

"I come to you to throw myself on your mercy," Vesha said. "I come to prove that *I* have been betrayed, twice now, and only that has prevented me from keeping my end of our bargains."

Moreyne made a clicking, serpentine sound.

Vesha continued, speaking as fast as possible without garbling her words. "Become patron of my empire," Vesha pleaded. "Become our goddess and our protectress. Make Erymaya your domain."

In the distance, the lava flows rumbled. There was a faint whispering swoosh as Moreyne's wings waved back and forth.

"Gaze upon me, mortal witch," Moreyne commanded.

Vesha looked up.

Moreyne wasn't human, but then Vesha supposed she had never been. She looked nothing like her portraits in chapels and cathedrals.

In those, Moreyne was a woman—a beautiful woman with skin like moonstone and hair that evoked the color of the night sky.

The creature towering over Vesha was at least eight feet tall. Leathery, batlike wings rose high above her head, a pale, albino pink.

Her heart-shaped face was human, but only barely. Pockmarks and scars marked her cheeks and forehead, reminding Vesha of the dark patches on Eponine, the moon that remained in the night sky.

She had a feline body with a slender tail that swished back and forth. Long, gangly limbs were roped in muscle and tipped with unnaturally pointed talons.

Vesha forced herself not to react.

"Would you have this be your goddess?" Moreyne growled. "This monstrosity?" Her teeth might have once been human, but now they too were pointed spikes, more fangs than teeth.

"I would," Vesha said, and she meant it. She had always

done what needed to be done. It didn't matter how she felt about her allies if they protected her people.

Moreyne roared, "Criin Moor!"

There came a whimpering from outside in response. "Yes, Mother."

"Search the Dread Marches. If you find Saan Thii, bring her to me," the goddess commanded.

Criin Moor whimpered their acknowledgement before the scampering sounds of claws retreated.

"If she is here," Moreyne purred. "I will know you are telling the truth." The goddess pulled herself to her full height. "While we wait…tell me, Vesha, Empress of Erymaya and witch of Caa Iss." Moreyne's voice rumbled with satisfaction as she sat back on her haunches. "What are the terms of my patronage?"

CHAPTER TEN

Amira

Amira checked her weapons again, making sure that they were secured to her waist and torso and wouldn't clank when she moved. If this worked, she shouldn't need them at all, but she wanted to be ready.

Daindreth watched her, the dappled patterns of sunlight dancing across his bare chest. "I don't want you to go." There was a sadness in his words and a tightness that betrayed fear.

Amira looked up from buckling on her boots. "We've discussed this."

"I know." He let out a long breath. "I just hate it."

Amira crouched down beside him, resting a hand over his heart. "Are you worried about me, love?"

His arms slid around her, pulling her closer. "I want you safe."

Amira kissed him, deep and slow—soft.

Their horses whickered as the wind stirred the treetops. The ground was wet, but it had stopped raining this morning. Amira and Daindreth had taken advantage of it, riding into the forest for privacy. It might be a childish thing to do, but they hadn't been alone together since leaving the Haven three days ago.

Amira would have met Daindreth in a barn if it meant they could have time together. Loving him was like drinking salt water, the more she drank, the more her need grew.

They'd found a place sheltered by trees with long grass that had soaked up most of the water. Amira had spread a blanket on the ground and though it had done little to keep them dry after the first hour, Amira and her husband made the most of it.

"Are you sure about this?" Daindreth asked, resting his forehead on her shoulder.

"No," Amira admitted, kissing his temple. "But I need to do it."

Daindreth exhaled and released her from his arms. "Yes. Time is short."

"Do you remember what you promised me the last time we were in these parts?" Amira whispered, fingers feathering along his collarbone. She loved kissing and touching this part of him. Loved the way his muscles bunched and tightened around them when he was on top of her.

"I'm afraid not," Daindreth admitted with a slight frown.

"A hot bath when we return to Mynadra," Amira said. "Big enough for us both."

"Oh yes." Daindreth smiled. "I promised to wash your hair."

"Yes." Amira kissed the stubble along his jaw. "Tonight will bring us one step closer to putting you back in the palace where you belong. As emperor."

Daindreth looked around them, one arm still looped easily around her waist. "This is hardly the right place for us to conceive our heirs, is it?"

Amira laughed at that. "Sair assured me I can't conceive right now."

"I still don't understand how she can tell," Daindreth said.

"A woman's womb flares with *ka* when conception is possible," Amira explained. "It's harder to sense *ka* in our own bodies, but Sair has been teaching me about it."

"I see." Daindreth stroked her back. "I do want a baby with you," he said. "Just…"

"Not right now," Amira agreed.

Daindreth nodded sadly.

"I will give you back your inheritance, Daindreth," Amira promised. "And then I will give you as many babies as you want."

Daindreth's mouth quirked at that. "As many as I want?"

"A palace full of imperial piglets," Amira promised. "With your eyes, my hair, and their Uncle Thadred's sense of humor."

"Gods help us," Daindreth muttered.

Amira giggled and kissed his cheek. "Come on," she beckoned. "We mustn't keep the others waiting."

◆ ◆ ◆

No one commented when Amira and Daindreth returned to

82

the camp. Everyone knew where they had been and aside from Thadred's knowing grin, no one felt the need to remark on it.

Amira saddled up her horse and Daindreth saddled his. He hovered close to her as they went over last-minute preparations and final details. Sair was the only other one with any recent knowledge of Lashera and Thadred had military training, so they would assist Amira.

Never before had Amira been this in control of an assignment. Everyone deferred to her, even Daindreth—rightful emperor and her liege lord as a Kadra'han.

Amira's job was to get inside, free Cromwell, and see what she could do to get close to her father. Sair would be waiting near an ore vein to take them all out through a portalstone to outside the city.

They rode toward Lashera as the sun began to sink behind the distant mountains. It was one of the busier times to arrive at the gates and in the press of travelers, no one paid them much attention.

Their group stopped near the edge of the city. Pulling to the side, they let the merchants and ox carts pass.

Daindreth and Tapios were to wait with the horses at the exit of the portalstone. Thadred had wanted that job, assuring them all that one trip along a portalstone had been enough, but Amira needed him with her.

They all dismounted, Thadred with much more cursing than was necessary. He'd claimed his leg felt much better now that he'd been learning to use more magic, but he still griped at times.

Daindreth dismounted, too and wrapped Amira tight in a final embrace. "Be safe, my love."

"I will come back to you," Amira promised, trying not to be annoyed by his concern. "Caa Iss is far more frightening than my father, love."

"I know, but..." Daindreth exhaled a long breath into her hair. "I've wanted you for so long and now I have you." He kissed the side of her neck. "I don't want to lose you."

"You couldn't lose me if you tried," Amira whispered back. "Now trust me and trust that I know what I'm doing." She pecked his cheek and pulled away, but letting her hands linger on his, their fingers knotted together for a few extra moments.

"Let's be going, you ginger terror," Thadred muttered. "Come, ladies." He ruffled his hair a little more and pulled out the worn wooden staff that would be serving as his crutch for now. His cane sword was strapped across his back and covered by his cloak.

Amira and Sair pulled on plain, nondescript linen dresses. After living in the rainy forest for several days, the three of them were grimy and dirty enough to be convincing farmers.

"Lleuad, listen," Thadred said, taking on a stern tone. "I'm going to be back tonight, but you need to go with Dain and do as he says, hear?"

The kelpie snorted and swished his tail impatiently. He had gotten to the point that he now allowed Dain and Amira to touch him and even lead him, but he was still leery of most other people.

"We can take care of him," Tapios assured Thadred for the fourth time since they had set out.

"See that you do." Thadred grumbled under his breath as he turned away.

Amira and Sair walked on either side of Thadred, each carrying baskets of herbs.

Daindreth remounted his sorrel, holding the reins of Amira's bay and Lleuad. The black stallion nibbled at his reins and his eye rolled wildly in the direction of Thadred, but he didn't panic as Amira had feared he might.

Tapios and Daindreth turned and took the horses off the main road to circle around the city to where they would wait. Amira watched them go with a sad kind of anxiety in her chest.

There was no need to worry about Daindreth now. He no longer had to vie with Caa Iss every time he left her presence, but...

He looked back one last time before disappearing into the trees. His eyes met Amira's and then he was gone.

Amira took a deep breath and marched alongside Thadred and Sair, heading toward the city gates.

Vesha's agents would be on the lookout for two men and a woman. They weren't expecting a man with two obvious women.

Amira covered her hair with a kerchief, but neither she nor Sair concealed their faces. The rain had started again and the guards huddled back, trying to stay dry.

The city guards waved them through just as the sun was sinking down below the horizon.

"I hate this," Thadred repeated for the fourth time as they sought shelter inside a packed hostel. The crowd wasn't as thick as Amira had seen before, but it seemed business was still good for the establishment.

"My contact should meet us here soon," Sair said.

"Good," Thadred said. "All this walking is taking its toll."

Amira nodded. "I will start my scouting, then." She ducked to the corner of the room, into a stairwell leading up to the main sleeping quarters. She sloughed off her dress and came back out.

She wore a dark brown leather hunting habit Cyne and the others had made for her. It was not unlike the one she had used in the service of her father, but this one was inscribed with runes and spells on the inside.

Amira could feel their power against her skin. There were spells to keep the leather supple and soft, a few to dampen noise, and many, many runes to make the hide stronger. If the tests Thadred and Tapios had done were any indication, these leathers should be able to block most arrows and blows from a spear or a sword. The blunt force of the strike, or an attack from mace or a hammer, would still be able to hurt her, but she would be better protected against most blades.

Some of the spells in this armor lay entirely dormant, waiting. All she had to do to breathe life into those spells was infuse them with more *ka*.

Amira handed her dress to Sair, keeping the cloak.

"We will be ready for you," the sorceress said. She nodded solemnly, gripping Amira's hand for just a moment. "Eponine's favor guide you."

Amira inclined her head to acknowledge the blessing and clapped Thadred's shoulder as she slipped back out into the streets.

Amira had snuck out of the palace many, many times. But

85

she had never had to sneak *in.*

With her hair still tied back under a kerchief and the hood of her cloak weighed down by the rain, few people noticed her. Amira stuck to the edge of the streets, making her way to her childhood home.

She circled the palace a few times, counting the guards and taking note of which entrances were opened and which ones were closed. There were six different servants' entrances and they all appeared to be open, though she noticed two armed guards posted at each one. A little unusual, but not wholly alarming.

On her second circuit, Amira dared to climb the roof of a mansion near the palace walls. She crouched behind a smoking chimney to study the palace for anything, *anything* that might be odd.

A guard came, making his rounds on the parapet. As he did, Amira's eyes caught the color of his uniform—black with a white crown and the number nine emblazoned across his tabard.

Amira chewed her lip. Her father's house was being guarded by imperial guards? Interesting. Would there be Kadra'han among them?

She waited, taking time to stop at a bakery just before it closed. She traded a copper coin for a dirt pie. No two dirt pies were ever exactly the same, but it was much like the one she had given Daindreth on their last visit to this city.

Perched on a deserted upper-level balcony, she ate it in silence and watched the palace, waiting for nightfall. Clouds remained overhead, though torches lit the darkened streets.

Amira tried not to let her mind wander into thoughts of Vesha or the court at Mynadra or anything that would distract her from the mission at hand. She had one assignment, only one—retrieve Cromwell.

That might put Cromwell's family in danger if King Hyle or Vesha decided to use them as hostages. But from what Sair had heard, Cromwell's family had already left the city. Rumor said they were in Affenshire, farther down the coast. Amira suspected that had been Cromwell's plan for his family for just such a circumstance.

Affenshire was in Hylendale, but it was two days' journey from Lashera and barely an hour's journey to Phaed. It would be easy to hop a boat to anywhere in the world from there.

The sun set and the streetlamps lit the night in a golden glow. Amira waited until the toll of the eleventh bell before slipping through the emptied streets toward the palace. The guard would be changed in an hour, so the guards on this shift would be tired and impatient to go home.

The assassin made her way around the palace to the side facing the gardens. A tributary of the river flowed straight through the palace, little more than a stream on most days, but after weeks of rain, it had swelled into an impressive current.

A drain released the river on the west side and Amira slipped around to the edge of the water, where a culvert ran under the walls. It let the water out into a stone-lined waterway that channeled into the rest of the city. The culvert was barred with iron, but over the years, two of the bars had rusted away, leaving a hole just large enough for a person to pass through. The bars had been near the center of the drain, so no one had bothered to fix it. After all, who could even reach the gap?

Amira waited until the guard passed overhead on the wall, counted to ten, and slipped down on the side of the waterway. It was sloped just enough that she could find grips and handholds despite the stones being slippery with rain. Scuttling sideways, Amira crawled just above the line of the rushing water until she was touching the palace wall. The culvert entrance was still a good ten feet away.

She poured *ka* into the runes on the inside of her gloves and the ones lining the soles of her boots. She hadn't had much time to practice using these runes, but she stilled her worries as she pressed a hand to the wall.

Her foot stuck, held by the magic in her boot. Amira cautiously put weight on that foot, relieved when it held. Next, she reached out a hand, pressing her palm against the stone, making sure she channeled enough *ka* into the runes as she did.

Her hand stuck to the stone, and she pulled herself out on the face of the wall. When it came time to move her first foot, she carefully withdrew the magic from the rune in that boot, careful not to withdraw it anywhere else.

Her foot gave way suddenly, her whole body jerking. Amira stifled a scream as her foot dangled down, touching the surface of the river below. But her hands and other foot held, keeping her glued to the wall.

With a deep breath, Amira pulled herself together and continued the slow process of reaching, sticking, and then releasing each of her hands and feet in turn.

As she reached the edge of the culvert, she took a deep breath before reaching down and sticking one hand to the side. Sliding around, Amira took her time, not wanting to overstep or rush this part.

Cyne had been sure the spells would be strong enough, but Amira found that now she was depending on it, she didn't have so much faith.

Dropping down, Amira crawled upside down along the top of the culvert. She focused on her breathing and going forward one step and reach at a time. She'd underestimated how unsettling this would be.

There was precious little light in the culvert, less than two feet above the river. The water was a black abyss beneath her, roaring too loud for her to hear her own breathing. It was normally quiet, but right now it would be strong enough to sweep Amira away before she could resist.

On the wall, she'd had a sense of safety and assurance that she would be fine. Here, the underside of the culvert was slick stone. If her magic failed her, Amira would go straight into the water. Gravity pressed against her, pulling her down. She moved slowly, despite her eagerness to have this over with. She couldn't afford mistakes.

Finally, Amira reached the other side of the culvert and pulled herself up the wall, looking around. She was in the outer courtyard of the castle, in the carefully built waterway that kept the river to one side of the palace.

The assassin reached for *ka,* but she could only feel the animals in the stables and the guards on the battlements. The darkness worked in her favor as she climbed out of the culvert's waterway and onto solid ground. Breathing deeply, she took a moment to be thankful she wouldn't have to do that again.

Amira shifted *ka* into the runes in the collar of her habit. Immediately, she felt the dreadsight spell wash over her. Unlike when she had used rabbit's blood to cast this enchantment, the runes in her collar could be withdrawn and re-cast at will, so long as Amira kept enough *ka* in them to power the spell.

The assassin broke into a brisk walk, heading into the stables. A hound by the entrance looked up, then looked away, large eyes not quite landing on her.

A sleeping horse stirred as she passed, but the animal didn't wake. Amira could sense the stableboys nearby, but they seemed to be sleeping, too.

From the stables, Amira was able to get to the gardens. She'd crept through the hedges and rose beds so many times over the years, she could almost find her way blindfolded.

Keeping a careful watch for the telltale warnings of *ka*, Amira reached a familiar set of windows. She stopped for a moment, concentrating. After confirming that there was nothing alive in the right window, she grabbed a familiar stone and pulled herself up.

Amira scaled the wall easily, even without magic, and slipped open the window, wary the whole time of traps or tricks. But she sensed nothing unusual.

Her old bedroom was clean and orderly. The bed was made, but empty. Her old clothes were still hanging in the wardrobe, including the black velvet dress she'd worn the night she met Daindreth at the banquet.

In the other room, she could sense the sleeping form of Fonra. A part of Amira ached to wake her sister, to tell her that she was safe, that everything would be fine. But even using this window to enter the palace was a risk.

The last thing she wanted was for Fonra to take the blame while Vesha and her loyalists were still at large.

Creeping to the hallway door, Amira slipped into the hallway of the palace. She pushed more magic into the dreadsight spell, but took care to move quietly all the same.

She had only been to the palace dungeons a handful of times. Most criminals were kept in the city jail or locked up in one of the handful of prisons around the countryside.

She didn't remember the last time that the palace dungeon had been used for more than holding people overnight—servants who stole the silver or guards who were caught being drunk and disorderly.

Amira walked down the hallway, hearing footsteps ahead. She thickened the dreadsight spell and kept walking straight on.

She rounded the bend and was a little surprised to see Corman, the footman she'd kissed once. He carried what appeared to be a quill and ink set.

As he came closer, he shifted slightly to one side to let her pass. Amira slid by him like a ghost. The dreadsight spell made people do that. They avoided Amira without even knowing they did it. Corman never quite looked at her. The dreadsight spell made his eyes slide off her like oil off water.

Amira continued and so did Corman. She passed her father's study and was a little surprised to see that light still spilled beneath his door. Why was he awake so late? Maybe it was one of his secretaries.

Amira made her way through the main residence to the guard barracks. The men inside were mostly asleep, but a few remained gathered around a card table in nothing but their trews, taking turns sipping from a flask.

They huddled closer together as she passed, heads angling away from her. Amira got by them easily and headed straight for the entrance to the palace dungeons.

There were no extra guards posted there, but a thick wooden door blocked her way. It sat across the small courtyard in plain sight of the guards, but they were preoccupied. The keys hung next to it—this had been built to keep people in, not out.

Amira hesitated. The dreadsight spell would make them avoid looking at her, but as soon as she started interacting with other objects...

Another guard came jogging to those who sat off-duty. He delivered a few short commands and though the other men seemed startled, they put their full attention on the man in front of them.

Amira seized the opportunity, grabbed the keys, and pushed

open the prison door. She shut it hastily after herself, clenching the keys tight to keep them from rattling.

For a moment, Amira wondered if the other guard brought news that there was an intruder. But she was sure she had left no trace in the palace thus far. There was no way they could know...

Unless they had caught Thadred and Sair...

Amira chose not to consider the possibility and focused on the task at hand.

The palace dungeon was one part of the palace that hadn't been updated in keeping with the times. Stone cells lined the walls with rusty iron grates across the front.

She could sense the *ka* of moss, mold, and mildew. The small shapes of mice scurried around the edges of her awareness. But the unmistakable shape of a man slumped in a cell near the middle of the aisle.

Amira marched straight toward it and stopped before the bars. A narrow shaft of light from a torch illuminated the cell.

She dropped the dreadsight spell, testing keys on the lock. "Cromwell," Amira called, keeping her voice down. "Cromwell, is that you?"

The shape stirred, then looked up.

"If I'm in the wrong place, just say so and I'll let you get back to your nap." Even as she said it, Amira tested a second key, then a third. "It's hard to see in here."

"Princess Amira?" a familiar voice replied from the darkness.

Amira smiled with a sense of triumph as she found the right key and the door swung open. "Good evening, Lord Cromwell."

"How?" he gasped, stirring off the floor. "What are you doing here?"

The triumph of surprising Cromwell was almost greater than the triumph of successfully infiltrating the palace.

Amira found his hand in the darkness and helped him to his feet. She could sense pools of *ka* splotched over his back, ribs, face, hands, and legs—wounds of some sort.

"I'm rescuing you," Amira said.

"I see." Cromwell cleared his throat with a wet sound that

sounded akin to a cough.

"What happened?" Amira asked. He swayed and she gripped his forearm to steady him.

"I was found out shortly after you escaped Lashera. The Kadra'han wanted to know where you had gone."

"Did you tell them?" Amira asked sharply.

"Of course I did," Cromwell replied, as if it had been a silly question. "But they already knew."

Annoyance flared through Amira, but she didn't say anything.

"The Kadra'han left, and the imperial guards came. They've interrogated me a few times, but I think they've given up. I'll probably be executed as a traitor soon." Cromwell's tone was calm, passive. No different from when he had discussed banking investments.

"Good news, Cromwell," Amira said with just a touch of sarcasm. "My husband has use for you."

Cromwell coughed and Amira thought that she would have to have Cyne and Sair take a look at him when they got him to the caves.

"Your husband? Should I call you empress, then?" Cromwell's tone was flat and maddeningly unreadable once again.

"Probably," Amira shrugged. "Right now, I would like to focus on getting out of Lashera." Amira couldn't see well in the dark, but from the *ka* splotched over his body, she could tell he was injured. "Can you walk?"

"Yes," Cromwell said. He straightened, coughing again.

Amira rested a hand on his forehead. He was hot to the touch. "You're sick."

"Damp and drafty cells aren't the best medicine for an old man, Your Majesty." Cromwell slipped easily into calling her by the imperial title, like it was nothing to call her empress of the largest empire in the known world.

"Hmm." Amira pulled the kerchief off her hair. Runes had been stitched into the fabric with embroidered thread. Cyne, Sair, and Thadred had all helped infuse the cloth with *ka* for this purpose.

"I'm going to put a spell on you to help us walk out of here. So long as you don't draw attention to yourself, no one will want to see you."

"*Want* to see me?" Cromwell skeptically repeated.

"It's a dreadsight spell," Amira explained.

Cromwell either knew what that was or didn't want to waste time on it. "Carry on then, Your Majesty."

Amira knotted the kerchief around his neck like a cravat. He let her tie it without resisting, even lifting his chin to make the job easier. Several weeks of beard growth and stubble scratched against her hands as she worked.

"Come," Amira stepped back. She pushed her own magic into the runes.

Before her eyes, Cromwell flickered and wavered. When she tried to focus on him, her eyes slid off and the spot between her eyes throbbed.

Amira looked away and motioned for him to follow. "We're going to cross the courtyard and then I will remove the dreadsight spell from myself so you can follow me. Don't speak, touch anyone, or make a sound."

There was the sense of a presence at her back, but she couldn't quite see or hear anything. It nagged at the corner of her mind, but all she knew for sure was that she had a vague sense of missing something, of being watched.

Amira finally understood why the dreadsight spell was called that.

She made it to the door of the jail, opened it, and waited several moments to give Cromwell time to get through. She revived the dreadsight spell on herself before stepping out, locking the door, and hanging the keys back on their hook outside.

The soldiers were still at their card game and didn't seem to notice.

Carefully, Amira ghosted back across the courtyard. The misty presence of Cromwell hovered nearby.

Amira was about to step through the door leading out of the barracks when a cough ripped through the air. She whirled around to see Cromwell doubled over, choking as he fought back another cough, but it was too late.

Cromwell stood in the middle of the courtyard in plain sight. The guards looked up and even with their wits muddled by alcohol, they recognized him.

"Hey, old man!"

In an instant, every one of the men was on their feet. They charged Cromwell and he tried to run, but they tackled him to the ground.

Amira could take them, but not without alerting the rest of the palace, including Vesha's agents who were somewhere nearby. She would have to kill at least a few of them and even then, she doubted she could get herself and Cromwell out of the palace. Fighting her way out wasn't an option.

Amira turned her back on Cromwell and ran.

CHAPTER ELEVEN

Vesha

Vesha breathed in the cold, clear air. After the Dread Marches, the air of the city felt light in her lungs, bubbly, even. She inhaled huge gulps, not sure she'd ever get enough.

She collapsed on the cobblestones, the clear night sky stretching overhead.

"Your Majesty!" cried a soldier's voice. "Your Majesty, you've returned!" There was a clatter and clank of his armor as the Kadra'han knelt in front of her. He took her by the arm, carefully. "My empress, are you hurt?"

Vesha looked up at him. She must indeed look a sight—covered in sweat, grime, soot, and the stench of brimstone and smoke.

"Your Majesty!" Vesha's handmaidens crowded around her the next moment. "My lady, your face! Your *eye!*" Gasps of horror echoed through the women.

A torch blazed over Vesha's head and she blinked. She could see out of her right eye, which surprised her.

She had scratches on her face where Moreyne's claws had ripped her eye out, not to mention the blood that still soaked her face and dress. Vesha had never known pain like that in her life.

Then the goddess had truly shocked Vesha. She had ripped out her own eye and crammed it into Vesha's bloody socket.

Moreyne had jammed it in, holding Vesha down as if she was a screaming mouse in a panther's grip. After a few torturously long moments, Vesha had suddenly been able to see.

The goddess's eye had settled into Vesha's skull. From that eye, the darkness made no difference. She could see across the courtyard as if it was only dusk, yet the torches seemed bright. Too bright.

"I am fine." Vesha waved her guards and handmaidens away. "A gift from the goddess."

"Your Majesty, what happened?"

Vesha didn't want to answer that. "How long was I gone?" The light of torches cast inconstant shadows over the attendants crowded around her.

"Two days, Your Majesty," the soldier answered. "We were going to wait for dawn and then carry out your orders."

Vesha touched the man's armored shoulder. She didn't remember his name right now, but recalled he had served under Darrigan for several years. "You did well," she said, her voice a rasp.

"Beautiful," grated a voice from behind her.

Vesha's soldier drew his sword and the handmaidens screamed as a creature on all fours with a rat's tail crawled out of the open portal at her back. The creature's coat appeared to be burned off in places so that raw flesh was visible, but if it was in pain, it didn't show it.

"Vaad Rii," rumbled a familiar voice. Caa Iss towered over Vesha, crouching possessively like a dog over a dead rabbit.

"Hello, brother," the creature simpered, lips pulling back to reveal a mouth with too many teeth. "I hear you are to lead us. For now."

Caa Iss growled, his massive hulk seeming to grow more solid.

Vaad Rii made a cackling noise that might have been a laugh and loped away, shimmering out of view like a mirage.

Next came a creature with wings like Caa Iss, its jaw positioned at an odd, unnatural angle as if it had been broken and reattached wrong. This creature didn't speak, only bowed to Caa Iss and spread its wings before launching into the sky.

"My empress," gasped the soldier, his hand shaking as he leaned closer, shielding her.

The handmaidens cowered around her, seeking protection.

By now, Vesha's inner circle were accustomed to seeing the cythraul. But few of them had seen them at this scale.

Darrigan had, but he was gone now. Vesha wondered—just briefly—if that could be coincidence. The man who had known the most about cythraul had been the most opposed to their use.

It didn't matter now. Even if there had been a better way, it was too late.

One of the maids screamed and Vesha realized then that her servants and soldiers were staring at Caa Iss. They could see him now?

They had all known Vesha was a witch. They had all known she communed with demons. That didn't stop them from looking on in horror as cythraul after cythraul came marching through the portal and disappearing into the night.

The edges of her right eye, the god-eye, itched. Vesha reached to touch it, but touching it hurt. The flesh was still sore.

When the imps had brought Saan Thii to Moreyne, the goddess had questioned Saan Thii, and tortured her by ripping off limbs and clawing off her flesh, then healing her.

Vesha had been forced to watch. The gruesome process would have made her vomit if she'd had anything in her stomach. She had wanted Saan Thii to pay for her betrayal—Saan Thii was the reason Darrigan was dead—but even she had to admit that what Moreyne did was beyond cruelty.

After she'd satisfied herself with answers, Moreyne had taken Vesha and forcibly replaced her eye. "To seal our pact," the goddess had said, "and mark you as mine."

The eye had allowed Vesha to see gateways out of the Dread Marches. More than that, it had allowed her to step back through this one. According to Moreyne, she would be able to open portals at any holy place to summon more cythraul.

Moreyne herself could not come through this portal. Something about it being too small. But there were gateways on the mainland. Sacred places. Vesha needed only to find her way to one and release Moreyne to extend her protection over the entire continent.

Vesha knelt, staring up as the parade of unholy specters continued before her eyes. She lost count of how many there were as they marched out of the portal before disappearing from view.

Dozens of little imps came scurrying out, giggling and laughing. She recognized Criin Moor and their pack of companions.

Vesha stared as her soldiers spoke and her handmaidens asked her questions. She could barely hear them. All she knew was that she had succeeded.

It had been a fool's hope and she had succeeded.

"Forgive me, my love," Vesha whispered, looking up to Caa Iss. The demon's teeth were exposed in a gruesome smile as he watched dozens, perhaps hundreds or thousands, of his kindred loosed from the Dread Marches.

Her husband had died to keep Caa Iss out of this world. So had Darrigan.

Vesha closed both eyes so she wouldn't have to watch as more and more of the creatures came through the doorway. A sickening dread washed over her.

This was the only way to ensure peace, to ensure the empire remained stable, to prevent war, famine, and disasters. This was the only way she could save thousands of innocent lives.

She had done the impossible. She had petitioned a goddess and gotten her request. Her nation would be saved because of her.

It was her moment of triumph. So why did it feel like this was the worst thing she had ever done?

CHAPTER TWELVE

Amira

I t was easy to find the window to her father's study. The lights were still on, and it overlooked the garden as did most of the royal family's rooms.

Climbing up the wall was hardly a challenge, either. Amira hovered just below the edge of the window, feeling for *ka* inside. Only one source.

Pulling herself up, Amira touched the window. It was latched from the inside, but she was able to slip the smallest of her knives through the crack and ease it open.

Amira strengthened the dreadsight spell around herself, hoping this would work. It was a risk, yes.

But she was committed.

Daindreth needed this alliance, and this was the best way she knew how to get it.

Amira slid the window open. The lone figure bent over the desk didn't move. She slithered inside and eased the window shut after her.

King Hyle sat hunched at his massive oaken desk. The remains of a late-night meal lay discarded to one side along with an empty ale mug. He was reading through stacks of letters, then ordering them neatly.

He rubbed his eyes and heaved a sigh. Amira noticed his hair had thinned and it was greyer than the last time she had seen him. He seemed frailer, less substantial. Had he really aged so much in mere months?

Amira felt out into the hallway but felt no additional sources of *ka* or anything else to indicate her father had left guards posted. He must have dismissed his servants.

Hovering just behind her father's shoulder, Amira studied the papers scattered across his desk. A familiar seal caught her eye. It was a twisting polecat, the seal of Cromwell.

Looking closer, she realized that all the papers were stamped with Cromwell's seal or addressed to him. Her father was personally going through Cromwell's correspondences.

Still holding her knife, Amira dropped her dreadsight spell—it would be easier to cast again if it wasn't broken outright. She clapped a hand over the king's mouth in the same moment she pressed a knife to his throat, hugging him against her.

"Don't scream, Papa," Amira whispered in his ear.

King Hyle thrashed, trying to throw her off, but she pressed the knife hard enough to draw blood and held on. He froze as red stained the collar of his doublet, leaving a dark smear on the velvet.

"Good," Amira purred. "Now. I am going to take my hand off your mouth. You are going to be a good little king and not call your guards. Do you understand?"

King Hyle made a sound that she took for agreement.

Keeping her blade against his throat, Amira lowered her hand.

"Amira?" King Hyle gasped.

"Now you know what they felt like, Papa." Amira's heart raced and her arm tightened around him, seemingly of its own accord. "All those people you made me kill for you."

"Release me and tell me what you're doing here," King Hyle demanded.

Amira flinched. For a moment, she could imagine the phantom pain in her throat. There had been a time when she would have been forced to obey him. There had been a time when she'd had no choice. But no longer.

Amira jabbed the knife tighter against his neck. His collar grew sticky with blood as she cut deeper. "I don't answer to you anymore."

King Hyle seemed to recover himself. "You're not here to kill me."

"Are you so sure?" Amira spat.

"If you wanted me dead, I would be dead already."

Amira grated, annoyed at the levelness of his response. He should fear her. He should be begging her mercy right now. "How many imperial Kadra'han are in Lashera?"

"One that I know of," the king answered. "And that's you. But there is an imperial battalion here."

"Who leads them?" Amira pressed.

"Captain Ohad Westfall. He was sent here with the empress's men."

Amira cursed internally. "Where is he right now?"

"I don't know. He has taken command of the guards and soldiers in the city. He sleeps in the barracks."

Amira considered her options. She could order her father to have Cromwell brought here, but that would get back to the imperial guards. If Amira got close enough to this Captain Westfall, she would be able to tell for sure if he was a Kadra'han or not.

"What happened, Amira?" King Hyle asked. His tone was quiet, but Amira recognized the old echoes of command in them. "Tell me."

Amira lifted her knife off her father's throat. He turned to face her and she smashed a fist into his jaw.

He wasn't expecting it and her blow knocked him back, blood spattering over the table and papers.

Her knuckles stung, but Amira grabbed his collar and pressed the tip of her knife against his bloody mouth. "That's the last time you give me a command, do you hear me?"

She could feel her chest tightening, her spine tingling. Fear gripped her even though she knew he held no power over her.

Her father's words couldn't hurt her anymore, but the memories were there—the memories of every time he had ordered her to silence, ordered her to stay in line, to grovel to her stepmother, to overlook every insult and barb. He had ordered her to risk her life, to crawl into the most god forsaken hovels, to maim for him, murder for him.

Amira grabbed a fistful of his hair, yanking his head back. "If you ever try to command me again, I will slice your tongue down the middle and I will smile as you choke to death on your own blood. Are we clear?"

The king watched her with wide eyes, but to his credit he didn't grovel or beg. He swallowed. "Forgive me, Amira."

Somehow, him asking forgiveness made it worse. Instant guilt washed through Amira, a heavy rock in her gut. He had never been a violent man. The violence was all her.

"Get on your feet," she ordered.

The king obeyed, if slowly. "Where is your sister?"

"In her rooms, I imagine."

The king fixed her in a look that lasted just a little too long.

"I would never hurt her," Amira said, realizing what he meant. "You know that."

"I *don't* know that, Amira," the king said. "You loathed her as a child and then…"

"And then I was bound by the curse?" Amira finished. "You think she was only protected by you?"

"And the queen?" King Hyle pressed.

"I haven't touched your bitch of a wife," Amira snapped. "Are you happy?"

King Hyle's face relaxed ever so slightly. Had he really been concerned for them? "What happens now?"

"You and I are going to take a walk." Amira jerked her head to the door. "Quietly."

This plan had been intended for a willing rescue, not an unwilling hostage. But Amira was determined to make it work.

"Are you doing this for him?" King Hyle asked. "The archduke?"

"Move," Amira repeated, grabbing her father's arm. She touched one of the brass buttons on his wrist and funneled just enough *ka* into it to make it burn.

The king flinched, swatting at his sleeve.

"That's a taste of what I can do now," Amira growled, her voice low as the rumble of an oncoming storm. "Do as I say. And don't try anything." She herded her father out the door as soon as she confirmed there was no one waiting outside.

"There's a lamp—"

"I don't need it," Amira interrupted. "Walk." The hall was deserted, but she helped him find his way in the dark with one hand on his arm.

The king obeyed, moving down the hallway. "My valet will come to check on me soon."

Amira shoved her father forward in response. "Then move. I'd rather not have to kill him."

"You would kill an innocent man?"

"Don't talk to me about innocence when you stole mine."

The king went quiet after that, letting her shove him along the passage. When they reached the stairs, he stumbled, but Amira grabbed his thinning hair and shoved him forward.

They reached the next level and continued down several hallways until they arrived at one lined with large, broad windows that faced toward the city. Amira counted down until she located the third one from the right.

"What are you going to do with me?" the king asked again.

"Whatever I want."

"Is this revenge, then? Retribution?"

"Shut up," Amira ordered. She watched the darkness of the street below. As a child, she would come here to observe the common people wandering about their common lives—free of her stepmother, the whispers at court, and her father's perpetual disappointment. "Be reasonable or we'll find out if Fonra is more reasonable."

"Are you saying you'll kill me?" the king asked quietly, almost as if this was the answer he had expected.

"If the mood strikes me," Amira quipped back.

In reality, she needed her father alive, and she knew it. They needed him on their side and while she doubted that she would be persuading him after this stunt, that would be Daindreth's problem. Let her husband figure out the diplomatic side. She was more for threats and coercion.

Amira watched the streets below. She might be a little bit early. She didn't have a timepiece to know and from this angle, the moon was obscured.

"Eponine help me," she muttered.

Movement caught her eye as a cart pulled by a pair of mules came clopping into view below. Two shapes hunched on the driver's seat and Amira breathed an internal sigh of relief.

The cart was piled high with hay, rising in a heap that seemed too big for the space of the cart. From one level up, it would be a rough landing, but not too rough. Her father would survive it.

"You're abducting me?" King Hyle's voice cracked just a little, surprised.

Amira didn't answer, studying the glazed window in front of

103

her. She pried at the latch.

King Hyle jerked away from her. He ran, robes flapping behind him as he ran. "Intruder!" he shouted. "Intruder in the east hall!"

Amira spun around and caught the sash of his robe. It ripped off, but she sped after him, catching him within two steps. She wrapped the sash around his neck, yanking him back against her.

"Bad choice," she growled in his ear. Amira forced *ka* into his skin, her power tingling through the veins and sinews in his body. *Ka* was power and it could heal, but Sair had shown her the trick of how to use it like a puppet's strings.

Amira laced her magic through his veins and yanked tight. The king's whole body seized and he stopped struggling. He let off a gurgling, whimpering groan, face going slack as he collapsed on the floor.

Amira released him and he coughed, choking and fighting to lift himself off the floor. "You should have obeyed me," Amira sneered. "You did this to yourself."

Her head snapped up at the sound of voices and bootsteps coming down the hall. Amira dragged her father to the window, drawing on *ka* for strength. She lifted him up, magic coursing through her in torrents strong enough to make her dizzy.

Her father struggled as the sound of shouts came around the corner. He fought to run, but she grabbed his hair and smashed his head straight into the window. The glass shattered into thousands of pieces, bursting out like a popped bubble.

The king swayed and Amira shoved him out the window, straight into the haystack. She leapt after him, scrambling down the exterior wall.

"Amira, what happened?" Thadred demanded from the driver's seat of the cart.

"Plan changed." Amira swung herself up onto the haycart. "Go!"

Thadred didn't hesitate, slapping the reins against the haunches of the mules. The animals sped off into a brisk canter, tails snapping as Thadred drove them faster.

Overhead, voices rose, and the alarm sounded through the entire palace. It echoed through the night like the bay of a hunting dog.

Amira gripped the side of the cart for balance as it swayed and wobbled under her. She grabbed for her father, lying dazed in the hay. She gripped him tight to keep him from flying off the cart. He didn't struggle at first, but as the mules careened around a sharp corner, he sat up.

"Unhand me, you—"

Amira backhanded him across the mouth. "Sair!" she shouted to the form beside Thadred. "Do you have rope?"

It was hard to see Sair in the dark, but a coil of rope flew at Amira from the front. Amira caught it just as her father regained his senses and tried to crawl for the back of the cart.

Amira pinned him down, straddling his back. She lashed rope around one wrist and dragged it behind him. He kicked and bucked, fighting to throw her off. The cart swayed as Thadred took another turn at breakneck speed.

Amira looped the rope around her father's neck and jerked tight. "Stop fighting," she snarled. "You'll only make it worse."

She couldn't tell if the palace guards were pursuing them or not. The noise of the cart disguised the noise of any pursuit and the city was already alive with *ka*. How would she be able to sort out more sources at this distance?

"Amira," Sair called from the front. "That's not Cromwell."

"I know!" Amira hissed back, grappling with her father.

He kicked, but she kept her arms around his neck in a chokehold.

"Damn it." Thadred added some more choice curses from the front, driving the mules as fast as he could.

It was dark and they had a head start on the palace guards. All the same, Amira was sure the guards would be onto their trail by now.

"Here!" Sair shouted, smacking Thadred's arm. "By the fountain."

Thadred reined in the mules and the sudden stop sent Amira and her father slamming into the front of the haycart. King Hyle tried to shout, but Amira already had a length of rope in his mouth and one knee digging into the middle of his back.

Her father was not a particularly large or muscular man, but

105

he was stout after a life spent mostly indoors. He had a least fifty pounds on Amira, and if she hadn't had the aid of *ka,* there was no way she could have wrestled him down. As it was, she had to drag *ka* from all around her and into her muscles to keep him contained.

"Amira." Thadred twisted around in his seat. "What happened?"

"I couldn't get Cromwell out, so I got someone who can."

"Amira," Thadred asked, tone wavering just a little. "Is that the king of Hylendale you're hog tying in our haycart?"

"It's my father," Amira said.

"Is that your father, the king of Hylendale, that you're hog tying in our hay cart?"

"We don't have time," Sair interrupted. "Come. Both of you. Before the soldiers find us."

Drawing in another draught of *ka,* Amira dragged her father off the haycart. He went limp.

Amira wasn't playing games. She let him fall to the ground and kicked his ribs. He coiled inward and Amira kicked his back.

"Amira! Stop beating the shit out of your dear papa and get over here," Thadred snapped.

Amira grabbed the back of her father's collar and heaved. He slid on the cobblestones thanks to the day's rain and she was able to drag him the few steps to where Sair and Thadred waited.

Behind them, Amira could hear the sounds of pursuit. The guards had been roused and were searching the city, though they might not yet all know the king had been taken.

"Hold onto each other," Sair ordered. "Make sure you are all touching each other's skin."

Amira grabbed her father's wrist, Thadred grabbed her hand, and held onto Sair. Sair planted one hand on the stone fountain.

There was a flare of *ka* so bright, Amira was momentarily blind. There was the sensation of being twisted, crushed, stretched, and tossed to and fro in a powerful current.

Amira felt herself flip upside down, roll sideways, back up, and then she was crashing into wet grass. Her stomach roiled and she coughed.

"Amira!" a familiar voice called. "Where are you? I can't

see."

"Daindreth." Relief shuddered through Amira even as the nausea threatened to make her hurl.

"Sair, is everything alright?" Tapios asked.

"No!" Thadred answered for their group. "Your wife's done it now, Dain! Just wonderful. Absolutely wonderful."

As if that was his cue, a flurry of motion to her right told Amira that her father had regained his senses. She whirled on him and sprang. She tackled him to the ground and they both hit with a hard thud.

He writhed and fought beneath her as they wrestled with his bonds. He ripped his gag off and let off a howl. "Treachery!" he shouted. "Treachery!"

There was no one to hear him in this place, outside the walls and in the middle of the night. But Amira didn't want to risk it.

Amira yanked out her knife and stabbed it into the back of his shoulder. "Shut up!" she ordered.

"Amira!" Daindreth shouted. "What are you doing?"

The king cried out, but he stopped fighting long enough for Amira to get the gag back in his mouth and lash his hands behind his back.

"Amira," Daindreth knelt at her side. "What happened? Are you alright?"

"I'm fine," Amira grunted. She looked up at her husband, the reality of what she'd done beginning to sink in. "I tried to get to Cromwell, but he was recaptured. So I..." She looked down to the bleeding and bound king.

"Amira." Daindreth rested one hand on her shoulder and ran the other over his face. "This isn't..." He exhaled a long breath.

"Let's get him to the horses," Tapios interrupted, ever the sensible one. He might not have the best grasp on geopolitical maneuvering, but he was strong on commonsense.

Daindreth helped Amira get her father to the horse that had been brought for Cromwell. They all but threw him atop the mare and secured his hands to the front of the saddle.

"Amira." Daindreth wrapped her in a hug the instant she turned to face him. He held her for a long set of heartbeats while the others mounted up on their respective animals. He kissed her hair, then released her, looking her from head to foot. "Are you alright?"

"Yes," she assured him, watching his eyes in the moonlight. He had every right to be angry with her right now, but there was no trace of anger in his tone or in the lines of his face highlighted by the moonlight.

"Good." He kissed her, soft and gentle. "I'm glad."

"Can you wait until we're safely away for that?" Thadred asked.

Amira pulled away from her husband as Tapios shoved the reins of her horse at her. From the corner of her eye, she noticed her father watching her with Daindreth, his expression unreadable in the partial darkness.

They mounted their horses and headed back to the main road, where they would ride for a few miles before slipping back into the forest.

Overhead, thunder rumbled again. There was another storm coming.

CHAPTER THIRTEEN

Daindreth

At least the storm was buying them time. Soldiers would be hard pressed to track anything in this weather.

"I didn't know what else to do," Amira said quietly. "We don't have much time."

"I know." Daindreth pulled her closer against his side. "I know, love. I'm just...thinking."

They had arrived back at the cave complex unhindered except for their horses stumbling once or twice. King Hyle was under guard by the Istovari in one of the grottos in the cave complex.

Amira and Daindreth crouched near the fire, drying off while considering what to do next.

His wife had abducted her father from his castle, smashed his head into a window, beaten him, then stabbed him. It was hardly a good way to start off an alliance.

Not to mention that once it was discovered that the king was missing, this entire countryside would be crawling with soldiers—imperial and Hylendale soldiers alike. All King Hyle had to do was wait and he would be rescued.

If they'd had Cromwell instead, they could have used his connections to bargain their way into an audience with the king. Maybe they could have done something about the imperial soldiers while they were at it.

By skipping straight to the king, Amira had shortened their timeline and raised the stakes.

Daindreth didn't want to be angry with her. Anger was hardly useful at the moment, but he couldn't imagine what she had been thinking.

Thadred on the other hand, had yelled at her for the better part of the past hour. Amira had argued at first, then fallen silent. She seemed to know she'd made a mistake. No point in harping the issue further.

Tapios, Cyne, Sair, and Thadred joined them around the fire. Rhis wedged between Sair and Thadred, nodding off against the knight's shoulder. Sair leaned against her son, also appearing to be asleep.

"This could be a good thing," Cyne said. Her voice took on a low, musing tone Daindreth didn't recognize. "We can force Renner to do anything we want. He's at our mercy now."

"We need him," Amira reminded her mother. "We need his support and we need his alliance."

"Then make him give it to us." Cyne's hands fisted in front of her. "The late emperor brought him to heel." She looked to Daindreth. "Why can't you?"

"Strength is vital for a ruler," Daindreth agreed. "But ruling by force should always be a last resort." That much he had learned from his mother. Despite the many things she had done wrong, that was one he agreed with.

"The man enslaved you." Cyne looked pointedly at her daughter.

Amira stiffened against Daindreth's side and she turned a hard look to her mother. He pulled her closer against him, comforting her. Amira had been jockeyed between her parents ever since the war. Left for dead by one and exploited for her power by the other.

At the same time, there were hard feelings between the parents, at least from Cyne. It did make sense that a scorned wife would be vindictive.

"I can speak to him," Cyne offered. "Make it clear where he stands."

Amira raised her chin. "You don't speak for the empire."

"I have pledged my allegiance to your husband," Cyne reminded her daughter. "This time, Renner is the traitor."

"He has betrayed everyone." Tapios's low voice rumbled from across the fire. "The Istovari, his own family. The attempt to assassinate Daindreth was a betrayal of the empire." Tapios seemed to count betraying the empire just as bad as betraying the Istovari.

"King Hyle will do what he believes is best for his kingdom." Amira sounded almost sad at that. "He will align with whoever serves him best."

"You know your father best." Despite Thadred's earlier anger at Amira, his tone was almost gentle now. Maybe even sympathetic. "Why don't you talk to him?"

Amira looked down at her bloody knuckles. Daindreth hadn't asked her for details, but he'd seen how battered King Hyle was by the light of the torches. He suspected that not all of it had been because King Hyle resisted. Sair had spent some time patching up King Hyle, but he was still quite disheveled.

"I'll speak to the king," Daindreth interrupted. "He will be my vassal. He will answer to me."

Not only that, but it seemed Daindreth had the least amount of bad blood with the man.

Amira exhaled and nodded. No one else protested, but hers was the only response he cared about right now.

"What he did to you was wrong. Nothing will change that." Daindreth picked up her closest hand and left a kiss on her knuckles, where scabs were starting to form. "But we need his help."

"I know." Amira avoided eye contact.

Daindreth released her hand and kissed her temple. "He will bow to you before this is done."

Amira stared into the flames of their campfire. Gone was the vengeful rage she'd had when she'd tackled her father on this side of the portalstone.

Rising, Daindreth rested his hand on Amira's shoulder. "You did well." He lifted her chin. "It's a powerful woman who can steal a royal from within his own home. But to do it twice?"

Amira smiled a little at that.

"Get some rest, love. That goes for all of you, too. We'll need it."

111

Leaving Amira and the others by the fire, Daindreth went to find his way to the grotto where several of the younger Istovari were keeping King Hyle contained. It was a few dozen paces deeper into the cave complex and he needed a torch to see.

He found the young Istovari—a man and a woman—with their torches, sitting with King Hyle against one wall. They jumped when Daindreth rounded the bend.

"Can you give us a few minutes?" Daindreth asked. "Wait at the entrance."

"Are you certain, sir?" the young man asked.

"Gavin, was it?"

"Yes, sir," the Istovari confirmed, seeming proud that Daindreth had remembered his name.

"I think I will be fine. But I shall call for you if I require assistance." Daindreth found himself slipping easily into courtly dialect, the words coming to him like breathing.

The two Istovari shuffled off, leaving Daindreth and King Hyle with just the light of Daindreth's torch.

The emperor staked his torch near the entrance, digging it into the soft soil of the cave. King Hyle had seated himself on a low rock and Daindreth took up his place on one facing the other man.

"King Hyle," he began. "I would say well-met, but that seems inappropriate under the circumstances."

"Archduke Daindreth."

Daindreth thought he caught a hint of sarcasm in the king's greeting. He didn't correct the title for now.

"I have many questions, as you can imagine." King Hyle's lip was bloody, and one eye had swollen. His dressing robe was ripped and he looked very much like a man who had lost a fight with Amira. Most of Sair's healing had been focused on his shoulder.

"I am sure," Daindreth agreed with a nod. "Understandable. First, I want to apologize for how this evening has played out."

King Hyle watched Daindreth closely, eyes wide and

unblinking. "My daughter mentioned you wished to speak with me. I cannot help but wonder if there might have been a less dramatic way to arrange it."

"Circumstances are unique," Daindreth answered vaguely.

King Hyle's expression gave away nothing. "You know my daughter is a Kadra'han?"

Daindreth almost smiled at that. "You handed her vows to me unintentionally, I believe." It wasn't a question.

"Then she has told you everything." King Hyle's voice was quiet, small.

"I know you sent her to kill me, yes."

King Hyle didn't move. He didn't speak. For all Cyne might think him a weakling and a fop, King Hyle showed no fear in the face of a man who was, for all he knew, possessed by a demon. "Do you still plan to marry her?"

"I already have," Daindreth answered, allowing himself a small smile at that. "Amira is my wife as of last week."

King Hyle took a moment to process the news. "My congratulations. I understood that the wedding had been delayed while you recovered from an illness."

"Illness?" Daindreth asked, not surprised at all. He'd known his mother would have to spin some story to explain his disappearance.

"The empress has informed us that you and your bride had taken ill and retired to the countryside." If King Hyle had been concerned by that news, he didn't show it now.

"I see." Daindreth considered how much he was willing to tell his reticent father-in-law. "Amira told me why you wanted me dead."

King Hyle shifted, eyes darting to the side.

"It's alright," Daindreth assured him. "In your position, I would have wanted to kill me, too."

King Hyle straightened, then winced, probably upsetting some of the bruises Amira had given him.

"I was ill, I suppose," Daindreth said. "But I'm better now.

113

In no small part thanks to your daughter."

King Hyle's brow furrowed. "Amira?"

"She's strong," Daindreth said. "Loyal and brave. The best thing that's happened to me, really."

"Do you not have other Kadra'han?" King Hyle asked.

Daindreth had to bite back his first reply to that. "Amira is my Kadra'han, yes. But I no longer have power over her." He wasn't sure if this was a good idea to tell her father or not, but now was the time to be bold. He was challenging Vesha, the most powerful woman in the world, for the seat of the empire. The time for caution was past. "Amira is no longer bound by my commands, though her power does continue to grow with service to me."

"You released her?" King Hyle asked, sounding the most surprised he had this whole evening.

"She released herself," Daindreth corrected. "She almost killed herself to do it, but her curse is broken. Now there is only power."

"How is that possible?" King Hyle shook his head, eyes wide over his beard. "No Kadra'han has ever broken their curse."

"No other Kadra'han that we know of," Daindreth corrected. He considered his next words carefully. "Your daughter will be my empress, King Hyle. She is my empress now."

King Hyle considered the archduke's words for a long time, the popping of the torch the only sound.

"I made a deal with her, you know. The day I learned she was a Kadra'han and you'd passed her leash to me. I agreed to spare her family if she would help me."

"When was this?" King Hyle pressed.

"The day I removed her from your care. After your wife attacked her. Amira wanted her family safe, and I promised her that, even then." He leaned closer to the king, resting his elbows on his knees. "You barely know me, Your Majesty. And I barely know you, but I see you are a pragmatic man, so I will be frank

114

with you. We are going to war."

The blood on King Hyle's lip had turned dark, shining in the flickering torchlight.

"I will take my birthright and become emperor, whether my mother is ready to step down or not. Amira and the Istovari have cast their lot with me. I would have you cast your lot with me as well."

"You have a strange way of asking, Your Majesty," King Hyle said. But despite his tone, he used the title for a reigning monarch, not the one for an heir.

"Circumstances are not ideal," Daindreth agreed. "The plan was to rescue Cromwell and sway him, then urge him to contact you." Daindreth shrugged. "Regardless of what you choose, my mother will not believe your loyalty once we go to war."

Even if King Hyle publicly denounced Amira, it would be hard for him to convince the empress that he was innocent twice. Vesha would most likely kill Hyle and have Fonra married off to the nobleman of her choice, then install that man as the new king.

"My mother will question you at every turn and may take you hostage against my wife," Daindreth pointed out.

"Can you sway more barons?" King Hyle asked. "More kings?"

"Yes," Daindreth said without hesitation. "It has been a long time coming. Vesha's reign must end."

"Vesha has been good to us," King Hyle countered. "The kingdom prospers under her reign."

"Does it?" Daindreth lifted his head at the sound of distant thunder. "How many days of rain have you had this spring, Your Majesty?"

The king blinked at him, not understanding.

"You knew of my curse, didn't you?" Daindreth pressed. "Maybe you didn't know the details, but you knew I was a monster inside."

King Hyle didn't answer right away. "I would have thought

Cromwell would have told you if he was your ally."

"He was thrown in prison and didn't have the chance to explain himself," Daindreth replied.

"I didn't ask who Cromwell's sources were," the king replied. "I never did. I only knew that he learned you were inhabited by a monster. A thing that would destroy us all." As he spoke, King Hyle's expression grew tight, like he feared that if he kept speaking, the beast would claw its way out of Daindreth's skin and attack.

"The monster and I no longer share a body," Daindreth answered. "You can rest easy."

King Hyle studied the archduke cautiously. "I was with your father at the battle of the tower. I saw the ruins. The remains of whatever dark ritual the sorceresses used my daughter for." King Hyle's voice faltered. "I begged Emperor Drystan to save her, and he gave the order to his Kadra'han. They kept the life in her veins." King Hyle looked down to his hands, bloody and scarred with bits of broken glass. "But Amira was different after that. Quieter. It was months before she would speak again and when she did, there was nothing but rage." King Hyle shook his head. "Cyne took away a laughing child. I got back an angry woman."

Daindreth had seen some of that. Amira was less angry these days, at least to his eyes, but the rage was still there, the fury that could be unleashed whenever she felt threatened.

"Your father came back changed, too," King Hyle continued. "He was a great man. When he walked into a room, you could feel it shift. He inspired men, made them want to follow him. I know what people say, but I didn't swear fealty because I feared him. I swore my fealty because he made me want to believe—his vision of a united Erymaya."

Daindreth didn't think that was a good enough excuse for King Hyle abandoning his wife and daughter but said nothing for now.

King Hyle looked up to Daindreth. "You inherited your father's curse?"

"I did," Daindreth nodded. "But I've been freed. And I couldn't have done it without Amira."

"The Istovari released the curse?" King Hyle sounded more surprised by that than anything else that had been discussed so far.

"No," Daindreth answered. "They couldn't. But we found another way. I am...myself now."

"How long ago?"

Daindreth had to take a moment to count the days. "A few weeks."

"I see. And the empress?"

Daindreth considered again how much to tell King Hyle. "My mother had a different opinion as to how we should deal with the cythraul."

King Hyle nodded. "It's true, then? Vesha is a witch?"

Daindreth was a little surprised that King Hyle had known that. Perhaps he had Cromwell to thank for it. "I'm afraid so."

"Her witchcraft has been to our benefit," King Hyle said. "She will pay the price for it eventually, but for now—"

"It's over," Daindreth interrupted. "There's too much to explain, but my mother lost her familiar when I was freed of Caa Iss."

King Hyle looked past Daindreth. Outside, thunder rumbled. "Is that why the storms are here?"

"I think so," Daindreth confirmed. "The whole empire has been suffering, as far as I know."

Thunder boomed, shaking the ground beneath them. It would be some time before the Hylendale soldiers were able to come for their king.

"You trust my daughter?" King Hyle asked.

"Obviously." It was a rude response, but it seemed like the sort of question that deserved a rude response. Amira had saved him from a fate worse than death when they had barely known each other. What he felt for her was not just love and trust, but a deep, burning gratitude. He was grateful not just to her, but for

117

her. The gods had brought them together, he had no doubt. "Amira has risked herself for me more than once. I trust her and Thadred more than anyone else in this world."

King Hyle looked down to his hands, to the signet ring that still flashed on his knuckles. "She serves you willingly?"

"Yes," Daindreth answered, fighting and failing to keep the annoyance out of his tone. "Your daughter loves me, and I love her. Is that so hard to believe?"

King Hyle was quiet for a time. "I don't know Amira at all." He shook his head. "She used to sing, did you know that?"

Daindreth didn't but doubted that was important.

"As a child, she would sing songs she'd heard. Some she just made up." A wistful smile flitted across the king's face. "After the tower, she didn't sing. She used to be such a good child, but she became vicious. She bit her nursemaids and would scream at them if they disturbed her."

Daindreth could, oddly enough, picture that.

"I didn't know what to do." King Hyle ran a hand through his hair. "Her mother had destroyed an emperor. I didn't know how powerful she would grow to be, but I couldn't wait to find out. Cromwell procured the Kadra'han spell for me and I had her swear the oaths."

It had all worked out. Daindreth might not have met Amira if this hadn't happened. He might not have been freed of his curse and he might not have married her. But he couldn't deny the simmering heat in his chest or how he found his hands clenching on his knees.

"I had her trained then, as a Kadra'han. She made Adelaide uncomfortable, so I sent Amira away as much as I could, to serve our kingdom."

"You made her a slave." Daindreth forced his voice low, not trusting himself to let it go louder. "You made her a slave and then you used her to do your dirty work."

King Hyle frowned. "Wasn't she the one you sent into that palace tonight?"

"Amira serves me of her own free will, not because a curse compels her," Daindreth snapped.

King Hyle's voice went quiet as if he felt it wasn't a good excuse himself. "I didn't know what else to do."

Daindreth exhaled a long breath again, steadying himself before he spoke again. "What you did to her was wrong. I will never be convinced otherwise. But because of it, she will be empress."

King Hyle raised his chin. "It is to be civil war, then?"

"I hope not." Daindreth thought that sounded weak even to his own ears. "My mother has lost her power. She should be persuadable."

"Just because she has lost her familiar, does not mean she has lost her power," King Hyle said. "Whether her power was from a demon or not, her management of the empire has earned her the trust and loyalty of barons and lords across the continent."

"Which is why I need your help to make her see reason."

King Hyle's brows rose in a skeptical expression that reminded him of Amira.

Daindreth pressed on. "You are my father-in-law now. I know you have always done what is best for your people and I respect that. But my mother's time is short. Her reign is at an end. And while I do not hold a grudge against you, I cannot say the same for your daughter."

"So, you know she is dangerous, then?" King Hyle asked.

"She is," Daindreth agreed. "And I am grateful for it."

King Hyle leaned back, probably wondering if he was being threatened or not.

"I meant everything I said when I proposed to your daughter. I want an alliance with Hylendale and I want your friendship. I am sorry things happened as they did tonight, and it was certainly not what I or anyone else had in mind for this evening."

King Hyle didn't answer right away. He watched the patterns

of firelight on the cave wall, not speaking. "You have a plan to deal with the imperial soldiers, I assume? Will they swear allegiance to you? Or are you marked as a traitor by the empire?"

"I had hoped you could tell me," Daindreth responded non-committedly. "I have been cut off from the empire for the past months."

"I don't know," King Hyle responded. "Officially, the imperial soldiers told me they were here hunting fugitives. I thought you and my daughter were ill. I never knew you had gone on the run."

Daindreth would have to ask Amira if she believed her father. "Cromwell? What of him?"

"They told me he had aided and abetted the fugitives." King Hyle said that as if it was a prompt.

"He helped us," Daindreth confirmed. "Then informed the empire of our presence in the city."

"Yet you wanted to rescue him?"

"In his defense, he did warn us they were coming." Daindreth didn't quite understand Cromwell or his strange relationship with the royal family, but he saw an opportunity for an ally.

King Hyle chuckled. "You have allied with those women." It wasn't a question.

"The Isovari?"

"They cursed your father," King Hyle pointed out. "Caused his death, indirectly."

Daindreth's mind caught on those words. Did Hyle know the circumstances of his father's death? Most of the empire had been told it was illness contracted in the north. In a way, it was true.

"They tried to murder Amira and they have been the cause of more pain and suffering than I can describe."

Daindreth considered that for a moment. "They wanted to kill me when we first met," he said. "But the past years have not been kind to the Istovari." Daindreth was loath to give away any secrets of his allies, but he needed to share enough to hopefully sway this king. "They are ready for change. But more than that, I need them to help fight against my mother."

"I remember the empire before your mother, you know," King Hyle mused. "We weren't a part of it, but I remember how the land changed after Drystan married her. Before Vesha, Erymaya was a confederation of nations and city-states held together by tradition and pride. After Vesha, came the roads, the academies, the orphanages, and the cathedrals. Before her, Drystan the Conqueror lived up to his name, but few of us expected his expansion to last long. After Vesha, we knew that this was a dynasty here to stay."

"What are you saying?" Daindreth asked, trying not to sound defensive.

King Hyle sighed, studying the damp walls of stone. Rain had begun seeping through the rocks overhead to soak the walls. "You fully expect me to give you my allegiance, don't you?"

"I do," Daindreth answered, not hesitating this time. "Because now I see why you shackled Amira—you're afraid of her. Terrified, even."

King Hyle's eyes widened so slightly it might have been a trick of the light.

"And we both know that if you betray me, not even the gods can save you from her."

Many people thought Amira was a monster. Daindreth saw her as a woman who had been through pain and had come through it with anger in spades. She wasn't a monster, but she could be monstrous. If King Hyle harmed Daindreth or even tried, he had no doubt the king would quickly find his way to a slow death.

"Amira…" King Hyle hesitated. "You would unleash her on me? Is that what you are saying?"

"No," Daindreth said. "I'm saying I wouldn't be able to stop her."

"You know what she's capable of," King Hyle blinked at

him. "Yet you married her? You sleep next to her?"

Daindreth wasn't sure how to respond to that. "She's my wife, so yes, we sleep together." It felt strange to say that to her father, but what did the man expect? "Amira stayed with me when I was cursed, and she knew I could turn on her at any time. She chose me when I was at my worst."

King Hyle straightened. "I still don't trust her."

"I don't expect you to," Daindreth said. "But Amira is your rightful empress."

King Hyle exhaled a long breath, looking around the cave. "I need to speak to Cromwell. I want his advice in this."

"The man you had imprisoned?" Daindreth thought it sounded like a delaying tactic.

"If I am going to switch sides, then he will be reinstated as my advisor, I presume."

Daindreth wasn't so sure. Amira would need people to help her navigate the perils of courtly imperial life and if they could make it clear that Amira's wellbeing was in the best interest of Cromwell, he could be a valuable ally.

"I'll be back in the morning," Daindreth said, rising. "Tell me then if you will pledge your allegiance."

"If I do not? Will you hand me off to the mercy of my daughter?"

Daindreth shrugged. "I haven't decided yet." And he really hadn't.

No matter how one looked at it, tonight had sunk them deeper into a stalemate while raising the stakes at the same time.

CHAPTER FOURTEEN

Vesha

Vesha tried not to touch her god-eye, though the skin around it still itched. Through it, she could see the world crisper and clearer than she had thought possible. But everything through that eye seemed slightly blue, like nightfall.

She was sure the eye had been much larger when in Moreyne's face. Had the goddess shrunk it down somehow?

"Excellent," Caa Iss rumbled, chuckling all the way back to her sister's residence. "Excellent work, my dear."

Vesha rode in her palanquin, once again carried through the streets of Iandua. "Can you see him?" Vesha asked the quivering girl who knelt at her feet, Shelaine. "My new familiar?"

The handmaiden nodded. "Yes, Your Majesty. He's...large."

Caa Iss lumbered a full head and shoulders above the tallest man Vesha had ever seen. His chest was wider than most doors and his limbs were roped in cords of veiny muscle.

"You're not afraid of him?" Shelaine asked.

Caa Iss grinned at her with his fanged smile.

"No," Vesha said, looking over Caa Iss mildly. "He knows he's better off with me than without."

"She's a pretty thing," Caa Iss leered down at Shelaine. "If only I had a body again."

Vesha narrowed her eyes at the cythraul.

"What?" Caa Iss snorted. "I was complimenting her."

Vesha didn't look away from the demon as they rounded a bend in the road.

"Fine!" Caa Iss huffed. "I'll stop staring at her. Better?"

"What's he saying, Your Majesty?" Shelaine asked.

"You still can't hear him? Fascinating."

A lean, flea-bitten urchin came stumbling out of the shadows in front of the palanquin. As the guards approached him, he didn't move.

"You!" the guard in front shouted. "Get out of the way!"

The urchin dragged his head upright, as if he had trouble using his neck. "Pardon me. It's been so long since I've had a body." The urchin blinked at the guards with bright red eyes.

The palanquin stopped. Vesha straightened, not sure if it was dread or excitement pooling in her gut.

"It's a little awkward at the moment." Despite his words, the urchin flourished a bow, smirkingHe looked past the guards to Vesha. "Maal Dree. At your service, my lady."

Another figure came swaggering into view, an old woman moving far more confidently than the frail shape of her body should have allowed. "Huu Maak, most esteemed empress." The second creature's voice had a sultry, smoky sound that sent shivers down Vesha's spine.

"Set me down," Vesha ordered her palanquin bearers.

They obeyed and she stood as more shapes emerged from the darkness of the streets. Their eyes glowed that telltale red, none quite as bright as Caa Iss and Saan Thii, but there was no mistaking them.

One came in the body of a child, barely out of nappies with a belly swollen by hunger. A large man smudged with soot and grime, still wearing his blacksmith's apron carried the child on one shoulder. Both were now cythraul. Next came an emaciated young man with pox scars riddling his face, though the creature now in control assured Vesha that he was cured of any contagion. A thin girl Vesha recognized as one of the prostitutes from a few days ago emerged beside him, a confident smirk replacing her fearful cower—eyes burning red.

Vesha stepped down from her palanquin with Caa Iss close beside her.

"Humans," Caa Iss mused with a low chuckle. "The desperate among you are always so eager to be possessed. After all, what could be better than being strong and powerful? Of never having to hunger or grow old? Never having to know pain?"

Vesha had known that hosts would have to agree to be possessed, but she hadn't expected so many to agree so quickly. Either the demons were truly persuasive, or she had underestimated the weakness of her own kind.

"You want to know a secret?" Caa Iss whispered in Vesha's ear.

Vesha didn't respond, but Caa Iss took that as permission.

"I have always admired that about humans. You will do anything—*anything*—to spare yourselves pain."

Vesha didn't speak. She had taken on pain her entire life, if only to spare others from it. First her parents, then her sister. Now her husband's entire empire.

"The others are still seeking hosts, but they shall be joining us as soon as they do," said Huu Maak with an elaborate bow.

A scream rent the night air.

Vesha and her guards all turned in that direction.

"Oh dear," Caa Iss muttered. "It would seem someone has spotted one of us."

More shapes shambled from the darkness as more and more cythraul found hosts and came to meet their new mistress.

Vesha turned in a slow circle as the figures came closer, hemming her and her retinue in on all sides. She knew the demons couldn't hurt her, but her guards and servants pressed closer, seeking protection or waiting for orders, she wasn't sure.

She turned to Caa Iss. "This isn't what I wanted."

"Did you offer the deal I told you to make?"

"Yes." Vesha raised her chin and stuffed down the vague sense of dread in her chest.

"Then you made a deal for the protection and prosperity of the empire in exchange for a new home for the cythraul. Did you ever forbid us from taking new hosts?"

Vesha shook her head, realizing she hadn't. "How is this possible? They had no rituals. No—"

125

"If a cythraul is released into this world with the proper permissions, they are free to make a pact with a host," he rumbled back. "I was summoned to bind to the Fanduillion bloodline, so I can bind with no other."

"What if I banished you back to the Dread Marches?" Vesha demanded. "Would that fix it for you?"

Caa Iss seemed amused by her suggestion. "If I was summoned back."

Vesha turned away. Each moment she seemed to have more power, yet less control.

"We await your orders, Your Majesty," said a cythraul who kept licking their mouth as if they were used to larger teeth. "What would you have us do?"

"We must return to the mainland," Vesha said. "We have work to do there. Secure the necessary ships and supplies."

The cythraul who appeared to have taken over a sailor raised his meaty hand. "My host knows about ships."

"Mine too," said the cythraul who had taken over the prostitute. "We can lead."

"Good." Vesha returned to the seat of her palanquin, exhaustion settling over her like a thick fog. "Good."

She had succeeded. She should feel victorious.

Instead, Vesha felt stained. Dirty. The filth of the Dread Marches smudged her clothes, her skin. She wanted nothing more than to tear off this dress and scrub away the feeling of pollution, but something told her she never would.

Vesha hung her head and buried her face in her hands as the screams in the city grew louder. She'd done the right thing, she knew she had.

She just wished it didn't feel like this.

CHAPTER FIFTEEN

Amira

Amira had found her way to the grotto she shared with Daindreth and fallen asleep without undressing. She woke when he crawled in beside her.

"How did it go?" she asked, her voice thick with sleep.

Daindreth kissed her temple. "It could have gone worse. We'll talk in the morning, alright?"

"Mmm." Amira curled against his side and fell back to sleep. She dreamed of a coastal city she didn't recognize. Red eyes stalked the shadows and screams filled the air.

Amira awoke with a jolt. Her pulse raced and it took a moment for her to realize she was lying beside Daindreth, safe in their grotto, not back in the nightmare.

"Daindreth." She sat up, cocking her head to the side.

The world was rich with *ka*, even in this cave. The rains for weeks had meant that moss, mold, and insects were thriving. The hungry northern plants sucked up the water.

Even with that, she could sense bodies through the nearby cave complex. Not far away were the rangers gathered around what she would guess was a fire. The horses were near them, and a cluster of bodies apart from them. Amira assumed the second cluster was her father and the Istovari guarding him.

But there was something else…something coming through the trees. Under normal circumstances, she might have been able to ignore it, but she could feel the *ka* of several large creatures…at least a few.

"What is it?" Daindreth sat up beside her. The blankets slid off, revealing his bare chest and torso.

Amira realized he slept naked and her heart thudded just a little faster before she forced herself to focus. "It might be nothing," she mumbled, tearing her eyes away from his lines of muscle. "It could just be deer, but I think something is coming."

Daindreth was already pulling on his breeches and boots. Amira slid off their pallet and started pulling on her own boots. Those were the only things she had bothered to take off.

"If it is the guards, I'm impressed anyone was able to track us this quickly after that rain," Daindreth said.

"Yes," Amira agreed. She marched from their grotto to find the rangers in the larger cave chamber. A meaty, savory scent filled the air.

Thadred was beside the fire with Rhis, showing the boy how to sharpen his cane sword with a whetstone.

Cyne was there as well, though Sair was missing. The other sorceress was probably still asleep after having to channel so much magic last night.

Tapios and several of the other rangers were around the fire, roasting a medium animal over a spit. They carved pieces off, eating with their hands with large leaves for plates. At least the Istovari were well equipped for life in the wilderness.

"Amira!" Thadred smiled, seeming to be in a better mood this morning. "How's—"

"Do we have guards posted?" Amira looked straight to Tapios, speaking over Thadred.

"Yes," Tapios answered. "Two, as you suggested. They're watching the wards we placed."

"Are you sure—"

A high-pitched whistle split the air and the entire cave went still. A second whistle followed.

Amira spun around to Daindreth to find her mute horror mirrored on his face.

A third whistle came, this time from the other direction.

Thadred cursed, climbing to his feet. "Well, good thing we've sharpened this. Rhis, go wake your mother. Tell her someone's coming."

The child scurried off as fast as his little legs could carry him.

Tapios had his bow nocked, and ready.

Amira checked the knives and short sword strapped to her body. She'd found them in the ruins of Kelamora and they were some of the best weapons she'd ever had.

One of the rangers was already kicking dirt over the campfire by the time one of the scouts came panting up the hill.

"Tapios!" The young woman ran straight to her leader. "Men through the trees on horseback. Ten of them and more coming."

"Describe them." Tapios was already checking his bow and quiver. The Istovari weren't much good in hand-to-hand combat, but the rangers were all on their feet and ready.

"Armor," the young scout said. "Green and white armor of Hylendale."

Amira looked to Daindreth. Her father's men had found them.

"Tapios!" the second scout stumbled into the cave, his hood pulled low to hide his red hair. It would stand out like a firebrand in the trees. "Another group approaches from the west."

Cyne stepped up beside Amira. "You might want to fetch your father."

"To what end?" Amira demanded. "A human shield?"

Cyne's mouth tightened. "He is leverage."

Amira rolled her eyes. "We use him as leverage, then what?"

They might be able to hold off the soldiers temporarily, but if they made themselves enemies of Hylendale, Amira didn't imagine it would end well. The goal was to get past the hostilities, but things had been escalating ever since Amira had kidnapped her father.

She knew now that hadn't been the best decision.

"There's too many," Thadred said. "We can't fight them even if we wanted to."

Amira clenched her jaw, thinking. The forest was full of untapped power. *Ka* simmered through the air like smoke.

She knew more spells now, more ways to shape and weave *ka*. There were spells in her grandmother's book she had yet to try. Spells that were dangerous, but Amira had never been one to hesitate from fear.

"We need more time," Daindreth grated. "We're not ready to confront them."

"We can mislead them," one of the rangers suggested. "They're still at least three hundred paces off. A few of us can lay a false trail and take them away from this cave."

"I can place a dreadsight spell over us," Amira offered. "But if we hide in the cave, we'll be trapped." They had found other passages and tunnels, but none that would allow all of them, much less their horses, through.

Daindreth nodded solemnly. "We'll still have a better chance than if we run." He was right, of course. The soldiers were too close and there were too many of them.

"I'll lead the distraction," Tapios said. "Anders, Vynn, with me. We'll see if we can lead them away."

"The king?" Amira looked to Daindreth.

"Secure him," Daindreth said. "If this goes bad, we'll need him for bargaining."

"I'll see to him," Cyne volunteered.

Amira arched one eyebrow at her mother. As far as she knew, her parents hadn't seen one another since her father had denounced his wife as a traitor. Cyne had taken Amira, then only four years old, and fled Lashera.

"I won't hurt him" Cyne said, almost making that sound like a concession. "I'll even be courteous."

Daindreth made the decision so that Amira didn't have to. "Keep him hidden and keep him safe."

"I'll place a second dreadsight spell over the entrance to his alcove," Cyne said. "And I'll keep him quiet."

Amira felt torn and she wasn't sure why. "Mother, if you're caught by them—"

"You'll rescue me." Cyne turned around and marched in the direction of where King Hyle was being held.

Amira let her mother go and followed Daindreth to the

horses. The animals had been picketed near the mouth of the cave, but they needed to be inside it if Amira's spell was going to hide them.

Tapios and the other two Istovari had already jogged into the pines. They melted skillfully into the undergrowth. As hunters who had practiced on the treacherous forests of the Cursewood, the game park of King Hyle was nothing.

Sair and Rhis emerged from the back of the cave. Sair's hair flew in every which direction, but her eyes were bright and alert.

"Sair, we need to get the horses inside," Thadred said. "Rhis, stand here and hold Lleuad for a moment. I need to grab the other horses."

Sair didn't argue, which was a testament to the seriousness of their situation.

"I get to hold the kelpie?" Rhis's eyes went wide despite the danger.

"Yes," Thadred said, not looking up as he helped another Istovari untie a horse from the picket line. "But if he tries to pull away, just let go, alright?"

Sair set to grabbing her horse, buckling on the animal's saddle in moments. It was easier to move the saddles if they were on horses.

The first Istovari headed for inside the cave, leading Tapios's flea-bitten gelding behind them. Thadred was next and he pulled Rhis along, the boy still leading Lleuad while Thadred wrangled two other horses on his other side.

"Follow Thad," Daindreth ordered. "Our goal is to avoid the soldiers, let them find this place, and come back out after they leave."

Amira grabbed her little bay mare and Daindreth's sorrel.

Lleuad stamped and sorted, tail held high. Thadred still used a bitless hackamore for the stallion, but when he was tugged toward the cave, Lleuad followed. The kelpie might still be half wild, but he was a fast learner.

They took the horses into the largest of the cave chambers.

The ground was rocky and lopsided in places, but the animals managed.

Amira cringed at the sound of so many hooves echoing through the cave at once, but it couldn't be helped. They huddled back as riders shushed their horses.

The alcove holding King Hyle was closer to the front. Amira hated leaving her mother behind. She hated it more than she would have thought.

Once the horses were gathered in the shelter of the largest chamber, Amira began casting the dreadsight spell over the entrance. A dreadsight spell over the entire mouth of the cave would take too much time and would be too delicate, but spells over certain cave chambers were easier.

There had been a time she had needed blood to cast the spell just on herself. Now, with her service to Daindreth making her stronger every day, she was only limited by her own concentration.

Amira felt the smog of *ka* that hung over the forest. She drew it in, eyes closed and brow creased as she shaped the spell. She'd never cast one this large before, but she hadn't hesitated to believe she could.

Sair stepped up behind her and a moment later, so did Thadred. The two of them joined their power to hers, and the work sped up. Amira wove the spell larger and larger, expanding it until it covered the entire entrance of this chamber.

Amira finished and drew in a deep breath. The passage behind them was unchanged to the naked eye, but Amira's handiwork was plain to anyone who knew what to look for.

By now, Amira could sense more clearly the shapes of the soldiers on the other side, closing in on the cave. She didn't think the soldiers had seen them. Maybe Tapios and the others had successfully caught their attention.

Amira glanced at Daindreth. "I'm going around to watch them."

The cave complex had several passages, this was just the only one large enough for horses. Another tunnel, much smaller and less accommodating, led around the other side.

"I'll come with you." Daindreth stepped after her.

Amira paused, glancing at Sair and Thadred. "Can you keep that up?" She jerked her head in the direction of her dreadsight spell.

Several of the horses whickered uneasily and the Istovari worked to shush them. Lleuad pinned his ears at a much larger gelding and Thadred scolded him in a low tone.

But all they could do now was wait.

Sair nodded, hands in front of her. "We can maintain it, yes. You've done the hard part."

"Thank you." Amira adjusted her weapons and headed for the nearby passage.

Amira moved more easily than Daindreth, but the two of them forced their way through the tight corners and narrow clefts to a narrow seam in the rock. The seam was barely wide enough for a person to pass through, but it offered a view of the clearing, if it was obscured by shrubs and vines.

Amira peered through as soldiers approached the cave. There were the banners of Hylendale and the green tabards of the Hylendale uniforms. They were all on horseback and well-armed as best Amira could tell. After them came a group of soldiers in black.

Daindreth stiffened at her side.

Amira frowned. Hylendale men didn't look like that. "Those are imperial soldiers?" Amira squinted, trying to make out the shape on the banner. It appeared to be the number nine beside a crown.

"No," Daindreth said, voice low. "Not soldiers."

"What?"

"Those are palace guards. The Ninth."

A jolt went through Amira's spine. "Could Vesha be here?"

"I don't think so. Not unless she rode to Hylendale personally." He frowned, squinting, then his eyes widened.

"Look."

He pointed toward the clearing, and a flurry of action caught Amira's eye.

A figure was dragged out between two soldiers, ruffled and bound. Amira couldn't make out many details from this distance, but she thought she recognized the man.

"One of the rangers?" Daindreth asked.

"It looks like Tapios." Amira added several choice curses under her breath. Caught already? She'd definitely give him a hard time about this later.

Several Hylendale soldiers entered the cave, their weapons drawn. The signs of habitation would be obvious inside from the soot marks and the remains of several meals. None of them seemed to spot the horses or the Istovari behind Amira's spellwork, though.

Amira hoped that her mother's dreadsight spell would hold up and that she and King Hyle wouldn't be discovered. She wondered how her mother was keeping the king quiet.

"They're questioning him." Daindreth crouched low, trying to get a better view through the branches. "What's this?"

"What?"

Daindreth's frown deepened. He spun to her. "Amira, do you trust me?"

The assassin shook her head in confusion. "Of course I do, but what—"

"I can't explain, but I don't think Vesha sent those men."

"But my father said—"

"They probably lied to him," Daindreth said. "This could be an elaborate trap, but..." He looked between her and the clearing. "They have Tapios."

Amira closed her eyes, swallowing down a hundred protests. Taking dangerous chances was her specialty, not his.

"Daindreth—"

He leaned over and kissed her. It was a hard kiss, like a final gulp of air before plunging underwater.

"Stay hidden," he said. "If something goes wrong, wait and come to rescue me once they've let their guard down."

"Husband." Amira grabbed his sleeve, her tone going hard.

"Trust me, love." He pulled away from her. "It's my turn to take risks."

Amira let him go, even as her mind screamed at her not to. This was an all-out gamble. They had no recourse if the soldiers turned on Daindreth. She wouldn't be able to do anything from this distance, not against that many men. There had to be at least fifty in the clearing—and more were coming.

Daindreth squeezed past her and out of the narrow passage. He stumbled through the briars for a moment before he caught his balance and made his way down, through the trees and toward the clearing.

The assassin watched him go, her heart in her throat and her chest tight. Trust him. She needed to trust him.

But that didn't mean she was going to stay behind. If she circled around, she would be able to approach from the far side and be at their backs when Daindreth approached the soldiers.

The assassin poured power into the dreadsight runes in her hunting habit until she felt the effects spread over her entire body.

Once Amira was sure her own dreadsight spell was in place, she squeezed out of the narrow cleft in the rock. Then she followed Daindreth.

CHAPTER SIXTEEN

Daindreth

Daindreth felt he'd made a mistake almost instantly. If he was wrong, he would be captured or perhaps killed. Either way, it would endanger Amira when she came to rescue or avenge him—and she *would* do one or the other, there would be no stopping her.

Daindreth forced his way through the undergrowth, as fast as he dared move. He didn't want to be shot before he got close enough to speak or be recognized. Several of the soldiers carried crossbows.

From here, he could see Tapios bound on the ground between two imperial soldiers in full armor, the emblazon of the imperial palace guard across their tabards.

Tapios's face was bloodied and he slumped at a concerning angle. A man on a white horse dismounted, removing his helmet.

Underneath it, the man had a thick black beard that had been trimmed with military precision. Even at this distance, Daindreth recognized him.

The commander crouched in front of Tapios. An exchange too low for Daindreth to hear passed between them. The commander backhanded Tapios with a gauntlet.

If Daindreth waited too much longer, this could get out of hand.

Soldiers guarded the perimeter of the clearing, but they were a few dozen paces back. He just hoped they wouldn't shoot him on sight.

Daindreth whispered a prayer to his family's patron god, raised his right hand in a gesture of peace, and stepped into the sunlight.

"Captain Westfall!" he shouted.

Instantly, at least ten crossbows pointed at his chest. The ring of steel rattled around the clearing as imperial and royal soldiers alike drew their weapons.

Daindreth kept his right hand raised, in plain sight. "Ohad Westfall," he repeated.

The armored man in front of Tapios leapt to his feet, one hand on his sword hilt. He had a scar cutting down the left side of his jaw, allegedly where a southern tribesman had slashed him in a tavern brawl. It was an embarrassing enough story that Daindreth believed it. Few soldiers would admit to being marked in a common street fight.

"Hands up!" cried one of the crossbowmen.

"Hold," Captain Westfall ordered. He kept behind the line of crossbowmen and didn't take his hand off his sword. He peered at Daindreth, probably just as shocked to see Daindreth as Daindreth had been to see him. "Your Majesty?" Westfall asked, head cocked to one side. He glanced around them, searching for movement in the trees.

Daindreth felt something was off but couldn't quite put his finger on it. "It's good to see you."

"Are you alone, Your Majesty?" Ohad kept one hand on his sword.

Daindreth wasn't sure what answer Westfall wanted but answered honestly. "I came alone."

He suspected that Amira was already in a position to slaughter everyone if something went wrong, but he had indeed come alone.

"I see you found one of my friends." He jerked his chin to Tapios.

Tapios looked up at Daindreth through bloodshot and bruised eyes. He was a little battered, but should recover.

Westfall whirled on Tapios, then back to Daindreth. "Your friend?" He said the word slowly, carefully, like he hadn't heard right.

"Yes. Could I trouble you to release him?"

Westfall signaled to the soldiers and they unbound Tapios. None of them helped him stand, but the ranger got to his feet

137

on his own. Standing, he was at least a head taller than the other men.

"Tapios." Daindreth looked him over. "Are you alright?"

Tapios nodded once, smearing the blood off his face.

That had worked. That had actually worked.

"We've been searching for you, Your Majesty." Westfall took several steps forward and stopped.

The Hylendale soldiers stood by mutely, barely moving and not speaking. The imperial guards stood at attention.

Daindreth then realized what was off—Westfall had called him *majesty,* the title reserved for the empire's ruler.

"You disappeared from the palace months ago and now your lady mother…"

"What of my mother?" Daindreth couldn't hold back the spike of alarm that shot through his chest.

"She's missing, Your Majesty. No one has been able to contact her or her Kadra'han for over a month."

Over a month—that would have been about the time they had all met at Kelamora, when Vesha had been betrayed by Saan Thii and the monastery had burned to the ground.

"Who knows she is missing?" Daindreth demanded.

It wouldn't have been unusual for kingdoms and fiefs in the empire to go months without hearing from the empress, but for her personal guards?

Westfall wasn't a Kadra'han. He was an officer in the imperial guard. In war time, they were the elite troops who rode with the emperors into battle. In peace, they served as the protectors of the imperial family and a kind of intelligence corps.

"We've been trying to find you, my liege. The empress is lost at sea as best we know. The courtiers are growing restless as are the ministers."

Daindreth considered that. He needed to get back to Mynadra at once and stabilize the court.

"Your Majesty, forgive me for asking, but…" Westfall glanced around at the woods and their meager surroundings.

"Where have you been?"

Daindreth suppressed a laugh at that. He had no idea how to even begin answering that question. "My mother and I had a disagreement," he said, even though he himself considered it the understatement of the decade. "I had hoped to settle it privately between us, but it seems that will not be happening."

"You have seen the empress?" Westfall asked, looking to a man in a lieutenant's uniform at his left.

"Yes," Daindreth confirmed. "But it was over a month ago, I fear. Captain Darrigan is dead."

Westfall's face paled and his eyes widened. He was either genuinely surprised, or an excellent actor. "Dead?"

"I'm afraid so." For now, Daindreth left out the fact that he had been the one to kill Darrigan.

Westfall shook his head. "My liege, we need you to return to Mynadra. Earthquakes have wracked the coast and volcanoes have erupted in the south. The empire needs leadership."

Daindreth processed the other man's words. His first impulse was to ask after the damages and loss of life, but he restrained himself. He focused on the captain's last sentence. It might be a trick from his mother, but he doubted it. Vesha wouldn't need to trick him like this. "You would recognize my leadership?" Daindreth pressed. "In full?"

Westfall hesitated just a moment, then nodded slowly as he caught Daindreth's intent. "The empress has ruled well, but you are of age, more than of age."

Daindreth was almost afraid to believe it. "Speak plain, Westfall." He glanced past the other man. This was a gamble. There was no way around it. But he was ready to cast the die. "Would you follow me, even if my mother and I were at odds? Because I fear it has come to that. So, tell me forthright, are you my mother's man, or mine?"

Westfall drew his sword.

A part of Daindreth knew he was vulnerable, understood he should be wary of a trap, but a gut feeling told him not to move.

"Long live the emperor." Westfall dropped to one knee, laid his sword flat in his hands, and presented it to Daindreth. "All hail the Emperor of Erymaya, High Prince of Galais, and Lord Castellan of Mynadra."

"Hail!" the imperial guards shouted their agreement at Westfall's back and one by one dropped to their knees before Daindreth.

"I pledge my sword, my loyalty, and my life to Daindreth of the House Fanduillion from this day forward," Captain Westfall declared. "I swear to uphold the throne of your fathers and the throne of your sons unto my last breath. May a curse be upon me and my line if I break this bond."

The soldiers echoed the vow. It was far more than Daindreth had dared wished for, and their oaths settled over him like a weight. He had done nothing to earn the loyalty of these men. His father had led men into battle, bled with them and fought alongside them. Daindreth was just a boy who had struggled with a cythraul for most his life—and barely won.

"You honor me." Daindreth extended a hand to Westfall and pulled the other man to his feet. He gripped Westfall's forearm as he might have done with Thadred or one of the other men at court. "I will seek to be worthy of the honor you give me."

Captain Westfall nodded shortly. "I know you will, my liege."

Daindreth looked past him to where Tapios stood, the soldiers around him giving him space. The men from Hylendale had bowed as well, recognizing Daindreth as emperor.

"Amira," Daindreth called. "Show yourself, my dear."

The air shimmered and rippled and Amira stepped out from behind Westfall. A dagger hung easily in one hand.

Westfall jumped, his sword raised. Several soldiers reached for their weapons.

Amira cocked her head at the armored man, staring Westfall down. She could have killed the soldier, and they both knew it.

"Captain Westfall," Daindreth gestured to Amira, "I don't believe you have met my lady wife, Amira Brindonu Fanduillion of Hylendale."

Westfall lowered his sword, stepping to the side so that he could face them both at the same time. He inclined his head to Amira, if a little stiffly. "She's a sorceress, my liege?"

"Yes," Daindreth confirmed. "My Kadra'han. And my empress." She hadn't been crowned yet, but the title was hers by rights.

Amira sauntered to stand beside Daindreth. She didn't touch him, but she stood close enough to convey ownership.

Daindreth looked back to Tapios. "Come here." He wasn't in the habit of commanding the Istovari, but if the imperial soldiers saw Daindreth was in command, they wouldn't see the Istovari as threatening.

"I think there is much catching up to do," Westfall said as Tapios came to heel on Daindreth's other side.

The ranger walked with a slight limp, but didn't appear to be bleeding. Sair and Thadred should be able to patch him up.

"I think there is," Daindreth agreed.

"We came into this forest tracking criminals," Westfall explained. He inclined his head to Amira. "Forgive me, Empress Amira. But your father is missing. He was abducted last night."

Daindreth didn't see if Amira reacted or not, but he made a split-second decision and spoke. "Yes," Daindreth nodded. "I needed to speak with him."

Westfall's dark brows rose. "Your Majesty?"

"I've been gone, Westfall," he said, dropping the captain's title. "I don't know who my friends or enemies are."

"You knew I was a friend?" Westfall glanced to Amira. He was too young to have fought in the wars against the Istovari, but he had been trained by men who had. There was no one in the empire who hadn't heard tales of their wrath and ruin.

"No," Daindreth said. "But I hoped you were."

Daindreth didn't add that Amira would have killed Westfall

141

or at the very least taken him hostage. She'd been able to walk into the middle of a clearing full of soldiers in broad daylight. Truly, her power was increasing.

"You know where the king is, my liege?" Westfall asked, not looking away from Amira.

"Tapios," Daindreth looked to the ranger. "Would you show two of Westfall's men to where the king is and fetch him here?"

Daindreth wanted Amira to stay with him, where she would be able to act if Westfall did turn on them. He also wanted imperial soldiers, not Hylendale men, to fetch the king.

"Stand down," Daindreth ordered the Hylendale soldiers.

Their leader hesitated, but Westfall took a sharp step forward.

"You heard the emperor," Westfall bellowed, his voice strong and stern, an army commander's voice. "Stand down."

That was one thing Daindreth had always appreciated about military men. They were decisive.

The Hylendale soldiers made room for Tapios and two heavily armored imperials to march into the cave.

Westfall turned back to Daindreth. "My liege, there are so many questions."

Daindreth smiled and rested a hand on the other man's shoulder. "I will give you what answers I can."

He had never been as close with Westfall as he had been with Thadred, but the other man had been part of his personal guard before being assigned to his own detachment. He had joined Thadred and Daindreth on many evenings of drinking and reveling, before Daindreth had realized impairing himself made Caa Iss stronger. Westfall had known his secret and, like so many others, had kept it.

"He's gone, Ohad," Daindreth whispered, using the captain's familiar name. "That's why I left. There was a chance, and it worked."

Westfall blinked at Daindreth in surprise. "You're sure?"

"Yes," Daindreth grinned, excitement welling anew like it

did every time he thought about it. "For a few weeks now. But I'm free."

Westfall smiled and clapped Daindreth back. He withdrew his hand instantly, as if remembering himself. That wasn't appropriate behavior with an emperor. He cleared his throat. "We shall have much to discuss indeed."

Westfall and Amira eyed each other—him in his full plate armor and her in her leather hunting habit. A fox and an iron bull. Neither seemed quite sure what to make of the other.

Voices came from the mouth of the cave and the soldiers of Hylendale stirred.

King Hyle walked between the two imperial soldiers, Cyne and Tapios following behind.

Westfall stared as the royal limped down from the cave. "He looks a bit rough."

"He tripped." Amira folded her arms across her chest.

Westfall leveled a look at her that was hard to interpret. "He tripped?" The words were flat, but at the same time skeptical.

"Twice." Amira's response was equally flat.

"No more tripping for anyone," Daindreth interjected, looking at Amira.

Westfall studied Amira, not speaking. He probably knew she was the one to blame for her father's disappearance and present condition. Westfall was probably wondering just *what* she was and what she could do. He wasn't used to women as warriors any more than Daindreth or Thad had been, but he was familiar with Kadra'han and he would know of sorceresses.

"Who's the other woman?" Westfall asked as Cyne and Tapios approached.

"Lady Cyne," Daindreth said. "My mother-in-law. I have revoked her exile."

Westfall shot him a sharp look but said nothing. Daindreth expected to hear much more once they were in private. Westfall would probably want to speak away from Amira and the others.

King Hyle walked on his own, but the bruises were dark

circles on his face. In daylight, Daindreth realized he had bits of broken glass shining on his forehead. When had that happened?

The king inclined his head, perfectly composed. "Captain Westfall. Good to see you."

Westfall looked to Daindreth. "Your Majesty?"

Cyne stood, her hands clasped before her. "Tapios said there has been a change of plans?"

Daindreth needed to take control. He had crossed a line somewhere and there was no going back. "King Hyle, if you would be so kind, I would like to continue our discussions in the comfort of your home."

King Hyle bowed, the veins in his forehead throbbing. "It would be my honor, Your Majesty."

What else was Hyle supposed to say? His men were outnumbered, and Westfall appeared to be on Daindreth's side, not to mention the two sorceresses.

Amira gripped Daindreth's sleeve. Her face taut as she leaned in, turning away from Westfall. "You want to go into the palace? With my father? Can we trust Westfall?"

"I think so," Daindreth replied, keeping his voice down. "I'm not sure, but he's a friend."

Amira grabbed the front of Daindreth's collar. "Husband, this could be a trap."

Westfall coughed awkwardly. Such intimate touching, especially of the emperor, would have been inappropriate back at court.

Daindreth kissed her forehead. "But it might be what we need."

There was no way to seize control of an empire, even one that rightfully belonged to him, without danger.

Amira nodded, releasing him.

CHAPTER SEVENTEEN

Vesha

Vesha slumped on the front steps of her sister's villa. She rubbed her temples, wishing the screams didn't make her head pound.

The screaming hadn't stopped since last night. At least she thought it hadn't stopped. Perhaps it had and she just couldn't get the echoes out of her head.

The sky was overcast and Vesha wasn't sure if it was smoke or clouds. After the wastes of the Dread Marches, her nose and throat were too raw to smell.

Was it morning? She wasn't sure.

Someone tugged on her arm. "My lady. Your Majesty, please, get up."

Vesha forced her head up. One of her maids leaned over her—Odette. Her hair was mussed, and soot and dirt covered her from head to foot, just like Vesha.

"Please, Your Majesty," the girl pleaded. "Come inside."

"How did we get here?" Vesha remembered the cythraul taking over the wretches of the city and coming to her and Caa Iss, then…

She didn't see anyone else. Not her guards, not even Caa Iss. None of her sister's servants were in sight, either.

"The city is burning," Odette sobbed. She cowered over Vesha, almost as if she hoped to shield the empress. "We were brought here by your guards and then…" A sob broke off Odette's words.

"What happened?" Vesha rasped, her throat tight and breath coming in sharp gasps.

"You…you ordered your Kadra'han to become hosts. Captain Cashun begged you not to, but you repeated the order." Odette broke down into sobs, folding herself in over the empress in an absolute butchery of all etiquette and courtly law.

145

Vesha slipped an arm around the girl. "The other men?" she croaked. "The soldiers who weren't Kadra'han?"

"Cashun and the others attacked them." Odette gestured weakly to the courtyard.

Vesha looked up and almost gagged. Bodies in imperial uniform lay strewn in front of her—their limbs broken at odd angles and their chests ripped open.

Entrails and broken bones had been spread across the white cobbles and the manicured shrubberies. Heads lay with jaws still open in final screams of agony. Their plate armor had been dented and peeled back like scraps of paper.

"Is...is that all of them?" Vesha gasped. "All the men who weren't Kadra'han?"

"No," Odette cried. "It's just the ones who wouldn't accept cythraul."

Vesha had no idea how many bodies lay before her. They were too mangled for her to tell them apart.

"Come inside," Odette pleaded again. "Let me...clean you up."

Vesha looked down at herself—covered head to foot in blood, ash, and filth. She didn't remember what it felt like to be clean. The shift she had worn into the Dread Marches was tattered and stained.

"I commanded them?" Vesha repeated. "I don't..." she shook her head as it throbbed sharper. "I didn't..."

Odette held onto her. "Come with me. Please."

"Where are the others? The handamidens?" Vesha asked. "Did the cythraul take them, too?"

"No, they fled," Odette replied. "Well, Shelaine took on a cythraul. I think she was frightened. The others stayed until they saw the city was burning."

"Why is the city burning?" Vesha rasped, her voice dry and scratchy.

"Some of the priests, I think," Odette answered. "They set the cathedral on fire when the cythraul tried to go inside. It spread from there."

"Fools," Vesha mumbled. "I'm saving them. The deal is to save them, so the…the demons can't hurt them."

Even as she said it, Vesha knew it wasn't true. Even with her head throbbing, she knew it wasn't true. What were the exact terms of the deal? The empire's protection and prosperity. She hadn't said anything about individuals, had she?

Vesha staggered to her feet. "Caa Iss!" she screamed, her voice harsh and broken. "Caa Iss! Answer me!" She stumbled and Odette had to catch her.

"Please, my lady," Odette wept. "Please come inside. Your sister is inside."

Vesha shook her head. "I don't want to see my sister." A fit of coughing overtook her and she doubled over. She might have fallen except for Odette steadying her.

Without waiting for permission, Odette began to pull her inside. Vesha stumbled after her handmaiden, breath coming in harsh rasps.

"What have I done?" Vesha needed to do something. She knew what it was, but couldn't quite remember. She'd made a mistake. She needed to—

A sharp throb went through her head and chased the thought away.

"Darrigan," Vesha whimpered. "I need Darrigan."

"He's not here, Your Majesty," Odette said patiently. "He died in Kelamora, remember?"

Vesha did remember, but she still needed him. Hot tears trailed down her face as the other woman guided her inside.

Vesha almost tripped on several shapes strewn across the foyer. Her foot slipped in something red. At first, she thought they were more of her soldiers, but then she recognized her sister's spaniels.

The little dogs lay with their carefully groomed fur smeared in blood, mangled bodies scattered like trash. Their silk ribbons were still perfectly tied around their necks in neat little bows, now stained scarlet.

"They wouldn't stop barking," Odette whispered, her voice little more than a wheeze. "Caa Iss had them all...well." Odette gulped.

Vesha's stomach recoiled.

Odette began crying quietly as she guided Vesha into the mansion. Apart from the carnage in the foyer, the rest of the mansion appeared empty.

"My sister?"

"She's in her rooms, I think," Odette said.

"Is she alright?" Vesha tightened her grip on Odette's arm.

"I think so," Odette said. "The servants ran or were taken by cythraul. But Count Serapio...he's one of them now."

"My sister's children?"

"I don't know," Odette answered. "I think the boy was with his father, but I'm not sure."

Odette guided Vesha into the residential area of the mansion, past drawing rooms and solariums. "Countess!" Odette called. "Countess!"

One of the doors cracked open, revealing part of a woman's silhouette. "Vesha!" Zeyna's face was red with tears. "Oh, Vesha are you alright? You're not one of them?"

Vesha shook her head, not knowing what to say.

"Come inside," Zeyna urged, her hair still braided for sleep. "Quickly."

Vesha didn't understand the point of moving quickly. There was no one else here and even if there was, the flimsy bedroom door wouldn't stop cythraul.

Through the door was a room that couldn't be anything other than Zeyna's personal suite. Hairbrushes, rouge bottles, and collections of silks, damasks, and brocades lay scattered on every available surface. A flower vase graced every corner, though the blooms had begun to wilt and hadn't been replaced.

The way Zeyna and Odette looked at Vesha reminded her of the way the servants had looked at her the night her husband lost control to Caa Iss.

Few people knew the full details of that night, not even Vesha's son. It could have been considered treason, but Darrigan had heard her screaming and broken down the door. The other household guards had protested, arguing they weren't allowed to disturb the emperor and his wife.

Darrigan had dragged Caa Iss off Vesha and held a blade to the demon's neck until he let her husband back into control.

The emperor had taken one look at Vesha and vomited. He hadn't ever been squeamish in the least, but Drystan the Conqueror was sick when he saw what he'd done to her.

Her face had been swollen and bloody. The physicians had said her cheekbone was fractured, her shoulder dislocated, and she had at least two broken ribs. And that was just what the male physicians were comfortable discussing.

Drystan had left that bedchamber with the guard captain. They had gone to the gardens and Vesha later learned that Emperor Drystan had ordered Darrigan to kill him.

"Darrigan," Vesha whimpered again, one hand covering her face. If only she had listened to him, she could have—

The throbbing returned, sending sharp pangs through her head.

It didn't matter. She had committed to this course, and she had to stay on it.

"Let's clean you up," Odette whispered.

"What happened to your face? Vesha, you're covered in blood! And your eye…" Zeyna whimpered, clutching hands to her mouth.

"I am…fine." Vesha knew that was less convincing when she was struggling to stand.

"Fetch us some water," Zeyna said to Odette.

"You will fetch it," Odette snapped. "I'm not leaving her majesty."

"Remember your place, young—"

Odette settled Vesha on a chair facing a wash basin and

149

mirror. "You're going to go fetch us water." She straightened, rising to take control. "I am going to find something for Her Majesty to wear."

Zeyna bristled. "I don't—"

"Go, Zeyna," Vesha ordered. Her head ached and every thought was sluggish, but she could tell Odette was the most sensible person in the room. "Listen to her."

"But sister—"

"Go!" Vesha's voice rose, grating into a roar. The wash basin rattled in its stand and the mirror cracked.

Odette swallowed, not letting go of the empress, but stiffened like a frightened animal.

Zeyna stumbled back, red face going pale. She stumbled out of the room and Vesha assumed she was obeying.

Odette went to Zeyna's wardrobe and returned with a clean dressing gown. She knelt before the empress. Carefully, she studied Vesha's feet. Odette peeled off the tattered shoes and examined the cuts and sores along Vesha's soles that she hadn't even noticed.

It was such a mundane task, seeming so common and trivial now.

Vesha finally dared to look into the splintered mirror. Her face was splattered in dark flecks of dried blood and massive stains marred her collar and the front of her dress. Several shallow scratches on her cheek, forehead, and temple marked where Moreyne's claws had held her down. Tears in her sleeves showed where the goddess had pinned her arms.

The god-eye itself...

It was blue. As crystalline blue as the azure waters of Iandua. It might have been pretty if not for the elliptical slit down the center, feline and predatory.

The flesh around it was puckered and red with irritation, like her body was loathe to accept the strange organ. The eye itched again and she could feel a headache returning.

"Odette," Vesha murmured, her head throbbing.

"Yes, Your Majesty?"

"This is how we save the empire." Vesha's voice came out as a croak. "This is the only way."

"Yes, Your Majesty," Odette answered softly.

Vesha stared at her own reflection, looking like a woman who had barely survived a housefire, not the empress of the known world. "I am doing the right thing," she said, more to herself. "I have to do it."

At her feet, Odette began to weep again.

CHAPTER EIGHTEEN

Amira

T he Lashera palace seemed smaller now. Amira couldn't quite explain what it was. A nagging dread weighed in her gut. It was more than just leaving Daindreth behind to speak with Captain Westfall.

At least with King Hyle in reach, she would have a hostage if anything went wrong.

After seeing Westfall pledge allegiance to Daindreth, King Hyle had become much more cooperative. Amira didn't know how much she trusted her father's compliance, but she planned to exploit it for now. She doubted he would do anything that put himself at risk.

Thadred had also been skeptical at first, but as best she could tell, he and Westfall were old friends. They certainly acted like it. In moments of seeing each other, Thadred was cracking jokes with the other man. It turned out they were around the same age and had trained together.

The Istovari had been less eager, but had followed Amira's lead when she had said they would be going to Lashera.

After nearly two decades, the Istovari were being invited back into the empire proper. Cyne and King Hyle didn't speak which was just as well.

The soldiers had stared at Sairydwen and Cyne, as well as the female rangers, but it seemed more curiosity than malice. Most of them had probably never seen a sorceress before.

Amira walked beside her father through the halls of the castle, still in her hunting habit. Some of the servants and guards recognized her, though few had seen her outside a gown.

King Hyle walked with a slight limp, but still managed to move with a stately grace, even with part of his head bandaged and bruised. He had changed out of his tattered clothes, but the wounds of last night's abuse still marked him.

They didn't speak. There was probably a lot to talk about, but words failed Amira. King Hyle had never had to treat Amira as an equal before, much less as a superior. Amira had never had to worry about protecting her husband's tenuous alliance.

They marched through the courtyard of the barracks with two imperial soldiers beside Amira and two Hylendale guards beside the King. It was strange to be coming in here now after she had snuck in only the night before.

The guards unlocked the door of the prison house and the Hylendale guards led the way with torches. Amira could sense the *ka* from inside Cromwell's cell. He was alive and still the only person imprisoned.

"Lord Cromwell, you have visitors." The guard began unlocking his cell door.

Stirring came from inside the cell. "So soon?"

One of the imperial guards went in ahead of Amira and took up a post inside. The other remained outside with the king and the Hylendale guards.

"Cromwell." Amira slipped through the door.

"My lady." Cromwell's eyes widened in surprise. "You returned."

Amira smiled at Cromwell with just an edge of a taunt. "You didn't think I'd just leave you here, did you?"

Cromwell blinked at her. "I did, actually."

Amira laughed at that, not sure why.

Cromwell made to stand but coughed. The coughing seized him, and he doubled over.

Amira crouched in front of him, steadying his shoulder as the coughing subsided. "Let's go, Terrence," she said lowly. "You're being promoted to imperial advisor."

Cromwell glanced between her and the imperial guard. The guard's visor was up, but his face might as well have been a steel mask. "Your Majesty?"

"My husband and I have discussed it and we'd like you to join my staff." Amira cocked her head to one side. "Do you

153

accept?"

"King Hyle?" Cromwell couldn't see his majesty in the darkened hall, not even by torchlight.

"He's not confident in your loyalties at the moment," Amira replied. "To be fair, I have never been confident in your loyalties. But as chancellor to the empress, my success will be your success and my failure will be your failure."

Cromwell nodded slowly, considering. Amira was transplanting him from his networks and carefully constructed web of favors and debts. He had plenty of contacts outside Hylendale, but in Mynadra, he would be a little polecat in a big forest. Amira had no doubt he would thrive, but someone like him would find it very difficult to change loyalties to someone else in the court. He was a nobody, barely a step above commoner. He would have to attach himself to a more prestigious name.

Unlike Amira and her father, no one else at the imperial court would be likely to see him for the genius he was. His only choice would be to create his own faction—a risky endeavor— or advance Amira.

Cromwell inclined his head to Amira. "I will gladly serve you, my empress. In whatever capacity you so choose."

"Let's go." She pulled him to his feet, not liking how easy it was to lift him. He'd lost weight. To make matters worse, he was covered in splotches of *ka* that denoted injuries.

"Yes, Your Majesty." He was able to stand on his own and follow her out of the cell, if a little slowly.

In the aisle, Cromwell stopped at the sight of the king.

King Hyle was marked by a black eye, numerous tiny cuts, and a bandage over his forehead. He stood with his hands in front of him like a true royal, glancing over Cromwell from head to foot as if to say *you still look worse than me*.

"Your Majesty," Cromwell said, an edge in his tone.

"Chancellor," the king responded coolly. Did he feel that Cromwell had betrayed him? Probably. When Amira had shared their intentions to recruit Cromwell for her staff, he hadn't argued, but he hadn't seemed to approve, either. "I hope you serve your new empress as well as you have served her in the past."

Did the king think Cromwell had been in her pocket this whole time? That was laughable, but neither Amira nor Cromwell corrected him.

"Come," Amira jerked her head to the older men. "Cromwell, we need to get you to my physician."

"You have a physician?" the king interjected. "Or are you appropriating one of those from me as well?"

"Sairydwen and I will tend to Cromwell." Her father's physicians had probably saved Amira's life more than once, but she didn't trust them with their sedatives and stern orders. They'd always treated her more like a slab of meat than a woman.

Cromwell stumbled on the threshold out of the jail. One of the guards reached to help him, but Amira caught him first. She grabbed his arm and hauled him out the last few steps.

"Come, chancellor. You might be old, but you have a lot of work to do yet."

Cromwell coughed again.

Outside, she let Cromwell walk on his own. They crossed the courtyard of the barracks as the entirety of the off-duty Hylendale garrison stared at them.

Amira took the lead with the imperial guards and Cromwell following. She headed back to the wing of the castle where Daindreth and the rest of their group were being housed.

The Istovari were uncomfortable being so deep in the territory of their longtime enemy, but Thadred was staying with them to assuage their concerns. He'd been to Hylendale before and stayed in that wing of the castle. Alongside the imperial guards under Westfall's command, he was securing the wing.

Cyne had been asked not to leave that wing. Amira would prefer that her mother and Queen Adelaide didn't meet, at least not right now.

Amira helped Cromwell up another flight of stairs. Torches lit their path and thick carpets muffled their footsteps. Amira sensed several sources of *ka* flickering through the castle around them, but that wasn't unusual. It was just after dusk in a royal residence. Servants and courtiers were usually bustling about for hours after dark.

A shape flickered at the edge of Amira's vision. A female silhouette in a white chemise and green overdress.

"Amira!" Fonra cried.

Amira spun around, heart in her throat. A sick, wretched feeling rocked through her, almost like she had been caught doing something wrong. "Fonra."

Her sister was on her in a moment, all hair, arms, and skirts. She clung to Amira's shoulders, gripping her sister like she'd never expected to see her alive again. Maybe she hadn't. Fonra shook and Amira realized she was crying.

Amira hugged her back, squeezing her sister tight as she could. Fonra smelled like lilacs and roses, some gentle perfume.

"I was so worried for you," Fonra whimpered. "None of my letters were answered and then the imperial soldiers came, and I thought—"

"It's alright." Amira pushed her sister back enough that she could wipe the tears from Fonra's cheeks. "I'm alright, little sister. Everything's alright."

Fonra took a steadying breath. "When I heard you were here, I didn't believe it."

Amira smiled. "Well, I'm here."

Fonra gripped Amira's arms with surprising strength. "You're here."

"Yes." Amira glanced to Cromwell and King Hyle.

Fonra seemed to notice them for the first time. "King Hyle." She dropped into a slight curtsy. "Lord Cromwell."

"Your Highness," Cromwell wheezed, another coughing fit threatening.

King Hyle took a breath. "Fonra—"

"Sister, it is so good to see you," Amira interjected, hooking Fonra's arm through hers.

King Hyle's mouth snapped shut, eyes flickering with annoyance.

"Come." Amira tugged Fonra after her. "Lord Cromwell, you as well. My healer is this way."

Amira couldn't keep antagonizing her father. She knew that. But perhaps he shouldn't have double crossed everyone who had ever held him loyalty. Even his most trusted advisor belonged to Amira now.

A part of her wanted to invite him to the imperial palace at Mynadra just to see him bow to her in front of the entire court. It would be poetic.

Then she reminded herself that she and Daindreth still needed to retake said court.

Amira hadn't intended her father to follow, but he and his guards did. Along with Fonra's maids, Amira's two guards, and Cromwell.

"We were so worried," Fonra whispered, leaning close to Amira. She didn't comment on her sister's hunting habit or the signs of grime and travel that marked the assassin.

"Forgive me," Amira said, inclining her head. "Circumstances have been rather unusual of late."

"Is the archduke here?" Fonra asked, her voice and body tense.

"My husband is here, yes," Amira replied. "He's meeting with his officers."

"Husband? You were married already?" Fonra rounded a sharp look at Amira.

"We were." Amira tried and failed not to smile at that. "I'm sorry you weren't able to be there."

Fonra shot a glance to King Hyle and Cromwell, as well as the guards trailing behind them. She didn't seem particularly concerned with her own maids overhearing.

"I love him, Fonra," Amira assured her, smiling because she

157

couldn't help it.

"He's good to you?" Fonra asked, hesitant.

"He's the best thing that's happened to me," Amira answered softly.

Fonra nodded slowly, considering. "I'm glad."

Amira patted her sister's arm. They hadn't been so casual in public before, but things had changed.

No longer was Amira the bastardized older sister. She had married far above her station, to the emperor himself. She had risen as high as any woman in the empire could hope to rise.

"What brings you to Hylendale under such…unusual circumstances? We weren't expecting you and this seems more—" Fonra swallowed, glancing back to their father again. "It seems more like your usual way of doing things."

Amira kissed Fonra's temple. "It is unusual, I admit. But circumstances arose, and we had to make hard choices." And Amira expected many more, but staying with Daindreth had never been one of them. Staying with him—loving him—was easy.

They rounded a corner and their small group entered another hallway, lit by candles tucked into glass lamps. Doors lined the hall of the guest wing, and many stood open. Servants bustled in and out with fresh linens.

At the center of it all, Cyne directed servants left and right, taking command like a seasoned general. Her hair was pulled back in a tidy braid and she had changed into a gown of blue linen instead of her usual undyed tunic.

"See to it that the corners are tucked," Cyne was saying. "Have hot water brought for this room and two tubs. Yes, one of them can be small."

Amira recognized Vylia, who oversaw the cleaning and care of the castle bed linens, relaying her mother's orders like a loyal lieutenant. Vylia was one of the few servants here who remembered when Cyne had been queen. One of the few who had seen the Hyle family through their entire turbulent saga.

Amira was sure she could feel the air thicken as King Hyle and Cyne caught sight of one another. The former queen raised her chin, squaring her shoulders as she faced her former husband.

"Empress Amira," Cyne greeted her daughter first. "King Hyle."

"Taking over my servants, I see," King Hyle remarked.

"Your lady wife hasn't deigned to appear to do the honors herself." Cyne offered the king a frosty smile. Normally, it would be the responsibility of the woman of the house to prepare for guests so prestigious as the emperor and empress.

A part of Amira wanted to see her mother and the new queen meet. But the part of her that was still trying to be a good politician knew better.

"She is Queen Hyle now," the king replied softly. "You will address her as such."

"Mother," Amira interrupted, blocking her parents' view of one another. "This is my sister, Princess Fonra."

Cyne appraised the girl in front of her with a quick head to foot glance.

"Fonra, this is my mother, Lady Cyne Brindonu of the Istovari."

Fonra dropped into a curtsy as graceful as a young swan. "A pleasure, my lady."

Amira kept her arm hooked through Fonra's. "Mother, I'm sure you remember Lord Cromwell." Amira gestured to the battered lawyer at her back.

"Cromwell." There was an edge of annoyance to Cyne's tone. She had been part of their discussions on making Cromwell Amira's advisor. While she had never spoken against the idea, she had not been particularly supportive, either.

"Lady Cyne." Cromwell stooped into a bow. "You haven't aged a day."

"You have," Cyne clipped. "More than a day."

"Prison will do that to an old man, my lady." Whether he

had intended it or not, Cromwell broke into another coughing fit.

Amira turned to her mother. "Where is Sair? I need her to tend him."

Cyne caught one of the servants by the arm. "You, boy, fetch Lady Sairydwen. Tell her we need her to tend a rheumatic and feeble old man who has been beaten within an inch of his life."

The boy frowned at that description but nodded and jogged toward one of the other rooms.

Cromwell inclined his head. "Much obliged, my lady."

One of the doors opened and Daindreth's head poked out. "Amira." He glanced to Cromwell standing beside her. He hesitated a moment at the state of the man but said nothing. "Good. We will be done in a moment."

Amira nodded. She was tired. More tired than she'd been for a long time.

People thought that danger was exhausting, but Amira rarely felt tired when she was facing a direct threat. It was after the threat passed that the exhaustion crushed her.

Amira wouldn't have to fight her father. They had a contingent of imperial guards on their side. And her sister was safe.

Sairydwen came to collect Cromwell and he bowed to her. Those two knew each other, at least. Cromwell had been feeding the Istovari information through her for years. Amira still didn't know how long.

King Hyle bowed to Amira as the now-chancellor was taken away. "I bid your leave, Your Grace," he said, using the title for a princess or imperial consort. "It has been a long day."

Amira inclined her head to him in turn. "Farewell, Father."

"Princess Fonra?" The king looked to his younger daughter.

"I would like to stay and speak with my sister for a time, if that please you, my king," Fonra said, gripping Amira's hand tighter. "My maids can attend me."

The king was quiet for a long heartbeat and Amira thought

he would protest. Then he nodded once and left, taking his guards with him.

"You may return to your posts," Amira said to her own guards. "I am safe in this wing of the castle."

The guardsmen were brusque and professional. Unlike some Hylendale guards, imperial palace guards rarely showed emotion. They bowed and left.

"Amira, there is so much you must tell me," Fonra whispered. "What happened?" She glanced toward the door where Daindreth had disappeared. "I know you said he was…"

Amira pulled her sister to a window seat, in sight of the bustling in the hall, but out of the way. Fonra's maids hovered nearby. "Things were more complicated than I thought," Amira admitted. "Daindreth…" She hesitated. "Fonra, there are many things I've never told you. Things I was forbidden to tell you."

Fonra nodded. Many people thought Fonra was naïve because she was softspoken and kind. Fonra was naïve in many ways, but she understood politics as well as Amira did. Maybe even better in some ways.

Amira took a deep breath. "I don't want to put you in danger."

Fonra looked outside where the sun was setting beyond the blue mountains that marked the boundary of Hylendale. "It hasn't rained today."

"What?" Amira glanced outside.

"It's rained every day for over a month. Some days there was lightning for an entire week and some days it only drizzled, but there was always rain. Then the day you come home, the sun shines."

Amira hadn't noticed that. She had been too distracted by swaying the imperials to their side.

"You said he was a monster." Fonra squeezed Amira's hand. "Now you love him?"

"What I said was true," Amira began, not sure how much she wanted to tell her sister. Not sure how much she could share without endangering her. "But not the whole truth."

"What do you mean?"

"That thing was a monster, but it wasn't Daindreth—wasn't His Majesty." Amira needed to get used to referring to him as the emperor, even with her sister.

"Tell me," Fonra said.

Amira took a deep breath. They weren't equals and they never had been. They'd grown up as the redheaded stepchild and the heir apparent. Now Amira was the empress and Fonra would be, by all appearances, a future vassal queen.

Secrets and machinations far beyond the control of either sister had stood between them for their entire lives. But if Amira could tell her sister the truth for once, if she could be honest without someone else's commands shackling her words, she would.

"Let's take a walk," Amira said, glancing to where her mother had gone back to speaking with the servants.

"We could go to your room," Fonra suggested. "The one where you are staying, I mean."

"My husband is meeting with his captains there," Amira replied.

"In your room?"

"We're sharing one," Amira simply answered. "I'll sleep easier knowing he's next to me."

And they had been sharing ever since their wedding.

Fonra's brows rose at that. A noble couple, much less an imperial one, rarely shared rooms. They might sleep together, but they usually maintained their own separate chambers.

But Amira didn't trust anyone to guard Daindreth except herself. She didn't think that would change any time soon, either.

"Come," Amira stood, pulling Fonra to her feet. "I have much to tell you. Have your maids walk ten paces behind us."

"The garden?" Fonra asked, glancing out the window. It was dusk, but the garden was usually the most private place in the castle.

162

"Yes," Amira agreed. "Let's walk in the garden."

CHAPTER NINETEEN

Vesha

Vesha woke up slumped on a settee in her sister's rooms. Odette's voice spoke from the corner, too low for Vesha to make out the words at first.

The empress's head still throbbed, but her throat no longer felt scorched and scratchy. Her feet ached. Her delicate ladies' shoes hadn't been meant for the abuse of the Dread Marches, but when she looked down, she wore a clean blue dress and signs of the long trek had been scrubbed away.

Her hair was neatly braided and though the many cuts and scratches on her hands were still there, the blood was gone. In some places, hints of dirt were still wedged in the wounds, but Odette had probably done her best.

"They're not going to kill us," Odette said confidently.

"How can you be sure?" Zeyna's question dissolved into a whimper. "The servants have fled, Serapio is one of *them,* and my sister lies senseless."

"If they wanted us dead, we would be." Odette had a sound head on her shoulders, it seemed.

Zeyna let off a horrified shriek that muffled into a groan.

Vesha smeared a hand over her face, forcing herself upright. Sunlight filtered through the window of the dressing room, though it was dim and overcast. Dark trails of smoke drifted over the sky. She couldn't hear the screams anymore, but a sick feeling told her that was because there was no one left to scream. "What have I done?"

A sharp pain shot through her right temple, radiating out from the god-eye and through her skull. She winced as the thought flitted away.

Fresh determination and focus came over her. She needed to keep her mind on what was in front of her. She needed to stay on task—keeping the empire together.

164

"Odette?" Vesha stood, leaning on the armrest of the couch for support.

The handmaiden stood before Zeyna, comforting the panicked woman. "My lady!" Odette jumped. "You're awake."

"Yes." Vesha inhaled, squaring her shoulders. She looked to her sister. "Have you found your children yet?"

"No," Zeyna moaned, a heaviness coming over her as she lowered her head.

"Hmm." Vesha turned her attention back to Odette, the only other useful person here. "Where is Caa Iss? I need to speak with him."

Odette shook her head. "I don't know, my lady. We haven't seen anyone else."

Vesha glanced around the room. She snatched up an overdress from one of the couches—Zeyna always had left her clothes lying everywhere. Vesha threw it on impatiently, flinging her braid over one shoulder.

"My lady, let me help—"

Vesha brushed Odette aside and stormed from the room, tying the sash of the overdress herself. "Caa Iss!" Vesha shouted to the empty halls of the mansion. "Show yourself!"

Odette and Zeyna followed her into the hall, huddling around her like nervous ducklings.

"Your Majesty," Zeyna whispered, shoulders hunched, glancing left and right. "I don't think we should—"

"Now!" Vesha snarled into the mansion, her voice rippling through the air like the crackle before lightning strikes.

Odette and Zeyna cowered back, the countess hiding behind the handmaiden.

"My dear empress," Caa Iss crooned from the shadows. One moment the hall was empty and the next moment, he filled the width of it. He towered at nearly twice the height of a man and three times the width of an ox. He had grown larger and not just in size. He was more substantial, the gleam of sweat on his scarred skin and droplets of blood shining on his fangs.

Imps scurried at his feet, a pack of simpering rats. The creatures had been terrifying back in the Dread Marches, but next to the horrific majesty of Caa Iss, they seemed like nothing more than pests.

Zeyna screamed, clinging to Odette. The handmaiden shielded her, eyes wide with horror at the cythraul.

Caa Iss shot a glance to Odette with a flash of teeth that might have been a smile. "That one has courage," Caa Iss mused with a throaty chuckle. "It was foolish of her to stay, of course, but the courage of a fool is courage all the same."

"Where is Flavius?" Vesha demanded.

Caa Iss sat back on his haunches. "I'm not sure I know what you mean."

"My sister's son," Vesha snapped. "Don't lie to me."

Caa Iss cocked his head to the side. "Have I met him?"

"Count Serapio was possessed by one of your brothers." Vesha wished for a moment that Caa Iss had a body, just so she could strike him. "Have him find Flavius."

"Ah Serapio, yes." Caa Iss nodded his great head. "He's possessed by one of my sisters, actually. She wanted a female body, but Serapio was the first to give in and she didn't want to wait for the girls."

"The girls?" Zeyna gasped.

"Don't worry, countess," Caa Iss snickered. "Your daughters escaped...for now."

"Where...where are my daughters?" Zeyna choked.

"Your eldest convinced her lover to take her and her sisters into the countryside. We haven't found them yet."

"Vespasia doesn't have a lover." Zeyna's voice was little more than a squeak.

Caa Iss chuckled again. "He was humping her in the stables when we returned yesterday."

Vesha felt heat rise in her chest, red-hot anger. Caa Iss should be rushing to obey, not stalling with these taunts to her sister. "The boy. Now!" she ordered. Her voice echoed through the hall, rumbling through the floor.

Caa Iss flinched. His weight shifted and for just a moment, his browless face wrinkled. He cocked his head to the side ever so slightly. "As you wish, my witch." The cythraul turned.

"Not you." Vesha jabbed a finger to stop him. "Send one of your lackeys. I have more orders for you."

Caa Iss heaved a great sigh. "You heard her," he mumbled, gesturing to the air.

The imps at his feet scurried away, chittering as they loped down the darkness of the hall. Vesha watched them, fighting back disgust. They were the lowest of the demons, little better than rodents and useful only as bottom feeders.

"What do you wish of me, my witch?" Caa Iss bowed his great head, though it seemed more a mockery than genuine respect.

"We must set sail for the mainland at once." Vesha had been given instructions from Moreyne. The goddess needed more if she was to protect the empire as Vesha wished. "How many of your brothers and sisters now have bodies?"

"A few thousand," Caa Iss answered. "I haven't bothered to count. The rest have taken to the countryside to find hosts."

"Call them back," Vesha ordered. "There will be plenty of hosts for them on the mainland."

"I see no reason for the hurry. We will be at full strength by the end of the month."

"I ordered you last night to secure ships and supplies." Vesha's nostrils flared. "I have been gone from my empire for over a month already. We have been rocked by disaster after disaster. Anything could happen in another month."

"We may not have enough ships for them all." Caa Iss shuffled his wings.

"What do you mean? We can easily transport the number who have bodies."

Caa Iss made a hesitant gesture. "Yes, but the longer we are in this world, the stronger our bond to you becomes. And the

167

more we bind to this world."

"That's good," Vesha said impatiently.

"Yes. And no." Caa Iss brought his hands together, talons clicking against each other. "It allows us to interact with this world, but it also limits us."

"The point?"

"Even without bodies, those of us who remain in our spirit form can't walk on water. And no, we can't swim the length of the Jaunty Straits or walk on the ocean floor, either."

"I never said we were headed through the Jaunty Straits," Vesha said.

"That's the fastest way to the mainland," Caa Iss replied.

Vesha inhaled a long breath. "Just get the ships we need and make it work."

Caa Iss glanced to the side.

"What?" she demanded.

"Many of the ships were taken," he admitted.

"Taken," Vesha repeated.

"Last night, many fled to the sea."

"And you let them?"

"The sea is the dominion of Llyr." Caa Iss sounded just a little condescending at that. "You can give us authority over land, but the sea will always belong to the sea god."

"I don't have time for superstition."

"Many superstitions are the echoes of old laws. Laws among gods," Caa Iss replied, speaking very slowly. "Llyr bows to only the moon and sky."

"Moreyne is a moon goddess!"

"Not anymore." Caa Iss enunciated each word with painful clarity.

Vesha inhaled sharply. "Fine. I don't care what you must do. But find the ships you need. We're leaving tomorrow."

Caa Iss shook his head. "We can't—"

"We need no provisions because cythraul need no food or water." Vesha was done with his excuses. "There will just be me and my handmaiden."

"You're leaving me?" Zeyna shrank back, hands clutching to her breast.

Vesha whirled on her. "Unless you would like to come with the cythraul."

Zeyna began to weep—again.

Vesha turned away in disgust. "Make the preparations," she ordered. "My patience is wearing thin."

Caa Iss inclined his head. "As you wish, my lady."

"You called for me?" crooned a glassy, noxious voice.

Behind Caa Iss appeared a child of around seven in boy's shorts and a small velvet coat stained with dirt and blood. His eyes glistened the crackling scarlet of an elder cythraul.

"It appears your brat of a nephew has been inhabited."

Zeyna let off a choked scream, collapsing to her knees on the floor. "No," she wept. "No, not my baby. Please…"

Vesha marched past Caa Iss, towering over the small child. The creature looked up at her curiously.

A tongue slid over its teeth as a smirk shaped its face. There was a time Vesha would have shuddered at the inhuman, unnatural expression, but she had seen too much to be afraid now.

"Get out."

The demon arched one eyebrow. "This child gave me full consent to inhabit him. I followed the rules."

Vesha leaned down. "I don't care." She spat out each word carefully. "I said, *get out.*" Vesha seized the air in front of the creature. She couldn't see what she was holding onto, but she felt something solid. She yanked it.

The cythraul was all limbs and knobby joints. Skin the color of dried blood was scored with scars and holes where white bone showed through. It tumbled out of the child, unfolding like a red silk kerchief. It collapsed on the floor, staring up at Vesha in shock.

The empress kicked it aside and the creature cowered. The

beast growled and Vesha fixed it in a hard glare.

Lowering its head, the creature tucked a spiked tail between its legs.

The child collapsed to the floor, crying.

"Flavius!" Zeyna pushed past Odette and rushed to her son. She tucked him under her chin and turned her back to the cythraul, shielding him from the creatures. "My sweet baby. Oh, my poor, sweet, brave baby."

Flavius sobbed as little boys did when they had been brave for too long. He clung to his mother, blubbering into her skirts.

"Be gone," Vesha said to the evicted cythraul still at her feet. "Find another host and spread the word that we need to make ready to cross the sea."

Caa Iss made a rumbling sound in his chest. "I told you. We need more time."

"There is no time." Vesha clenched her hands into fists. "We leave tomorrow. Even that is too late."

Caa Iss shook his head, but it seemed more of a nervous gesture. "I cannot stop you."

That was an odd thing to say. Since when had Caa Iss admitted to weakness?

"If these are your orders, we will carry them out."

"These are my orders." Vesha straightened. "Send some of the imps here. I want at least six of them ready to carry my messages at any time. And have twenty of those who now inhabit bodies to come here."

"So you can cast them out, too?" grumbled the evicted cythraul at Vesha's feet.

The empress grabbed the creature around the neck.

The creature scrambled and scratched, but its claws went right through her.

Realization sunk in that Vesha could hurt them, but they couldn't hurt her. A rush of excitement rippled through her.

For weeks now, she'd felt helpless. She had been fighting to regain control, retake mastery of her world.

170

Lying on the floor of Moreyne's cave, she had come to her lowest. At the feet of the fallen goddess, she had known true helplessness, true weakness.

Even as empress, she had known that she was only as powerful as she could make the world believe her to be. There were always nobles to appease, barons to assuage, or vassal kings to shepherd back into the fold. Even once she had bonded Saan Thii, she had to abide by the terms of their contract.

Now—now the demons cowered before her.

Vesha dragged the cythraul toward her. Veins popped across the cythraul's skin and patchy spots on its hide where pieces of bone showed. The creature was disgusting.

"Beg," Vesha ordered.

"What?" the cythraul choked, staring into her right eye, the one that had come from Moreyne.

"Beg me," she repeated, her voice going soft. "Beg me for the honor of finding a new host. Or I banish you back to the Dread Marches and tell your mother of your impertinence."

The cythraul's eyes bulged and it writhed in her grip.

Caa Iss stood by with his wings raised, like a bird unsure of whether to flee or not.

In truth, Vesha had no idea if she could make good on either threat, but she felt that she could. She felt that she could do anything.

"Forgive me, my lady," the cythraul wheezed. "I should not have been so bold. It will not happen again."

"Good," Vesha mused. "But as a reminder not to do it again—" Vesha jabbed the nails of her free hand into the creature's eye.

Her nails dug in easily and raked it out, leaving nothing but a bloody gash. The creature howled in pain, its whole body twisting and writhing in her grip.

Vesha's hand came away covered in black gore. She flexed her hand, feeling the tarlike sensation of the demon's blood. It was strange to be truly powerful. To be truly strong.

171

"Go," Vesha said mildly, releasing the creature. "Do as I have commanded. Time is short."

The offending cythraul limped away, muttering and weeping and sobbing.

Zeyna stared at her in horror, her son still nestled in the safety of her bosom. Odette stood aghast. Even Caa Iss watched her closely, shoulders hunched as if he expected a blow.

"Mother gave you more than a bargain, didn't she?" Caa Iss rumbled.

"What do you mean?" Vesha demanded.

Caa Iss stared straight into her face, focusing on her right eye.

Vesha fought the impulse to look away.

Caa Iss took a step back, then another. He lowered his great head toward the ground. "I will obey you," he said. "We shall make ready to sail at once."

"You will call your brothers and sisters back from the surrounding countryside?" Vesha demanded.

"Yes." This time Caa Iss didn't argue.

Vesha noticed then the tatters and tears in his wings, the places where the bones were set at unnatural angles.

For an instant, she saw his wings snapping in her hands. She envisioned white claws gripping them and tearing the soft membrane down the middle until he was too maimed to ever take to the skies again.

Vesha blinked and the image was gone.

"Good." She nodded curtly. Finally. They were getting somewhere.

"I will send the imps and the guards as you commanded," Caa Iss added.

Vesha turned to her sister and handmaiden. Neither had moved and both stared at her. Their eyes were wide, mouths shut tight. Utter horror painted their faces. They feared her—or perhaps the cythraul. Possibly both.

"Come." Vesha beckoned impatiently. "We must make

ready to depart." Scowling at her black-stained hand, she looked to Odette. "Fetch me something to clean this off, would you?"

CHAPTER TWENTY

Amira

The sun was shining. That would not have been of great note on any other day, but after weeks of rain, Amira couldn't help feel it was a sign. The clouds were gone. The rain had stopped.

Amira lay beside Daindreth, watching the sunlight in his sandy hair. She stroked the curve of his shoulder blade, admiring how cords of muscle rippled in his back and arms.

He was beautiful. The most beautiful thing she had ever seen. Ironically, they shared the same bed she had once feared he would force her into.

Daindreth looked almost childlike in sleep. She thought she could picture the boy he had been, back before the demon had stolen his youth.

Amira flattened her hand against his back, feeling the steady rise and fall of his breathing. Part of her wanted to wake him, but a greater part of her didn't.

Waking would mean sending for the servants and readying their retinue—such as it was. It would mean more meetings with King Hyle and discussions with Westfall and Cromwell and Cyne.

Outside, she could hear thumps and shuffles—the telltale sounds of a castle stirring. She thought she heard Westfall's voice, then Cyne's. It might have been them or her imagination, but she nestled closer to Daindreth.

Here in this moment, everything was peace and beauty.

Daindreth's eyes peeled open, still groggy. "Good morning, wife."

Amira shifted, bringing herself closer to him. "Good morning, love."

Daindreth shifted to better face her. "What's wrong?"

Amira shook her head. "Nothing, I just…" She exhaled a

long breath, then looked down.

Daindreth caught her chin in his hand. "Tell me."

Instead, Amira kissed him. "I love you," she whispered against his lips.

Daindreth rested a hand on her side, tracing her scars. "I love you, too. Amira?" Daindreth searched her face, now fully awake.

"I just…" Amira pulled herself closer against him, heart beating faster. "I want to be with you."

"You are with me," he said, resting his forehead against hers. "Nothing is going to change that."

Amira wished she could believe him. She wished her fears were so easily put to rest. She reached for him, but the blanket was in the way. She kicked it off, leaving them both naked on the bed. Amira closed the distance, straddling him.

"Easy, girl," Daindreth chuckled, then grew serious when he saw her expression. He rested his hands on her thighs, stroking gently the way he might pet a spooked horse. "Tell me," Daindreth murmured. "Tell me what's wrong."

"Something's going to happen," Amira burst. "I don't know what it is yet, but something is going to go wrong. Vesha will rally the army or Caa Iss will return to you or—"

"Caa Iss is gone," Daindreth said firmly, almost like it was a command. "And we can take my mother. Look at Westfall— we've already won over part of the army."

Amira rolled her eyes. A battalion of palace guards hardly counted as part of the army.

"We're already preparing as best we can," Daindreth said. "Worry only makes us suffer twice."

Amira made a strangled whining sound, not sure what it meant herself. She lunged, her mouth crashing into his.

Daindreth seemed startled by her sudden passion, but returned her kiss, hands finding their way to her back.

She broke away from his mouth to kiss his jawline, his throat. Her kisses came faster and harder the lower they went, growing in intensity. When her teeth sank into his thigh, Daindreth grabbed her and wrestled her under him.

"Damn it, Amira." He shook his head, pinning her down. "No biting, alright?"

"I want you," Amira panted, heart beating fast already. "I just…want you." She wasn't sure how else to put it. She writhed under him, not really struggling, but twisting against his hold.

Daindreth brought his head down and their lips met again. "You just had to ask." His lips found her neck, caressing gently.

"Faster," Amira gasped. "I can hear the servants waking up and—"

"They can wait," Daindreth shot back, "and so can you," he added with a mischievous lilt to his words.

Amira whimpered in protest as he took his sweet time. His lips caressed her like every inch of skin was the most exquisite wine, like he wanted to savor every taste.

"I'm here," he said, placing a kiss against her throat. "And here." He kissed her collarbone. "And here." His mouth wandered down to press between her breasts.

"I want you inside me," Amira panted, getting her arms free to wrap around him. "Please."

Daindreth's brows rose. "Are you going to beg for me, dearest?"

"Do I have to?" She tried to shift to open her thighs, but he kept her locked in place.

"Why the rush?" Daindreth studied her closely. "We have all the time in the world." His voice dropped low.

"You don't know that," Amira protested. "We could die tomorrow."

"No," Daindreth said, pressing her harder into the bed to emphasize his words. "We are the most powerful man and woman in the known world. We have tamed kings and conquered demons. No one can stand against us and live."

Amira smiled despite herself, even though she didn't quite believe him. "You sound like a herald."

"You married a poet. Or did you forget?"

Amira ran her hands along his sides, feeling the tense muscles through his body. "Make love to me," she asked, the request soft and pleading, nothing like her initial demand. "Make poetry with me."

"I can do that." Daindreth shifted, sliding one hand between her thighs, though he didn't let them part just yet. He gently explored, reaching up to finger the wetness between her legs.

Amira gasped, twisting in protest. "Please," she panted.

Daindreth's fingers stopped moving. "Do you not like it?"

"No," Amira shook her head. "I just want more."

"More?" Daindreth's fingers went to work again, and Amira moaned, half in frustration, half in pleasure.

"Please!" Amira shouted, almost shoving him away.

"Alright." Daindreth's hand stopped what it was doing. "Alright, then." He pressed one knee between her thighs and Amira spread them eagerly.

A sigh of relief escaped her as he slid inside her, but he did it too slowly. "Daindreth," she groaned, grinding her hips against him. Her back arched in frustration. "We don't have much time."

"We have time," he said quietly. "We have all the time in the world." He thrust his hips slowly, pushing in and out of her to a steady rhythm. "All the time in the world." He leaned down, dropping onto his elbows to cover her with his body.

Amira wrapped around him, clinging as he made torturously slow love to her.

"Shh," he breathed into her ear. "Just hold onto me." He tucked her shoulder under his chin and breathed in the scent of her hair.

Amira relaxed in his arms as he moved over her, still holding onto him. "If anyone walks in on us, that's your fault."

Daindreth chuckled, pulling back enough to see her face. "You locked the doors last night."

"Someone could still knock," Amira countered. "Westfall or

Thadred."

"I don't want you thinking about other men right now." Daindreth pushed into her harder, making the bed creak.

Amira pulled him against her, savoring the weight of him, the warmth of him, and how he covered her entire body. She traced her tongue along his collarbone, tasting sweat.

Their lovemaking grew more intense, little by little so that she hardly noticed it until the frame squeaked in protest and her moans filled the room.

Daindreth finished first, collapsing heavily against her. Amira held onto him as he panted against her breast, his body pressed to hers.

Amira could have held onto him like that for a while, letting him rest in her arms. For a moment, the room was as still and quiet as it had been in the moments before he had awakened.

Peace. Comfort. Safety.

Daindreth pulled away and she let out a whine of protest. "It's your turn," he said, kneeling between her legs. "Easy, Amira," he murmured, pressing her back into the bed when she tried to rise. "Let me pleasure you?" It was something in the way he said it, almost like a request, like it would be a favor to him.

"You did all the work just now," Amira protested, but leaned back into the pillows.

"You've been working your whole life." Daindreth kissed the inside of her leg, hands gliding up. "Rest, Amira. Just enjoy me."

Amira opened her mouth to speak, but then his mouth pressed down on the apex of her legs. The words she had planned came out as a gasp that turned into a moan. She sank back, a swelling sensation deep in her core.

This was luxury. Indulgence. Like being drunk, but so much better.

"You're going to get me so fast." Amira's back arched as the pressure built, rising and rising.

Daindreth made a low, throaty sound of amusement, but his

tongue didn't stop stroking her.

Amira's climax came in starbursts of pleasure that shot through her whole body. A cry of ecstasy escaped her best efforts to hold back.

Daindreth rested his cheek against the inside of her thigh, watching her with a faint smile.

"Are you proud of yourself?" she asked, choking a laugh.

"A little," Daindreth shrugged. "I like giving you pleasure."

Amira reached for him, still breathless. "Come here?" She shivered, suddenly cold.

Daindreth slid up on the bed beside her, one arm around her and his face nestled in the hollow of her neck.

Amira breathed in the smell of him as her breathing slowed to match his steady rhythm. "I love you," she whimpered not sure she would ever say it enough.

"I love you, too." Daindreth ran his fingers along the curve of her hip. "Everything is going to be alright, my love."

Amira could almost believe him. Lying here, flushed with delight, feeling more loved, cherished, and pleasured than she had ever thought she would, anything seemed possible. She could almost believe that everything was going to be alright, that they wouldn't lose each other, Fonra, Thadred, or anyone else dear to them ever again.

A knock came from the door.

Amira jumped, though a part of her had been expecting it.

"Dain?" Thadred called from the other side. "Amira? Stop swyving each other and get up. We have problems."

Amira covered her face with her hands. So her feeling of imminent doom had been correct. Of course they had problems.

"Do you have clothes on?" Thadred continued, not waiting for a response. "Can I come in? Not that I mind if you're both naked."

"A moment, Thad," Daindreth called back. He rose from the bed first, wrapping one of the discarded blankets around his waist. "Amira?"

179

She was already on her feet and making her way to the dressing room. Her hunting leathers had been cleaned and oiled and she found a fresh tunic and pair of her old doeskin breeches—Fonra had them sent over last night.

Amira dressed with easy efficiency. By the time she reemerged, Daindreth had let Thadred into the sitting room outside their bedroom. Though the emperor was half naked, Thadred stood fully dressed with his cane at his side.

Thadred tapped the cane impatiently against the ground, not standing still for more than a moment at a time. He glanced at Amira, lashing her hair into a braid. His brows rose just a little. "There you are. Good. We have a problem."

Daindreth faced her and from the way his brow furrowed and one hand rubbed the back of his neck, Thadred's news was indeed bad.

"We found Vesha." Thadred's voice was heavy. It was the sort of tone one might use to relay the death of a close family member. "At least, we know where she was a couple days ago."

Amira raised her chin, bracing herself.

"She was in Iandua, one of the old colonies in Kelethian."

"Kelethian?" Of all the places Vesha could be, Kelethian had never crossed Amira's mind.

"Yes, it was surprising to me, too. There was a report at least a week old saying that Empress Vesha was confirmed in residence with the Count and Countess Serapio, her sister."

Amira hesitated, not sure if she should mention it.

"My mother, yes." Thadred waved his hand impatiently as if it didn't matter. "There were several ships that just landed in Phaed. It seems the reports were picked up by Cromwell's spy network days ago, but he only just now was able to receive them—for obvious reasons."

Amira swallowed, that feeling of dread that had been growing all morning became a rock in her stomach. "Go on," she urged, afraid of what he might say but needing to know all the same.

"The ships were people from Iandua," Thadred explained. "Refugees. They have some interesting stories. The spies didn't know exactly what to make of them, but it seems a good portion of the city changed."

"Changed?"

Thadred inhaled a long breath, jaw clenching. "Most of the reports were incoherent," he said. "Cromwell shared them, but they make little sense. I think the people were just afraid and confused, but at least three of them mentioned their loved ones changing—their eyes turned red, their voices altering."

Amira's body went cold all at once. "That's not possible," she breathed.

"It gets better," Thadred continued. "They found one of the infected had snuck on board."

Amira was bursting with questions, but she didn't dare interrupt.

"A young boy had been dying of leprosy when he was put on the ship. By the time they docked, he had killed eight of the passengers before they managed to trap him below decks."

"Where is he now?" Daindreth's voice was quiet, small.

"At last report, the magistrate's men had the ship burned," Thadred said. "It took hours, but the boy eventually stopped screaming. They recovered his body a day later."

Amira looked to Daindreth. Just as she had feared, their brief interlude of peace was over. The war had found them again. "We need to get to Mynadra."

As emperor, Daindreth would have the power and authority he needed to deal with this. As emperor, he would be able to stop his mother once and for all.

Daindreth kissed her forehead. "I'll get dressed and meet with Westfall. Prepare your sorceresses and whoever else you want to come with you. We'll leave at first light tomorrow."

That was an odd statement—*her* sorceresses. But she supposed the women were under her command now.

Daindreth looked to Thadred. "While I get dressed can you

send a message to Phaed? Tell them they did the right thing and that if any other infected are found, they are to be destroyed. No exceptions."

Thadred nodded. "I can do that."

Amira finished her braid and set to pinning it in a circle around her head. It was hardly the hairstyle of an empress, but she wasn't an empress today. She had been Daindreth's assassin, but now he needed a sorceress.

Amira had barely made it out the door of their rooms when she was joined by two imperial guards. Daindreth had made it clear he wanted her always guarded. He said it was for appearance's sake, but she suspected that he didn't want to risk her being alone.

Heading straight for Sair's room, she found it empty, but the maid making the beds told her that the sorceresses were breaking their fast with the king. That seemed suspicious to Amira, but she headed straight for the private dining hall the royal family used most of the time.

It was a long chamber with narrow windows that could be sealed during the winter months. Rushes lined the floor and sleek hounds sprawled on the ground, hoping for stray morsels.

Servants and cooks bustled in and out of the room. Most of them recognized Amira and bowed to her as she passed.

Some called her *majesty*, *highness*, and still others called her *my lady*. No one seemed certain what she was now. Amira wasn't sure she knew herself.

Amira had been subjected to many awkward family meals over the course of her life, but she doubted any of them compared to this.

King Hyle sat at his usual place at the head with several untouched slices of bread and ham on his plate. At his right was Queen Hyle, Adelaide. At his left was Fonra. Beside Fonra was Cyne, the former queen. Istovari occupied the rest of the table. Sair, Tapios, Rhis, and all the female rangers.

Fonra refused to look at either of her parents, eyes fixed on her own plate.

Cromwell sat between Cyne and Sair, looking better, but still unhealthily pale. To think he had already been checking his spy network today was remarkable, but this *was* Cromwell.

He made eye contact with the king and queen easily, shamelessly, though he didn't speak. Cromwell rarely spoke anyway.

Breakfast with his former wife he had banished, her clans people he had also banished, and the former advisor he had jailed. What a morning King Hyle must be having.

King Hyle caught sight of Amira and stood, the rest of the table following his lead. "Empress, good morning. Will you be joining us?"

Amira shook her head. "Forgive the intrusion, but I have need of my sorceresses and my chancellor." It was odd to call them that, odd to have a claim over people. "It's urgent," she said, looking at Sair and Cromwell.

Cromwell bowed to the king. "By your leave, Your Majesty." He pushed back his chair, no readable expression at all. It was almost as if he had been expecting her.

Sair, Cyne, and the other Istovari followed suit.

Fonra stood next. A servant rushed to pull back her chair, but not fast enough.

"Fonra," Queen Adelaide chided. "Finish your breakfast."

Fonra inclined her head to her father, bowing, then to her mother. "By your leave, my king. My queen."

Amira wasn't sure what was happening there, but she took her advisors into the hall, gesturing quickly. She hooked her arm through Cromwell's. "Who else knows?" she whispered.

Cromwell seemed to know what she meant at once. "Lord Thadred and Captain Westfall. And whoever they have told by now, I suppose."

"Amira, what has happened?" Sair came beside her, looking out of place in her plain linen dress surrounded by the lush tapestries of Hylendale castle.

183

Amira glanced to the servants bustling past them. "Not here. Somewhere private."

"We can use my study in the castle," Cromwell offered. "It's not far from here and the key has been returned to me." He wheezed, a coughing fit seizing him for a moment.

Amira looked him over, feeling at the *ka* in his body. There was a great deal of it congealed in his chest and mid-back, where the lungs were. His body was still damaged but working to repair itself. "Do you need to rest?"

"I've been resting for days in that cell," Cromwell muttered. "I don't want to rest anymore."

Amira thought she might have to order him to rest if things got much worse, but for now she needed his help.

"Amira!" Fonra came running after them, bursting into the hall. "I want to come with you."

Amira blinked at her sister. "Fonra, we're about to discuss—"

Fonra shook her head. "I volunteer to serve as your lady in waiting."

It took Amira several heartbeats to realize what her sister had said. "What?"

Often imperial women had staff made up of high-born noblewomen. They were usually relatives or the daughters and wives of loyal vassals. Amira had once offered herself as Fonra's lady in waiting, back when they had thought she would be the one to marry Daindreth.

"I know you're leaving soon." Fonra swallowed, glancing to Cromwell.

Amira's eyes narrowed at the older man. Had he told her sister something?

"I want to come with you."

"It will be dangerous."

"Regime changes are always dangerous," Fonra insisted. "For everyone involved. But this is Hylendale's chance."

"Chance?"

Fonra nodded quickly. "I am the heir to Hylendale and my sister is now the empress. We are the nearest kingdom to your new allies, the Istovari." Fonra wasn't telling Amira anything she didn't already know, but she seemed to be interpreting it differently. "If I go to Mynadra as your companion, it will be my chance to create alliances for Hylendale. Which will create alliances for you and your husband as well."

"It will be politics, Fonra," Amira countered. "Hylendale is a small puddle compared to the very large pond that is Mynadra. It would be like swimming with snapping turtles."

Fonra's nostrils flared. "You need allies, sister. And I am not without my own. The Bolesses, to start, have every reason to hate you."

The Bolesses were Fonra's relatives on her mother's side. They had been leading supporters for Fonra's match with Daindreth. From what Amira understood, they had been furious with Amira's substitution. Granted, she hadn't had much time to worry about them these past few months.

Fonra grasped Amira's hand. "I can win them to your side."

Amira stared at her sister—her sweet, innocent sister. Fonra had no idea what the court was like, she was certain of that. And now, with the threat of the cythraul landing on their shores, how could she risk having her sister with her?

Fonra stepped closer, voice dropping to a whisper. "And father wouldn't dare turn against you if I am at your side."

Amira bit her lip. For just a moment, she tried to think as an empress, not a sister.

Fonra was right about the last part. Amira had worried how to ensure her father's loyalty. If he decided to side with Vesha after all and cut them off from the Istovari clan in the Cursewood, it would be disastrous.

But if Fonra was at her side—his only other living child— she could serve as a hostage as much as an ambassador. Even better, she just might be able to sway the Boless family. They had lost their chance at having an empress for a cousin, but if

185

Fonra were to tie her own fortunes to Amira's, that would put Amira's success in their best interests.

Taking Fonra with her began to make sense and Amira was immediately seized with a tightness in her chest.

"Fonra, the cythraul might be coming for us," Amira said. "I don't know what tricks Vesha might be about to unleash. Until we find a way to banish them, there will be danger."

"In that case, the safest place for me to be is with you," Fonra answered shortly.

"What? No."

"Yes," Fonra insisted. "According to you, you've already fought one of them and won."

"It wasn't that simple!"

Fonra looked to Sair, then Cyne. "Am I wrong?" She looked back to her sister. "It's better for us both if we stick together."

Amira spun a glare at Cromwell. "You put her up to this."

"How?" Cromwell's tone was dry, unoffended. "I was locked up until last night."

"I'm not a puppet," Fonra insisted. Her shoulders tensed and she pulled herself up a little straighter. "I came up with this idea on my own."

Amira shook her head. She just wanted her sister safe. This whole thing had started because she wanted her sister safe.

"It would be helpful to have another lady you could trust," Cromwell interjected. "Lady Cyne and Lady Sairydwen are invaluable, for certain. But as sorceresses, they will be mistrusted by most the court, at least in the beginning. Princess Fonra will bring legitimacy and a certain measure of *convention* to your staff."

Amira glared harder at Cromwell, but he was unruffled.

"I support the princess's proposition." Cromwell inclined his head to Fonra in approval. "It is a shrewd measure."

There was a time Amira would have torn into them both, but now she bit her tongue. She had wanted Cromwell as an advisor for a reason. And Fonra was making sense.

Amira clenched her eyes shut. "I will speak to my husband."

Fonra's face lit, though she didn't quite smile. She dropped into a curtsy. "Thank you, Your Grace."

It wasn't agreement, but Fonra acted as if it was. Unfortunately, Amira had a feeling Daindreth would side with Fonra.

Fonra was likeable and unassuming, but also knew how to keep secrets. She was connected, but young and seemingly harmless. She wouldn't be seen as a threat. At the same time, she was a potentially valuable ally, not to mention a potentially valuable marriage alliance.

Even the likes of Dame Rebeku wouldn't want to cross her outright for fear of who she might marry or how powerful Hylendale might become now that it was homeland to the new empress. King Hyle would be held in check and Amira would gain a trusted confidante in what she herself had called a pit of vipers.

Fonra would be the perfect lady in waiting.

Amira just wished it didn't make her stomach churn with worry.

CHAPTER TWENTY-ONE

Thadred

Thadred traced the patterns of spells around his hip and upper thigh again, concentrating in the mirror to make sure he shaped the spells correctly. He had a long day in the saddle ahead of him, so he wanted to get this right.

He pulled his breeches on, then his shirt and boots. When they got back to Mynadra, he would need to get himself a squire. In the court, it would be shameful for him to prepare his own clothes every morning. He was the emperor's right-hand man now.

A knock came from the door.

"Come in," Thadred called.

He had been expecting Dain, but the door opened and Sair floated in. She took a few steps, then drew to a halt. Her brows arched when she saw his shirt still unbuttoned but said nothing.

Thadred's face heated and he found himself fumbling to finish the buttons faster. He wasn't sure why. Plenty of women had seen him in far less. "Can I help you, my lady?"

Most women would have commented—either to express embarrassment or interest. Sair just made eye contact. She was shameless as an army general.

"Amira wanted to know where you were."

"Amira?" Thadred shot a sharp glance to the sorceress. He supposed they needed to stop calling her that. She would be "Her Majesty" once they returned the palace. Or maybe "Her Grace." Official titles hadn't been decided.

"Her sister is accompanying us."

"So I've heard." Thadred didn't have much of an opinion on the idea. Dain had agreed to it and Amira needed to start her own staff, anyway.

Sair watched as Thadred struggled with the buttons of his

shirt, fumbling now that she was watching him. "We're ready to leave as soon as Westfall's soldiers are ready."

"Yes," Thadred agreed. "Have you traveled by sea before?"

"No," Sair replied.

"It will be fun," Thadred said. "Rhis will enjoy it, I think."

A smile tugged at the corner of her mouth. "He looks up to you."

Thadred shook his head with a sigh. "I keep telling him not to do that."

Sair laughed, more a snort than a ladylike giggle. She picked up Thadred's coat from the back of the chair. "You're a good man, Thadred Myrani."

She held up his coat. Thadred hesitated.

It was a bold move, helping him dress. In the palace of Mynadra, an unmarried woman usually wouldn't even be present while a man was dressing. But Sair was Istovari and didn't have the same sensibilities.

Thadred turned around and let her help him. She smoothed his collar and helped button up the front. Her fingers seemed to be back at full function now, deft and skillful.

"Because of you, my son will grow up in peace."

Thadred frowned. "Because of me?"

"Yes." Sair looked up at him with that open, guileless face of hers. "You saved me from the Kadra'han. Because of that, I put in a good word for you with the Mothers, and now we've made an alliance."

"I think you skipped a few steps." Thadred straightened his collar. "Mainly the part where Amira and Dain took on a demon and won."

Sair shrugged. "Either way, I am grateful. We all are. Even if there are still challenges ahead."

Thadred wasn't sure what to make of that. Sair finished adjusting his coat and stepped back.

"Your things are already with the horses. Are you ready?" There were no games with Sair. No flirtations or double

189

meanings.

Sometimes, Thadred thought her words were intended as more than those from friend to friend. Other times, he thought perhaps it was that he had never had a woman as *just* a friend.

Amira, perhaps, but she hardly counted. She'd been Dain's woman from the start, and they had a somewhat antagonistic relationship as it was.

"Let's be going, then," Thadred agreed.

Outside, the guest wing was almost empty. Servants were at work, already stripping the beds and dusting out the rooms.

Several of the Istovari rangers were headed downstairs, nibbling at biscuits with their bows and arrows slung over their backs.

It had been decided that the Istovari would be serving as scouts for now as well as personal guards for Cyne and Sair.

"Rhis told me he wants to be a knight," Sair said.

"Oh?" Thadred used the handrail of the stairs to step down. It was a habit and after a few steps, he remembered the spell on his body. Letting go, he found that he could walk without the support. Awkwardly, but he could do it. Perhaps someday he would be able to perfect this spell to the point he could walk without even a cane.

"He wants to be like you," Sair said.

Thadred laughed, but Sair didn't. "Wait, you're serious?"

Sair smiled sadly. "Yes. Why wouldn't I be?"

The two of them reached the level of the courtyard. At least a hundred horses were saddled and bridled. Soldiers packed gear and several lady's maids worked to collect all Princess Fonra's things into a few trunks.

The rangers were easily spotted to one side. All of them wore their hoods up except Tapios, like they were trying to hide from the strangers around them.

Rhis was with Lleuad, assisted by his uncle, of course. Lleuad now allowed other Istovari to handle him, but the kelpie was still a kelpie. None of them knew just what he might be capable of or what he might do if frightened.

"Rhis has only rudimentary magic," Sair said. "I gave too much of mine away before he was born, I think."

The Istovari sorceresses has sacrificed seven tenths of their power to create the Cursewood, the poisonous forest that had protected them from the outside world for years. Unfortunately, that also lessened the power of all children born since. Thadred and Amira were exceptions because they had been born before the creation of the Cursewood and hadn't been part of its casting.

"I thought I had rudimentary magic," Thadred countered. He was still learning to use the power he had, but he *was* learning. It was possible. "Now I cast spells every day."

Sair stared straight ahead. "Then perhaps you can teach him."

Thadred's chest tightened at that. He'd only been half-joking when he said he'd told Rhis not to look up to him. Thadred knew, deep down, that he wasn't someone a little boy should want to emulate. He wasn't someone a little boy should admire.

Even if Thadred had grown fond of this particular little boy. Even if the boy's mother was the most fascinating woman he'd ever met.

Thadred knew he'd only disappoint them both.

"You said Amira wanted me?"

A flicker of disappointment was Sair's only reaction to his change of subject. "Yes, she and Daindreth should be here shortly."

"Myrani!" Westfall emerged from behind a large dappled grey destrier, in full plate armor.

Daindreth's stag emblazon marked his breastplate as well as the breastplates of the other men. Banners of stags fluttered above their heads—and Vesha's white raven had been removed. If any imperial citizen with any measure of education saw those banners, they would know a member of the imperial family was on the road.

"Westfall." Thadred met the other man, feeling like a dandy in his embroidered riding coat.

"I've assigned ten guards to his majesty and six to her grace," Westfall said.

Thadred quirked a brow at that. "Why so few for Empress Amira?" As Daindreth's sorceress, Kadra'han, and his primary link to the Istovari, she was strategically vital. As empress, it was Amira's role to ensure the continuation of the imperial line. Either way, she should at least have as many guards as her husband.

Westfall looked over to where the Istovari were readying their horses. Sair had joined her brother and son in readying Lleuad. The black stallion seemed to be at least tolerating their attention.

"I understood that the empress was to be guarded by her sorceresses and rangers."

A good explanation. Thadred wasn't convinced it was the reason, but he would let Westfall get away with this one. "Assign two more men to Empress Amira. I will make sure her sorceresses know they are to guard her."

Thadred was quite proud of himself for that response. He'd let Westfall know that Amira was important without chastising him and Dain would never need to know about this.

Westfall inclined his head curtly. "I will."

Chapter Twenty-Two

Amira

Mynadra first appeared on the horizon as a sprawl of brown and grey shapes. As they drew closer and closer, Amira was able to make out the form of the white palace with its high spires and towering walls.

The sun was just rising behind the city, casting it in golden sunbursts. It reminded Amira of the cathedral murals of Alshone, the metropolis of the gods.

She braced her hands against the railing as the ship bobbed and swayed. Below deck, Thadred's kelpie had nearly gone mad when the ship began to rock, but Amira found something soothing in the swelling of the waves.

She was aware of Daindreth's approach as he crossed the deck, followed at an easy distance by a pair of guards. Her own guards were also a few paces back, standing at attention.

It was strange to be always followed by men, but she supposed she would have to get used to it. This was her life now.

"You're quite the sailor, my love." Daindreth slid up behind her, lacing his arms around her waist.

Amira leaned back into his chest. "I've sailed a few times. My father's errands took me many places."

Daindreth kissed her hair. "It's a pity the rest of your Istovari brothers and sisters do not have your experience."

Tapios and most of the other rangers had puked their guts out for the first day. Cyne had fared somewhat better. Most of them were recovered now, but Tapios was still pale and had refused to come up from below decks.

Gulls squawked overhead, a sure sign they were nearing land.

Amira and Daindreth sailed in a ship called *Wavecleaver*, a large vessel intended for a merchant's use. On either side of them were the two smaller but much better armed ships. Amira hadn't bothered to learn their names.

Captain Westfall rode aboard one and his lieutenant in the other. Their job was to protect the main vessel, though there had been no attacks thus far.

Last night, Amira and Daindreth had made love then laid awake listening to the rocking of the waves. Amira found herself straining in the dark, trying to hear any sign that there was danger, any hint that Vesha was drawing near. She knew deep in her bones that Vesha was coming, and a storm was coming with her.

Amira and Daindreth had spent all day yesterday in their cabin—leaving only to eat and meet with their advisors. The rest of the time they had spent tangled up in each other, whispering in the dim light of the cabin and trading caresses in the dark.

Daindreth said everything would be fine, but Amira suspected he feared what they might find, too. She felt like he was snatching up final moments of comfort and respite as surely as she was.

Sometimes she could fool herself into believing that there was no danger. Unfortunately, this time of peace wasn't going to last.

A fishing vessel passed them on its way to the deeper waters, then another merchant ship, and a large caravel. They were entering Mynadra's port.

"Shall we run the colors, Your Majesty?" asked the captain, a gruff naval officer in an impressively starched coat.

Daindreth nodded. "Run the colors." He kept his arms around Amira as the order was passed on.

Shouts leapt from ship to ship and there was the snapping of ropes and cloth as the red imperial banners were raised. On the other two ships, the stag banners also rose, announcing their trio of ships as an imperial convoy.

Amira swallowed heavily. They didn't know for sure that they were the first ones to reach Mynadra. Vesha could already be here and then they were just giving her forewarning.

But they'd discussed this at length—Daindreth was the

194

rightful heir. The rightful heir shouldn't sneak into his rightful palace. If they wanted the people to accept him, he needed to fit their idea of what a rightful emperor would do.

Even though Amira preferred stealth whenever possible, they were no longer playing by only the rules of the shadows. They had to play by the rules of the light as well. The rules of pomp and circumstance, the rules of spectacle.

"We should be docking within the hour, Your Majesty," the captain said.

Daindreth nodded. "Thank you." He turned back to his wife. "You look lovely."

"Thank Fonra," Amira said, nestling closer back against him.

This dress, ironically, had been another gift from Cromwell, but from several years ago. It was black and grey brocade with silver accents and a close-fitted bodice that left her shoulders naked.

Fonra had added a mink mantle for Amira's shoulders and silver earrings. Fonra and her maids had pinned Amira's hair up and covered it with a netted veil in the modest fashion of a Hylendale matron.

"Clothes are not just clothes," Fonra had said to her that morning. "They are banners that send a message." Stepping back to admire her work, she had smiled proudly. "This says that you are a Hylendale noble and a married woman, but also bold and unafraid of scandal. The earrings draw attention to your husband's means, but they aren't so large or flashy as to overdo it."

"They're your earrings," Amira had reminded Fonra. "I'm borrowing them from you."

"Yes, but no one will know that when we arrive in Mynadra."

Amira had been skeptical, but she trusted her sister's judgment.

"Are you ready for battle, my empress?" Daindreth asked calmly.

"I've been fighting Vesha's legions from the beginning," Amira said.

"Not the demons," Daindreth chuckled. "No, I meant the court."

"I will be fine." Amira wished she could make herself believe those words. "I will have Fonra and Cromwell to help me."

Cromwell was like Amira—he had risen to a station he should never have had. Cromwell had not only held his position but continued to rise—as was evidenced by his position now as Amira's chancellor. Fonra had been Daindreth's original intended and had been much better educated to navigate the imperial court.

Amira thought she had done well, all things considered, but she was no longer the future archduchess. She was the new empress.

"I'm glad you have them," Daindreth said, rubbing her bare arms. "You feel cold."

"It's the wind. It's always bad at sea."

Daindreth wrapped his cloak around both of them. His was much longer than her mantle, trailing to the ground. "Better?"

"Much." Amira snuggled back against him.

They stood together, watching the shore grow closer and closer. The sailors called to each other in preparation of docking.

More and more vessels floated past them, veering away to make room as the imperial banners were spotted.

Amira squinted, watching the docks and the palace. "Do you think they've spotted us yet?"

People on land should have seen the imperial banners approaching. Word would spread quickly through the palace and then the rest of the city.

"Yes," Daindreth answered. "I expect they saw us shortly after we raised the banners."

The larger merchant vessels gave them a wide berth as they came closer into port, but the smaller boats drifted closer. Fisherman's sloops bobbed in the water, their crews stopping to gape up at the imperial convoy.

"They're staring," Daindreth said flatly. "They knew I was gone."

"People always stare," Amira interjected.

"Yes, but not this much." Daindreth exhaled, pulling her closer against him. "Look at the shore."

Amira had been looking at the shore, but when she looked back, the docks were crowded with a motley assortment of figures in all colors from muted browns to flamboyant reds. People crowded around the beach near the docks, small pockets of people gathering here and there.

"Vesha's not here," Amira said, not sure she believed it. "Vesha's not here and they know it."

Against her ear, Daindreth nodded. "They wouldn't be this excited unless…"

"No one is sitting the throne," Amira whispered. She had a creeping sensation then, not unlike the times when she had been stalking through a castle, unable to find the guards she knew were there.

The best-case scenario had been that they would arrive in Mynadra to find it unoccupied, but this raised new questions. If Vesha was not in residence and people knew it, who had been running the empire?

In the forest, when an animal died and left its burrow empty, *something* moved in to fill the space. Thrones were no different.

From the docks, flags raised, waving where there was space for their small convoy to dock. Thadred and Westfall's ships docked first, anchoring to let the bulk of the soldiers and their personal guard out.

Amira spotted Thadred, walking without the use of his cane, but still recognizable by the hitch in his gait. He led the lines of armored soldiers down to the dock where Amira and Daindreth's ship would anchor, leading them in two neat lines as they pushed the crowds back.

Though Daindreth and Thadred seemed to trust Westfall,

Amira was glad Thadred was the one tasked with meeting them when they landed. Westfall led the contingent now pushing people back from the docks, making sure that the imperial group would have the space safety required.

Daindreth nipped the top of her ear.

Amira jumped, shooting him a sharp look. "That's unfair, Your Majesty."

"Unfair?"

"Teasing me when I can't do anything about it."

"Teasing?" She could feel Daindreth's grin as he pressed his cheek against hers. "You haven't even begun to see me teasing, my dear."

Amira opened her mouth to reply, but the ship's anchor dropped then, chain rattling over the side of the ship.

"Your Grace!" Fonra came rushing from the cabin of the ship along with her gaggle of maids—now Amira's maids by default.

Amira reluctantly left the shelter of Daindreth's arms. "Fonra."

Her sister wore a fine brocade dress of silver and white, a fine complement to Amira's. She was lovely, Amira thought. She always had been.

"Are you ready?" Fonra fussed over Amira's hair, fixing the strands the wind had blown loose and adjusting Amira's mantle one last time.

Amira was done answering that question. "I'm ready to get this over with."

Fonra nodded, gripping Amira's hand tightly. "You'll do magnificent."

Cromwell emerged, dressed in his usual black velvet. He had his typical black cap and hose, but a gold chain now fastened his mantle, marking him as a noble. His cough was gone, but he was still deathly pale.

Fonra stepped up beside Amira and Cromwell stepped behind Fonra, followed by the entourage of maids. Amira hooked her arm through Daindreth's and the ramp lowered to let them off the ship.

The guards marched down first, joining Thadred and the other men below. Thadred grinned up at them, looking rather proud of himself. He swept a bow, his armor glinting with polishing as he did.

"We have reached Mynadra, your majesties," he said. "Allow me to be the first to welcome you home."

Daindreth inclined his head to acknowledge the words and led the way off the ship. The plank swayed and Amira had to hold her dress with one hand.

Horses were readied at the end of the docks to take them to the palace. The growing crowd swelled around the docks as word spread that Daindreth was indeed here.

The city was alive with *ka*. Amira had felt it before, but she hadn't remembered it as quite so *bright*.

Mynadra fairly glowed. So many bodies all in one place. So much death, decay, rebirth, and life. She could feel the layers of the city, left by the generations of people who had lived and died here, stretching back thousands of years.

Mynadra was an ancient place, a powerful place. For just a moment, she could believe the city had been founded by a god.

Amira and Daindreth were escorted down the docks to where their horses waited. Carriages weren't an option because they hadn't brought one and they didn't want to wait for one from the palace.

Amira's little bay mare was there, as was Daindreth's sorrel. Lleuad stood to the side, his bridle held by Tapios. The swamp horse's ears flicked nervously, but he seemed to be cooperating.

Amira's horse had been outfitted with a sidesaddle to account for her skirts.

"Can you ride sidesaddle?" Daindreth asked in her ear as they drew closer to the horses.

Amira almost laughed. "I'm not a savage, love."

Daindreth shrugged. "I've never seen you use one."

Amira kissed his cheek and allowed one of the soldiers to give her a boost onto her mare's back.

The rest of their party mounted up, at least those who had horses. The sorceresses, Thadred, and Westfall and his officers had mounts, but most the soldiers and the rangers didn't.

Tapios and his rangers walked surrounding Amira on one side, with the soldiers circling around them. Fonra had a small gelding and Cromwell had a large white beast that was almost a destrier.

Amira took up her horse's reins. She surreptitiously surveyed the crowd, the upper story windows, and the dock. As best she could tell, there were no threats, but there was so much commotion, she couldn't be sure.

"To the palace!" Daindreth shouted, giving the official order.

Westfall echoed the command to the rest of the troops.

Amira had ridden through the city in a carriage and prowled through it on foot. Each time it had seemed different and now was no exception.

The air still crackled with power, the cathedrals, libraries, and opera houses still formed their grandiose display. But it felt…less impressive. Or perhaps less frightening.

All of this was Daindreth's and by extension hers. As empress, every person who gaped at her and every child who pointed would be expected to show her deference.

When she had come here the last time, she had been unsure she would survive the month. She'd never put much thought into what being empress actually meant.

People pressed around the streets, but soldiers held them back. People called to Daindreth and shouted blessings to his majesty. Most called out his old title of archduke.

They rounded a corner in the street toward the palace to take a shortcut through the industrial quarter. Someone exclaimed and Amira looked up, sure her eyes must be deceiving her, but no.

The industrial quarter—with its coopers, weavers, tanners, and other craftsmen—was in ruins. Broken boards, crumpled stone, and heaps of rubble were all that remained.

The imperial procession came to a halt. Amira looked to Daindreth to see her own shock mirrored in his face.

Several of the soldiers spoke with locals and one of Westfall's troops approached the captain. He spoke with Westfall for several moments, then returned to his post.

Westfall twisted in his saddle to address Daindreth. "It seems that an earthquake struck over a week ago, destroying much of the industrial quarter."

Amira looked out at the neat, sharply outlined destruction in front of her. "An earthquake?" She found that hard to believe.

"That's what the people are saying, Your Grace," Westfall replied. "I will have men investigate the matter further once we arrive in the palace." From the shortness in his tone, Amira suspected that Westfall was more disturbed by this sight than he wanted to show.

The city's industrial quarter here in Mynadra was the largest in the empire. Raw goods arrived from around the continent—wool, hides, ore, and flax—and left as cloth, leather, linen, and metal ingots. Much of the goods were even transformed into finished products like saddles, cloaks, boots, shovel heads, or…spears.

Amira glanced to Thadred as the thought struck her. The knight rode beside Daindreth, looking grim.

If they went to war, the Mynadra industrial quarter would have been vital to equipping an army. Yes, Erymaya had a sizable standing army, but if the need came for them to raise a larger army or even just take the soldiers they had on march…

"Shall we go around, Your Majesty?" Westfall asked.

"No," Daindreth replied. "I want to see it."

"Some of the way may not be clear," Westfall protested.

"I want to see, Ohad," Daindreth repeated. He used the other man's given name, emphasizing the gravity of the situation.

"As you wish, my liege." Westfall passed the order along.

"None of the other buildings look damaged," Fonra said in a hushed voice from behind Amira.

"I noticed that, too." Amira glanced around them to where the industrial quarter ended—immediately, buildings rose at the edge of the warehouses, appearing to be intact from the outside.

This could only be witchcraft. Amira could think of no other explanation.

The road through the industrial district had been wide to begin with and most of it had been cleared. It seemed that the recovery process was underway, but...

Vesha was to blame somehow, Amira was sure of it. She just didn't know how.

The workers shoveling through rubble stopped their labor and looked up. Many waved and saluted, excited to see the imperial banners just as those on the docks had been.

The devastation to the district appeared absolute. Equipment parts jutted up from the rubble here and there like the bones of great metal skeletons. Amira felt as if she were riding through some kind of industrial graveyard.

They reached the other side of the district and the rest of the city appeared fine. People came running to meet them in the streets, held back by the soldiers. Others leaned out of windows and cheered at the sight of the imperial banners.

Amira glanced over to Cromwell. The man looked serious, but then again, he always looked serious.

Their party reached the gates of the palace to find them already open. Messengers had been sent ahead to warn the palace and it appeared that they had made an effort to be welcoming.

Daindreth and Amira rode under the white arches of the palace's outer courtyard. Looking up, Amira wondered again how men could have built something so massive.

Fonra stared, craning her neck to see the tops of the walls.

Her mouth formed a small "o" at the sight of the palace. It was one thing to live in Hylendale and know that you were a small, insignificant northern kingdom. It was quite another to see it up close. The Hylendale palace could have fit in the courtyard of the Mynadra palace.

Cromwell took a single glance around at the palace and then focused straight ahead again. Nothing impressed that man. On second thought, Amira wondered if Cromwell had been to Mynadra before. She knew he had spent time abroad, but just where he had spent time was often a hazier subject.

Daindreth was greeted with the sound of trumpets. Nobles came rushing out in hastily adjusted court attire, though some appeared to have arrived in their everyday clothes.

Servants lined the steps leading up into the palace, ready surprisingly fast, all things considered. Courtiers dressed in various levels of finery stood by, clustered around the steps, crowding windows and balconies overhead, and standing at the edges of the courtyard. A number of courtiers watched from carriages and atop horses, having been on their way in or out of the palace.

Westfall was first to dismount. He approached a man in an officer's uniform from the imperial household and they traded low words for several moments. The officer nodded and signaled to the rest of his men.

Westfall turned and saluted Daindreth. "Welcome home, Lord Emperor."

A herald appeared at the top of the steps with a trumpet. He declared Daindreth's various titles and honorifics, voice booming over the crowd.

Amira waited for her husband to help her down from her horse as was proper. He kissed her hand as she landed, his fingers stroking the backs of her fingers. No doubt, he wanted the show of affection to be witnessed by the court.

The rest of their party dismounted and formed into ranks around them once again. Daindreth headed for the main steps of the palace with Amira on his arm.

Courtiers and servants alike bowed and curtsied around them. Amira kept her chin up, focusing on the steps.

At the top of the stairs waited a woman in a black wimple with a headband of pearls. Her waist was likewise roped in pearls. Her thick wrists rattled with them, and Amira wasn't sure she had ever seen someone wear so many.

"Dame Rebeku," Amira whispered to her husband, fighting the urge to bristle.

She had no fond memories of the woman. Last time she had been here, Rebeku had made it clear she would try to manipulate Amira at the very least and oust her at the worst.

Rebeku had held power at court for longer than either Amira or Daindreth had been alive. She had been at court even before Vesha. Like an oak tree, she had grown stronger with age.

"I see her," Daindreth said as they closed the distance to the matron.

Dame Rebeku swept into a curtsy, the first real one Amira had seen her give. On her left and right stood her daughters, Gisella and Melonia. Amira couldn't remember which one was which, but the younger of the two winked at Thadred.

Amira resisted the urge to turn and see if he winked back.

"Dame Rebeku." Daindreth's tone was mild. If he shared any of Amira's annoyance at seeing the woman, it was hard to know.

"Emperor Daindreth," Rebeku greeted him with a pearly smile.

"My wife, Empress Amira Brindonu Fanduillion."

They had made the decision to keep Amira's Istovari name as part of her title. It reminded people she was a sorceress and just which clan she had brought into this marriage alliance.

Dame Rebeku's eyes flickered for just a moment to Amira. Amira wasn't sure, but she thought she saw frustration.

Amira and Daindreth were married and Daindreth had just declared it in front of at least a hundred watching courtiers. She would not be so easy to get rid of now.

"Empress Amira," Rebeku said, dropping into a curtsy as one was supposed to do for the empress. She looked back to Daindreth. "Your Majesty, I have been serving as chatelaine since your mother's departure. I do hope you find everything to be in order."

Amira cursed inwardly. Vesha had left Rebeku in charge when she'd left? What was she thinking?

"I am sure we shall," Daindreth said. "If you would see the banners raised and the word spread that I have returned."

Amira studied the guards lining the palace walls. Fifty-eight of them were in sight, not counting those she and Daindreth had brought with them. They appeared to be in the official palace uniforms, their *ka* a healthy golden color—human.

Westfall was now speaking to a different officer. Amira had to wonder who was acting as captain of the guard since Darrigan had left with Vesha.

"It has been a long journey, Dame Rebeku," Daindreth apologized. "My wife and I are in need of rest. But we shall send our people to speak with yours as I am sure you are quite eager to be unburdened from the tasks of running the palace."

Daindreth sounded so sincere and congenial that Amira could almost believe he was genuinely concerned for the strain such a task would place on the old woman. He acted like the perfect emperor.

Amira felt coarse and uncultured by comparison. Empresses were supposed to be ornamental, beautiful creatures who aided their husbands through court schemes and games. Amira could play games and she was no stranger to intrigue. But when it came to lying, to pretending she liked people she'd rather skin alive, she had a lot to learn.

Mistress Galidge, Daindreth's housekeeper, greeted them at the entrance to his wing of the palace. The plump woman wept as she bowed and kissed Daindreth's hand. Many of the other servants joined in her weeping, echoing how happy they were to see him. It was like he'd been thought dead. Perhaps he had been.

Amira wondered just how much they knew about what Vesha had planned on that night months ago. From their tears, she guessed they knew more than they were supposed to.

"Would you like your old rooms, my love?" Daindreth asked.

"I don't care," Amira answered simply.

Daindreth didn't take long to consider it. "Mistress Galidge, would you see my wife's staff set up in her rooms?"

"Would you like her to take the one beside yours, Your Majesty?" Mistress Galidge asked. "We've cleaned your rooms out thoroughly."

"No, the same rooms she had as before, thank you." Daindreth's expression remained kind, but his shoulder tensed ever so slightly.

His rooms had been *cleaned*—Mistress Galidge meant that they had scrubbed the death out. Daindreth's valet, Taylan, had his throat cut in Daindreth's sitting room by Vesha's men. His body had been left there to bleed out on the floor.

Amira didn't blame her husband for wanting her to keep her old rooms—that meant he could sleep well away from his.

Mistress Galidge scurried off to prepare the chambers. Fonra and the lady's maids went with her along with a few footmen who appeared to be Daindreth's staff here at home.

A clerk came to deliver a report to Daindreth. The emperor thanked him and clipped back a few short sentences about a time to address the whole of the assembled court. No sooner had the clerk left than one of Westfall's squires came bowing before Daindreth.

"My liege, Captain Westfall has found that Lieutenant Garvic has been in command of the palace guard since his departure. With your permission, Captain Westfall would make himself acting guard captain until further notice."

"Granted," Daindreth replied without a second thought.

Odds were that Westfall would be official guard captain before too long. No one wanted to be hasty, but right now Westfall was the most qualified and seemed to be the most loyal.

"We've probably given them enough of a head start," Daindreth remarked, gesturing to where Galidge and the others had disappeared. "I think we can follow them now."

Amira stepped into her rooms to find it seemed she had never left. The bed was freshly made and the curtains were drawn, but her hairbrushes and perfume bottles still lay where she had set them. Her dresses still hung in the wardrobe, too.

Sair met her at the doorway and nodded. "The room is safe. No traps or snares that we can find."

"We're addressing the court in two hours," Daindreth said, as much to Amira as to everyone else in the room. "Meet me in the throne room for it." Daindreth kissed Amira's cheek, his lips brushing her ear. "See if you and your women can find anything in my mother's rooms she left behind."

Amira nodded quickly. "Lady Cyne will be able to tell us what's important." Amira glanced toward her bedroom. Just outside, there was a white quartz pillar capped with silver crescents—a shrine to Moreyne. "I would like to remove Vesha's places of veneration to Moreyne. And destroy the witch's wheel as soon as we can."

Daindreth nodded. "See it done."

"Just like that?"

"Why not?" Daindreth cocked one brow. "Am I missing something?"

"No, I just thought you might not be so eager for me to start ripping apart your palace."

Daindreth shrugged. "I want the cythraul out of my lands."

Amira swallowed. She wanted the creatures out, too. "I will give the orders at once."

"Good. In the meantime, I will find out what I can about the state of the empire and just who has been running it." Daindreth kissed the back of his wife's hand. "Mistress Galidge?"

"Your Majesty?" the plump housekeeper squawked from across the room.

"My wife and her women are to have full access to everything—including anything owned by the former empress." Daindreth gestured to Amira and her sorceresses. "Help them with whatever they need."

Daindreth squeezed Amira's hand one last time before marching out the door with Thadred and the rest of the guards.

"Your husband seems quite loved," Cromwell remarked. "That will be useful."

CHAPTER TWENTY-THREE

Vesha

Cythraul were many things. It turned out that "sailors" was not one of them. Their ships had run aground off an abandoned coast. Despite many of the creatures insisting that their hosts had been sailors, either the hosts had lied or the cythraul were not so good at following directions.

The ships had begun drifting toward land early this morning. No matter what the cythraul had done after that, the vessels had drifted inexorably toward shore until they ran aground, slamming into what must be a massive sandbar. Some of the ships had even smashed into each other.

After it had become clear the ships were stuck, they'd been able to climb into rowboats and come almost to the beach, but their cythraul crewmen only brought the boat partway up the surf. Impatient, Vesha had climbed out.

She slogged ashore with Odette gripping her arm. The handmaiden held her skirts in one hand and Vesha in the other, pulling them both to land.

Around them, cythraul in bodies and some not, flailed and floundered to land. Most had also climbed into rowboats, but some had stumbled to land, screaming the entire time. The creatures howled when they touched water, shrieking like cats.

"Useless," Vesha muttered. "Absolutely useless."

Vesha and her handmaiden made it to the shore, covered in sand and seawater. The empress looked down along the length of the beach to see hundreds of cythraul crawling out of the ocean. The ships sat not far offshore, the ragtag collection of vessels bunched together like leaves in a drain.

"How did this happen?" Vesha demanded, grabbing the first cythraul who came within reach. "Dozens of ships, and you ran them all aground?"

Vesha didn't know the name of this cythraul, but the creature was in the body of a pockmarked boy. He licked his lips nervously. "Forgive us, witch." He ducked his head.

"Not good enough," Vesha snarled, gripping the boy's jaw in one hand. She dragged him closer. "Who should I punish for this failure?"

"Llyr," Caa Iss rumbled from her back. "He's playing with us."

Vesha dropped the boy and spun on her familiar. "The sea god?"

Caa Iss bobbed his head. His shoulders hunched and his head hung low, oddly subservient.

Vesha didn't know when Caa Iss had begun groveling to her, but she liked it. "Why not sink us on the open ocean?"

Caa Iss tilted his head to one side. "Perhaps he does not wish to declare outright war against Moreyne. But inconveniencing her vessel is fair game."

"Her what?"

"This is a minor setback, my lady," Caa Iss said, pointedly not answering her question. "We shall regroup here and make our way inland."

"Your mother is not patient, and neither am I!" Vesha swore and cast about the beach. "Where are we?"

Pine trees lined the beach. Dark sand gave way to dark rocks worn smooth by the tides. Massive logs of driftwood littered the shore, the skeletons of ancient trees.

They could be anywhere north of Mynadra, in Hylendale for all she could tell. They should have reached the capitol city tomorrow, but that was before they had been blown off course.

"I do not know, my lady," Caa Iss replied, not making eye contact.

Rage surged through Vesha's whole body. Her face flushed and sweat hinted at her back despite the chill breeze. "You had best find out."

Caa Iss bowed and didn't quite lift his gaze from the ground.

He feared her now. That felt good. He backed away and spoke to several cythraul now in bodies, voice too low for her to hear.

Around them, cythraul in their motley shapes and forms staggered out of the water. Those with hosts rolled in the sand, scrubbing at themselves like they were trying to get the seawater off. Many yowled and whimpered, pawing at their faces and exposed skin. Some even began to strip, tearing off their waterlogged clothes.

Vesha was disgusted.

"My lady."

Vesha spun around.

A cythraul faced her, but not one she recognized. He had no host yet, standing exposed in all his naked glory. This creature was ashy grey with notches in his hide and a gaping hole in his ribs that would have been deadly to a mortal creature. What struck her most about him was his posture. This one stood erect like a human, overlarge hands clasped behind his back.

"There is a farmhouse some distance back through the trees. We have secured it. You may wish to take refuge there while you wait for us to gather the troops."

"I don't want refuge, I want answers." Vesha had no intention of being placated.

"I understand, my lady. But I do not have answers for you at the moment. The best I can offer is shelter while we restore order."

Vesha frowned at the cythraul. This one was different. "I haven't met you before."

"I am Araa Oon, my lady. Master of the hunt."

"Hmm." Vesha glanced to the clear skies. "Show me this farmhouse, Araa Oon. Before the others burn it to the ground."

"Yes, my lady." Araa Oon bowed and led her back into the trees.

Araa Oon walked calmly, leading the way along a narrow footpath. He moved eerily like one of her imperial soldiers, like her Kadra'han had before they were turned into hosts. Vesha tried not to think about them too much.

The smell of woodsmoke was her first warning that they neared a farmhouse. Pigs squealed and human voices screamed. Bile rose in the back of Vesha's throat and she gulped it back. Now wasn't the time to be squeamish. Not the time.

They came into a clearing some hundred paces or so back from the beach. Nestled in the shelter of a rocky outcrop, a thatched farmhouse with a nearby barn and pig pen came into view.

Several imps that still lacked bodies chased the pigs around the pen, laughing and cackling. Chickens scattered in all directions. A dog barked from somewhere Vesha couldn't see. Then it yelped and screamed before falling silent.

Vesha tripped on something and glanced down, then wished she hadn't. A severed arm draped across the path. Several steps away laid the rest of the body, an old man with his mouth still open in a final scream, chest freshly clawed open.

Vesha gasped before she could stop herself. The old man wore a farmer's simple tunic and trews, a basket of fish strewn on the ground beside him. Her gaze caught on the many careful patches in his clothes. Someone had lovingly repaired every tear and hole. Had that person ever thought, as they mended his tunic, that he would die in it?

Odette shuddered at Vesha's side, clutching the empress's arm.

Araa Oon grimaced. "You may want to wait here, my lady."

Vesha took a shaky breath and forced herself to walk past the body. She held onto Odette and it was hard to know which of them supported the other. "No," she said to Araa Oon. "Take me inside."

Vesha didn't want to go inside the farmhouse. Voices cried out and whimpered inside. Imp voices laughed and cackled, but she needed to see. She had to see just how high the price of her empire's salvation had risen.

Araa Oon didn't argue further, leading her up the worn path

to the farmhouse. The wattle and daub house had been built on a packed earth floor with small windows carefully cut in the walls. Through the windows, flurries of motion fluttered back and forth as imps without hosts chased shapes to and fro.

They stepped inside and Vesha felt she had stumbled upon a nightmare.

Children huddled under the table in a bundle of limbs and snotty, tear-stained faces. The body of an old woman with her skull smashed in lay beside the hearth. The remains of a large man lay spread over most the kitchen, blood and entrails splattered everywhere, as if he had just burst like a rotten fruit.

Imps harried the children, circling the table and biting at them, laughing when they shrank back. The children didn't seem to realize the incorporeal creatures couldn't hurt them.

A cythraul in a man's body towered over a kneeling woman. He looked up when Vesha and Araa Oon entered, and she choked back a gasp.

It was Cashun, or at least his body. The young man had always been serious, perhaps a little too much so. Now his face was twisted in sadistic glee, teeth splattered in blood and eyes glowing red with the taint of the cythraul.

Araa Oon stared down the cythraul in Cashun. "Our bargain is to save this empire, not ravage it."

Cashun shrugged, still holding the woman by her hair. "The bargain grants us bodies, hunter. We're just taking what's owed us."

Araa Oon shot a glare to the imps chasing the children. Oddly enough, they stopped. Several dropped onto their haunches, though they didn't back away from their prey just yet.

Strange. Vesha had assumed that all the high-ranking cythraul had already taken bodies, but this one…

"Release this woman," Vesha ordered Cashun's host.

The cythraul snickered. "Your Kadra'han isn't in command anymore, empress. I don't have to obey you."

The woman at Cashun's feet didn't look that much older

than Vesha. Her apron was stained and worn, but her woolen dress was clean. She stared toward her children huddled beneath the table, tears streaking her face.

Araa Oon studied the ceiling and the careful rows of onions, carrots, and root vegetables above. He then turned and studied the children. His insubstantial tongue slid over his teeth, the way many of the creatures did when they were thinking.

Vesha bristled, stepping closer despite the seeping horror at seeing Cashun in this state. She'd ordered him to take a cythraul. Even if she didn't remember doing it, she was to blame for this. Her right temple throbbed again, and it was all she could do not to wince in pain.

"You would defy me?" Vesha demanded.

Hesitation flickered in Cashun's red eyes. Just the barest sign of uncertainty.

"It's my right—"

Araa Oon dropped into a crouch in front of the farm woman, so that he was at her eye level. "Yours?" He pointed to the cluster of children beneath the table.

The woman nodded, breaths coming in ragged gulps. "Yes."

Araa Oon glanced back at them. "Impressive."

"What?" the woman choked as Cashun pulled her hair too far back.

Araa Oon didn't seem to care. "All those children, but…" He glanced into one of the rooms beyond the kitchen. "Such…order."

The small farmhouse appeared to be made up of three rooms, two bedrooms adjoining the kitchen and work area which took up most of the space. A loft overhead appeared to be where the children slept.

The woman trembled, shaking in Cashun's grip. "Please let them go," she rasped. "Just let them go."

Araa Oon nodded calmly, thinking. He glanced back to Vesha, as if asking permission. For what?

Vesha looked to the children. At least five of them. The

oldest was barely small enough to fit under the table and the smallest clung to an older sister, sobbing and begging for their mother.

Something caught in Vesha's throat. This was the way it had to be. Everyone had to make sacrifices. It was for the empire. The empire had to be saved. If Vesha didn't make the hard choices, if she didn't—

But this was wrong.

Pain shot through her whole head, so sharp her vision went dark. Vesha doubled over and Odette caught her arm.

When Vesha was able to look up again, Araa Oon held a clawed, insubstantial hand toward the woman.

The woman trembled as she took it.

Araa Oon sprang forward, diving straight for the farmwife. His form rippled and smoked, and the woman's eyes flashed, then glowed a steady red. The farmwife, now Araa Oon, sprang upright, shoving back Cashun's cythraul so hard he slammed into the opposite wall.

Cashun's cythraul snarled in annoyance. "That was unnecessary."

Araa Oon flexed his neck to one side, then the other. "Secure the farm," he ordered. "Enough play. We have work to do."

Cashun's cythraul snarled but slunk to obey. He marched past Vesha, sneering lecherously in her direction as he headed out the door.

"Mama?" one of the children wept.

Araa Oon's host had been neither tall nor short, but her frame seemed to tower now. Thin shoulders pulled back and her chin rose. "I am not your mother," the demon's voice said simply. He looked to the imps. "The young ones are free to go."

That was met with howls of protest from the imps. The small demons scratched at the floor and bellowed their disapproval.

"That was the deal with my host," Araa Oon said. There was

215

no venom in his voice, only flat recitation of fact. "Go, children. You will not be harmed by cythraul for as long as you live."

Relief coursed through the empress. Araa Oon had made the decision for her.

The eldest child looked to Vesha and Odette. "Who are you?"

"I'd listen to him." Vesha raised her chin. "Get out of here before we change our minds."

"Mama," cried the youngest, reaching vainly toward Araa Oon.

Pain wrenched through Vesha's chest this time, an altogether different ache.

"I want Mama. Please, Mama."

Vesha looked away.

Thankfully, the eldest child was smart enough to take their chance. She grabbed her younger siblings and shoved them toward the door, past Vesha and Odette.

Outside, the children let off cries of horror and grief, but through the window, Vesha watched until they disappeared into the forest beyond the clearing. Araa Oon was right—none of the cythraul now swarming the farmstead came near them.

"You let them get away!" howled the imps at Araa Oon's feet. "Five perfectly good bodies!"

Araa Oon ignored them. Most cythraul stumbled and flailed somewhat when they first entered a new body. Araa Oon flexed methodically, first one arm, then the other. He tested the balance of his new limbs and cracked his head to the side. His face remained eerily expressionless.

Cashun's cythraul chuckled, looking over Araa Oon's new form. "Limber, this new vessel of yours, Hunter." He leaned closer. "Would you like to test it more?"

Araa Oon cast Cashun's cythraul a flat look. "I want a tally of how many imps have made it to shore."

Cashun grumbled. "Haven't we earned a break from work?"

"You haven't worked a moment since taking that body,"

Araa Oon clipped. "Gather the imps. I don't want them wandering off. We have scouting for them to do, and we need to learn where we are."

Cashun, to Vesha's surprise, obeyed. "Yes, Hunter." He stepped past Vesha and Odette, pausing to leer at the younger woman.

She looked away and he chuckled.

Vesha glared at him and the thing that used to be Cashun broke eye contact, stepping outside the farmhouse.

Vesha turned back to Araa Oon. "Hunter?"

Araa Oon faced her. "Yes, my lady?"

"You said imps could be sent to scout. They don't seem like the most responsible creatures."

Araa Oon shook his head. "No, but they are obedient. And they can travel faster than the rest of us, especially now that we are on the mainland."

The flick of Araa Oon's eyes was Vesha's only warning before a shape darkened the doorway behind her.

Caa Iss stooped to enter the farmhouse, snorting at the sight of the two murdered humans on the floor. "Ah, Hunter." He glanced over Araa Oon from head to foot in his new form. "Interesting."

Araa Oon touched the apron of his host, feeling the wool. "She will do."

"You might want to go speak to the imps outside," Caa Iss said. "They'll run those pigs to death before they remember what pigs are for."

Araa Oon snapped his chin in agreement, the movement sharp and militaristic. He marched out of the farmhouse, eyes straight ahead. He seemed to forget to move his arms when he walked. His whole upper body stayed rigid.

Araa Oon might be different from the other cythraul, but he was still *wrong*. They all were.

Vesha's head throbbed again, faintly.

"You want to send a scout to Mynadra?" Caa Iss asked.

"Yes," Vesha replied. "More importantly, I want word from Mynadra."

"Don't trust your regent?" Caa Iss cocked his head to the side. Whatever deference or even fear he had shown before was gone now.

Vesha exhaled sharply. "It has been weeks since Mynadra would have last heard from me. I have not been gone so long from the capitol in years."

Caa Iss shrugged. "I would not be worried."

"Well, I am!" Vesha fought to stop her voice from cracking. "The longer it takes for us to..." Vesha grasped for the words to describe her mission, her task, but they slipped away. It was there, driving her on like a whip on the back of a cart horse, yet like a whip on the back, it seemed just out of sight. Vesha shook her head. "We must send a scout. I need to know what's happening and if my son...Daindreth...the boy..." Vesha hissed in annoyance as the thought fled away. "Just make sure a scout is sent!"

Caa Iss looked downright mocking as he stooped into a bow, "As you wish, my lady."

CHAPTER TWENTY-FOUR

Thadred

Thadred had never had to pay much attention to state addresses before. He'd usually stood at the back or wandered through the crowd. But this one he actually wanted to hear.

Nobles milled in the massive ballroom, speaking in low tones and whispering to each other as they waited for Amira and Daindreth. Some had spoken to Thadred, but most gave him a wide berth, eyeing the strange woman at his side.

Sair was not dressed for court. The black dress with a simple fur mantle and the lack of ornamentation marked that she was *not* one of the gentry. But it suited her.

Sair was a thing of nature, of rocks, trees, and mountains. What was the ephemeral beauty of the court compared to the timeless power of a sorceress?

Her dark blonde hair hung loose today, unbound down her back. Thadred had overheard several people say she looked like a savage, but he liked it. Even if he kept fighting the impulse to touch it.

"Can we go to the stables after this?" Rhis tugged on Thadred's sleeve.

"Yes," Thadred promised. "If you're good."

Rhis hopped in front of Thadred. The boy seemed to hop as much as he walked, like a little frog. "I want to ride Lleuad."

Thadred fought to keep his face composed. "You can. If you're good."

"Rhis, quiet now." Sair gave him a stern look. "We're at court."

Rhis looked up at the massive chandelier. "How did that get up there?"

"Pulleys and hooks in the ceiling." Thadred turned his attention to the head of the room, noting several imperial guards taking up posts around it. "The servants lower them to light the candles and then raise them back up."

"Do you think they could raise it if I was on it?" Rhis wondered. "Then I could see everyone."

Thadred shrugged. "I can ask them. But if you fall and go *splat,* don't blame me."

"Thadred!" Sair chided, though she didn't sound truly upset.

Rhis giggled. "I wouldn't go *splat.* You and Mama would catch me."

Thadred raised one eyebrow. "We would?"

"Yes." Rhis grinned and hugged Sair's waist.

"Rhis, you need to calm down." Sair patted his head. "We're at the imperial palace of Mynadra."

Rhis exhaled, then ducked his head shyly.

That was Thadred's only warning.

"Sir Thadred."

Thadred startled at the familiar voice, a little embarrassed. "Melonia!" He coughed. "I mean, Lady Melonia. A pleasure to see you." Thadred fought the urge to step between Sair and the noblewoman.

"Or is it, Lord Thadred? I heard you've been given lands." Melonia was the eldest daughter of Dame Rebeku. She was stern and cold to most the world, but that was in public. In private, with the right company, the carefully trained lady shaped by her mother's discipline became someone else entirely.

"Lord Thadred is correct. Thank you." Thadred had enjoyed many evenings with Melonia and a few with her younger sister, too. For years he had proudly considered himself the chief means of rebellion for young noblewomen at court.

Melonia's smile was polite, but her eyes sparked with interest as they settled on Sair. Her gaze lingered on the sorceress a little too long, then slid down to Rhis, huddled at his mother's side. "I don't believe I've had the pleasure."

"Forgive me." Thadred cleared his throat, recovering himself. "Lady Melonia Rebeku, this is Sairydwen of the Istovari and her son, Rhisiart."

Melonia hesitated just a moment. "One of the Istovari sorceresses?" The noblewoman's voice cracked ever so slightly on *sorceress*.

"Yes, my lady." Thadred straightened just a little. "She is a member of Empress Amira's personal retinue."

Melonia glanced to the dais where more guards were being readied. "Empress Amira? I thought the wedding was being postponed."

"On the contrary," Thadred said. "It was held several weeks past. I officiated it myself."

Melonia barked a laugh, then clasped a hand over her mouth, as if it had come out by accident. "You? Officiated a *wedding?*"

Thadred frowned. "Yes. Why is that strange?"

Melonia cleared her throat. "A surprise, is all." She looked at Sair once again. "You'll have to forgive me. I've never met a sorceress before. Is it true that your kind veil your eyes in public?"

Thadred didn't like the way Melonia said *your kind*.

"We once did, Lady Melonia," Sair responded calmly. "But we didn't wish to frighten the court."

"Wise of you," Melonia agreed. "Our court can be rather suspicious of outsiders as it is."

Thadred's jaw tightened as he caught the implication—Sair was an outsider, as were Rhis and Amira.

"How much things can change in a single generation." Melonia's face held an amiable expression, but she didn't smile. "Emperor Drystan and Empress Vesha hunted sorceresses to the ends of the earth and now…well. It seems the archduke has married one."

"Emperor," Thadred said cheerfully.

"I'm sorry?"

"Emperor Daindreth," he said. "And it is true that the dowager shared her husband's dislike of sorceresses. But as you said, much can happen in a generation." Thadred glanced past

Melonia. "Is your mother well? I heard she has been running the court in the dowager's absence."

"She is," Melonia replied. "She has been frightfully busy with affairs of state these past months, but I believe the emperor shall find his empire in good order."

Months might be a bit of an exaggeration, unless Vesha had left Mynadra as soon as they did.

Was Melonia implying that Dain owed a debt to her family now? If Rebeku had indeed managed the empire, truly managed it, and not just the court...

Problems for later.

Trumpets sounded and heralds announced the arrival of Daindreth Fanduillion, followed by a string of titles and honorifics that had suddenly gotten longer.

Melonia clasped Thadred's hand in both of hers. It was a bold gesture. "Be careful, Lord Thadred."

Thadred couldn't miss the warning in that, but he responded the way she would expect. He cast her a cocky grin. "It is you who should be careful, my lady. Word might get back to your betrothed."

Thadred had heard she'd been recently engaged—very recently. It seemed the announcement had been mere weeks ago.

"You are a memory to me," Melonia said simply. "But a fond one." Her gaze flickered briefly to his lips before she met his eyes again. "Keep careful watch."

Thadred inclined his head, hoping Sair wasn't listening too closely. "What should I watch for?"

The trumpets sounded again, and Melonia leaned over to whisper in his ear. "My mother is not one to be lightly cast aside." Melonia left a brief kiss on his cheek before dropping into a curtsy.

Thadred recovered himself enough to bow in response. He glanced to Sair. The sorceress stood with one eyebrow raised, Rhis staring wide-eyed at her hip.

Thadred cleared his throat. "An old friend."

A smile quirked Sair's mouth. "The emperor is my friend. I don't kiss him like that."

Thadred opened his mouth to defend himself. Sair had no right to judge him. She'd had her own lovers, and the evidence now stood quietly, staring at Thadred and glancing to where Melonia had disappeared back into the crowd.

"Friends, citizens, esteemed members, and guests of the court." Dain's voice rose clear and crisp over the ballroom.

Thadred bit back what he had been about to say and did his best to look calm beside Sair. Had he warned her about this? He couldn't remember. He'd never had to warn a woman about his well-earned reputation. It had always proceeded him.

"I am glad to have returned and I am glad to find you all here." Daindreth looked like an emperor as he spoke. That was good.

Amira stood a little behind him with her hands clasped in front of her. The pose might have been demure if not for her squared shoulders and raised chin. She looked ready for battle.

Good. A court used to Vesha would expect a strong empress.

Westfall watched the crowd a little to the side of the emperor, dressed in the full imperial regalia. His eye caught Thadred's and Thadred nodded once.

No trouble here. At least not yet.

"I know my absence was sudden and unexplained. I confess I do not know what stories were told of my absence. But I did meet with my mother, the dowager empress, in the north."

That much was true.

"The regency of Dowager Empress Vesha is ended," Daindreth said.

A stir went about the room at that. The courtiers would not object out loud, not during an imperial address. No, here they were too polite for that.

Thadred watched their reactions carefully. Most looked surprised, but it was hard to read them beyond that. He wished he could see Rebeku, but he hadn't seen her since she had greeted them on their arrival. Was her absence itself a slight?

"Much has happened these past months and I know there are many questions." Daindreth addressed the entire room, looking every bit the rightful emperor.

Cromwell and Cyne had helped Dain craft this speech. They needed to be in control without giving away too much. They needed to tell the truth while holding back the complicated parts that would be controversial or misinterpreted.

They all would have preferred to wait until they understood more about the court's situation. Just how much had Vesha told the court? What version of the truth? Who here might still be loyal to her?

But they needed to begin their own narrative as soon as possible. They needed their own version of the truth to begin circulating.

Legitimacy, strength, and confidence. That was what they needed right now.

"The time for answers will come. I appreciate those who have tended the court and our empire in my absence." Dain reached for Amira's hand and led her forward to stand at his side. "My wife and I are grateful."

The whole room stirred at that, shifting with barely contained gasps of surprise. No one had expected an imperial wedding to be done in private. Had the archduke—the emperor—really eloped?

"Our empire is facing crises from all corners," Daindreth continued. "I have received word of many recent misfortunes, but I am sure there are more."

Thadred noticed several courtiers grimace at that. There were probably a good many calamities Dain hadn't yet heard of.

"I have returned with a new bride and a new alliance." Dain gestured to his other side and Cyne stepped forward.

From their reactions, no one knew who the stately woman was. Cyne carried herself proud and tall, like her daughter. But where Amira stood like a warrior, Cyne stood like a queen. She reminded Thadred a little of Vesha.

"Lady Cyne, my mother-in-law, has come as a pledge of loyalty from the Istovari."

The courtiers nearest the dais visibly drew back. Several choked gasps sounded around the room.

Thadred had expected that, but it still made him grimace. There was too much fear and superstition around the sorceress clan. They'd known this, but it was still something that would have to be dealt with.

Just what story had Vesha told? They were fairly confident she hadn't spread any irreparable rumors, just because she wanted to keep her deal to let Caa Iss rule through Dain.

If possible, Dain wanted to avoid discrediting his mother. He seemed to think Vesha could be forced to surrender, but he was the only one who thought that. Perhaps he was reluctant to declare open warfare on his one remaining parent.

"I shall be accepting meetings in the coming days to answer your questions and accept your fealty." Dain said it calmly, as if it was a given that everyone here would give him fealty. "You have all served my family with loyalty and honor in the past."

That was a bit too generous in Thadred's estimation. To his left, he spotted Duke Peppin, a southerner who had some involvement in a revolt not five years ago. There were others present who'd had their hands in various plots and schemes. But such was court. Everyone pretended that the imperial crown was indomitable and somehow that made it so.

"I trust that we shall lead Erymaya into an age of prosperity and abundance even greater than we have seen." Dain smiled in that courtly way of his. It earned him a few hesitant claps.

"There is much work to be done in the coming days, months, and years. I have inherited a great legacy. My father, Emperor Drystan, expanded this empire as no ruler has done before. He united the continent beneath a single banner and ensured peace for years."

Sair stiffened at the mention of Drystan, but most the court nodded in solemn agreement.

"My mother, Empress Vesha, guided the empire after his death. She *kept* us united, and led us into prosperity, all while preparing me to one day succeed her."

That was true, after a fashion. Vesha had helpfully spread rumors she would be stepping down after Dain's wedding. People were now willing to believe it.

"I know I am heir to a great legacy, but also great expectations. While I know that to many of you, I am untried. I am confident I shall be a steward worthy of this empire." Dain inclined his head, a gesture of humility. "I am honored by the burden of this mantle and take it upon myself with all solemnity. May Demred grant me strength and Eponine her favor."

Thadred hadn't expected that last part. Besides his own family patron, Dain was invoking Eponine, the patron goddess of the Istovari. He was implying that Amira had brought more than just sorceresses and spellbooks into her marriage.

The young emperor and his wife bowed to signal the end of the speech. There were dutiful cheers and cries of fealty.

It was hard to know just how sincere those cries were. Even after a lifetime at court, Thadred often found it hard to tell.

"Will they follow him?" Sair asked quietly, watching as Dain and Amira disappeared back the way they had come.

Thadred smiled as another noble made eye contact. "They have to."

Sair cast him a sideways glance. "Do they?"

"He has the strongest claim to the throne."

"They followed Vesha," Sair reminded him.

Thadred had no retort to that, but Daindreth *did* have the strongest claim to the throne. No one could dispute that. Daindreth was the last person to bear the Fanduillion name. Fanduillion men tended to be great warriors, but great warriors rarely lived long.

There were of course distant relatives in surrounding vassal states. Several had rebelled after Drystan's death. One fourth cousin had tried to assert his claim to the throne against Vesha and then nine-year-old Dain.

That fourth cousin was dead now, along with all three of his sons.

"Rhis?" Sair looked all around her frantically. "Where did he go?"

Alarm spiked through Thadred, then he spotted a small figure against the wall—right by the lever for the chandelier. "There!" Thadred leapt past Sair, shuffling through the crowd. "Pardon me." He shoved past a middle-aged woman he didn't recognize. "Forgive me, madam."

Thadred reached the far wall. "Rhis! Don't touch that." Thadred scooped the boy up without thinking. He checked the ropes and the knots, relieved to see them still intact. "Do you want that thing to drop on the heads of the whole court?"

Rhis wiggled in Thadred's arms. "I want to see how it works."

"You can't just play with things like that. People could get hurt." Thadred shook his head, exasperated. Had he ever been so much trouble?

"Sir Thadred?"

Thadred remembered to smile as he turned around, Rhis balanced on his side. "Lady Leena," he greeted the newcomer. "A pleasure to see you again. I trust your uncle is well?" He didn't bother to correct her on the title.

Leena bobbed a curtsy, curls bouncing around her face as she did. She'd always been a playful thing, bouncing and flouncing here and there. As much a dream as a woman. She always seemed so innocent and naïve. Few would guess she'd trysted with him all through last winter. But she was cunning as a polecat when she truly wanted something. Luckily, the things she wanted were usually harmless.

The expression on her face now gave Thadred pause. "My uncle is well." She looked to Rhis. "Is he…yours?"

"Yes." Thadred took a moment too long to realize Leena had been asking if Rhis was *his*, not if he was responsible for the boy. "No! I mean, no, he is my friend's son."

No one at court would be surprised if Thadred had a bastard of his own. Thadred himself half expected one to emerge every year. But Rhis wasn't his—not in that sense.

Rhis rested his elbow comfortably on Thadred's shoulder, like he belonged there and was daring Leena to disagree. Damned kid.

"Oh." Leena cleared her throat. "Forgive me."

"What's wrong?" Thadred stepped closer, lowering his voice.

Leena shot a glance over Thadred's shoulder. "I don't wish to see any harm come to you, Sir Thadred. But nor do I wish to cause trouble."

"Leena." Thadred rested a hand on her shoulder, the one not hanging onto Rhis. "What is it?"

Leena smiled then, her usual smile. "Are the sorceresses truly safe?"

"To us? Yes. Amira is loyal to the emperor. Maybe even more than I am, if that's possible. The others will follow her lead."

"I see." Leena clenched a fan in her hands, twisting it around.

"Is there something else?"

Rhis twisted around to see over Thadred's shoulder, shifting his weight and making Thadred grunt with the effort of holding onto him.

"Stop squirming, boy."

"Regime changes are dangerous things, Sir Thadred. Especially for those closest to the rulers." Leena leaned forward, close enough to whisper in Thadred's ear. "But you have friends in this court. If you need us, you have only to ask."

With that, Leena stepped back and dropped into a curtsy. She was gone before Sair caught up with them.

Thadred considered Leena's words and Melonia's. He was on good terms with all his former lovers, as far as he knew. He was still a little surprised that they would be this protective. Could he trust them?

"Another friend of yours?" It was maddening how calm Sair could be, sometimes. Her face showed nothing but mild curiosity.

"Yes," Thadred said. "An old friend. Former friend." He swallowed.

Thadred had always thought he didn't care what people thought of him. But he had to admit now that he cared what Sair thought of him.

He could be responsible. He could. He wanted Sair to know that. He didn't see her as just another diversion.

Sair smiled. "Thank you for catching Rhis." She turned a stern look to her son. "You know better."

Rhis shrugged. He held onto Thadred's shoulder, clinging like a squirrel to a branch.

"Alright, down." Thadred peeled the boy off, setting him on the ground. "We have work to do. But first, I'm getting you a leash."

"You wouldn't!" Rhis's eyes went wide.

"You act like a puppy, I will treat you like one." Thadred caught one of Rhis's hands and Sair took the other.

He realized how it looked. Half the court was still in that ballroom. All of them would see Thadred wrangling the boy and make their assumptions. He'd walked straight into that rumor trap.

Everyone would think he'd had an affair with an Istovari sorceress and had just now claimed the resulting son.

As much as Thadred wanted to rest after their journey here, there was still work to do before tonight. He needed to make sure that all the proper appointments and reports were set for tomorrow.

He'd once told Amira that politics was one great game. In

the past, he'd played it as an amusement, almost ironically. Then he had been the bastard cousin of the archduke and a crippled knight. Now he was one of the emperor's most trusted advisors and an envoy to the Istovari—their strongest allies at the moment.

Thadred could no longer play for fun. The lives of his friends and family were at stake. He had to start playing to win.

Politics was a web of half-truths, secrets, threats, bargains, bribes, and compromises, all delicately balanced on a knife's edge. Agreements made within this palace, both spoken and unspoken, could change the course of history for centuries.

Thadred had returned from the savage wilderness of the Cursewood to a different kind of battlefield. But what was a warrior without a war to fight?

Thadred had been born for this as much as Daindreth. He'd trained for this as much as Amira. This empire was theirs by rights and they belonged here.

All three of them had suffered, bled, and almost died for the sake of this empire. Shunted aside, manipulated, controlled, abused...they had gone through all of that. The gods owed them this.

Even if they would have to fight for their inheritance, they were meant to have it. As Thadred walked out of the ballroom with Sair, Rhis held between them, it felt good to be home.

CHAPTER TWENTY-FIVE

Vesha

Vesha had headaches most days now. She'd come to accept it as yet another price for power.

Their strange fleet of fishing sloops, carracks, and argosies still sat offshore, stuck in the sand bar. Many of the ships were probably now stuck for good, but their cythraul crews didn't care.

They'd set up a base of sorts at the farm. The tilled garden and pasture beside the house now served as a gathering place for the cythraul.

Vesha had a pavilion set up with couches and a rug. The cythraul had procured wine and cheese for her, too, though she didn't ask from where.

Hundreds of cythraul had made the journey on the ships with countless more of the creatures still in incorporeal form. A swarm of them had stormed onto the mainland after getting permission.

Vesha and Caa Iss now waited as more and more cythraul returned by the day as they found hosts.

A ragtag group of fighters stood in ranks on the tilled earth. There were men, women, and youths of all ages. There were few similarities between them. Some had been blacksmiths, goodwives, prostitutes, beggars, sailors, soldiers, clerks, or just nobodies. There were even a few pigs—imps were able to inhabit pigs, but not other animals. Vesha didn't know how she knew that, but she did.

Yet they all stood in ranks, going through drills while Araa Oon paced back and forth in front of them. He still inhabited the farmwife, dressed in loose trousers now with her hair pulled back into a severe bun.

Caa Iss was usually more than happy to discuss his brethren and sistren and their exploits. When it came to Araa Oon, he would only say that the demon had served Moreyne well and that there was no finer general among the cythraul.

"When are you taking a vessel, Caa Iss?" Vesha asked, sipping her wine. Wine was one of the few things that dulled her headaches. The eye of Moreyne throbbed in her skull. The flesh around it was red and sore. Vesha wondered if she'd lose the eye eventually. She had no hope of regaining her old one. That thought should have concerned her, but she hardly cared anymore.

"I can't," Caa Iss answered. "Not just yet."

Vesha cocked her gaze in his direction. "No?"

"My bargain with the Istovari."

Vesha blinked at him. The edges of her vision were fuzzy, even the usually sharp vision of the god-eye. How much had she drunk? "The Istovari?"

"My first contract. The one that brought me into this world."

It took Vesha a moment, but she realized he meant the one that had bound him to her husband's bloodline. She downed what remained in her cup. It wasn't the best wine and burned her throat. "That contract was broken. You were cast out."

"Yes," Caa Iss answered slowly. "That is the problem."

"What do you mean?"

"The Istovari never fully completed their end, either. As you'll recall, their sacrifice survived." That was why Caa Iss had never been able to possess Daindreth at will the way most cythraul could with their hosts. "When I was forced out of Daindreth, that broke the bargain on my end, as well. But I still agreed to it, and it binds me. I cannot take back Daindreth without another bargain, but nor can I take another host."

Odette refilled Vesha's wine cup without needing to be asked.

Vesha nodded to the girl, signaling that she was to keep the wine coming. Looking back to Caa Iss, she took another sip. "What a tragedy to be you."

Caa Iss bristled his massive, broken wings. "What do you mean?"

Vesha smiled over the rim of her goblet. "Your brothers and sisters are even now becoming lords of this land, but you," she gestured to his massive, insubstantial bulk, "are stuck being my familiar. Forever, it seems."

Caa Iss growled. "I am doing the will of my mother."

"With none of the rewards," Vesha answered simply. "You can't feel the grass, the sunlight, or the wind." There was no wind in the Dread Marches, only gusts of heat from the lava flows. "You couldn't taste this wine." Vesha tapped the side of her cup even though Caa Iss wasn't missing much on that account. "Are you jealous of your brothers and sisters?"

Caa Iss's lip curled, revealing a jaw stuffed with too many teeth. Vesha was reminded of how hideous his true form was.

"Did you see the *revels* on the beach last night?" Vesha asked. At least two hundred of the creatures had participated—those not impressed into guard duty by Araa Oon.

"Everyone saw it," Caa Iss snapped back. "Everyone heard it, too."

"You must have been jealous, surely. You do enjoy that *human* experience, don't you?" Vesha stared at Caa Iss pointedly. "I know my son was celibate as a monk. That means it's been, what? Almost twenty years now? How desperate you must be for another lay."

Caa Iss snarled. He swooped down, mutilated snout so close she could have bitten him. His face twisted in fury, then relaxed. A wicked grin split his mouth and he showed her his fangs. Notably, he stared at her left eye, her human one, when he spoke. "I admit I can't stop thinking about my last one. You were *such* a good lay."

Vesha's heart raced, and she fought to stay still, fought not to move.

For just a moment, she saw Caa Iss's gaze burning out of Drystan's face. She still remembered that moment, hadn't been able to forget it.

Vesha had been a young empress. She could have remarried or taken lovers as she pleased. Who would have stopped her? But she hadn't.

People thought she had remained faithful to Drystan out of love for his memory and it had been true for many years. But more recently, every time she had entertained the idea of taking another lover, she had seen that moment.

Caa Iss leered down at her. He knew. He knew she still saw him in her nightmares. He knew he had tainted the memory of the only man she had ever loved. And worse, he knew that she needed his help now.

It was cruel. Twisted. And exactly the sort of irony that delighted cythraul.

"Your Majesty." The steady voice of Araa Oon interrupted them.

Vesha turned, grateful for a distraction. "Yes?"

Caa Iss withdrew, stepping back from Vesha.

"Forgive me if I am intruding." Araa Oon was one of the few cythraul who seemed to have a sense of propriety. "Criin Moor has returned."

"Already?" Caa Is straightened.

Araa Oon nodded brusquely. The woman's body had already been thin, but since the cythraul had taken over, the lines of the jaw had become sharper, the face gaunter. It had become a face that gave away nothing but steely resolve.

"Where—?"

A shape stumbled under the canopy. Vesha wasn't sure how cythraul could stumble when they lacked corporeal form, but the imp did.

"Forgive me for bearing bad news, my lady," Criin Moor groveled. "I know you shall not be pleased. But I am only the messenger." Criin Moor bobbed their head in rapid succession, paws grasping at the air. "Yes, only the scout. I can't help what I see. I can only be truthful, yes?"

"Enough." Araa Oon booted the creature. Oddly, Araa Oon's kick landed and sent the imp sideways.

Vesha had noticed before that cythraul seemed able to affect each other whether they had bodies or not. Interesting.

"Report," Araa Oon ordered.

"The archduke has returned to Mynadra, as you feared."

Vesha braced herself, already sure she knew what words would come next.

"He has declared himself rightful emperor and has begun demanding fealty from the nobles."

Vesha remained still, but her mind raced. As best the empire knew, she had sailed into the north never to be seen again. Why wouldn't they rally to Daindreth? What would stop them?

No one wanted a power struggle for the throne, not really. Wars of succession were bloody, messy things and rarely had any true winner.

Declaring for the legitimate son of the last emperor and empress was the logical thing to do.

Cursing, Vesha clenched her wine goblet. Her chest bubbled with heat. How dare that boy? How *dare* he?

Her children should know by now that—

Vesha's brow wrinkled at that thought. Children? She had only one child. One.

And he *was* the rightful heir under the law. What had she expected?

Criin Moor whimpered at Vesha's feet, sniffling and pressing themselves against the ground as they had done when facing Moreyne. "There is more, my lady. Forgive me. I hate to bring you bad news. Forgive me."

"Continue," Vesha ordered, barely recognizing her own voice.

"The sorceress has begun searching your things. She has found your vault of books. I heard before I left that she plans to have your shrines to Moreyne torn down."

"Who?" Vesha finished off what remained of her wine and

passed it to Odette. "What sorceress?"

"Daindreth's sorceress. His wife."

"Wife?" Vesha's drunken mind reeled.

"Yes," Criin Moor muttered. "The Istovari Kadra'han."

Amira Brindonu. Daindreth had married that girl? Vesha hadn't thought he would go through with it. Amira had been an unpopular choice with the court. Not to mention her stepmother's family would probably cause problems for years over this.

But no. Vesha realized she should have known better. Daindreth was his father's son.

Caa Iss looked ready to speak, but Vesha interrupted him.

"So, Amira Brindonu has taken my crown and my empire." Vesha wasn't as angry as she had expected.

"She has brought sorceresses with her, my lady. Her mother and several others." Criin Moor flinched as if expecting a blow.

"Of course, she did." Vesha exhaled a long breath. She looked toward the moon—Eponine. Perhaps Llyr was not the only one determined to sabotage their efforts.

"But some of your servants remain loyal, yes. Some still stand by and await your return."

Vesha looked back to the imp. "Who? And how do you know?"

Criin Moor licked their lips again, paws still kneading on the ground. "I overheard whispers in the palace. Some do not trust the Istovari girl. Many think she has ensorcelled your son and that is why he loves her."

"I see."

"Many wonder if perhaps the Istovari girl had you murdered."

Vesha laughed. She had no doubt the Istovari girl would have preferred that.

"The archduke's coronation is set for the end of the month," Criin Moor continued. "His wife is to be crowned empress with him."

"Does he control the army?" Araa Oon demanded. "How many troops are under his command?"

"I don't know," Criin Moor replied. "He had guards. A lot of them."

"Were there Kadra'han?" Araa Oon demanded.

"Only two," Criin Moor replied. "The Istovari girl and the knight."

Vesha swallowed another gulp of wine. So Daindreth still had both his Kadra'han.

Vesha's own Kadra'han were now possessed by cythraul. She tried not to remember their names, tried not to recognize their faces. She'd ordered Araa Oon to find assignments for them away from her, especially the one that now inhabited Cashun.

Araa Oon, unlike Caa Iss, hadn't taunted her about it. Araa Oon had simply nodded and said it would be done.

Vesha looked down into her wine goblet, thoughts lumbering through her head like sailors their first day back on land. "So Daindreth seeks to be emperor."

"Yes, Your Majesty," Criin Moor confirmed.

"Amira…she brought her clanswomen with her?"

"Yes," Criin Moor chirped, head bobbing again. "I was able to learn she brought her mother and another sorceress as well as her sister."

Vesha blinked several times before that made sense. "Princess Fonra? She is no sorceress."

"No," Criin Moor mumbled, fidgeting awkwardly. "But she is Amira's lady-in-waiting."

Vesha considered it for a long moment. "Hylendale must be allied with Daindreth, then." She cursed inwardly. "This changes nothing. As soon as my roving children find bodies and rejoin us, we march inland." Though where they were going, Vesha wasn't entirely sure. Toward Mynadra, but not Mynadra. Near it, but…

Araa Oon and Caa Iss shared a look. It was brief, but just

237

long enough that Vesha caught it.

"What?" she pressed, glaring between the two of them.

Araa Oon looked pointedly to Caa Iss, standing at attention like a good little soldier.

"Nothing," Caa Iss answered. "I'm sure it's nothing."

CHAPTER TWENTY-SIX

Amira

A mira had felt as if something was watching her all yesterday. She'd never quite been able to make it out, but again and again, she'd felt a presence hovering at the edge of her vision.

After three days juggling the rush of the court, Amira thought it might just be lack of sleep. Neither Daindreth or anyone else could sense it. Whatever it was, the feeling was gone today and they had tangible work to do.

Workers had already finished removing and dismantling all the known shrines to Moreyne in the palace. There had been some questions, but she'd given orders for Vesha's koi ponds to be restored to their original design. It should make the structure useless to witches while also taking less time than outright destroying them. Those changes should be done within the week.

Fonra had found Vesha's cache of personal books in a cleverly concealed compartment in the empress's old rooms. It seemed the gilt work on the mantle was a few shades too light and that had raised the princess's suspicions. Inside were stacks of old letters, reports, and a motley collection of spiritual treatises, spellbooks, and grimoires.

Amira and Cyne, along with several of the other Istovari women with light magic had been rifling through Vesha's book cache for the better part of the morning.

They had started by looking for anything similar to the spells outlined in the spellbook of Amira's grandmother. The older sorceress had written out what she remembered in general terms, but so far, Amira had seen nothing even close in Vesha's cache.

Cyne had noticed that several of the books had come from the Akiran Library, all attributed to the same scribe. Sair and Thadred had been sent on an errand this morning to find what

239

they could about this Scribe Egrid. It was possible he knew something about Vesha, but it was also possible he just happened to specialize in the kind of texts that had interested Vesha. There was only one way to find out.

Daindreth had been caught up in meetings and reports. Amira was also supposed to have meetings with ministers and nobles, but she had Cromwell clear her morning schedule so she could spend that time raiding Vesha's cache.

Amira had one of the spell books open on the table before her and a book, also of Nihai origins, that seemed to be speaking of the rules of balance. The book was written in Erymayan, but the script was in an odd style that took time to decipher.

This book was a short work on the ideas of balance titled *A Treatise on Equilibriums*. Amira wasn't sure why this book was with Vesha's witchcraft collection, but Vesha rarely seemed to do anything without a reason. It was worth checking.

When anything is pulled too far in one direction, an opposing opposite reaction may be expected. Just as pulling back a pendulum leads to a forward swing, so do moral reforms lead to moral oppression which leads to moral liberations back to moral reforms and so on. In the same way, we see anything outside the natural order of balance will create a backlash.

Amira rested her cheek in her hand. The concept was fair enough.

Great empires must also experience great downfalls, though these downfalls can be mitigated or possibly prevented should their leaders understand that equilibrium must be honored.

Amira came to the end of that page, then stopped at the heading of the next section. She took a slow breath, reading the heading again—*On the Principle of Sacrifice.*

Amira braced herself. She had a feeling she wouldn't like what she was about to read.

One common substitution for equilibrium is sacrifice in its many forms. Many will think of sacrifice as a ritual to appease the gods, but this is a misunderstanding. In accordance with the God Pact of the Second Millennium, the gods surrendered all claim to the mortal world.

Amira flipped to the cover of the book. The front listed the name of three or four monks, but only as translators. Translators from what language? She looked at the first page, but it was just the same information repeated. There was no original author or any indication of the original source.

She skimmed down the page, then slowed as a new passage caught her interest.

Today, the gods may only interact with our world to the degree they are given permission to do so. This permission must come from a mortal authority. We have seen the greatest influence from gods granted by kings and priests.

This was perfectly illustrated when King Cashal of Galindra began publicly venerating the goddess Ekin in place of Anu. Famine ended and his people thrived, but when they next went to war against the southern raiders, they were met with slaughter.

For this reason, I warn strongly against the wholesale adherence to a new god. Not having a patron god at all is far worse, however, as it will invite a struggle over the region as different gods vie for control.

Amira glanced across the study. Fonra and a few of her maids occupied the seats beneath the windows. They were hard at work stitching Amira's coronation gown. Fonra had taken over the designing and creation of the dress. It was black and had plenty of brocade. Beyond that, Amira trusted her sister to handle it.

As soon as Amira and Daindreth had entered Lashera, the storms had stopped. The storms Caa Iss claimed were Moreyne's revenge. But no, that wasn't quite true. The storms had stopped after Amira and Daindreth were welcomed into the palace…after King Hyle had given his allegiance.

Amira looked back to the book. She skimmed down several anecdotes and a few pages of rambling until another passage caught her attention.

While it is true I cannot explain why prayers so often seem to go unanswered or ignored, I would urge you not to grow weary. It is possible that you have petitioned a deity when another deity's influence is too strong in that region. This is why I recommend making supplications to all gods to some degree as they are more likely to allow another god's aid should you need petition them in an area they hold sway.

Amira had never heard of gods being limited to regions before. There were areas where some gods were venerated more than others, but she'd never thought that would make their power greater.

Vesha's bargain had been with the cythraul. That was how Amira had always thought of it.

As Cyne had explained it, the Istovari had been able to curse Drystan because of what he had done to their families. He took their families from them, so they were able to take his bloodline from him.

Vesha had been able to give the cythraul jurisdiction over the land because she ruled it.

Did that mean that throwing the cythraul out of the empire would be as simple as telling them to leave?

What about Demred? He had been the god of the Fanduillion bloodline—the god of retribution and dominion. Before Vesha's reign, he'd been venerated as the patron of the empire. Publicly, he still was. Wouldn't he be stopping the extermination of his descendants if he could?

"Sister." Fonra stood, setting aside her needlework. "I believe it's time for us to go."

"Hmm?" Amira looked up from the treatise in her lap. "So soon?"

"Yes. Dame Rebeku will be expecting us."

Amira nodded. She had no desire to spend time with Dame Rebeku, but she was empress now. She had to spend time with people she didn't like. Amira closed the small book and returned it to the pile.

Fonra and the other ladies adjusted her dress and changed the combs in her hair. Like squires preparing a knight for battle, they put a circlet about her brow and a heavy collar of emeralds around her neck. Fonra had selected cuffs of gold for Amira's wrists and a golden sash to complete the look.

"There you are," Fonra said, looking Amira head to foot. "Perfect."

Amira was sure that every piece had been chosen to make a statement. "Thank you, Fonra."

"Of course." Fonra smiled back at her.

Never had Amira relied on Fonra for anything, but Fonra seemed to prefer this. Perhaps she enjoyed being able to finally play a role that suited her. A vital role where she excelled.

"Let's go, then." Amira nodded to her mother and Sair. "I will return after. Send word if you need me before then."

"I am sure we can last a couple hours," Cyne assured her. "Off you go, daughter. Enjoy yourself."

Amira didn't think her mother understood the point of this luncheon. It certainly wasn't enjoyment.

Fonra led the way from the room, alerting the guards in the hall before they stepped out. Fonra wore white as she usually did with emeralds as well, though much more understated settings. A silver circlet rested on her head and Amira was sure she'd put just as much care into choosing her own dress.

The guards fell into rank and file around them in the hall, stepping up to ring their empress and the princess. Amira recognized a few of them as being from among Westfall's men. That was good. She didn't yet feel comfortable letting anyone else guard her.

Odd that she now felt safe with Westfall's troops, but she did. He was loyal to Daindreth and wouldn't move against her for that reason. At least not directly.

Fonra hooked her arm through Amira's, and they walked as if they were girls again. "My uncle will be joining us," Fonra said.

"Your uncle?"

"Baron Boless," Fonra replied. "He was added this morning. My cousin, too. You remember Elton?"

Amira thought carefully for a long moment. "Shaggy-haired fellow with the mastiff?"

"He's cut his hair and the mastiff is no longer with us, but yes," Fonra answered.

Amira hid a grimace. She had met Elton Boless before, but only briefly. He hadn't known who she was then. Not that he would have cared. Amira had been nothing but the king's bastard after his marriage to Cyne had been annulled.

They came to Rebeku's apartments much too soon. Dame Rebeku's palace lodgings were sumptuous as any court lady could wish for. Chandeliers dangled from the ceilings and white columns supported the receiving room.

Rebeku had been the most powerful woman at court—next to Vesha—for over twenty years. She'd schemed to get one of her own daughters married to Daindreth, but Vesha had rejected it out of hand. Whispers at court said that it was because the late Emperor Drystan had lost his virginity to Rebeku, long before he had married Vesha. A match between her daughters and Drystan's son would have been borderline incestuous.

Rebeku met them herself in the foyer. She must have been waiting for their entry for some minutes. Her wimple was held back with her usual headband of sapphires, though today they were accented with diamonds.

She clasped her hands before her, head canted slightly to show respect. At sight of Amira, she dropped into a curtsy.

"Lady Amira," Rebeku said, "soon to be empress. Welcome. I am so glad you could join us."

"Forgive me, your ladyship but it is empress now." Fonra spoke with just a hint of a titter. "Empress Amira."

Something flashed across Rebeku's face at the correction, but it was gone a moment later. Perhaps the older woman was not used to being corrected, but Fonra outranked her and was right. Amira *was* empress, she just hadn't been crowned yet. There was nothing Rebeku could do without breaking protocol herself.

Rebeku smiled brightly, showing a mouthful of teeth. "Forgive me, Your Majesty. Come, I am having my attendants pour the wine now."

Amira uttered mindless pleasantries back, words so common she could speak them in her sleep. "How are your daughters? I hope you are in good health. What did you think of the rain yesterday?" and so on.

Rebeku's quarters were on the ground level with a magnificent dining room overlooking the palace gardens. It was not the imperial banquet hall, but it was still large enough to seat at least a dozen nobles comfortably. Servants in livery uniforms bustled about.

Amira had seen enough ordinary villages and farms to know that this dining chamber was the size of most houses. She'd seen entire Hylendale families huddled in cottages no bigger than this.

Wealth. Power. Opulence.

No wonder Caa Iss had wanted to rule this empire. No wonder men and women schemed to rise through its ranks.

Two men spoke at the far end of the dining chamber, beside the windows. Both had glasses of sherry and their clothes were the same dark blue velvet, but that was where the similarities ended.

One was a portly man with a chest that seemed ready to pop out his coat. The other was a young man with dark hair who held scant similarity to the boy Amira had met back in Lashera.

"Baron Boless and his son, the Honorable Elton Boless." Dame Rebeku introduced them with a flourish of her hand.

The two men bowed to Amira and she inclined her head. She wasn't required to curtsy, being empress. She no longer had to curtsy to anyone except her husband and perhaps foreign rulers.

Amira held out her hand and Baron Boless kissed her knuckles. "Your Grace," he said.

"Your lordship," Amira replied easily.

Elton did the same. "Empress Amira," the younger man said. It was hard to know if that sneer in his tone was real or Amira's imagination.

Next, Boless kissed Fonra's hand. "You are even lovelier than when I last saw you, niece."

"Thank you, uncle," Fonra smiled. She kept her head canted down in the demure way young women were supposed to. She'd perfected the look to be just a little coy.

Amira had only ever looked like a growling dog when she'd tried it.

"Princess Fonra." Elton clasped both Fonra's hands in his. "What a pleasure to see you again. I am sad that it is not your coronation we will be witnessing."

Amira's eyes narrowed on the nobleman. Was he saying he wished Amira wasn't empress? Everyone knew the Bolesses felt that way, but for them to say it out loud in front of her was brazen indeed.

Baron Boless shot his son a look.

Fonra tittered, slipping into the role of the insipid debutante. "You tease me, Elton," she said, dropping his title. "My sister is a far better match for his majesty, I assure you." Fonra dropped her voice, leaning toward him as if to share a secret. "Though I was quite taken with his majesty, I knew from the moment I first saw them together that they were perfect."

"Did you, now?" Elton asked, slipping easily into a cordial, perhaps even indulgent tone.

"Indeed!"

That was a lie. The first time Fonra had seen Amira and Daindreth together, he had confronted her in a ballroom over her attempted assassination.

Still, Fonra spun the tale perfectly.

"Well, I suppose you are a romantic," Elton said. "You must get that from our grandmother."

Fonra rested a hand on Elton's shoulder, her doe eyes looking for all the world as empty and hollow as a blower's glass. "How is Grandmama? I haven't seen her since we visited for Midwinter."

Elton and Fonra slipped into conversation as Amira faced

Baron Boless.

"A pleasure to formally meet you," Amira said. "I have heard so much about you."

"Oh, Your Grace, you must not judge dear Wilman on the words of vicious gossips," Dame Rebeku interjected, patting Baron Boless's shoulder.

"The rumors are most likely true, I fear," Baron Boless replied. "I am indeed quite fond of a good sherry, appreciate a fine hunting dog, and am a horrible chess player."

Amira smiled. "Then we shall have to play chess. I would appreciate someone of my own skill."

Baron Boless chuckled amiably. "Indeed."

According to Thadred, this man had worked himself up into a rage over her betrothal to Daindreth. Nonetheless, he was excellent at trading pleasantries now. It was a reminder that people could put on friendly faces when they wanted to.

"How is His Majesty today?" Baron Boless asked, glancing over Amira's shoulder as he asked it.

"My husband is well," Amira answered, trying not to let her discomfort show at the question. She was loathe to give away anything about Daindreth.

"I heard there was a disturbance in the gardens last night. Is everything well?"

Amira had heard of no such disturbance. He was probably making it up. "We have worked late these past nights, but nothing a little rest can't fix," Amira answered easily.

"Hmm," Boless replied.

Amira realized she had just confirmed that she and Daindreth spent their nights together. That was hardly surprising, being newly married, but they were an imperial couple.

"His Majesty is quite fond of you," Baron Boless said. "You must feel like a fortunate woman indeed."

"I cannot begin to tell you, Baron Boless." What was it that this man was trying to find out?

"To fall in love so quickly, one might think you had put a spell on him."

Amira fought to maintain her composure. From the corner of her eye, she noticed both Fonra and Dame Rebeku had gone silent, watching. "Many people do think as much. But that is not how magic works, your lordship. I cannot bind a man's will any more than you can."

Baron Boless raised his eyebrows and he shifted away from her ever so slightly. "You admit to being a sorceress, then?"

It was Amira's turn to raise her eyebrows. "Admit? I have made no secret of it. Nor has my mother or my Istovari companions. If anyone had a different impression, it is no fault of mine."

Fonra was there a moment later. "Don't frighten my uncle, sister," she chided, a teasing lilt to her voice. "He isn't used to sorceresses where he comes from."

Amira was grateful for the intervention, but tension hung in the air. There was a threat of something imminent, something unspoken yet undeniably present.

They thought she had bewitched Daindreth. They thought she had used magic to ensnare him. There had been whispers to this effect when she had last been in Mynadra, but it seemed the rumors had only grown.

In the same way, the Istovari had been sure Amira's loyalty to Daindreth was because of her curse and nothing else. They hadn't known Amira broke her curse and freed herself.

"Indeed," Baron Boless agreed, playing along with Fonra. "Forgive me, I meant no insult."

Amira was sure he had, but she smiled and let the slight pass. "Of course."

"Please, let us sit, Your Grace," Dame Rebeku urged. "An old woman's bones aren't used to standing for this long."

Amira allowed herself to be seated with Fonra on her left and Baron Boless on her right. It occurred to her that she should have brought Thadred with her today, but he was in the city on another errand.

It was now Amira and Fonra versus Baron Boless, Dame Rebeku, and Elton. She didn't like being outnumbered, even if she was only outnumbered by one.

Amira and the others exchanged pleasantries that flitted between them as if they were part of a script. Dame Rebeku shared her thoughts on the latest shipment of flowers that had been brought in for the coronation. It seemed the traditional roses were out of season and lilies were being made to suffice.

Servants came to pour them tea and serve finger cakes and powdered candies. Their white uniforms and sleight movements reminded Amira of ghosts.

"How fares my sister?" Baron Boless asked, glancing to Fonra. "She must be most grieved to see you go."

Fonra smiled demurely in that practiced way. It made her look innocent and guileless. "She was sad, uncle. But she plans to visit court soon and I shall see her then. Perhaps even for the coronation."

Baron Boless nodded. "I suppose she was expecting to be parted with you much sooner."

Amira watched Boless from the corner of her eye. She held her spoon daintily, careful not to scrape the ceramic bowl as she scooped up a bite. How many times did the man plan to bring up that this should have been Fonra's coronation?

"Yes! We were blessed to spend many extra months together. I was most grateful." Fonra took a bite of her soup. "Oh Dame Rebeku, this is exquisite."

"Is it not?" the dame replied. "My cook is the best to be found in this entire city. Brophy is simply a master of his craft."

"That he is!" Baron Boless leaned forward with his knees spread apart, one fist resting on his thigh while the other hand shoveled food into his mouth. Despite his gusto, he used his spoon expertly, not losing a single drop of soup.

Amira reached for her own glass of sherry and resisted the impulse to down the whole thing in one gulp. "Baron Boless, I have been told that you are quite an accomplished huntsman."

"Ah has my niece been speaking too highly of me, again?" Baron Boless chuckled with a fond glance to Fonra, but the girl was speaking to Dame Rebeku. "Yes, I do fancy myself an outdoorsman. I served Emperor Drystan in my younger days. Rode with him through no less than three campaigns."

Amira showed no reaction to that. She already knew that Boless had ridden with the army that drove the Istovari from Hylendale.

"Do you have a favorite courser?" Amira asked, trying to change the subject. Was it her imagination, or did the man keep angling the conversation to make her uncomfortable?

"I do! A fine gelding I had imported from the south. Astergold bloodlines, you know."

"Indeed." Amira didn't know much about horse breeding, but she recalled that the Astergold horses were said to have been born from the shards of a star that had fallen into the sands. They were known to be swift and courageous, and the southern lords made it a rule to only sell geldings and mares, never intact stallions.

"Rochester is his name," Baron Boless went on. In a conspiratorial whisper he added, "Named after my own uncle." The lord burst into laughter as if it was some great joke.

Amira laughed politely.

Beside Amira, Fonra was asking about Elton's latest romantic blunder and getting Rebeku to offer advice. Ribbing Elton looked much more fun than conversing with his father.

"Are you planning to make a match for your son soon?" Amira asked, keeping her tone calm, conversational. As a married woman, she was now permitted to ask such questions.

"Dame Rebeku and I are in negotiations," Baron Boless answered. "For her daughter, Melonia."

"Ah I see." Amira tried to remember which of the daughters was Melonia. Was that the younger or the older?

"Melonia is well-bred and cultured. I can think of no better match for my son," Baron Boless replied. "She's connected, skilled at court—"

"And rich?" Amira cast Baron Boless an innocent look.

Boless burst into laughter, his whole chest shaking. "You know the way of it! Yes, indeed. She has an impressive dowry."

The rest of the table was still engrossed in their own conversations. Amira took another sip of her sherry, glancing to the grandfather clock near the door. It was only a quarter past. She had another forty-five minutes until this ordeal was over and she could get back to important work.

"How was your wedding, if I may ask?" Baron Boless asked. "I had hoped to attend, but I understand what happened was rather unconventional."

Amira studied him over the rim of her sherry glass. What did he want? He was lying—he'd left court shortly after she had arrived. All indication said he had planned to boycott her wedding.

"The emperor and I were married by Lord Thadred in an Istovari ceremony." Amira saw no point in keeping it secret. "My father and my husband's retainers will attest to it."

"Never fear, empress," Baron Boless said. "I wasn't questioning its validity, only curious."

Amira smiled because that seemed the best response. "I know."

Perhaps Boless *was* questioning her marriage's validity. Perhaps he and Rebeku's allies were trying to get her marriage annulled so that Daindreth could still marry Fonra. Their efforts were for nothing, of course. Their plan would require both Fonra and Daindreth to betray Amira and that would never happen.

But still. It could be a problem.

Amira continued conversing with Baron Boless, then Dame Rebeku and the rest of the table. Their words fell into an easy rhythm, circling nothing and everything.

The servants came to clear away the soup and plated the next

251

course—a quiche.

Amira took a deep breath, steadying herself as she reached for another sip of sherry. She tried to center herself, focusing on the ebb and flow of *ka* around her.

She felt Fonra beside her, Dame Rebeku, Elton, and Baron Boless. Dame Rebeku's *ka* was faded, but strong. The sign of a woman past her prime but determined to keep on like an old tree. Fonra and Elton were both bright and healthy, though Elton might have a blister on his left big toe. Baron Boless's *ka* was the most concerning—threading through his body in reedy lines and large clumps. He might want to lay off the sherry.

Beyond the table, she could feel the servants bustling around them. Past the doors, Amira was aware of the *ka* of her guards and the servants bustling around the apartments.

Two sources of *ka* lingered at the door. She glanced up, but the two people couldn't be seen past the doors.

Baron Boless cracked a joke, something about his horse being able to outrun his bowel movements. Amira pasted a smile on her face and pretended to laugh as the footman placed a plate in front of her.

A faint click and rattle came from the door. It was faint—barely audible. Amira wouldn't have thought anything of it if she hadn't known that two people had been standing outside for several moments.

She looked up in time to see the doors jostle. Outside, she could feel the two people fleeing. Why were they running? Unless—

Elton's head jerked up from his quiche to the servant behind Amira. His mouth tightened and his shoulders hunched.

That was all the warning Amira got before the man's arm came up behind her, his *ka* a golden glow.

Amira dropped to the side without thinking, shoving Fonra. Fonra spilled onto the floor as Amira twisted around to deflect the man's second blow.

The footman loomed over her with a knife in hand, more of

a dirk, really. He stabbed for her again and Amira grabbed his wrist. She yanked forward, causing him to overshoot. His knife thunked into the table.

"Idiot," Amira snarled. She pulled at *ka* and let it surge through her. She snapped her elbow back, her augmented blow smashed into the man's jaw. She felt distant pain, but her attacker staggered back, knocked to the floor.

The second footman jabbed for her, and Amira was on her feet, bringing the chair up between them. Her emerald necklace smacked against her collarbone as she spun.

"Amira!" Fonra screamed.

"Get her!" Baron Boless shouted.

Amira was aware of the lord rising to his feet, drawing his own knife.

Fonra was there, blocking his path. "No!"

"Fonra, move!" Baron Boless shouted.

"You'll have to kill me first," Fonra snarled, sounding fiercer than Amira had ever heard her.

Amira hated putting her sister at risk, but she had bigger problems. At least it seemed that Boless wanted Fonra alive—probably so he could have her marry Daindreth once the emperor was widowed.

Amira blocked the second footman's attack with the chair. He slammed his weight into her.

Amira felt the table hit her lower back. It screeched as the second attacker shoved into her, moving the table across the floor.

Dame Rebeku squealed in shock. "Get on with it, man!"

Amira grappled with the second footman, cursing to herself. So Rebeku was in on it.

Excellent. Just delightful.

"Guards!" Fonra screamed. "Guards!"

"Quiet, girl!" Baron Boless shouted. "I'm doing this for you!"

Fonra wasn't listening. "Guards!"

Amira pulled at more *ka*, letting the strength infuse her. The first footman was back on his feet, though he staggered as if dazed.

"You're a shit assassin," Amira growled, straining against the second footman. "Want me to show you how it's done?"

She twisted sideways, wrenching the chair. The second footman lurched forward without her to support him, spilling over the table. Plates crashed as tea, cake, and quiche rattled to the floor.

Dame Rebeku screamed again. Good. Amira hoped she'd die of fright.

Amira whirled on the first footman. She had two steps until he reached her.

Many people thought the worst part about fighting in dresses would be the skirts. That wasn't the case in Amira's experience. The worst part was tight sleeves and bodices that restricted her arms. Good thing Amira's arms were bare thanks to imperial summer fashion.

Amira closed the distance between her and the first footman. His knife slashed the back of her forearm. Amira was aware of the cut, but her mind didn't register pain just yet. Amira ignored the wound and slid past his defenses. She grabbed his knife hand—his right—pulling it to her left.

Shoving forward, she twisted so that her back was to his chest. Grabbing his wrist with both hands, she dropped and spun around, bringing his arm over her head and twisting it down, then up behind his back.

He let off a shout of surprise as she wrenched harder. Filled with the strength of *ka*, she felt his tendons rip and his shoulder pop out of socket. He dropped his dagger out of reflex.

Amira caught it before it hit the ground. She jabbed it up without hesitation and felt the blade meet his ribs.

There was that familiar feeling of metal squishing into flesh. Amira drove the dagger straight to the hilt as skin and organs gave way to the blade.

The second footman charged, already halfway to her.

Amira dropped down to miss his strike. He stomped on her skirt, trying to pin her in place.

His blade came for her breast. Amira blocked with her left arm, fighting to keep her balance. That blade bit her arm, slicing through skin. Blood spattered and Amira wasn't sure if it was hers or the dying man's.

The second man tried to grab her knife with his free hand and missed. He stabbed for her neck, probably expecting her to duck. Amira only tilted her head to the side. She felt his knife graze the side of her neck, slicing deep, but missing the vital veins of her throat.

Amira slashed for his inner thigh. Her blade was sharp and she sheared through his livery pants. Blood bloomed instantly and the footman gave a shout as red pulsed down his leg.

"Missed me," Amira spat. She came back up and stabbed straight into his throat for good measure.

He dropped his dagger to grasp his throat. Amira shoved him back and his foot came off her skirt.

Amira snatched up his discarded knife and whirled on the first footman. She found the man slumped against the wall, clutching the wound in his side.

Now Amira noticed that his shoulders were just a little too broad for his uniform, his hair cropped a little too short. "You're a soldier?" she guessed.

"Die, bitch," the soldier spat.

"We're all going to die," Amira replied, testing the weight of the two daggers in her hands. "But you much sooner than me." Amira was ready for the first footman to fight back, but he didn't resist as she jabbed a dagger straight through his eye.

She let his body hit the floor and whirled around.

Now that she had a moment to take in the room and feel out *ka*, she could feel the flurry of energy in the other room that denoted guards rushing into the apartment. Westfall's men must have heard Fonra's screams.

Dame Rebeku had retreated to the window, face even more pale than usual. Baron Boless goggled Amira, his knife still held in one hand.

The doors smashed open, wood splinters flying, and guards spilled into the room. The men took in the sight—their empress covered in blood, dress torn, standing over the bodies of one dead and one dying man.

Baron Boless held a dagger and Dame Rebeku held a kerchief to her mouth, shaking.

"Empress!" the head of the guards shouted, a lieutenant. "Empress, are you hurt?"

"A few scratches," Amira answered, chest heaving. "It would seem Dame Rebeku and Baron Boless felt particularly brave today."

Baron Boless sprang into action. He grabbed Fonra's arm and yanked her against his chest. Pressing a knife to her throat, he glared at Amira. "Call your men off."

Baron Boless shook, his knife rattling against Fonra's skin. If he didn't control himself, he would cut her by accident.

Fonra met Amira's eyes, her face white with shock and fear. But she didn't weep or cry out. She was brave.

"Unhand the princess, Baron Boless," ordered the lieutenant.

"Tell this witch to stand down," Baron Boless snarled. His *ka* flared bright and sporadic as fear coursed through his veins. "You may have ensorcelled our emperor, but not all of us are fooled."

Amira forced herself to remain calm. Until she got Fonra out of this man's grasp, she needed to be reasonable.

Boless had wanted to protect Fonra, but now it seemed he would prefer to protect his own life.

Amira examined her two stolen weapons, taken from her would-be assassins. "I'll make a deal with you, Baron Boless." Amira set the two footmen's daggers on the table. The blood seeped into the tablecloth, a gory red mark on the white linen.

"If you surrender and let my loyal guards take you into custody, I will let the emperor decide your fate."

"You let us leave this room. Or your sister dies." Baron Boless jerked his arm against Fonra's neck and she yelped.

"Amira," Fonra whimpered. "Tell me what to do."

Amira's chest clenched and it took everything she had not to charge Boless and rip his throat out with her teeth. Instead, she knelt beside the dying man on the floor, the one whose throat she had cut. The second footman was still bleeding out, though he wouldn't be for much longer if the massive red pool was any indication.

Dipping her fingers into the dying man's blood, Amira traced the outline of a sigil on the floor.

"What are you doing?" Boless demanded.

"Last chance, Baron Boless," Amira said quietly, watching him from the corner of her eye. "Will you face the empire's justice?" Amira completed several more strokes and laid her hands on either side of the rune. She looked up at Boless as she fed the rune power. "Or mine?"

The bloody mark simmered and bubbled, then turned a bright gold. Power sizzled against the stone, roiling and popping.

"Boless…" Amira growled.

"Alright!" Baron Boless shoved Fonra away and dropped his weapon.

Amira lunged, grabbing her sister's arms and dragging her out of Boless's reach. Without hesitation, the guards were on him, grabbing his arms and searching him for other weapons.

Men seized Dame Rebeku and Elton. Dame Rebeku tried to resist, but Westfall's men were not in an understanding mood.

"Are you alright?" Amira clutched Fonra's face, looking her sister over from head to foot.

"Am I alright?" Fonra choked. "You're bleeding."

"It's a few scratches." Amira stroked Fonra's hair, letting relief flood through her.

Two men each grabbed Boless and Elton, while a younger

guard was assigned to Dame Rebeku.

"Find a few nice cells for them," Amira ordered the guards. "Separate ones. They are to have no visitors. And search them again once you get them to their cells. I don't want any of them being brave and trying to take their own lives."

"As the empress said," the lieutenant ordered.

The guard dragged the old woman from the room and Elton after her. Baron Boless was still shaking, now staring at the bodies of his dead men on the floor.

He looked up to Amira as the guards bound his hands. They didn't have shackles but were making do with a bit of cord from the drapes.

"How?" Boless asked, gaping at her. "How did you do it?"

"I'm Daindreth's goddamn assassin." Amira picked up what remained of Baron Boless's sherry, oddly one of the few things on the table that hadn't been knocked over. Amira downed the contents and gestured to the guards. "Take him away."

CHAPTER TWENTY-SEVEN

Thadred

Thadred didn't like being shorter than the other riders around him. On foot, he was tall enough to hold his own against most men. On Lleuad, he was a head or more below the others.

Lleuad didn't seem to like being short, either. He nipped at the other horses when they came too close, baring fangs at the much larger geldings.

They had ridden out into the city early this morning. Amira had planned to come, but she had gotten roped into a luncheon with Rebeku and Dain had to deal with planning a coronation and getting an empire under control.

Vesha wasn't gone. Not yet. There were still loose ends, though thankfully Amira had found a few threads to follow.

One of those threads had led them here, to the monastic quarter of the city. Hooded monks and clerics moved past, eyeing the armed riders. Some looked on with fear and others with the haughty air of people who know they are the gods' favorites.

Sair had volunteered to come with Thadred. He'd needed a sorceress's help and she had stepped up. Unfortunately, neither of them really knew what to expect.

Not all monks and nuns lived in the monasteries. Those with the means usually had vocations and families outside the monastic quarter. Very few orders required total asceticism, though a few did.

But here was where the real work of serving the gods was done. The monastic quarter was home to several universities, public infirmaries—and the Grand Akiran Library. And many books within Vesha's vault had come from there.

Most of them had also been transcribed by the same scribe. It had seemed too great a coincidence to ignore.

The Grand Akiran Library was hard to miss—sprawling over one side of the street. The building had been cobbled together in a mesh of architecture styles as it had been expanded over the course of several generations. The entrance to the courtyard was open and their party made themselves welcome inside.

Thadred dismounted and handed Lleuad's reins to one of the soldiers. "If he bites, just let him go. I'll catch him when I come back."

The soldier stared wide-eyed at the kelpie.

"He hasn't bitten anyone in a few days, so you're probably fine," Thadred added, then realized that was probably not as comforting as he had hoped. He offered a lopsided smile. Nothing he could do for it.

Sair joined him and took his arm.

Thadred still used his cane on his right side. Even if he could use magic to compensate for his injury, it was a useful and discreet way to bring a sword everywhere he went.

Several guards fell in around them as they entered the library. Monks and nuns scurried to and fro in their long, drab smocks. Akira, the god this library honored, was depicted in the foyer as a young man with a shaved head, stack of books in each hand. The bronze statue towered far above the people below, staring upwards. Like most scholars, he looked too busy with thinking to worry himself with everyday people.

Sair and Thadred made it all the way to the edge of the foyer before a young monk with a shaved head met them at the edge of the foyer.

"My lord. My lady." The monk bowed. "Welcome to the Akiran Grand Library. I am Jossen of the Akiran Order of monks."

"Lord Thadred Myrani." Thadred held up his signet ring, the one that bore the imperial crest and granted him Dain's authority. "This is Lady Sairydwen of the Istovari. We are here on behalf of the emperor."

Jossen's thin neck bobbed as he swallowed, looking at Sair. No doubt, people had heard of Empress Amira's sorceress attendants. "We were not expecting you."

"It's short notice, we know." Thadred put on his most easy-going, relaxed expression. This monk was already tense and tense people weren't the most cooperative. "We're here looking for a monk of your order. His name was Brother Egrid, we believe."

Jossen's face fell. "Scribe Egrid ascended into Akira's light some years ago."

Thadred blinked, somehow not surprised. "He's dead?"

"To us, yes. He lives now in the glorious enlightenment of Akira's wisdom."

Thadred exhaled, trying to stay positive. "Is there anyone who might have worked with him? Anyone familiar with his research?"

Jossen glanced between Thadred and Sair. He seemed to expect Sair to do something, but Thadred couldn't guess what. "Allow me to take you to the abbess."

Thadred smiled. It seemed the imperial seal was good for many things. "Thank you, Brother Jossen."

Jossen bowed. "I am Scribe Jossen, my lord. But thank you. Right this way. Your guards may wait here."

"Our guards will come with us," Thadred answered.

"My lord, this library is quite safe.

"I'm sure. But my men are most eager to see the inside. They've heard many stories about the library, you see."

At his left and right, Thadred's soldiers stood mute and motionless. They wouldn't care either way, but of course that wasn't the point.

Jossen cleared his throat. "Some of the passages are quite narrow."

"Never fear, my good man," Thadred kept smiling. "We will march single file. Lead the way."

Jossen shot a glance at Thadred's signet ring, as if to confirm once again that it was real. Then he finally bowed and led the way into the library.

Thadred followed the monk. The guards fell in around them, four men in the imperial armor and livery. Bringing this many soldiers might be overkill, but Thadred would rather be safe.

The monk led them through narrow rows of shelves and sure enough, there were places they had to march single file.

Thadred kept Sair close against his side, which meant they had to squeeze tight together at times, but she never complained and never made to pull away from him.

"I wouldn't be surprised if Vesha had Egrid disposed of once he outlived his usefulness." Thadred kept his voice down, watching Jossen's back.

"It's likely," Sair agreed. "She might have been covering her tracks."

The maze of bookshelves was cramped and tight. Thadred could barely fit through in places and understood suddenly why all the monks and nuns were rail-thin—they had to be. The winding shelves were labeled and neatly ordered, but at the same time, the shelves were cobbled workmanship at best. Many sagged with the weight of the books on top and only seemed to be held together by the books below. This whole place had the feeling it might topple over at any moment.

Jossen took them to the abbess, a small woman with a cramped frame stooped from a lifetime hunching over books. She had been overseeing a small team of scribes who worked to recopy dozens of volumes, transferring the text in the old books into new tomes.

Several scribes gawped openly at Thadred and his imperial retinue, but just as many didn't even seem to notice them.

The abbess's thin brows shot up her forehead when she heard Thadred's name and saw the imperial signet. Thadred would guess they didn't get many visitors from the palace. She confirmed that Egrid had been dead for several years.

Thadred tried not to show his frustration. Just like that, their trail had gone cold.

"Do you know of anyone who might have helped in his research?" Sair asked. "Particularly his research for the empress?"

"For the empress?" The abbess's brows rose yet higher, which hadn't seemed possible. "Egrid's work hardly earned such notice."

Thadred imagined far more people had taken notice than this woman realized. "Did he have any apprentices? Assistants?"

The abbess nodded, resting one hand on the stack of books before her. "The boy, Kaphen," she said. "Yes, I think he is still here. He might be able to help you, but you are the first imperial visitors we've had since I have been abbess." Something about the way the abbess added that last part implied she had been abbess for a very long time.

Thadred bowed solemnly. "Good lady, if you could direct us to this boy Kaphen, we would be most obliged."

The abbess seemed puzzled by the whole thing, hand stroking the spines of the books like some women did their favorite pets. "Kaphen is…?" The abbess glanced to Jossen quizzically.

"He's sorting the new Dumali texts this morning, Head Scribe," Jossen offered.

"Good. Take our guests to him."

"Much obliged." Thadred inclined his head.

He braced himself as they thrust their way back into the maze of books. He felt like a bee forcing its way through a honeycomb. Their guards had to shuffle awkwardly, careful to keep halberds from catching on the books overhead.

"Is there a particular reason you are interested in the late Scribe Egrid's work?" Jossen sounded almost eager. "I might be able to offer a few selections. What topics are of interest to the emperor?"

"Right now, Kaphen is of interest." Thadred tried to make that as casual-sounding as he could.

"I warn you, Kaphen is a junior scribe," Jossen said. "We had high hopes for him, but he's shown no real talent as a scholar."

Thadred wasn't sure what that was supposed to mean. What did talent have to do with reading and organizing books?

"You know him well?" Sair's tone was light and airy.

Jossen made a noncommittal sound. "I was a novice when he first entered the order. He showed great promise, but then Scribe Egrid took him on. He's spent all his allotted time since studying rumors."

Behind Jossen's back, Sair cast Thadred a significant look. "Rumors?"

"Scribe Egrid was obsessed with obscure references to communing with the gods." Jossen took them around another corner, his lean frame bending expertly through the twists and turns of the shelves. "He even tried a few rituals over the years, but beholding the faces of gods is not for the living."

Sair looked pointedly at Thadred. He nodded back.

What if Scribe Egrid had more success than his colleagues realized? And what if he had found a way not to commune with gods, but demons?

Jossen led them through a set of doors into what appeared to be a newer portion of the library. Here the ceilings rose at three times the height of a man and the shelves just as high. The shelves were in neat, segmented rows. It was a refreshing break from the rest of the library. Jossen took them to a corner stacked with dusty crates of scrolls and assorted volumes with at least a dozen different languages on the spines. A group of monks were hard at work sorting the books, their shaved heads glistening with sweat.

"Brother Kaphen?" Jossen looked straight to a gangly young man wrestling a pile of books.

A hesitant set of eyes peered around the bookstack.

"We have visitors here from the imperial palace," Jossen explained. "They want to ask you about Brother Egrid's work."

Brother Kaphen took one look at Thadred and Sair. He dropped his books in an avalanche of vellum, parchment, and paper.

Kaphen spun around and bolted.

"Brother Kaphen!" Jossen shouted.

Well, on the bright side, Kaphen clearly knew something.

Sair made to run and Thadred grabbed her arm. "What are you doing?"

"I can handle a monk, darling. Caught you, didn't I?" Sair gave him a look that was—no. It couldn't be flirtatious, could it?

She freed her arm from his grip and raced after the fleeing scribe.

"Circle around and cut him off!" Thadred ordered the guards.

Kaphen scrambled headlong between the shelves, heading for the door.

"Brother Kaphen!" Jossen cried out, indignation coloring his tone. "Come back at once!"

Thadred's soldiers raced ahead to intercept Kaphen. Sair's swishing footsteps rushed in hot pursuit.

Did the monk actually think he could escape them? They were here on the authority of the emperor.

A yelp came from somewhere in the shelves.

Thadred caught a shout from Sair and a curse from one of the soldiers. That monk must be fast.

Thadred limped as fast as he could toward the door. If Kaphen wanted to get out, it would likely be that way.

He heard footsteps rushing in his direction and limped faster. He could make out the sound of Kaphen running down the length of shelves to his right, about to catch up.

The monk came dashing out in front of Thadred, swerving around the corner of the shelves.

Thadred stuck out his cane in a flash.

The monk squawked and fell sprawled on the ground. He clutched at his shin, breathing in sharp gasps. "Ow, ow, ow," he whimpered. "That hurt. Ow."

The soldiers were on him the next instant, seizing his arms and dragging him to his feet.

"It's a bad look, Kaphen." Thadred checked his cane, making sure it wasn't damaged. "Running away like that certainly makes you look guilty."

Sair trotted up beside him, breathing heavily. "I almost had him."

Thadred turned to her with a flat expression. "Of course, my dear."

Sair laughed at that, eyes shining with mischief. Sair touched his arm lightly, then let her hand fall at her side. She bit her lower lip for just a second and Thadred felt something snap in his head, thoughts falling into place like armor plates locking together.

I'm not just *her friend.*

"I didn't know who she was!" Kaphen howled, cutting off Thadred's happy realization. "I swear to you, please! I never wanted to—"

"Shut up!" Thadred ordered, glancing over his shoulder. Several monks including Jossen came jogging down the shelves. It seemed none of them were as fast as Kaphen.

"Brother Kaphen!" Jossen fluttered his hands, clutching at his breast in shock.

"Brother Kaphen is under arrest for suspicion of treason," Thadred said. "If you would show me back to the abbess, I will explain the situation to her."

"No!" cried Brother Kaphen. "I never wanted to—"

Sair placed her hand over the man's mouth. "Shush," she said, her tone gentle, almost maternal. "We have a few questions is all."

Thadred had *many* questions, and this young man obviously knew the answers to at least a few of them.

Finally, they were making progress.

CHAPTER TWENTY-EIGHT

Daindreth

Daindreth did not remember the last time he had been this angry. He paced around Amira's bedroom again, raking a hand through his hair. "Treason," he spat. "It's outright treason!"

"Yes, I would say stabbing your wife over tea is treason," Thadred agreed, toying with the head of his cane sword.

"I knew the court was resistant to our marriage, but for two such prominent courtiers to conspire against me is an outrage!" Daindreth resisted the urge to kick over a chair. "In broad daylight without pretense."

"If it's any consolation, Baron Boless about pissed himself after I dropped his men." For a woman who had nearly been killed a few hours ago, Amira was remarkably calm. Then again, she was no stranger to people trying to kill her.

Daindreth turned to face his wife.

She sat on the couch beside the window, her neck and arms exposed. The surgeon finished the stitches on her neck and two apprentices finished bandaging the cuts on her forearms. Cyne looked on, supervising from the side.

Sorceresses could heal, but Amira was strong enough as a Kadra'han that she would be healed in a few days anyway. The way it had been explained to Daindreth, Amira just needed the stitches to hold her skin in place while her magic worked. She might be able to speed the process more by having Thadred force healing, but with Thadred's lack of experience came a higher chance of scarring. Daindreth wanted her healed as soon as possible, but he didn't blame her if she wanted to avoid new scars.

"Amira." Daindreth wanted to touch her, wanted to hold her, but he didn't dare get in the way of the surgeon's work.

Westfall had interrupted Daindreth's meeting with the

267

master of coin and told him he needed to come at once. When Westfall had said it was about Amira, Daindreth had feared the worst.

When he'd arrived and seen her covered in blood, his heart had stopped for just a second.

"At least the food wasn't poisoned," Amira sighed. She winced as the surgeon's needle threaded through her wound again. They said they had numbed the wound, but it seemed they hadn't numbed it all the way. "Or the daggers."

Thadred's mouth twitched. "I'm sure you were never so sloppy in your own work," he chuckled. "Boless really has the worst luck, doesn't he? I mean, of all the women he could have tried to murder."

Amira surprised Daindreth by giggling. Perhaps the drugs were having some effect after all. "It was rather unfortunate for him, wasn't it?"

Daindreth glared between the two of them. "This is serious."

"I know," Amira replied, her face going grave. "We have to decide what to do about it."

"The punishment for treason is death." Daindreth had never thought himself bloodthirsty before, but this level of treachery…no Fanduillion had ever been assaulted in their own palace before.

Amira was his wife and that made her a Fanduillion. Boless and Rebeku's attack on her had been an attack on the family they had both vowed to serve.

"If you kill them, you will lose the support of the Bolesses," said a voice from the shadows. "Not to mention Rebeku's rather vast network."

Daindreth had almost forgotten Cromwell beside the door. The old lawyer had barely shown any emotion this entire time.

"I can't allow them to get away with this!" Daindreth's anger echoed against the gilt ceiling, making the surgeon jump. Daindreth took a deep breath and straightened his shoulders. "Forgive me."

"I am not suggesting they go unpunished, only that you can't kill them. At least not all of them."

Daindreth shook his head. "I can't leave Rebeku free."

"No," Cromwell agreed. "She must be dealt with."

Daindreth looked to Amira. She cast him a sad smile.

"I'm angrier that he threatened Fonra than anything else." Amira tilted her head for the surgeon to keep working on her neck. "That's something I won't forgive."

"Think, Your Majesty." Cromwell stepped away from the door. "Every crisis is an opportunity. Your enemies have given you a gift."

"A gift?" Daindreth scoffed.

"They overplayed their hand. Your lady wife is the victim here, not matter how one presents it. If we play this right, no one will be able to speak against her without being associated with the traitors."

Daindreth exhaled. "I've been away from court for too long."

Cromwell inclined his head. "If I may, Your Majesty. Empress Amira is not popular, but you still are. We can salvage this."

Daindreth stared at Cromwell. He tried to think clearly, tried to see like a politician instead of a husband.

"Your father also chose an unpopular bride," Cromwell said. "She eventually ruled—illegitimately—for almost twenty years. We can learn something from them."

Daindreth wasn't sure what there was to learn. His father had chosen Vesha against the advice of those closest to him. It had worked out for his parents in the end, but as far as Daindreth knew, no one had ever tried murdering Vesha.

The surgeons finished and began cleaning away their tools and equipment. The head surgeon promised to pass on instructions to Amira's servants regarding care for the wounds, though Daindreth expected her mother and Sair would be tending them—if they needed tending at all.

The surgeons left, bustling out. The door closed behind them, the latch clicking into place. Daindreth came to Amira's side, wrapping an arm around her, careful of her stitches. He kissed her temple, breathing in the smell of perfume mixed with blood and astringents. He waited until the sound of the surgeons' footsteps faded down the hall.

Cromwell continued. "Your parents did this successfully, but they did not make more enemies than necessary. That often meant ignoring or pardoning offenses."

"They tried to kill my wife!" Daindreth roared.

How could he pardon these people? They'd tried to murder Amira. After everything they had been through, after facing horrors unimagined by most, would court politics and petty jealousies be their undoing?

It was wrong. It was unjust. And what was an emperor if he could not right wrongs and bring justice? What was the point of ruling nations if he couldn't protect the woman he loved within their own home?

The whole room went still, Cromwell, Cyne, and Thadred staring at him.

"Love." Amira held out a hand to him, beckoning.

"I'm sorry." Daindreth swallowed, catching her offered hand. "I'm sorry, I just…after everything, I thought we were finally making progress."

"You are," Cromwell said flatly. His words were so cold, so pragmatic, it was hard to doubt him. "Westfall is loyal to you. Your staff is loyal to you. So are King Hyle and at least half this court. *I* am loyal to you."

"You're worth at least two kings, Cromwell," Amira said, her fingers knotting into Daindreth's.

"Never fear, my empress." Cromwell raised his chin curtly. "I know it's the surgeon's drugs making you say that."

Amira giggled.

Daindreth realized the analgesics must be affecting her more than he had realized. He should be the one comforting her, not

270

the other way around. He kissed her cheek and then her neck, above her line of stitches. "Thank you."

"What for?"

"For surviving." He kissed her forehead, then addressed Thadred and Cromwell. "See the court gathered tomorrow. I will pass judgment on the traitors then. No sense in waiting."

Cromwell bowed his head. "Agreed."

Daindreth still wasn't sure what he thought of the man. Amira seemed to trust him and she had good judgment. Not to mention she had rather ingeniously tied their fates together.

"Very well, then." Daindreth had at least one decision out of the way.

"Do you know what you'll do to them, yet?" Thadred asked.

"I could forgive them trying to kill me," Amira said. "Who hasn't, after all? My grandmother, Thadred." She cocked her head at Daindreth. "Even you at one point."

"That was Caa Iss," Daindreth argued.

"Still." Amira took a deep breath. "But they endangered Fonra. Threatened her." She shook her head. "No, that I can't forgive."

"She did seem quite shaken," Thadred added.

"She was brave," Amira countered. "But I'm angry that she had to be brave."

A knock on the door sounded.

Thadred answered and exchanged a few short words with the person outside. He closed it and turned to Daindreth. "A messenger from Westfall. He says you might want to address the court soon. Rumors are spreading that Rebeku has been arrested."

"She *has* been arrested," Daindreth ground out.

"People are still not pleased with the news," Thadred answered just a little sardonically.

Rebeku was practically the grandmother of this court. She wasn't the oldest courtier, but she was the court matriarch. Only Vesha had ever quite held her in check and just barely.

The Bolesses were also powerful and there were more of them at court than just the father and son. Boless nephews and cousins crawled this palace, some of them didn't bear the name, but still held the loyalties.

"You should address them," Cromwell said. "Tell them the trial will be tomorrow."

Daindreth inhaled a slow breath. "Amira."

"I'm fine, husband." Amira nodded. "Go. Be an emperor. I'll keep Cromwell and my own guards with me this time."

Daindreth turned to Thadred. "I want her guard doubled. She is to be protected at all times. Tell the men to kill anyone who threatens her. I don't care if it's a king or a cook. Do you understand?"

Thadred nodded solemnly. "Of course. Assuming your lady wife doesn't get to them first. She handled those two—"

"I mean it!"

Thadred recoiled slightly. "It was a joke, Dain."

The emperor drew a deep breath. "I'm sorry." He knew Thadred was joking. At the same time, he wasn't about to lose Amira.

"Don't worry about it. I'll double that guard, give them permission to be stabby, and keep your wife safe for a few hours while you control the rumors. Deal?"

Daindreth nodded slowly. "Thank you." Amira was hardly helpless and Thadred was right, but it still eased Daindreth's mind to know she would be protected by his cousin.

"The other sorceresses will be here shortly," Cromwell said. "They wouldn't dare let harm come to her."

Daindreth nodded. "Thank you." He braced himself and stepped out the door to where his own guards waited.

It was time to do damage control.

CHAPTER TWENTY-NINE

Amira

Amira marched into the throne room with her head held high and her shoulders back. Fonra had suggested covering her stitches, but for the first time, Amira overruled her sister's fashion choices.

Amira wanted everyone to see she'd been wounded and survived anyway. She wanted no doubt as to the severity of the attack, no question about Rebeku and the Bolesses' guilt.

This was not a misunderstanding. This was not a row over tea. This had been attempted murder.

Amira left her stiches visible, grotesque and unsightly. Let everyone see what her enemies had done to her.

Westfall had determined that no one else had known of the plot against Amira. At least, no one who was talking. Rebeku had said nothing in her confinement, but Baron Boless had been willing enough to speak—after Thadred paid him a visit.

Daindreth marched at her side, his arm through hers. He wore an imperial red coat with black boots. He looked like a man about to lead an army and perhaps that was the intent.

Amira's dress was black with a plunging neck that left her arms bare—showing her old scars and her fresh wounds alike. The crown on her head felt welded into place. Fonra had made sure the servants had braided it securely onto her head.

The heralds shouted their names as they filed into the throne room, surrounded by guards, servants, and attendants. Cromwell and Fonra followed close at Amira's back while Daindreth's valet and Thadred followed him.

Amira and Daindreth ascended to the two thrones that lorded over the room. The emperor saw his wife seated before taking his own place beside her.

Amira settled into the cold, hard marble. Vesha had once occupied this seat, first as consort and then as regent.

The assassin finally had time to survey the court. It seemed that everyone was gathered. The room was packed with courtiers, their servants, and what appeared to be lesser nobles who were probably here to witness and report on behalf of those they served.

Guards circled the main dais and Westfall's men had been posted at intervals around the room. Still, this was as public as things could get in the Mynadran court.

Before the dais, the two Boless men and Dame Rebeku had been forced to their knees. Westfall's soldiers held them in place.

Shortly after meeting Daindreth, Amira had pictured this scene again and again. Only in her imaginings, she had been the one kneeling before the thrones, about to pay for her attempt to assassinate the archduke.

Westfall stood at the head of his men. He bowed to the emperor. "My liege, I have brought the traitors to face your justice."

Daindreth nodded. "Let the charges be read."

A herald read a summary of the charges. Amira watched the rest of the room. Every whisper and shuffle, every stomp and shift. She recognized plenty of courtiers, picking them out and making them meet her eyes when they looked her way. Most of them dropped their gazes the moment she met theirs.

Witnesses were brought forward—Fonra was the first to testify. She repeated the story of what had happened, from the invitation to the luncheon, the attempted stabbing, then being taken hostage by her uncle. Amira noticed her sister shake, but she didn't waver when she spoke.

Next, one of Rebeku's own porters testified. Apparently, Westfall's men had spent the whole night finding one of Rebeku's servants who was willing to talk. The porter claimed that he and another man had been tasked with locking the doors to the hallway outside the apartments so that Amira's guards couldn't get in. Another pair had been tasked with sealing the dining room.

The lieutenant responsible for Amira's protection that day also gave a report, telling of what they had heard and what they had seen once he and the other soldiers broke the door down.

The lieutenant was a military man and he spoke without embellishment or sidestepping the facts. He reported that Amira had stabbed her two attackers to death with their own weapons, that they were confirmed to be Boless soldiers by the men in the imperial garrison.

Westfall also reported his findings from overnight. It seemed that several of the Boless soldiers had been approached for the task and had refused before those two men had volunteered.

This trial wasn't necessary. Daindreth was emperor. It was fully within his power to have these people executed right now.

It was all for show. This was to drive home the truth that the Bolesses and Rebeku were traitors.

The trial dragged through the morning. Testimony was given, more witnesses were called. Rebeku and the Bolesses were not given the chance to speak.

Scribes in the corner jotted down every word. Copies of this trial transcript would be shared throughout the empire.

Amira pulled out the book from Vesha's library. It was the same one she'd been reading yesterday. Cromwell quirked one brow at her but didn't say anything.

Her mother looked on disapprovingly from beside the dais, but Amira went back to the book and ignored her.

Brother Temain of the Holstead Parish has devised a most cunning method for ensuring the proper number of prayers are offered. His people have begun lighting small candles, to track the length and frequency of their prayers. Since beginning this practice, his parish has seen great results in their harvests and every one of their sheep bore twins in the last spring.

Amira paused and went back to the beginning of the page. Votive candles? Was this author describing the beginning of prayer candles? How old was this book? Amira had never heard of Holstead Parish, but the name sounded northern.

She kept reading the treatise, realizing it seemed to be a

collection of letters from a traveling priest to his fellow monastics. But from when? The place names sounded like they were from within the empire, but at the same time it made no sense.

The court broke for a short meal and a rest. Daindreth spoke with his clerks about other projects and reports that were still important despite the trial.

Amira let her mother and Sair apply fresh salve to her wounds and kept reading.

The Istavi priestesses do not approve of our efforts to seek the aid of the gods. They have opposed the building of shrines and chapels in our baronies, namely those devoted to Demred.

Last month, a band of armored young men came to the anchorage of Sister Cassra and harassed both her and her flock. No one was harmed, but the young men identified themselves as Cleavers.

Amira reread that passage as she had done so many others in this book. *Istavi* sounded a lot like *Istovari*. It would have been so much more useful if she'd had some idea of when or by who this was written.

"Empress Amira." Daindreth's voice spoke through her thoughts. "It is time, my love."

Amira closed the book and handed it back to Fonra for safekeeping. "Let's get it over with, then."

They returned to the main throne room and took their places once again overlooking the court. Some people had left, but it seemed that even more had forced their way inside, packing every inch of space allowed. More guards had been brought in to keep the crowd back.

Amira and Daindreth took their places at the two main thrones. The herald announced that the trial was once again underway.

"Baron Boless," Daindreth began, his voice stern and steady. "You have heard the accusations against you. What would you say for yourself?"

Baron Boless had seemed such a jovial and lively man

yesterday. Today, it seemed as if he was weighed by a great heaviness. "In truth, my lord, I have nothing to say. I did indeed plot against Amira Brindonu. I did—"

"You will refer to my wife as your empress," Daindreth snapped.

Baron Boless inclined his head, realizing he had overstepped his bounds. "My only interest was ever for you, my liege."

"By trying to murder my wife?" Daindreth demanded, his voice dangerously cold.

Amira glanced to him. He was doubtless far angrier than he was showing even now. She'd thought he'd had time to calm himself since yesterday, but she supposed not.

Baron Boless inclined his head. "The Istovari are enemies of the empire, my liege. You were young, but I remember how they afflicted your father with the sickness that took his life."

Daindreth's knuckles went white on the armrests of his throne. Boless had no idea what he was talking about.

Amira reached out and touched her husband's sleeve. He wouldn't want to lose his temper in front of the court.

Daindreth seemed to brace himself. He pulled away from Amira, but when he spoke again, his voice was calmer. "And yet the Istovari have stood by me unquestioningly. They have not defied me, and they have not betrayed me."

"I would never betray you, my liege," Baron Boless insisted.

"But you did," Daindreth said, voice dangerously soft. "You spoke against my wife when I chose her for my bride. You dared raise your voice against me and my lady mother on the matter."

Baron Boless's face flushed, and he lowered his head stiffly, as if forcing himself into obeisance before an ornery child. "My liege, I have only your best interests and the interests of the empire at heart."

"Did you or did you not conspire to have my wife killed, Baron Boless?" Daindreth clipped.

"My liege—"

"If the next word out of your mouth is anything but yes or

277

no, I will have you stripped naked and whipped by my squires."

Amira herself was a little surprised at that threat, but her husband seemed to mean it.

Baron Boless was silent a moment, as if fighting some internal battle. "Yes, my liege," he answered. "Yes, I did as you say."

Daindreth raised his chin, inhaling a deep breath. "Dame Rebeku?"

"My liege, I have served your family faithfully for years," Baron Boless protested.

"Guards," Daindreth said, not looking at Boless, "if he speaks again without my permission, you are to strike him in the mouth."

Amira watched Daindreth from the corner of her eye. He was tense, rigid. He looked ready to snap.

When this was over, she needed to have a moment with him.

"I too gave your father faithful service," Dame Rebeku began.

"Yes, madam," Daindreth interrupted. "All the court knows of your *service* to my father. The question at hand is if you tried to murder my wife."

The court stirred. Even as a criminal, the court would expect a certain level of deference be shown to Dame Rebeku. She was an elderly woman who had been loyal to House Fanduillion that entire time, one of their most public supporters.

From what Amira had heard, Vesha would probably have been ousted by jealous nobles years ago if not for Rebeku's support.

Amira lifted her head, looking to Daindreth. "My love," she said quietly. She reached over and touched his hand.

Daindreth exhaled a long breath and looked to her.

Amira was aware that the room had gone quiet, watching the two of them. She could feel hundreds of stares pressing on them, but she had only eyes for Daindreth.

"This isn't how we win, my love," she said.

Daindreth blinked at her and swallowed. He turned back to Dame Rebeku. "Please answer, madam," he said, his tone softer this time. "Do you confess to knowing of Boless's plot? Of supporting his assassination of your empress?"

Dame Rebeku made eye contact with Amira. She looked straight to the assassin. Something flashed in those eyes, something hard and defiant. She whirled back to Daindreth. "Yes, I am guilty," Dame Rebeku sneered. "Guilty of seeking to protect my emperor from the wiles of an Istovari witch. Guilty of fighting to protect our empire from her schemes. Even now, she blinds you."

Daindreth bolted to his feet, face red.

Everything happened in an instant.

Amira caught Cromwell's eye from beside the dais. His expression was hard, but from the slant of his head and a furtive glance to the crowd, she saw her own fears mirrored on his face.

Daindreth couldn't lose control in front of the court. Daindreth couldn't be the one to pass judgment.

The crowd jumped with sick excitement, horror, and delight on their faces in equal measure.

Daindreth had lost his temper. He had shown he wanted these three people dead. The court would be scandalized and speak of how their emperor preferred his new Istovari wife and her sorceresses to his own most loyal retainers.

This was a disaster, but in every disaster lay an opportunity.

"Westfall," Daindreth snarled, looking to his guard captain. "Take them into the city square and—"

"My liege!" Amira grabbed her husband's arm. She pulled him down so his ear was level with her mouth. "Let me do it," she whispered. "Let me pass judgment."

Daindreth shot her a look. "I can't let them go free, Amira," he insisted. "A flogging isn't sufficient and—"

"Let me." Amira held his stare.

Daindreth drew a deep breath.

Westfall and the whole of the room watched them

expectantly. Amira was aware of her mother pulling more *ka* from the room. She was preparing to use defensive spells if needed.

"Trust me, love," Amira said. "It seems fitting I pass judgment on my would-be murderers. I promise not to do anything more drastic than what you had in mind."

Daindreth nodded. He stepped back, addressing the three convicts before him. "You have all confessed to attempting to murder my wife. So you will face her judgment."

The room stirred at that announcement. Amira could feel their stares on her as surely as that time she had marched onto the archery field, what seemed like a lifetime ago.

The assassin stepped off the dais, a pair of royal guards trailing not far behind. What was the fitting punishment for these crimes? Her husband had just made it clear he wanted them all dead, so anything she did short of that would be seen as mercy.

Amira reached the bottom of the steps and stopped just a few paces from the two Boless men and Dame Rebeku.

Though Rebeku still carried her chin high, up close she seemed frailer, smaller. Still proud and still strong, but she was greatly lessened. She had been stripped of her silks and jewels and now wore an unadorned smock.

The Boless men were little better, stubble bristling their faces and the stench of prison on them. Their fine doeskin breeches were stained and the younger Boless, Elton, had a dark purple mark on his jaw.

"You tried to kill me," Amira said, looking down at Dame Rebeku. "It's a shame. We could have been great friends." Amira looked to Elton. "You are your father's only son, correct?"

Elton ducked his head, swallowing hard. "Yes, Your Grace."

"Hmm. My guards told me you were armed when they searched you. You planned to help finish me off, if necessary, didn't you?"

The young man ducked his head. He was older than her by

a few years, but in that moment, he struck her as a boy. Just a boy who had known too much peace to understand the true cost of violence.

"Baron Boless and the Honorable Elton Boless," Amira said, raising her voice. "You had your soldiers attack me. You attacked my sister yourself. But you failed to harm either of us. I think this counts as half a crime so I will give you half a punishment." She raised her chin. "One of you will leave this throne room a free man. The other will die."

Amira felt the room stir around her. She wanted to look to Cromwell, she wanted to ask his advice. But she needed to be in control, not her advisors.

Baron Boless swallowed heavily. He looked past Amira, seeking Daindreth.

"You think my husband will help you?" Amira asked, her voice cold. "He would rather have you all beheaded in the city square."

Baron Boless looked back to Amira. Gone was the arrogance and the confidence. Boless had been a soldier and good soldiers knew when they had lost a battle.

"I will let you choose," Amira said, the idea occurring to her as she spoke. "Which of you will get a pardon?" She looked pointedly to the halberd in the fist of a nearby guard. "And which of you will get the ax?"

"Me," Baron Boless shouted without an instant of hesitation. "Take my head. Let my boy go free."

Amira looked back to him, a little surprised that he had decided so easily. "You're very brave, Baron Boless," she said. "I do wish things were different."

Elton shook in his bonds. His eyes watered and he twisted around to see his father. "Papa," he said, voice trembling. "Papa, I—"

"Chin up, son," Baron Boless said. "You're about to be a baron."

Amira snapped her chin to Westfall. "Bring me an ax and a

block."

If the captain was surprised that she wanted to get it over with right here and right now, he gave no sign. He signaled to one of his soldiers and the man leapt to fetch them as he was ordered.

Amira stepped past the two men to Dame Rebeku. She was a little surprised to find she felt nothing toward the woman. Nothing at all. "Dame Rebeku," she began, her mind hard at work as she spoke, trying to remember every lesson she had ever been taught about politics.

Rebeku was dangerous because she had allies. Martyrdom could make her more dangerous.

"You have my respect, madam," Amira said. "You cared for the court in the absence of my husband and the former empress. You have been a leader and a strong supporter of our house for your entire life."

Amira could feel the shock rippling through the crowd in their movements and the way they whispered.

"I am grateful for that. Truly." Amira let genuine sincerity show in her words. "But change has reached this court. Change is sweeping this empire. If you refuse to be a part of that change, then your time is done."

Dame Rebeku held her chin high. Amira realized she expected a death sentence. She expected to be executed like Baron Boless.

"I hearby strip you of all titles and honors," Amira said. "On the morrow, you will begin your journey to Gunchester Convent. You will never leave the convent grounds under pain of death. You may not receive letters from the outside world nor more than two visitors per year." Remembering that Rebeku had wanted to marry Melonia to Elton, Amira continued. "Your daughters and their inheritance are now wards of the crown. The crown will choose their husbands and the crown will dispense their dowries."

The headsman arrived, carrying a stained block. From the

color of the stains, Amira guessed it hadn't been used in a while.

"You're going to behead me here?" Baron Boless demanded. "In the very throne room?"

Amira ignored him as well as the stirrings about the court. The headsman set the block in front of Baron Boless. Amira held out her hand for the ax.

The headsman hesitated, eyes going wide under his slitted hood, but who was he to defy the empress?

Amira took the ax, finding it heavy, as she had expected. She studied the edge, noticing the tiny notches in the blade. It had been recently sharpened from the look of it. "This will do," she said, planting the end on the ground as she turned back to Baron Boless.

He had to die. He was an admitted traitor and he had threatened Fonra.

But if Amira killed him herself, that would make her the villainess to Boless's kinsmen. In ten, twenty, or even thirty years, Baron Elton Boless might exact revenge for his father's death. If she had the headsman do it, the effect would be much the same. She wanted them to fear her more than that.

"Release the Honorable Elton Boless," Amira said to the two guards. When they seemed unsure, Westfall signaled for them to obey.

The two soldiers released Elton and the young man blinked up at her. He was pale and looked as if he might vomit. He had probably never been this close to death outside a fox hunt.

"Stand." Amira beckoned. "Come here."

What was he going to do? Defy her while imperial men surrounded him, and she held an ax?

Elton stood, though he trembled, and came to her side.

Amira patted his shoulder and he flinched. Good. "You stood by while your father's men tried to murder me," she said, her voice rising so that everyone could hear. "You knelt quietly while your father offered his life for yours." She grabbed his shaking hand and pressed the ax into it. "No more standing by

283

and watching, Your Honor."

"No," Elton gasped, trying to wrench his hand away. "No, I can't."

"Yes." Amira grabbed his jaw and forced him to face her, nails digging into his neck. "You are going to take your father's head. Right now. In front of the court. Admitting that he is a traitor." Amira's voice dropped as she glared harder into the frightened young man's face. "You will share in my blame just as you share in his."

By having Elton swing the ax, Amira would make him equally responsible for his father's death. It would make it hard for him to justify any revenge later and it would make it almost impossible for any uprising to rally with him as a figurehead.

Amira stepped behind Elton, her hands on his shoulders.

Westfall's men pushed Baron Boless down on the block, holding his arms behind his back.

Baron Boless glared up at his son. "Stop being a pansy, boy," he snapped. "Get on with it."

"If you don't take your father's head," Amira whispered in his ear, "I will. And then I will take your hands." She shoved him toward the block.

Elton trembled as he stepped forward. "I don't—"

"Do it!" Baron Boless screamed.

Elton made a strangled whimpering, mewling sound that reminded Amira of a wounded animal. The ax smashed down onto Baron Boless's neck. It opened a massive gash in his skin and Amira saw the flash of white bone before blood poured out.

Elton screamed in horror. Several ladies recoiled in the audience.

Amira didn't flinch. "Again," she snarled. "Finish it!"

"Finish it," Baron Boless screamed, his voice garbled and hardly audible. "Do something right for once, you pathetic—"

Elton brought the ax down again and something crunched. Baron Boless's head still didn't fall, but he stopped screaming.

Amira exhaled impatiently. She wanted this over with.

Everyone did.

Elton let off an animal scream that echoed with horror, grief, and frustration. He brought the ax down again and again, smashing until Baron Boless's head hit the white marble with a thud.

Elton stood heaving with the effort. Blood splattered him from head to foot and the guards who now held Boless's limp corpse.

Amira stepped up beside the young man and pulled the ax from his hands. His grip was so tight she had to yank it to get it free.

The moment she did, Elton doubled over, retching. Vomit mingled with blood, spattering the guards and Dame Rebeku who still knelt nearby.

Amira handed the ax back to the headsman. "Baron Boless, you are free to go." Amira looked to Rebeku's guards. "Take her to a holding cell. Her daughters may visit her to say their farewells, but for no more than a quarter hour. She leaves for the convent tomorrow."

Elton crumpled to the ground sobbing, sinking into his father's blood and his own vomit.

Amira addressed Westfall. "Have the remains burned and the ashes scattered into the harbor."

The captain inclined his head once. "It will be done, Your Majesty."

There would be no shrine to the late Baron Boless. Amira would leave no place for any supporters or mourners to revere him.

No one spoke, no one moved. There was barely any sound but Elton's sobbing.

One of the soldiers reached for him, but Amira raised a hand to stop the man. "No," she said. "Let him stay there as long as he needs."

Some might think it was compassion, but Amira had other ideas. After this display, no one would dare think the new Baron

Boless was fit to lead a rebellion.

Amira turned to her husband, still watching her from the dais. He waited on the last step, watching her with his hands locked firmly behind his back. She bowed to him, sinking into a deep curtsy.

The court needed to see her as powerful, but they also needed to see her as beholden to the emperor. They needed to know she respected him as the rightful heir. She did not control him.

"It is done, my liege," she said, calling him by the title used by vassals and servants.

Daindreth held out a hand to her and she took it, head still canted down in obeisance. "Judgment is passed," the emperor said. "The court is dismissed." He stepped down off the dais to join Amira on the ground.

Without waiting, he led her toward the hallway back to their quarters. Cromwell, Cyne, and their flock of retainers and guards followed them.

As if some spell had been broken, the room erupted into whispers and gasps at their backs. People jostled to get out of the throne room to spread the news of Amira's draconian justice.

In the safety of the hallways with two sets of doors between them and the chatter of the throne room, Cromwell appeared at Amira's elbow. "That was risky," he said. "Killing a lord so summarily."

Amira glanced to him. "My husband was going to kill them all."

"Yes," Cromwell said, glancing to Daindreth. "A good compromise. I will have to make sure that the story is shared accurately."

Amira grimaced. That was true. It was possible that the story would still be twisted into making her the villain.

"I think you effectively neutralized the Bolesses and the Rebekus," Cromwell said. "Our only concern now is if someone tries to take vengeance on their behalf. It's good you let the Bolesses and the Rebeku girls keep their lands. Loss of life, nobles can forgive, but not loss of land."

Amira had seen as much from her father's court. Men were far more likely to revolt over grazing rights and boundary stones than they were over the deaths of brothers, sons, and fathers.

"How old is your son, Cromwell?" Amira asked as they continued to walk down the hallway.

Cromwell shot her a sideways glance. "He's nearing twenty, my lady."

"Not married?"

"No, my empress."

Amira glanced to her husband. They needed harmless men to marry Rebeku's daughters. Men who were tied closely enough to their own power so as not to be interested in turning against them.

Daindreth seemed to catch on. "You may pick one of the Rebeku girls for him," the emperor said. "Whichever you consider most suitable."

Cromwell inclined his head. "Thank you, my liege. May I consider this honor more before I accept?"

"Of course."

"If I may ask, would this be to honor the house of Cromwell or shame Rebeku?"

"Bit of both, I suppose." Amira thought it was a good compromise.

Cromwell had been born a blacksmith's son and spent time as a common soldier, maybe even a mercenary. A few weeks ago, he had been imprisoned for treason. If everything went according to plan, his grandchildren would be nobles and his great-grandchildren might be anything.

If his children and grandchildren were as effective as Cromwell himself, who knew? Perhaps Cromwells would one day intermarry with the imperial line itself.

Meanwhile, Rebeku's line would be absorbed into a minor

Hylendale house. It was a way of tying more lands to northern families, back to Amira's base and by extension, Daindreth's.

One day, Fonra would be queen of Hylendale. Amira trusted support from the north would be stable for her lifetime.

They reached Vesha's former apartments. Amira and her sorceresses planned to spend a few hours today deciphering the clues left behind by the former empress.

Daindreth kissed Amira outside, one hand stroking her forearm.

"Did I do well?" she asked him softly.

"Better than I would have," the emperor said, resting his forehead against hers.

"Did I go too far?" Amira asked. "Making that man kill his own father?"

Daindreth closed his eyes. "I don't know." He pecked her nose softly. "I understand why you did it. I just..." He exhaled heavily.

"You didn't try to stop me," she said. "You could have."

Daindreth briefly glanced to Westfall, standing behind Amira. "I am the kind of man to hold an empire, wife. I know this. Conquest is not my strength."

"What does that mean?"

"I know I can run this empire," Daindreth said. "I know I can bring it prosperity and peace. I do believe that now. But we must secure it first." He cradled the side of her face. "My father was the conqueror, and my mother was the administrator. I think perhaps we are switched."

"I take after your father, you mean?" Amira wasn't sure if she should take that as a compliment or an insult.

"You are fierce like him," Daindreth said. "Strong, like him. You can...do the unpleasant things. The things that make me sick. And you don't hesitate to do them."

"I sicken you?" Amira tried to keep her voice soft, but she was firmly aware that their guards, Cromwell, her mother, and a small army of attendants watched them.

"No," Daindreth assured her. "No, never. But some of the things you've had to do, yes." He kissed her again, lips pressing to hers softly. "I need you, Amira. The empire needs you. Your strength, your ferocity, and sometimes, yes, your brutality."

Amira wasn't sure what to say. A numbness hung over her, a numbness she had put on the moment she stepped down from her throne. She had thought of it as a fight—a fight to strike a healthy fear while also showing that it was good to be her friend.

Daindreth stroked a thumb over her cheek. "I'll see you tonight, very well?"

"Tonight." Amira forced a wan smile.

Daindreth still had many meetings and duties to attend today. He had mountains of letters from foreign vassals and stakeholders from across the empire. They wanted to know that the heart of the empire was stable, that the throne was indeed occupied by a strong claimant.

Amira left him in the hallway, letting her guards open the doors for her. Already, several armored men were posted around the room.

She stopped at the sight of Fonra. Beside the window, her sister sat surrounded by handmaidens and lady's maids, several with handkerchiefs out as they tried to console her.

Fonra's face was red and splotched with tears. She looked up at Amira's entry, choking off the end of a sob.

The sorceress stood there, frozen. Not sure what to do. She hadn't considered that, despite Baron Boless threatening her sister, Fonra might still have felt some affection for the man. He was her uncle, after all. Amira had never really considered that Fonra might be close to him.

She remembered the way he had addressed Fonra, how easy it had seemed for her sister to converse with Elton. She'd assumed that was just her sister's natural cordiality, but perhaps...

"He brought it on himself, Fonra," Amira said.

"Did you have him killed him because of me?" Fonra

whimpered.

"No, sister," Amira answered, doing her best to keep her tone soft and patient. "I had him killed because he was a traitor and there had to be consequences." Vengeance for his threats against her sister was just a bonus.

"And poor Elton," Fonra wept. "You made him kill his own father."

"I did," Amira said. She clasped her hands in front of her. She realized that, prior to yesterday, her sister had never actually seen her as the assassin. Her sister had never actually seen someone die.

"Why?" Fonra sobbed. "He didn't attack anyone."

Amira stiffened. At her side, Cromwell stood quietly. "Elton was an accomplice."

"He just stood by," Fonra protested.

"Exactly." Amira had felt nothing when she had given the order and very little when it was carried out. She had felt some shame when she faced Daindreth, some fear of his reaction, but at Fonra's accusations, something writhed and simmered in her chest. "Elton agreed to my death but was too coward to take my life himself. So, when he agreed to his father's death, I made him face it."

"Why?" Fonra cried, her voice cracking. "Why did you do that to him?"

"They don't get to pretend anymore," Amira said, voice cold. "Men and women like him—like Rebeku, like *Father*." Amira spoke her father's name as a sneer. "They send other people to do their dirty work and then pretend they're better than us, but they aren't."

Fonra shook, swollen eyes widening at her sister.

Amira bit back the rest of her words, averting her eyes. She inhaled and exhaled, counting to ten. "You may rest for today. My sorceresses can attend me." She turned her attention to the piles of Vesha's books arranged on the shelves and tables. She didn't think she owed Fonra an apology, but she couldn't shake the feeling she had done *something* wrong.

"Do you hate Papa?" Fonra asked. "Did you have Elton do that to his father, because you wish you could do it to ours?"

Amira swallowed, raising her chin. She was aware of her mother, Cromwell, and a room full of maids and guards looking at her. "King Hyle and I have too many sins between us to ever judge the other," she said. "But I will never fear him as much as he fears me."

CHAPTER THIRTY

Thadred

Thadred expected the judgment of Amira to be immortalized in rumors, if not songs and poems. That had been a brilliant bit of statecraft, but he wasn't sure if history would remember her as the hero or villain.

It didn't really matter, he supposed. As long as they won, he himself was fine with being called a villain.

He met Sair outside Amira's chambers and they began the walk to the room where Kaphen was held. The monk had been housed in a room meant for a lesser noble or a high-ranking clerk.

Guards had been posted outside his door and his windows barred shut. Thadred didn't want the man trying to escape and falling to his death.

"Will they hate her for it, do you think?" Sair asked.

"I don't know," Thadred admitted. "These things can be hard to predict. I suspect it all depends on how long Daindreth keeps the crown."

Sair shot him a quick glance. "You think your cousin will be overthrown?"

Thadred shrugged. "If he is, it won't be our problem."

"It won't?" Sair sounded almost indignant. "You're his Kadra'han. I am Amira's vassal."

"Exactly. If he's overthrown, we'll already be dead. You, me, Amira, Cromwell, Westfall, Cyne...all of us."

Sair went quiet.

This was why they had to make sure Vesha was beaten once and for all. She was the only one who could rally enough support to threaten them. Thadred was sure that Amira's assassination had been planned out of loyalty to Vesha. Even if Vesha hadn't given the actual order.

The knight and the sorceress came to a stop outside

Kaphen's door.

"Has he given any trouble?" Thadred asked the guards.

"None, sir," the soldier answered. "Asked a few times when he would be let out, but none of the crying from yesterday." The guard's lip curled a little at that.

Kaphen had not been the most dignified of prisoners, to be sure. He'd cried most of the way back to the palace.

Thadred nodded. "We're here to question him."

The soldier scoffed. "Good luck, sir." The men opened the door and Thadred stepped through first, Sair on his heels.

Kaphen sat on the bed, hands folded in his lap and shoulders hunched. His breakfast from that morning lay mostly eaten beside him. He stood on seeing Thadred, eyes wide as a fresh colt's.

"Kaphen. How are you feeling today?"

"You said you would come to see me last night," Kaphen said. "I waited for you."

"I was distracted," Thadred drily retorted. "You see, someone tried to assassinate Empress Amira."

Kaphen's throat bobbed, and he glanced at Sair, then back to Thadred. His scalp and face bristled with dark stubble since he hadn't been able to shave. Thadred had denied his request for a razor for obvious reasons.

The door shut after them. Thadred grabbed the two chairs from beside the hearth, one for himself and one for Sair. He saw her seated before taking the chair beside her.

"Kaphen, I think you know why we came for you."

Kaphen's hands knotted in his lap. "I didn't know who she was," the monk whispered. "She would come to the library with a single guard. I thought she was just some noblewoman. I didn't…" He shook his head.

"Who was she, Kaphen?" Thadred pressed, leaning forward. "I want to hear you say it."

Kaphen licked his lips. "Empress Vesha."

Sair shifted beside him.

"Am I going to be executed?" Kaphen clutched at his knees, clenching the fabric of his robe. "Are you going to torture me?"

Thadred rolled his eyes. "Do you want us to?"

"I…" Kaphen swallowed. "You said I was being arrested on suspicion of treason."

Thadred shrugged and opened his mouth. Sair touched his arm, stopping him before he spoke again. "The emperor wants certain information," she interjected. "If you will provide that information, the emperor is willing to give you a pardon."

Thadred had heard no such thing. They'd barely had time to discuss this with Dain at all.

"That depends if your information is useful," Thadred added, fixing the younger man in a hard look.

Sair offered a gentle smile to their captive. "Can you tell us about what Empress Vesha wanted?"

Kaphen shrugged. "She came looking for Scribe Egrid. He didn't know who she was, either, so he told me to answer her questions." Kaphen turned wide eyes to Thadred. "I never meant for her to actually use those texts. They were just experimental. Brother Egrid had me working on his theory of realms."

"Realms?" Thadred blinked.

The earth I give to the sons of men," Kaphen said. "He was obsessed with that passage. He wondered if the gods had given us this world, but they could still touch it, if we might be able to touch theirs. He wanted to truly know the gods, to see them face to face."

Thadred wasn't sure what that was supposed to mean.

Fortunately, Sair did. "He was seeking a way to walk between the Veils."

"Yes," Kaphen admitted. "Or the study of them, anyway. He had me reading through old books and finding mentions of people traveling between this world and…others."

Even Thadred caught the meaning there. "What did you find?" The knight hadn't meant for that to sound harsh, but

Kaphen shrank back.

"Nothing!" He cleared his throat. "At least, not what Scribe Egrid wanted."

Sair cast Kaphen a smile that was a little warmer than Thadred thought necessary. "But what did you find?"

Kaphen swallowed. "Humans…we belong to this world…or at least our bodies do. Unless the gods grant it, we can't travel between worlds. But unless we grant it, nothing can travel into ours, either."

"So you taught Vesha how to summon gods, Thadred clipped.

"Gods?" Kaphen coughed. "No, not gods."

"Cythraul." Sair rested a hand on Thadred's knee, like she was bracing herself. "You're the one who taught her to summon cythraul." It wasn't a question.

Kaphen shook his head quickly. "No, no, I showed her early research. A compendium of sources. I didn't realize what she'd done with it or who she was until…until it was too late."

Thadred studied the squirrely man. Vesha had to have known he would crack like an egg if interrogated. He knew a good many of her secrets, but she had left him alive? Odd. Maybe the bitch had a heart after all.

Thadred was still surprised that Darrigan hadn't arranged a fortunate accident for the young man.

"You helped her become a witch," Thadred mused. "And you helped her nearly overthrow the rightful emperor."

Kaphen's eyes widened. "She just wanted to protect the empire. That's what she told me. I begged her not to, but…" He shook his head.

Thadred looked to Sair and they shared a grim look. They'd finally found someone with useful information. Someone who could tell them how Vesha had gained her power and how they could stop her.

"You're a very lucky man, Brother Kaphen," Thadred said. "You happen to be worth more alive at the moment. Would you like to stay that way?"

Brother Kaphen gulped again. "What do you want to know?"

"I am going to send for a quill and as much ink and parchment as you need. Then you are going to write down your confession for the emperor." Thadred shrugged. "If your answers satisfy me, I might even consider *not* torturing you."

Sair's eyes widened at the same time Kaphen's did.

Thadred didn't really mean it, but Brother Kaphen didn't need to know that. It was best that Kaphen feared him, best that the man felt like Sair was his only friend. She would have most the detailed questions and she was the one he would need to do most his answering to.

"I will tell you anything," Kaphen vowed. "Please just...don't hurt me."

Thadred nodded. Finally, one thing was going right.

CHAPTER THIRTY-ONE

Daindreth

"**S**o my mother gave Moreyne access to our empire through her own allegiance?" Daindreth asked.

"Yes," Amira replied. "At least according to the monk."

Daindreth let a long breath out his nose. His valets worked to adjust his epaulettes, making sure the gold cords hung evenly on his shoulders. Another footman knelt, polishing his boots one last time.

His wife was a vision in a shimmering black dress that reminded him of the sea at night. The fitted sleeves and bodice accentuated the shape of her body and the skirts pooled around her legs like water.

It was elegant, striking, and understated.

Meanwhile, Daindreth had been dressed to stand out in bright red and gold with high black boots. He found that he looked more like a military officer or a huntsman.

"It seems Vesha contacted cythraul through a blood pact, which is really just a roundabout way of harvesting *ka.*" Amira spoke of blood pacts and witches the way Daindreth's ministers discussed trade routes and seasonal goods. "It doesn't always work. The way Kaphen explained it, something else—a god or a demon—must accept the offering." The young empress exhaled. "So there are some similarities between her bargain and what my grandmother and the Istovari did. But their bargain was for revenge. Vesha's was for power."

They had just a few minutes before they were supposed to appear at the palace courtyard for the long procession to the coronation. Every moment was precious.

Amira and Daindreth didn't know how much time they had. Vesha could appear with her denizens any day.

He needed to be emperor and she needed to be empress.

They had a long road ahead of them and there was much work to be done to save the soul of the empire.

"What does this mean for us, Amira?" Daindreth asked, lifting his chin so that a valet could finish buttoning his collar.

"It means we need to take the empire out from under Moreyne."

"How shall we do that?" Daindreth tried not to sound angry, but so far, it seemed that all their efforts to fight his mother had been in vain. How did you fight a god without the aid of another god?

"You must take authority over the empire and cast Moreyne out," Amira answered. "That is the only way we have found."

Daindreth exhaled a long breath.

"Authority means something to the gods, even fallen ones."

Daindreth had said much the same thing to Amira before. Cythraul cared about authority, just as they cared about jurisdiction. If they weren't invited by someone, they couldn't wield influence. The problem was that they only needed to be invited by one person.

Was it possible that they could be banished by one person?

"Vesha wasn't able to allow the demons full access to the empire without the proper sacrifices," Amira acknowledged. "So I don't think we can throw them out without the proper rituals, either."

"Any idea what those rituals might be?" Daindreth lifted his chin as another attendant fixed his collar for what must have been the fifth time.

Amira shook her head sadly. "Not yet."

Daindreth shrugged which made his epaulettes uneven and a servant rushed to fix them. "We must find out then. I want the creatures banished for good." They no longer took care when speaking of the monsters.

Daindreth batted the valet away as soon as his epaulettes were fixed. "If it's not perfect by now, it never will be." He looked to Amira with a heavy sigh. "Is this what it was like to be a bride?"

His wife smirked at him. "Similar. Though they didn't make you bathe in cold goat's milk."

Daindreth's brows rose. "They made you do that?"

"Yes, actually."

The low murmur of trumpets sounded outside, announcing the beginning of the festivities. The imperial procession was ready to depart.

"Come, my love." Amira rose to her feet.

Fonra and several other ladies in attendance rushed to fix her dress. Amira was lovely, her hair pinned up in the style of an imperial matron, lips and cheeks rouged perfectly and kohl making her eyes smolder.

"Let's get you crowned." Amira hooked her arm through his. He leaned down and pressed a kiss to her temple.

"Your Majesty!" Fonra protested. "Mind her hair!"

Daindreth chuckled. "Yes, this does feel like our wedding."

"My liege." Captain Westfall appeared at the door, offering a bow. "The road to the cathedral is secured. We are ready."

Daindreth and Amira followed Westfall out of the parlor where Daindreth had been prepared for the past several hours.

They began the long walk from the imperial apartments to the palace courtyard. Along the way, the halls were lined with holy men and women, councilors, ministers, courtiers of every variety, military officers, and servants.

It seemed everyone who was anyone had appeared for this coronation. Even if this celebration would not be as large as that of Daindreth's grandfather and certainly nothing compared to that of his father. It was but a steppingstone.

Daindreth was a young emperor, the youngest to take the crown in over a century. That meant his reign might be the longest, but it might not.

With the beheading of Boless and the banishment of Dame Rebeku, he and Amira had far more enemies than before.

If the people had their reservations, no one showed it as

Daindreth and his sorceress made their way across the courtyard to the carriage that awaited them. It was not the open-air carriage that had originally been planned, but one with a solid roof.

Westfall had wanted a closed carriage after the attempted assassination, but the people expected to see their sovereign. A compromise had been struck and they would have a partially open carriage with spells lacing the outside.

Any crossbow bolts, arrows, or other projectiles would have a challenge getting to the imperial couple. That didn't mean it was impossible, though.

Four black mares had been hitched to the carriage, their manes in elaborate braids plaited with red ribbons. The mares stomped eagerly, anticipation thick in the air.

Daindreth scanned the crowd gathered in the palace courtyard. All the most important people were already at the cathedral, awaiting Daindreth's arrival. The faces looking back at him were for the most part unfamiliar, but they appeared happy. People cheered in a cacophonous roar. Red and white rose petals showered from the ramparts. Even the soldiers wore garlands of white daisies and sashes of red over their chests.

Daindreth stepped into the carriage first. Amira followed, her attendants helping to arrange her long skirts. The doors closed and the four black steeds snorted.

"What's wrong, husband?" Amira asked as the two of them settled side by side in the carriage.

"Do you think they're happy? The people loved my father. My mother, too. But me?"

Amira's hand slid down from his arm to clasp his hand. "They will love you. How could they not?"

Daindreth exhaled. "They loved me because of my parents. I fear that even now there are those who will defect to my mother if given the chance."

Vesha was still out there somewhere. Daindreth hated not knowing where.

Amira squeezed his hand, leaning over to kiss him. "You are

rightful heir to the empire," she said. "The gods are on your side."

Daindreth arched one eyebrow. "Have you become a woman of faith, my love?"

"I have faith in you." The way she said it reverently, almost like a prayer, made his chest swell.

Daindreth could only hope he would prove worthy of her trust.

The signal was given, and the horses leapt into a high-stepping trot. The carriage jolted and the small army of guards and attendants moved to encircle them.

"I have seen Caa Iss. I have seen Saan Thii." Amira looked ahead of them, smiling for the benefit of those who watched them. She raised her hand, waving demurely. "If they are real, then Moreyne must be real. And if Moreyne is real, then her sister, and Demred, and Teshner, and all the rest."

Daindreth straightened and waved, following his wife's example. They needed to preserve appearances, after all. On this day especially.

"I never took you for a pious soul."

"I never doubted the existence of Vesha or the need to respect her," Amira countered. "But nor did I grovel before her in her absence. The same is true for the gods."

Daindreth decided that was fair. "The gods left me to suffer with Caa Iss. I suppose I have long doubted their power."

Amira's expression remained the same as she looked toward the crowd—their subjects. "Have you ever wondered, my love, if perhaps I was the answer to your prayers?"

Daindreth chuckled despite himself. "Yes. Once or twice."

Amira squeezed his hand, still waving and smiling like a dutiful empress. She was fitting well into the role. "The gods have answered all my prayers. Just not as quickly or in the ways I would have liked at the time. But it was better, in the end, I think."

"What are you saying?"

"I don't know yet." Amira leaned over and kissed his cheek. "But I am beginning to realize that perhaps the gods are more limited than we think them to be."

"What do you mean?" Daindreth asked.

"Something that monk told us. *The earth I give to the sons of men.*"

"What is that?"

Amira shrugged her pretty shoulders. "A line from an old text about a thing called the God Pact."

"From my mother's collection?"

"There are several books in her collection that mention it, yes." Amira looked out at the city, her brow furrowing slightly. "The monk Sair and Thadred found has told us something of why."

The carriage rounded a corner in the street. Flower petals rained on them. People crowded the streets.

Even with this coronation being smaller and on much shorter notice than most, every person in the city appeared to have made their appearance for the event. This was a once in a lifetime opportunity. At least it should be.

Daindreth hoped his heir would not be taking the throne for many, many years yet. Especially since he didn't have an heir just now.

"Turns out it's considered an apostate story, telling of a time when the gods were banished."

"You mean Moreyne?" Daindreth asked.

"No," Amira answered. "All the gods."

"I have never heard that before."

"Me neither."

"Who banished them?" Daindreth's brow furrowed. This was the first stretch of uninterrupted peace he and Amira had experienced for days, outside sleeping.

"That's the thing," Amira answered. "There isn't a name. Just someone called Old Man or perhaps Old Woman. The translator made a note that he wasn't sure."

"Are you sure you aren't reading too much into it?" Daindreth asked. "My mother kept many books. It's possible she kept that one for its academic value."

"So far, every book from her vault has references to magic, the gods, Moreyne, witches, or the cythraul."

"Then I don't know what to tell you, my love."

Their procession reached the cathedral. The horses drew to a halt as guards fell into formation around the carriage.

Westfall stood out in his red uniform and shining armor. He perched on his destrier, high above the heads of the crowd. His helmet was down, and he was only recognizable by his captain's sash.

Westfall directed soldiers right and left, calling out orders. The crowd leaned forward, but men from the city watch held them back.

At Westfall's signal, a footman opened the door of the carriage.

Daindreth stepped out first. The sun seemed brighter than it had been before. He squinted against it, smiling and waving as Amira stepped out after him.

Seemingly from nowhere, ladies' maids were there, helping arrange her skirts and checking her hair. One of Daindreth's valets checked his coat and epaulettes one last time before the trumpets sounded.

Daindreth was to be crowned in the same cathedral where his father and many other emperors had been crowned. It was a cathedral to Demred, patron of the empire. Allegedly, the Fanduillion bloodline descended from Demred and a shepherdess, Yelevna.

According to the story, her sheep had been stolen by a neighboring clan because she had no brothers and no father to protect her. She had petitioned Demred, the god of retribution, and he had heard her pleas. Not only had he restored her flocks, but he had been so impressed with her courage that he made her his consort.

Motifs and friezes depicting portions of the story layered the cathedral from foundation to spire. The whole building was painted in red dye, symbolic of the blood Demred had spilled on his lover's behalf. As emperor, Daindreth was to spill blood on behalf of his people, to avenge the wrongs against them, and stand for order.

Amira and Daindreth entered the doors of the cathedral. The outer sanctuary was bright red, floor to ceiling crimson tiles decorated everything in sight.

Attendants flocked to them as the doors closed at their backs. Daindreth's valets removed his epaulettes and replaced them with a massive red cloak that dragged behind him on the ground.

He checked the inside, near the collar, and found a name embroidered in a flowing script—*Drystan Fanduillion Augustus*. So they had been able to find his father's coronation robes after all.

Amira had one similar, though hers was black lined with white ermine. She'd flatly refused to wear Vesha's coronation robes and had her own made.

The bells tolled inside the cathedral and Daindreth felt as if he was at his wedding again. His heart beat faster and he was grateful for the gloves that disguised his sweating palms. A choir began to sing and it was not at all unlike his moment before walking down the aisle to meet Amira.

"Are you ready, husband?" Amira's voice was gentle with just a hint of teasing.

Daindreth coughed. "I never thought I would make it this far."

"What do you mean?"

Daindreth looked to her, ignoring the valets, maids, ministers, and councilors for just a moment. "I never thought I would live to be crowned."

Amira knew what he meant. Even if no one else in earshot did. Her face softened with understanding and a bit of sadness. She smiled at him and reached out to touch his arm again.

"You'll live much longer than this, my love."

The doors swung open in front of them and Daindreth straightened. His train was too wide and long for them to walk side by side, so he walked down the aisle of the cathedral first.

The cathedral was its own palace. Able to seat hundreds, the massive arches and gilded walls had been adorned over centuries by thousands of craftsmen. A thick red carpet—recently replaced just for this event—made sure Daindreth's steps made no sound.

Light from the upper windows shone down, meant to symbolize the favor of the gods. A massive statue of a broken spear clenched in a fist dominated the head of the apse—the symbol of Demred's retribution.

People watched. Hundreds of them. Nobles in their finest array, priests, and priestesses in ceremonial robes, even a few of their servants who had been lucky enough to be brought along. The youngest guests were held in the arms of their nurses and the oldest had to lean on the arms of their grown children.

The weight of their stares—their judgment—fell upon him as heavily as the cloak around his shoulders.

Every person in this room was his responsibility. Each one was his charge. As emperor, he would answer for every single one of their fates. They were his to protect and his to guard. His to judge and his to punish, when necessary.

He looked to the giant fist above the cathedral's apse. What god had thought to place this weight on a single man's shoulders?

Daindreth knelt at the velvet-covered steps of the main dais. It was the last time he would ever be called to kneel. When he stood, he would be Daindreth Fanduillion Augustus, lord and ruler of the empire of Erymaya.

Before him towered the red-clad Bishop Havershal, head of the church of Demred. Several other bishops and were present to represent other churches as well as abbots and abbesses from several monastic orders. Daindreth spotted the blue robes of

305

Llyr, the white of Dyani, the purple of Anu, and even the pale yellow of Teshner.

He searched a moment longer before he glimpsed Cyne in her silver damask, eyes veiled in the way of a sorceress. A crescent moon hung over her brow, marking her as a representative of Eponine. Since they were waging war against Moreyne, it had seemed necessary to have her rival represented at Daindreth's coronation.

From the corner of his eye, Daindreth was aware of Amira at his right shoulder, just a few steps behind. Her black silhouette was comforting. She would be with him to whatever end. She'd proven that.

"Today is an auspicious day," the bishop began. "A long-awaited and joyous day. Since mourning the loss of the great Emperor Drystan, we have looked forward to the ascendance of his son and rightful heir."

Daindreth swallowed, hoping the bishop wouldn't push it too far. Vesha had made herself his enemy, but she still had many friends. Not everyone saw siding with Daindreth as siding *against* Vesha.

"The gods are smiling down upon us," the bishop continued. "As I know your esteemed father is, as well."

Daindreth kept his head down and closed his eyes. He remembered his father, but in flashes and echoes.

His father had been gone most of the time, away bringing the northern countries to heel. Expanding the empire he had wanted to give his son.

Everyone who had known Drystan said Daindreth favored his father. Some people still swore they sometimes mistook him for the late emperor.

But they were nothing alike. Daindreth was a scholar. He wrote poetry. He was not the conqueror or the great general his father had been.

The bishop was still talking. "It is my great honor to present the crown of Emperor Drystan to his son. Your Imperial

Majesty," the bishop turned to Daindreth. "Do you swear your fealty to your empire, to love, protect, and uphold the unity of Erymaya? To destroy her enemies, to defend her poor, to seek justice for all her subjects, and to serve her prosperity for as long as you shall live?"

Yes, this very much felt like a wedding.

"I do so swear," Daindreth answered, pleased his voice didn't shake.

"Do you swear to take up the office of emperor with all its duties, obligations, and responsibilities, for so long as you will live?"

"I do so swear," Daindreth repeated.

The bishop nodded. A pair of boys came carrying a massive golden crown.

It was the ceremonial crown used only for the most scared rituals. Though Vesha had claimed all the offices and duties of a regnant empress, not even she had touched that crown.

Solid gold, set with rubies, sapphires, emeralds, and pearls, the crown had been made for the coronation of Daindreth's great-great grandfather. The design reflected a bygone age of excessive gemstones and overwrought metalwork, but it was a magnificent piece, nonetheless.

Towering over a foot tall, the crown was heavy enough to make the bishop's hands wobble as he lifted it. Adjusting his grip, the bishop carefully settled the crown on Daindreth's head.

The weight was massive. Daindreth had to strain to keep his neck straight.

"People of Erymaya, brothers and sisters from across the empire," the bishop addressed the people before him. "Do you swear fealty to your new emperor, to uphold his office as one chosen by the gods, to honor him as Demred's chosen, and to serve him for so long as he shall live?"

"We do so swear," the crowd echoed, speaking traditional vows.

"Should these vows be broken?" the bishop called.

"May his blood be upon us and our children."

Daindreth flinched at that. Those words were a part of the ceremony, but he doubted most people understood just how binding such vows could be.

The bishop slid a massive signet ring onto Daindreth's right hand. It was the ring that had been worn by generations of Fanduillion emperors. From father to son, uncle to nephew, brother to brother—passed between them for hundreds of years. Forged from bronze, the outer layer had been re-plated in gold several times. Why were all the symbols of his office—the robes, the crown, the ring—so heavy?

The bishop then stepped back to join the gathering of the other priests, priestesses, and clergy. As one, they spoke, voices echoing through the rafters of the cathedral.

"As the voice of the gods, we give you Emperor Daindreth Fanduillion the First. Behold your emperor. Long may he reign."

The cathedral erupted with cheers, shouts of blessings, and whooping from every corner.

Daindreth rose to his feet, now carrying the weight of the crown along with the weight of the imperial robes. He faced the crowd.

Everyone in sight stood to cheer. They cast prayer scrolls into the aisle and shouted good wishes for their new emperor.

It was surreal. Did they mean it?

The favor of the court could be fickle, much less the favor of the people. Was he truly worthy in their eyes? Would they truly follow him when the time came?

Daindreth allowed them to cheer for a time before he raised his hand for silence. "You may be seated."

A rumble went through the cathedral as the audience obeyed.

Daindreth turned his attention to his wife.

Amira had stood behind him, hands clasped. Her head was angled downward, showing deference to her emperor as the ceremony dictated.

Daindreth reached for her. "Come, my love."

It had been a long time since an emperor and empress were coronated together. The rules for this ceremony were hazy, so they were taking liberties.

Amira knelt before him in the same place he had knelt before the bishop moments ago. Her hair had been pinned up, leaving her pale neck exposed. He noticed the wound on her neck, mostly healed, but still visible up close.

"My love." Daindreth clasped her hand in both of his. "You have proven yourself to me more times than I can name."

Amira looked up at him, and the bishop stiffened at Daindreth's side. This wasn't part of the plan.

"You have faced death from my enemies and some of my friends." He offered her a wan smile. "Through it all, I have never had reason to doubt your loyalty. You have saved me, time and time again. The empire would have been doomed without you. I certainly would have."

The audience went quiet, watching intently. According to Cromwell and his spies, few knew what to make of this wild northern bride.

Yes, they had seen her perform in a tournament, dance at a ball, and pass judgment on her enemies. But conflicting rumors dominated the court.

Had she placed him under an Istovari spell? Was she secretly controlling him? Who owned her loyalty?

Daindreth wanted to make it clear that Amira was his and he was hers. Attacking one of them was an attack on both. If there was any lingering doubt over that, he wanted to end it here.

"I will not swear to love you more than I love our empire. But nor will I swear to love our empire more than you."

Amira swallowed, not looking away even as her eyes misted with tears. She seemed to be wanting to ask him a question, but she remained silent.

"You fought for me when I would not fight for myself. Time and time again you have proven the fierceness of your devotion." Daindreth leaned down so that they were almost at eye level. "Will you accept the title of empress, my love?"

Amira had agreed to it a long time ago, but he wanted to ask again. She nodded slowly. "I do," she whispered, voice hoarse.

Daindreth straightened, falling back into the agreed-upon script. "Do you swear to take up the office of empress with all its duties, obligations, and responsibilities, for so long as you will live?"

Amira watched him, not blinking. "I do so swear."

"People of Erymaya, brothers and sisters from across the empire," Daindreth repeated the words of the bishop. "Do you swear fealty to your new empress, to uphold her office as one chosen by the gods, to honor her even as you honor me, and to serve her as if she were me for so long as she shall live?"

"We do so swear," the crowd echoed.

"Should these vows be broken?" Daindreth called.

"May her blood be upon us and our children."

Two acolytes appeared on perfect cue. They carried a second crown, one much more recent, little more than a century old.

The empress's crown was a circlet that glinted with black star sapphires and pearls. There had been several empress's crowns over the years, but the one Amira chose had been worn by Daindreth's great-great grandmother, a woman who had been a devout worshipper of Eponine.

Daindreth settled the crown on his wife's head, feeling that it fit her perfectly. "I give you Empress Amira Brindonu Fanduillion. Long may she reign!"

Daindreth had feared that there might be some resistance to that declaration, but the crowd followed along.

"Long may she reign!"

Daindreth had given Amira the same declaration as himself. She wasn't a consort. She was co-ruler. His father had done him the favor of starting the tradition and he meant to carry it on.

Daindreth helped Amira to her feet and to stand beside him. Her ladies bustled to fix her dress as she stood.

Side by side, Daindreth faced the crowd with his wife on his arm.

"Long may she reign!" the crowd echoed, following along.

"Behold your emperor and empress!" the bishop called.

Cheers roared even louder, shaking the rafters. The people seemed genuinely happy.

Perhaps they were just glad that they now had an emperor on the throne again. Succession had been established and with a young wife, succession would soon be continued.

"Hail the emperor!" the crowd chanted. "Hail!"

Daindreth looked to Amira as the crowd roared their approval.

She smiled up at him from beneath her circlet. "Long live the emperor," she mouthed.

Daindreth smiled back at her, even as the weight of the train and the crown pressed down on him, heavier by the moment.

EPILOGUE

Vesha

Vesha's head ached as it usually did these days. She swirled another cup of wine. When she could no longer swirl it or when she started spilling, that was when she made herself stop.

She hated turning to wine, but it was the only thing that seemed to dull the piercing sensation in her head.

"Your Majesty," a distant voice called. "Your Majesty?"

Vesha set the wine down and forced her head up. By the dim candlelight, Odette's face was pinched. The girl worried for her, and Vesha couldn't blame her.

"Your Majesty, it's late."

Vesha wasn't sure why Odette was bothering to tell her this. "Very well." Vesha squinted down at the table.

They were still in the appropriated farmhouse. Day by day, more cythraul trickled back to them. Araa Oon said they would be ready to head inland soon. When that happened, Vesha needed to have a clear idea of where they were headed.

Moreyne had not been able to come through the well at Iandua. Vesha wasn't entirely clear on why, but that portal had not been strong enough. They needed a larger gate. A greater source of power. Not even Vesha's witch's wheel would have been large enough, she realized.

But there were other places of power on the mainland. Other holy sites that might serve her purposes. She had to remember where they were. But how was she supposed to remember when she had never been there?

Odette didn't turn back. "My lady, you can finish your work tomorrow."

Vesha looked over her notes spread across spare papers, scraps of blank journals, the backs of nautical maps, and even parts of the table. She'd sketched out the same map at least twenty times, each time a little closer to what felt right. Unfortunately, Vesha didn't recognize the map. The only familiar part of it was the coast of Mynadra and even that was off. The angles too sharp, not yet worn by centuries of the crashing surf.

To release Moreyne, they would need a larger portal than the one that had unleashed her children. They would need one of much greater power indeed.

"There's so much work to be done," Vesha groaned. Her hands ached and her vision blurred, but as fast as Moreyne sent her revelations, she had to draw them before they fled her mind.

"My lady." Odette inhaled a deep breath. "Scouts returned today. They report that your son has been crowned."

"Already?" Vesha couldn't mask her surprise.

"We've been here for several weeks, my lady." Odette glanced around the small farmhouse, but it was just the two of them. The cythraul had left them alone. "My lady, forgive me. But I know you love your son. Are you sure you wish to go to war against him?"

"War against him? No. But he cannot save the empire." Vesha looked down to the sketches of the maps. "Only I can. Only Moreyne can."

Odette knelt beside her. "My lady, please. I'm worried about you. Let me help you to bed."

Vesha patted the girl's shoulder. "You're worried for me." Vesha would have been worried for herself if she hadn't given herself up for lost days ago. "This is all I have to do, my dear girl," Vesha said quietly. "That's the deal."

Odette shook her head. "Please, my empress."

Vesha rubbed her face with her free hand. The god-eye was swollen and painful tonight, not just itchy. "I have to finish this. Then Moreyne will care for my empire and I...can rest."

Odette pressed her face against Vesha's shoulder and wept, shoulders shaking.

Vesha patted the younger woman's arm and went back to

sketching. The more she drew, the more Moreyne was able to reveal, showing new clues.

Vesha needed to know where they were marching once the cythraul were gathered. Araa Oon and Caa Iss seemed to think it would only be a matter of days.

From beyond the veil between worlds, Vesha could feel Moreyne guiding her, teaching her.

Outside, the red eyes of cythraul occasionally lit the dark. Vesha could hear them reveling, training, or sometimes fighting. Darkness meant little to creatures that had been formed from shadows.

Not much longer now. A part of Vesha knew that without a doubt. It wouldn't be long before her work was done.

Coming January 2024

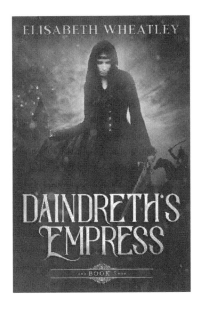

Fifth and final book in the *Daindreth's Assassin* series.

Visit elisabethwheatley.com/empress

About the Author

Elisabeth Wheatley is the author of High Fantasy with Epic Romance. She lives in Austin, TX with her husband Christian and her geriatric Jack Russell Terrier, Schnay.

You can find her at elisabethwheatley.com

Made in the USA
Columbia, SC
06 February 2024